THE
SUMMER
I
DROWNED

THE SUMMER I DROWNED

TAYLOR HALE

wattpad books **W**

wattpad books **W**

Copyright© 2020 T.D. Joyce. All rights reserved.

Published in Canada by Wattpad Books, a division of Wattpad Corp.
36 Wellington Street E., Toronto, ON M5E 1C7

www.wattpad.com

First Wattpad Books edition: May 2020
ISBN 978-1-98936-518-2 (Softcover original)
ISBN 978-1-98936-519-9 (eBook edition)

Library and Archives Canada Cataloguing in Publication
information is available upon request.

Printed and bound in Canada

1 3 5 7 9 10 8 6 4 2

Cover design by Michelle Wong
Images © lassedesignen via Adobe Stock

AUTHOR'S NOTE

Note that this story deals with difficult subject matter that may be sensitive for some readers. This story explores topics of death, violence, and mental illness. Please be aware of the potential emotional response this could cause. Thank you for reading.

To my readers: thank you for always believing in me

PROLOGUE

Growing up in Caldwell Beach, there were rules hammered into our heads designed to keep us safe. Don't swim too far out into the ocean, or the undertow will pull you in. Don't climb trees if they extend over the water, because you'll fall with them if they break.

Like most little kids, I didn't listen. My friends and I swam deep into the Atlantic Ocean every chance we got and hoped someday we'd reach the spot where the sun sparkled on the horizon. We'd get tired before then, of course, and the waves would carry us back to the rocky Maine shore. But even when the undertow pushed and pulled at my feet, I was never scared—a girl like me was made for the water. Sometimes I fantasized that if it did get me, it would carry me to the land of mermaids, right where I belonged.

But one rule was repeated so often, it became more of a superstitious warning: never, ever play on the cliffs. Especially the one by the lighthouse.

I obeyed that rule—when I was in kindergarten, fifteen-year-old Samwell Ellis cracked his skull open as he scaled the cliff's edge, and our teacher told us a sea monster had taken him. Our town was small—we believed nobody died unless they were old or sick—so it made sense a monster was responsible for the boy's death. The Ellis family then packed up and moved away, calling the town a curse, which fueled the legends and rumors that dominoed through my classroom.

It wasn't until I was old enough to question my parents that they finally told me the truth. Monsters didn't kill anyone; it was an accident brought on by teenage recklessness.

Even years later, that story still spiraled in my head; it was all I could think about as I gripped the flimsy rope fence, my toes only inches away from the cliff's edge. I wiggled them until the white rubber of my Vans moved. I'd heard you could get a better grip climbing rock without shoes, but only if your skin was strong enough to withstand the jagged edges. There's no way anyone's skin could be that thick.

Sure, teenage recklessness had killed Samwell Ellis in this very spot, but I wasn't a teenager—I had just turned twelve. I clung to that fact, as if it would protect me.

Cool wind licked my bare arms and legs. The ocean sloshed fifty feet below, inky and terrifying, and jaw-like rocks lined the curve of the cliff. One wrong move and I would fall. My body would become a waterlogged lump of flesh and disappear into the ocean, rot away like the whale corpses they showed us on *Planet Earth* in class. Maybe a shark would eat me, or maybe I'd become food for a school of fish.

The thought was almost enough to make me turn back.

"Liv, stop," Miles said from behind me. "Seriously, we're going to get in trouble!"

His blue-green eyes came into focus. The lighthouse faded into the churning clouds. Miles's curls whipped around his face as the thunder growled, and light rain began to sprinkle onto my arms.

Miles is right, this is stupid.

But then Faye Hendricks's face flared in my mind and said I was *way too chicken* to complete the cliff challenge. Faye had done it as some sort of initiation into being accepted by the older kids, and now everyone in our class thought she had more guts than me.

Screw that. All I had to do was climb down the cliff, reach the one rock called *checkpoint*, and climb back up. Piece of cake.

"Your sister's a jerk, Miles. Take a video. Don't worry, I'll be fine."

Miles whimpered as my bare knees sank into the cold, soggy grass. Icy rain pelted me until my skin was bumpy and purple, the veins on my hands, thin blue snakes. A deep breath and I climbed over the edge. Concentrated adrenaline coursed through me, but the rocks, though slick with water, kept me in place.

Breathe. You can do this; just breathe.

One step down. And another. I was going to make it. Just a few more steps.

But right before *checkpoint*, my foot slipped—and I fell.

My scream was so loud it grated my throat. Rocks sliced into my palms, but I couldn't hold onto anything.

The last thing I saw was a full moon blotted by the clouds. Dark water swallowed me, and a freezing current thrashed me back and forth. I kicked and flailed, but it was useless. Water, seeping with seaweed and raw fish, filled my mouth. My throat sealed shut and blocked my gasps for air, but only for a moment before the ocean rushed into my lungs.

I was going to die. Every cell in my body fought that reality until it was impossible to deny.

But when the final breath squeaked from my airways, the fear melted away. Everything slowed, as if I were an insect fossilized in amber. A quiet, frothy calm passed over me as I floated beneath the surface, silvery light pouring through the water above. It was a deep, indigo blue, like the depths of space. My hand extended up, reaching,

reaching—but I couldn't touch anything anymore. My head became weightless, my energy drained in a way I didn't know possible. The thrashing had stopped.

Somehow, none of that mattered anymore, because memories of those days under the sun with Miles and West ebbed through me; how I dreamed of mermaids and mythical underwater worlds. Suddenly I was closer to them than ever before.

So when the world slipped—faded behind a screen of black—I let the ocean take me.

1

FIVE YEARS LATER

The walls of Dr. Levy's office are dark red, but she sets the ambient lighting to blue because it calms me. I've always felt stupid sitting here with my eyes closed, but I've learned to trust her. Years of confiding in someone once a week will do that.

"Breathe, Olivia," Dr. Levy says. "Good, you're doing great."

The aquarium bubbles, the air conditioner hums, and the clock ticks. I count from *four, three, two, one*, and then I'm staring into her gray eyes again. They're kind and gentle, hidden beneath glasses with thin crimson frames. Behind her sits a mahogany desk with a bonsai tree and a photo of her thirteen-year-old son. The wall is covered in plaques commemorating her degrees and awards in psychology.

Our family has been short on grocery money every month for the past five years so I can sit in this office. Dr. Levy deals with rich kids—like from the Upper West Side—not kids like me. But my parents wanted the best treatment, no matter the cost.

Behind the wall of translucent blinds, Manhattan stretches forever under the afternoon sun. We're on the twentieth floor of a skyscraper, but from up here you can see the south side of Central Park, with Gapstow Bridge and the pond attached to it. Something about the wilderness being confined to that one space comforts me, and the high buildings of the city sometimes keep my panic attacks at bay. But tomorrow, I'll be by the ocean again. My stomach gnaws.

"The counting isn't helping," I say, breath ragged, and my knees bump together. The leather couch is cold under my thighs. "I'm still nervous."

"That's totally normal." Dr. Levy crosses her legs beneath her pencil skirt, her blond hair clipped back in a tight bun. "You aren't having a flashback right now, but if you experience one while you're in Caldwell Beach, you can try any of the coping methods we've been working on these last few weeks. You know how to help yourself."

I snap the elastic band against my wrist and take comfort in the shock of pain. Dr. Levy's brows pinch—she's trying to teach me ways to calm myself that don't involve chafing my skin, but so far, this helps more than anything.

"Olivia, are you sure you want to do this?" she asks. "It's never too late to back out."

"Now you sound like my mom." I laugh uneasily. "I'm okay, really. I want to go back. It doesn't matter if I'm nervous. I'm ready."

"Of course. I was ecstatic when you said you wanted to visit your hometown. But make sure you're going for the right reasons, and not because of what your classmates said."

A week before summer began, Dana Long, the captain of my volleyball team, invited me to a party. For the first time since I started at Manhattan High, I felt included; Dana's parties are a pretty big deal, and it was right before the year ended so I was still a junior.

I showed up to her stepdad's apartment building wearing a hoodie in case it was cold on their thirtieth-floor balcony. But as it turned out, the place had an indoor pool—so everyone brought the party there.

All throughout high school, I've managed to avoid pools. My other friends on the team live in apartments like mine—small and lower-middle class—so it's never been a problem. I couldn't go near the water; I knew that. But I did it anyway, paralyzed from the fear of being judged and rejected. Everyone started swimming. And when they told me to come in, the fact that I hadn't brought a bathing suit wasn't enough for them. Jensen Fletcher pushed me into the shallow end.

The moment I was in, the air was nonexistent; his hands pressed against my back, and then I was plunging into coldness. Chlorine-saturated water mixed with the taste of the ocean in my memory. My screams pierced the small room, and when I scrambled out of the pool, crying and dry heaving, everyone gawked at me.

The room burst into laughter. I cowered beneath a towel and ran out, just in time to hear Dana call me a freak.

But as terrible as that memory is, I won't let it overwhelm me—I need it in order to stay resolute.

"It's about more than them," I say. "I want to swim again, Dr. Levy. I miss my old life and my old friends. I hate it here, I—" I stop myself. "Sorry. I don't like it here, but I'm still glad we met."

"Don't worry. I understand." She pauses. "Facing your fears head-on can work sometimes, though I do still worry about you. You've made significant improvements in coping with everyday triggers, but PTSD and the anxiety that accompanies it is unpredictable. You know this."

"The aquarium isn't bothering me. And I still love the color blue."

"I'm being serious, Olivia. Your condition is very real."

Silence seeps into the room, and my thumb rubs along the elastic. "I know. But going back to the place it happened is the only thing we haven't tried yet. If I go there, maybe I can actually learn to swim again before senior year."

"I want that for you."

It's hard to imagine now, but in Caldwell Beach, everyone thought I would become an Olympic swimmer. Either that or a marine biologist, considering how obsessed I was with sea creatures and wildlife in general. Now I can barely shower without being transported back to the worst night of my life.

Sometimes it isn't even just the thought of being trapped under water that terrifies me. It's that moment of calm that came before I blacked out. The fact that I was *okay* with just dying—sometimes I stare at my ceiling for hours fearing it.

Dr. Levy continues. "How are your nightmares?"

"Good. Better."

It's not a lie, really. My nightmares have gotten better.

"But you still have them?"

"Sometimes."

"Tell me about the last one you remember."

Tempted to snap the elastic again, I sit on my hands. "I keep having a new one. It starts with me chasing Miles down the beach. We're kids, it's really sunny out, and I'm not afraid of the water. As I chase him, he gets farther and farther away. Then I find myself on the cliff, and . . ."

"And then you're falling," Dr. Levy finishes.

"Yes, but it's not happening as often, I swear."

"Good, that means the sertraline isn't making them worse. I'll let your psychiatrist know. How does the dream make you feel?"

Thinking about it is like reaching into water, trying to grab something I can't see—the feeling is there, but I have to search around to find it. "Empty, I guess. Because when I wake up, that same sadness is there, just like when I moved away. I thought Miles and I would drift apart, and we did."

The last time I saw my childhood friend in person, he and my other best friend, Keely, along with their parents, had met my family and me on the outskirts of town so we could all say goodbye. Ever since my fall I'd been jittery, and my teeth chattered even under the blazing July sun. Miles and I hugged, and he smelled like spring laundry, a scent that was so familiar to me. When we pulled away, he gently held my wrists.

"Don't go, Liv," he whispered so our parents wouldn't hear. "It's all my fault you fell. I messed up big—I shouldn't have let you go up there."

"If it's anyone's fault, it's Faye's. And my parents said I have to." The road behind him led into town, but it was empty. "Where's West? Is he coming?"

Miles kicked at the dirt. "Sorry, Liv . . . I haven't seen him."

Tears wet my cheeks, so I hugged Miles again.

"We're still going to be friends, right?" he asked.

"We'll always be friends. And we can talk online!"

At that point, almost everyone in our grade had made Instagram accounts behind our parents' backs. We weren't old enough, still in the sixth grade, but it was easy to lie about our ages. It comforted me knowing my friends would only be a few clicks away—but the idea of leaving without seeing West again created a hole inside of me.

He never came. My parents loaded me into the car, and Caldwell Beach disappeared through the back windows. Miles reached his hands far in the sky and waved, and I waved back.

We've talked online a bit since I left, but now, we're virtual strangers. A lot can change in five years. Miles doesn't look like the same awkwardly skinny kid with swoopy blond hair on Instagram, and most of his pictures are him on sets of high school plays, in which he apparently always scores a lead role. On top of that, he appears to have taken up the mantle his bloodline made for him—his profile has become increasingly more lavish over the years, with pictures of his dad's cars and their insanely expensive vacation spots all over the world. But Miles Hendricks has never been one to be a douche about his family's wealth, so I don't know why I'm so worried he'll be someone else now.

"You'll see Miles again tomorrow," Dr. Levy says. "How does that make you feel?"

"Happy, I guess. I'm pretty nervous, not going to lie."

"I'm sure it will go more smoothly than you expect. You can update me on your progress after the summer. And Olivia, if you do decide to try swimming again at any point, please make sure an adult is there."

I'm seventeen now, I want to say, but Dr. Levy means well. "Don't worry, there will be adults. And probably lifeguards too."

"Good, you can't be too careful."

"I know."

The buzzer on the desk dings. "That's our time," Dr. Levy says. "Let's leave it here."

I sling my burlap purse over my shoulder and stand. Dr. Levy holds her hands together.

"I'm proud of you, Olivia. You've come so far."

"Thanks." I smile, unsure if I believe her.

o o o

New York City is beautiful, but it isn't where I belong. It's pigeons, high rises, and concrete, instead of seagulls, sand, and the sea. I've felt like a fish out of water in this place since we moved here after the accident, but up to now, I've also always been too scared to visit home. After this summer, I'll be a high school senior. It'll be my last chance to join the swim team. To go to a pool party and not freak out. Maybe, if I'm lucky, I could even feel like myself again.

I never used to be able to imagine living anywhere but our old house in Maine. Our bungalow had white paneling, green shingles, and a garden full of azaleas native to the area. Afternoons were spent dancing in the sprinkler on my front lawn with Miles and Keely, or digging holes in the backyard to bury the pretty stones I liked. Studying wildlife used to be fun, and I was obsessed with the unique birds and fish that populate the state.

Here, everything is different. I get off the 7 on Eleventh Avenue and climb out of the station, avoiding the piers as I head straight for Tenth and blend into the sidewalk's heavy traffic. The air is humid and heavy, thick with the smell of frying hot dogs and salty pretzels from the food cart. I barely see any animals here other than squirrels and rats, and we're far enough back from the ocean that the sweltering heat has no cool breeze to mediate it. The long streets, darkened by shadows of tall buildings, trap me in. But when I was a little kid roaming the shores of Caldwell Beach, I didn't hide from the sun, I bathed in it.

Now I unlock the front door of an apartment building above a fried chicken shack in Hell's Kitchen. The vestibule stinks faintly of mildew and cat urine. I haul myself up the cramped stairwell to the third floor. Rent isn't cheap, but the apartment is within walking distance of my parents' thrift shop.

"Livvie, is that you?" Mom calls when I get inside.

"Yeah, it's me." Tossing my keys on the console table, I drop my bag and kick my Vans onto the mat. So much has changed since I was a kid—I've moved, switched schools, lost and gained friends, but I've always had this style of dark blue shoes.

A warm light emanates from the living room, and my dad's laughter bounces off the walls as *Seinfeld* plays on our small flat-screen TV. Mom's bead kit is scattered on the coffee table, and she looks up from the necklace she's stringing. My mom and I both have wintry-pale skin and straight, dark brown hair, but I have my dad's blue eyes. And unlike Mom, both Dad and I can absorb tans instead of turning into lobsters.

"Hey, kiddo," Dad says.

"How was your appointment?" Mom asks.

I leaned on the arm of the love seat. "It was good. Dr. Levy seems more confident that I'm ready."

Mom hooks an emerald gem to a gold chain. "That's bad news for me, because you know how I feel about this trip."

"She'll be all right, Carrie," Dad says. "Roger's going to watch her the whole time." My best friend's dad is a cop, and when Keely's parents agreed to take me in for the entire summer, my parents finally gave in.

"I'm allowed to worry, Allen."

A picture hangs on the wall of them holding me when I was a baby. As the only child, I've always been the center of their worries and disagreements, especially when I was younger. But since the accident, I've become that kid who'd rather watch a movie with her parents than go to a party. The thought of being away from them for an entire summer terrifies me, but that's why I need to go. I love my parents, but sometimes when I'm with them, I feel like a total loser.

Mom says, "And I have a bad feeling about that thing they found downtown. It's very disturbing."

With a sigh, Dad mutes the television. "I talked to Roger about that. The police don't think it's anything to worry about right now. There's been no sign that anyone's in danger."

Caldwell Beach hasn't had a known murder since the '60s, but last month, someone scattered half a dozen butchered and skinned squirrels around town, strategically placed for people to find. On church steps, the fountain by town hall, even one at the elementary school.

"We lived there for years and it was always safe," Dad says. "For all we know, there could've been another reason they were there. Maybe another animal dragged them in."

"And skinned them alive with a knife?" Mom shudders dramatically. "It gives me the creeps. They say that's how serial killers start out."

"Roger's the cop, and he says there isn't any danger," Dad says.

Mom faces me. "Are you *sure* you want to go, Livvie?"

The news report creeped me out—but if Roger Myers isn't worried, I shouldn't be. "Of all the things I'm scared of in Caldwell Beach," I say, "that's a little lower on the list, not going to lie."

"Cheeky monkey," Mom says, focused back on her beads. "We need to pick up the rental car first thing in the morning to beat traffic. Are your bags all packed?"

"Yeah, think so."

"Go check, please. Make sure you have your medication, and don't forget to pack Aqua."

"Come on, Mom. I'm not a little kid."

Annoyed, I go to my room and shut the door behind me. Of course I'm bringing Aqua, my childhood stuffed animal. She's already packed. But after hearing Mom say that, I don't want her. I shouldn't need a freaking toy with me; I'm way too old for it. Ripping Aqua out of my suitcase by her chromatic scaly fabric, I toss her on my bed. She has buttons for eyes and stuffing bursting from the seams, but she's been a constant in my life since the day I was born. Dr. Levy thinks it'd be good to bring her too. Two sessions ago we spent a half hour discussing how it would be helpful to have something that holds memories of a time before the accident.

A knock at the door, and Mom peeks her head in. "I wasn't trying to annoy you, sweetheart."

I flop on my bed and sit like a pretzel. There's a gaping hole in the bottom of my left sock, which was white at some point in its life, and I rip at it. "I might be feeling a little moody," I mumble.

After shutting the door, Mom sits next to me. "Are you nervous to see Miles again?"

"Yeah, who knows what he's even like now, Mom? I mean, Miles grew up in a borderline castle. Everything I own is thrifted." I tug at my blue *California* T-shirt. "I've never even been to California."

"Olivia, you've never complained about your clothes before. And Miles never cared that we don't have much money, remember? He adored you as much as you adored him."

True. I loved everything about Miles Hendricks, even his quirks: no peanuts or crustaceans near him or he'd puff up like a blowfish; no talking about clowns because they've given him nightmares ever since he saw the television adaptation of *It*. Miles never wanted to do daring things like climb trees or test how long we could hold our breaths under water—in that sense, I had more in common with his brother, West. But Miles and I were still inseparable, even with our differences.

"I know, but . . . how Miles and I even became best friends still boggles my mind sometimes," I say.

"Well I know exactly how you became best friends," Mom says. "I'll never forget your first playdate. I had been making you grilled cheese at home. You remember, right?"

"Of course." Mom's grilled cheeses are just Wonder Bread and processed cheddar slices, but they're always the best. She's told me this story a million times, but I let her continue.

"Then there was a knock at the door, and Beatrice Hendricks— one of the richest women in town—stood on the other side. I wish I could've seen my own face. I think I felt like I was somehow in trouble for something. Anyway, Beatrice said, and I'll never forget it, 'My son Miles has taken a liking to your daughter and would like to bring her to our estate for a playdate. If you could have her ready, we can drive you both immediately.' She didn't even ask! Just made the arrangements."

We both laugh. "Yeah, Miles's mom is terrifying, period," I say.

"Yes, but her children were sweet, even the one you had problems with. Don't worry, I'm sure you'll blend right back in with your friends there."

"Yeah. Thanks, Mom."

The conversation makes me a little warmer, but once Mom leaves the room, the anxiety kicks back on. I pick up Aqua again. I *will* need something to comfort me while I'm there, but . . .

No. Even though part of me hurts, I put Aqua back on the dresser with the other relics from my childhood: the collection of seashells and stacks of Maine wildlife books. I throw on one of my volleyball hoodies, plug in my headphones, and head out for an evening run to clear my head. It doesn't alleviate my stress the same way swimming used to, but I like the reverberation in my muscles as my feet slam concrete, and the way my lungs heave for air. I inhale breaths like I never drowned.

This trip isn't just about getting over my fear of the water—it's about growing up.

2

Through the window of the rental sedan, the familiar sight of the sea peeks over the trees. A mirage distorts the view beyond the hood of the car, and it's impossible to tell where the asphalt ends and the ocean begins. Sun-bleached pines grow farther apart as we reach the coast. We've been driving for over seven hours—past the granite mountains, through the dense forests of Maine.

All this time to prepare, but I still don't know how to feel. Caldwell might be where I was born, but it doesn't feel like I'm returning home, not the way I had hoped. I'm nervous. I sink in the backseat as the weather-torn sign appears: *Caldwell Beach, Population 3,089.*

This place has never been a hotspot for tourists like other coastal towns in Maine. Maybe it's the undying morning fog, or the way the wind howls through the mountains late at night—but it's one road in, one road out, forgotten by the rest of the world. Nothing more than where people go to outrun their pasts, where the rich cling to old estates, or where fishermen go to live out the rest of their days and die in solitude.

My parents came here for a fresh start. They've told me the story a million times, how they found each other at the Met in New York City, at an exhibit centered on the sea. They both dreamed of ocean air and clear skies. No light pollution to block out the stars. When my mom got pregnant, they made a decision: they would move somewhere remote, raise me to love nature, and live a happy life. And that was exactly what I had.

None of us could have anticipated how this place would affect me, least of all me.

Dad whistles from behind the wheel. "Been a long time since we've seen this, huh, Liv?"

I nod but say nothing. Mom glances at me from the passenger side, and her stare lingers before she perks up. "Oh look, Livvie, Roger and Keely are already here!"

On the side of the road, Keely hops up and down as we pull into the carpool lot. As freaked out as I am to be back, Keely Myers has been my anchor since our parents introduced us as playmates in pre-school. We were the type of friends who operated as a single unit; we always looked for the prettiest butterflies, but showed them off to our classmates together instead of competing. She visits me every summer, but now, for the first time, I get to visit her.

Sand and stone crunch beneath the wheels as Dad parks the car. Outside, the ocean air envelops me. The warmth from land blends with the cool breeze from the Atlantic. It's the smell of sulfur, salt, and sunscreen. My childhood.

"Liv!" Keely's body slams into mine. She wraps her arms around my neck, and I breathe in the scent of vanilla-pineapple on her curly hair. "I can't believe you're finally here." Keely grabs both my hands.

I look up at her. "Wait, how freaking tall are you? You're a giant!"

She puts her hands on her hips. "Five ten."

"When were you going to tell me?"

"I wanted it to be a surprise." Keely glows, like she has the sun's glitter speckled on her copper brown skin. "I randomly hit a growth spurt this year, and now I'm like, the tallest girl in school."

"Wow, jealous."

While my parents talk to Keely's dad, I look out at the town that descends the cliffs, the buildings all boxlike and multihued. They remind me of a coloring book scribbled on by a kid who can't stay within the lines. On the water, sailboats soar to and from the harbor. Seagulls float against the wind. The ocean rocks in its constant, live motion.

Roger puts his hand on Keely's shoulder while Mom takes the opportunity to trap me in a hug. We don't have a lot of money, but she always manages to find a way to afford her Chanel Allure perfume. That smell is warm and inviting, an instant antidote to my anxiety—but soon she'll be hours away from me for the first time in my life.

"All right, Liv," Dad says. "We better head back, it's going to be a long drive. We talked things out with Roger, so if you feel safe, we'll hit the road."

Roger's eyes glint with concern. I'd overheard Dad on the phone with him a week ago, and they talked about my violent night terrors and the five years I've spent seeing a psychologist regularly. I don't blame Roger for being nervous about looking after me for an entire summer.

"We *can* stay if you want us to, Livvie," Mom says. "We could Airbnb a cottage. And remember, it's never too late to go home."

"No, it's okay, Mom. You should go—Dad's right, it's a long drive. I'm fine, and I can handle this."

But I'm still not a hundred percent sure I can. On the cliff down by the beach, the lighthouse is blood red against the ocean backdrop.

Since Caldwell was founded in the 1800s, fourteen documented deaths have occurred on that cliff. It's because of the unique shape: a semicircle eroded in the rocks. When the waves are heavy, they swirl to create a vortex.

I know what it feels like to be swallowed by it: freezing and violent.

Mom touches my arm. "You're right, you can do this. I have faith in you. And I trust you and Keely to stay safe."

"Of course we will."

After smothering me with hugs, my parents drive away. Roger and Keely smile warmly, disintegrating my doubts. After all, it was Roger Myers who pulled me out of the water all those years ago. Miles told me that after I fell, he'd been frozen. Bawling, he screamed for help until police lights flashed up the street and Roger hurried out of his cruiser. Even with the dangerous rapids, Roger dove into the ocean without hesitation and managed to save my life without getting hurt.

I wish I knew what it felt like to be carried to land, but the last thing I remember before waking up in the hospital is the feeling of water in my lungs, and the eerie calm that fell over me. Not even two weeks later, my parents packed up and moved me away.

Roger places his hand on my shoulder. I'm as close with him as I can be with my best friend's dad, but to me, he'll always be a hero.

o o o

Downtown is only a short drive away, but every street brings back memories. The wheel of Roger's SUV clunks in the same pothole that's always been there, and we pass the old fire hydrant painted to look like an otter. The fish 'n' chips shop shaped like a pirate ship still hasn't repaired its electric sign, and the ropes lining the sidewalks are frayed and thinning. But not everything lines up with my memory. That burger shop used to be my parents' store. That tree in the park was just a sapling. Most of all, the way I feel is so different, it's hard to believe I ever lived here at all.

Roger parks outside of Coffee Cabin. "All right, Olivia, I'll put your suitcases in the guest room. And Lemon"—he looks at Keely with "cop eyes"—"you be responsible tonight, okay?"

"Yes, Dad. I know."

We get out of the car and watch Roger disappear around the corner.

"What does he mean *be responsible*?" I ask. "I thought we were getting iced capps and going to your place."

"Are you kidding? It's your first night back, Liv. As if I'm boring enough to *not* have plans for you." Keely unzips her yellow backpack. Inside is a huge bottle of Smirnoff vodka.

"Wait, your dad lets you drink?"

"No, obviously not. But he trusts me. I'm his *Lemon*. Don't worry, he won't blame you if we get caught. Now c'mon—I told Miles to meet us, so he should be here any minute."

Oh man. *Miles*. I'm not the headstrong girl I used to be. Will he even like me now?

The warm interior of Coffee Cabin hasn't changed a bit, and the smell of espresso roasts in the air. After we order our drinks, we grab a booth by the window. Keely tugs at the bracelet around her wrist; hers is yellow and purple while mine is green and blue, but it's around my ankle. We made them with Mom's kit last summer as we'd sat cross-legged on my living room rug.

"Nervous to see Miles?" Keely asks wickedly.

"What? No."

"Yeah, right. Still think you two are going to get *married*?"

"Oh my God, Keely. Stop. Don't say anything like that to him, *please. I* never said Miles and I would get married, everyone else did."

"Oh, chill out. You know I'm not that much of a bitch."

The door dings, and a guy in a seafoam-green T-shirt and tan shorts walks in.

"Olivia?"

"Miles?"

I stand, but stop myself from saying something stupid. Miles Hendricks used to be shorter than me. Not anymore, but he still has the same pale skin kissed red from the sun and sandy blond curls.

"Miles, you're so . . . different!"

"So are you." He flicks a strand of my hair, just like he used to when we were kids. A string of shark teeth hangs around his neck, and his dimples pronounce when he smiles. Of course I've seen pictures of him, but he looks better in person. Keely scooches over in the booth so Miles can sit across from me.

"All right, Miles," Keely says, "I've got the booze. Can we hang out at your place, or will your dad freak out?"

"Aren't we going to Carter's?"

A pause.

"Well . . . no," Keely says. "I don't know."

"Why? What's going on at Carter's?" I ask.

"Houseboat party," Miles says. "Everyone from our grade is going. It'll be the perfect time for you to like, re-meet everyone, Liv."

"But, Miles." Keely slaps his arm. "It's on a *boat*."

"Oh, right."

I tug at the elastic on my wrist. Being the center of attention is the worst. And crapping all over Miles and Keely's plans just because I'm scared of water would be so lame. I can't be who I was in New York, not here.

"I don't know," I say. "I'm here to get over my fears, Keely. Not hide from them."

"Wait, so you're down for the party?" Keely says. "Oh my God, yes, seriously Liv, you're going to love it."

Will I, though? Maybe I shouldn't have brought it up. Wanting to change the subject, I face Miles. "So, how's your dad? Or Faye? And your brother?"

"Everyone's fine. Faye has her Summer Intensive for ballet, so she won't be around until tomorrow."

"What about West? He seems to have dropped off the earth even more than I have."

I'm trying to play it cool, but my curiosity about West has been eating at me for literally years. His name sounds so foreign on my tongue now. The truth is, I don't even know what West Hendricks looks like anymore. After I moved away from Caldwell Beach, I followed everyone who wasn't already on my list on Instagram, and almost everyone accepted. Miles's older brother didn't. He picked up his phone, with its request from Olivia Cathart, and clearly ignored it. Years later, he's still never accepted the request.

After he didn't say goodbye to me, it wasn't surprising, but God, it still stings. It really, really stings. Because West was the strongest person I knew, and I'd thought our friendship—on at least one level—meant something to him, even with our problems. Not accepting my stupid request was the final nail in the coffin.

"West is . . . actually, my parents kind of disowned West," Miles says. "I haven't spoken to him in a while. But I'm sure he'll say hi if you see him."

Miles obviously doesn't want to talk about it, so I don't press, but *disowned* is such a strong word. I have no idea what happened with West and his parents, but it doesn't take much to fill in the blanks of what went wrong with him and Miles—mostly because their relationship was never "right" to begin with.

Somewhere down the shoreline, in an inlet where the rapids are calm, there's a floating dock off the beach where we used to play Pirates and Mermaids as kids. Miles, West, and I always went out on days when the sun glistened like crystals off the ocean and the sky was clear and blue. I would be the mermaid in the water; West the evil pirate king on the dock, and Miles the prince I needed to save. The battle always ended up between me and West. If Miles was on the dock, West was winning. If Miles was in the water, I was winning. It was more *Pirates of the Caribbean* than *Peter Pan*.

But one day, after West had grabbed him, Miles threw a tantrum on the dock. I climbed on, my limbs constricted by my life jacket and floaty wings. Other kids were involved, too, so when Miles started screaming, the dock quickly filled up, mostly with boys in West's grade. Miles and I were eight, so West would have been ten.

"It's not fair," Miles sputtered, boogers dripping from his nose, his big blue-green eyes filled with tears. "You guys always decide everything. *I'm* going to be the pirate king this time! This game is stupid."

"No way, you little freak," West spat, his black hair spiked in wet blades over his forehead. "I'm the pirate king and you're the wimp. That's just how it is."

"I'm telling Dad you said that!"

"If you do, I'll ruin your life!"

"You already do!"

Then Miles directed his anger at me—maybe knowing he couldn't take his big brother—and shoved me into the water, making me cry. West gave him a wedgie and booted him in after me. Miles screamed that he hated both of us, then cried and paddled to the beach, where the parents had already gathered as they noticed the conflict on the water. Then, because of Miles's crying, they called everyone back to shore. I crawled out of the water, West at my side. Miles and Faye were attached to their mom's hip.

"It's Olivia's fault!" Faye exclaimed and pointed at me. "She did it, she made Miles cry!"

"What? I didn't do anything!"

"That's right," West agreed. "Miles is being a baby. If he can't play by the rules, then he can't play with us."

"Exactly!" I said. "West is right!"

I was angry at Miles for pushing me in the water. I stood my ground, but the sight of Miles whimpering behind his mom's leg was enough to make me question whose side I should be on. *He* was my best friend, after all. West was just his older brother. Yet whenever West was around, I felt this unearthly need to impress him.

Faye kicked sand at me with her pink flip-flop. "If you love West so much, why don't you marry him? Come on, Miles, you don't need those jerks."

But Miles ignored her. "It was all West, Mom," he said.

"It was not!" West shouted.

"That's enough," Beatrice snapped, and we all fell silent. She had that effect on every kid, even West. So when she snatched West's forearm and dug her nails into his skin, I said nothing, despite the warning bells that clanged in my head. My mom had never grabbed me like that.

"Your father will deal with you, Weston," Beatrice said and pulled him away.

"Stop!" West's feet dragged through the white sand. "You're hurting me!"

She tugged harder until his legs went limp, and I wondered if this was all my fault—that if I wasn't there, Miles wouldn't have pushed me in, and then maybe West wouldn't have pushed him, and he wouldn't have ever gotten in trouble.

My parents soon found me through the crowd, but I was already crying. That was probably one of the last times we ever played like that together. It didn't take long for West to think of us both as "little kids" and stop hanging around with us in favor of the boys from Scouts. He left me in the past.

But the older I get, the more that day bothers me. I never told my parents about the way Beatrice grabbed West because somehow, in my childish mind, I thought I'd get in trouble.

Still, even with their dysfunctions, I imagined Miles and West would grow older and figure out their relationship. Maybe it's not my place to feel sad that they don't talk anymore; maybe I never understood their family at all.

"Hey, don't worry about West, Liv." Miles nods toward the window. "He's not dead or anything. He's working right over there."

The sun blares over downtown. At the auto body shop across the street, a guy with dark hair wipes his blackened hands on a rag as he ducks from under the hood of a rusty pickup truck. I don't recognize him at all.

3

By the time night falls, murky clouds stripe the sky like undulating seaweed. We've been walking the path to the beach for five minutes, and the waves lap against the shore. Brine and salt fill my nose as a pit forms in my gut.

Earlier, Keely picked up a few bottles of soda, dumped half of each one out, and filled them with the vodka from her backpack. She sips hers like water. I can't find the courage to tell her I don't drink due to my prescription of sertraline, the new antidepressant Dr. Levy has me on, so I nurse the bottle of vodka and cream soda I have no intention of drinking. I wish I could.

Cool, damp sand seeps into my shoes at the shore. A row of docked boats extends into the sea—some houseboats, some with tall masts and shrouded sails that flap in the wind. Silhouettes of bodies dance behind the white-curtained windows of what must be our destination. Bass-heavy music reverberates through the night. *The Rebirth* is written in cursive along the white, glossy exterior. It isn't a cruise ship or anything, but it's bigger than I thought it would be. Maybe that's a good thing—I might feel more leveled in a sturdy vessel like that. Still, part of me wished the walk here would last forever.

"Beauty, isn't it?" Miles says.

A lump forms in my throat. I haven't been this close to the shore since my fall. The boat doesn't bother me so much; it's the finality of the ocean behind it. The waves that devour each other the same way they devoured *me* all those years ago. Up the coastline, the rocky cliffs are topped by pines that reach into the sky, camouflaged by a hazy nighttime fog.

"You still up for this, Liv?" Keely asks.

"Not a hundred percent sure . . ."

Miles throws his arm around my shoulder. "Hey, don't worry. We'll check it out, and if it makes you feel uncomfortable, we can leave, okay?"

Breathe. You're not going in the water, just near it. You can do this.

"Okay," I mumble. "Let's go."

The next thing I know, I'm looking past my feet at water through the cracks of the rickety dock. It's three feet wide, but I wobble over it like it's a tightrope, arms stretched out and everything. Breathing deeply distracts me from the fear. Keely glances over her shoulder, and her dark curls fall down the back of her crop top. A sun pattern is weaved into the cotton fabric. I focus on that, and not the erratic rhythm of my heart.

"You going to be okay, Liv?" Keely asks.

"I'll make it." *Hopefully.*

"She's fine," Miles says from behind me. "Liv's always been a champ."

Not so sure about that.

Keely hops onto the deck of the boat and extends her hand. Swallowing my nerves, I steady my balance with the cold metal pole. Keely whips open the door, and the boyish smell of aftershave and soap wafts into the warm night.

Carter Bonnet's fake-tanned face peers out of half the pictures on the mahogany walls, mostly him on golf courses wearing pale-green polos. There's a lot of old money in Caldwell. The Hendricks and the Bonnets rival each other in community fundraisers every year, holding extravagant parties and barbeques at their opulent estates. As a kid, that world never made sense to me: why Miles's parents would dress him and Faye up and present them to the local media like show pets. West was always left out of those things, but he told me once he wouldn't be caught dead in a suit and bowtie, anyway.

Even though there's a lot of space in here, it's nauseatingly hot and stuffy. Two guys funnel beer into another guy's mouth in the saloon while some others play beer pong on a wobbly table, unsurprisingly dropping cups all over the floor. The whole structure sways. Music pounds my skull. I don't know what to expect—will people make a big deal out of me being back, or will they even care? But as I pass Bailey, June, and other girls I recognize from Instagram, someone says, "Is that really Olivia? I heard she was back for the summer . . ."

I keep my head down, just as a guy in a white T-shirt bumps into us and spills his beer on the vinyl floor. He steadies himself by gripping Miles's shoulder, and the pickaxe-shaped scar on his forehead shines pink under the dim light. His tanned cheeks are flushed, his eyes glazy and red.

"Whoa, Olivia Cathart?" he says. "Keely said you were coming into town, but damn, didn't expect to see you so soon."

"Hey," I mumble.

"It's me, Dean, Dean Bowman. You didn't forget me, did you?"

"No! Of course I remember you."

I do, but we were never friends as kids. Dean is a year older than me but he was held back a grade. He was always the guy who lived around the corner from the house I grew up in, who drove my dad nuts by blocking the street off with road hockey.

"Damn, you got hot," he says.

"Thanks . . ."

"Heard you moved away and became a city girl. How's that working out for you?"

Back home, I'm from the middle of nowhere. Here, I'm a city girl. Guess that means I don't belong anywhere. "It's okay."

"Anyway, Hendricks, you've got to see this." Dean grabs Miles's arm.

"Wait, Miles!" I shout.

As Dean drags him into the crowd, Miles yells, "I'll catch up with you in a bit! Promise!"

"Wow," I say to Keely. "We *just* met up and he's already gone. Keely?"

Turns out I'm speaking to no one, because Keely's already on the other side of the boat, leaning up against someone who I'm pretty sure is Dean's cousin, Shawn Watters. I wasn't sure what to expect everyone to be like—sure, I had a window into their lives through social media, but being here in person is totally different. I can't expect Keely to stick with me all night. She's moved on with her life.

The floor shifts, and bile rises. Crap, I'm not going to make it. My arm sticks to another girl's as I slip past her. Vomit on my tongue, I stumble outside, land palms-first on the dock, and hurl into the water.

"*Damn it.*"

No one's out here to see me wipe my mouth, but embarrassment is hot on my face. It is so like me to throw up without even drinking. Leaning over the dock, blackness flows beneath me. Vertigo makes the world wobble as I stand on shaky legs and hold tight onto the side of the boat. Catching my balance, I head for the shore, and once on land, my breathing slows.

There are so many boats out here that the crowded waterfront adds to my suffocation. A short walk up the beach will bring me to a small field, and then, the cliff. The place I came back here to confront. In a sick way, I want to see it again, to experience the place that has existed only in my nightmares for so many years. Pins and needles numb my legs, but soon the sand becomes grass, and I'm sloping up the hill that leads to the cliff. I don't know why, but I look up.

The lighthouse.

It reaches into the starry sky like a never-ending tower. I'm still far back, but close enough to see the texture in the chipping paint. Cold air swirls around my body as the trees flutter nearby. I stand there, frozen, and stare at it like a weirdo tourist. All I can do is hear. Hear, and remember.

"Liv, stop! Seriously, were going to get in trouble!"

The door to the lighthouse cranks open and cuts my flashback short. A man exits and locks the door behind him. I should get out of here, but then he says, "Olivia?"

My name is husky on his tongue, and my hair stands on end. I look at him. He wears a twisted expression, and my jaw drops.

"West?"

He jogs down the hill as a gust of wind whispers through the grass. A certain scent engulfs me—like earth and cologne—and catches me off guard.

"No shit," he says, "is that really you? I heard you were coming back, but . . ."

"Yeah . . . here I am, back for the summer," I say, awkward as hell.

He steps into the moonlight. A square jaw; strong, thick brows; the faintest stubble. Those are new. But the dimples, the messy black hair, the olive-toned skin—that's West. He's always looked different from his pale, blond-haired siblings. All they have in common are those eyes: deep, sea blue with feathers of green and yellow.

"It's been a minute, Mermaid Girl."

"Don't call me that," I say and try to keep my cool, but seeing him again—hearing how the years have made his voice masculine and gravelly—creates a static charge in my veins. His eyelashes are long and sooty, like they were when we were kids, when I thought of him as my friend. I wonder if he thinks I grew up to be pretty—then curse myself for being so dumb.

"Why not?" he asks. "You used to love it. All those mermaid necklaces, keychains . . ."

"That was before the ocean tried to kill me."

"Tried to. But it failed, right? You were stronger than it."

"I don't know about that. Roger was stronger, that's for sure."

When I shut my eyes, the waves *whoosh* around me, rain sticks in my ears. For a moment, it's nostalgic—but then I'm sinking into the depths of blackness until I can't breathe. I snap the elastic on my wrist and I'm back on the cliff with West, not dead. My life didn't end that night. Maybe he's right. Maybe I am stronger than it.

"I never saw you after you fell." West slides his hands into the pockets of his jeans. "I'm glad you're okay."

Part of me wants to say, "*You're five years late, West,*" but I don't. "What were you doing in the lighthouse?"

"I do some work for the town sometimes. Just some extra cash in my pocket to go up there and make sure the light's working okay. It always is."

"Your family is loaded, I never thought you'd have to do odd jobs." *Right, Miles said he was disowned . . . why did I say that?*

"Things are different now."

Of course they are. A million questions rush through my mind, but mostly I wonder why he and Miles aren't on good terms anymore. Sure, they fought and all, but they're *family.* The longest I've ever shunned either of my parents is like, three hours. Maybe I don't get it because I don't have siblings.

But I can't blurt all that out, so instead I say, "You never accepted my follow request on Instagram."

"What?"

"I tried to follow you. Like, years ago. And you never accepted."

"Oh . . . yeah. Sorry about that. I didn't think you'd notice."

"Why wouldn't I notice?"

"I don't know."

"That kind of hurt my feelings, West."

He laughs. "You haven't changed. Still not afraid to tell me how you feel, huh? Look, sorry. This probably sounds dumb, but my Instagram's kind of private. I didn't accept the request because I didn't think I'd ever see you again. I didn't think there was a point."

Old feelings of rejection resurface, and it's hard to look at West now and not think of him as that same jerk who didn't even say goodbye to me. But he's being nice. The years have changed us both, given us height and experience. He must be at least six foot one now. A loose-fitting black shirt hangs off his defined arms, and the *V* of his hips pushes through it. Heat touches my cheeks, and I tear my eyes from his torso.

"Hey," West says. "It really didn't mean anything. Me ignoring you on Instagram, I mean. It doesn't mean I didn't . . ."

This is all too heavy to drop on him within five minutes of meeting again. "It's okay. Sorry, I'm not trying to be dramatic."

"Don't worry."

The ocean stretches beyond the cliff's edge, the smell of sulfur strong in the air. Normally I'd be terrified, but I'm so far back from the edge. I'm safe. That's the thing about PTSD: it's in control. It decides when and where it flares up. Sometimes a shower will trigger me. Other times, apparently, I can stand in the exact spot it happened and be totally fine. It's a strange sensation, to be at peace with the one thing I fear the most.

"You see my brother yet?" West asks.

"We were at some boat party down the shore earlier. Keely too."

"Yeah?" West kicks up grass with his boot. "What took you so long to come back to Caldwell?"

"I was scared. But . . . I'm seventeen now. I'm seventeen and I'm scared of *water*. You know, I bet I don't even know how to swim anymore."

"You came back to what, get over it?"

"I guess."

"You haven't been in a pool or anything?"

"I tried to go to a pool party last semester at school and it did not go well . . . but nope, I haven't even had a bath."

He laughs. "Oh."

"Which means I *shower* instead."

"I know, I know. Maybe you're just loaded, but you've gotten kind of defensive, Olive."

Olive. West is the only one who's ever called me that. To everyone else, it's either Olivia, Liv, or Livvie. But to West, it was always Olive.

"I'm not drunk," I squeak out.

"Could've fooled me." He pauses. "Hey, I'm just teasing you. Anyway, you probably want to get back to your party. I'll let you go."

I do want to leave, but I feel like if I let him out of my sight, he'll slip away forever, and I'll be thrown back into that reality where I'll never know what West Hendricks thinks of me.

"Okay," I say.

"Bye, Olive."

"Maybe I'll see you around?" I say to his back. God, I hate the pathetic hopefulness in my voice.

He lightly waves. "Maybe."

And then he's gone. West gets into an old chromatic sports car that reminds me of a model on Dad's bookshelf. It revs as it starts, and the lights momentarily blind me before the car rumbles away. The pungent scent of gasoline carries on the wind as his taillights disappear, and strange clouds of emotions rain over me. I feel weird, I guess—a little hollow, a little sad. But I feel alive too.

With a knot in my chest, I go back to the party.

o o o

"Oh my God, Liv!" Keely stumbles off the dock, and I catch her so she doesn't fall face-first into the sand on the shoreline. Her bloodshot eyes find mine. "Holy shit, I was looking for you everywhere! Are you okay?"

"I'm fine, I just needed some air. How wasted are you?"

Tangles of her hair stick to the sweat on her forehead as she laughs a little too loudly. "Okay, maybe a teensy bit, but we started doing shots and—" She shoves her bottle in my hand. "Come on, drink with me."

"I can't, it messes with my pills," I mumble.

"Fine, more for me." Keely knocks back a huge swig. I've never seen her drink so much. Two summers ago, before I started my medication, Keely and I stole four of my dad's beers and two of my mom's wine spritzers. It was more than enough to get us wasted. We hid in my bedroom all night and laughed our asses off at videos of cats running into walls. Though it was one of the only times I ever drank, I had a lot of fun—but that Keely was different than this Keely. This Keely can't even stand up straight.

"You're not going to be sick, are you?" I ask.

"Don't give me that, Liv," Keely slurs. "I can handle myself, trust me! You've missed out on a lot."

Ouch. Obviously I missed out on a lot, but it still hurts to hear. Keely keeps drinking from the plastic bottle. Mine must still be on the boat—not that I care.

When the door to the houseboat flies open, voices shout and cackle as Miles falls onto the deck with a dopey grin on his face. He's probably as wasted as Keely.

I'm happy to see my childhood friends again, but I expected our first night together to be a little more . . . personal. They're both right in front of me, yet there's more distance between us here than when I was 450 miles away.

"There you guys are." Miles jogs down the dock, and his sandals squish against the sand when he hops off. The smell of stale beer and cologne radiates off him. Judging by the huge wet patch on his shirt, he got involved in one of the drinking games. Miles doesn't need to know I ran into West; he might get upset if I bring him up again.

"Hey." I rub the goosebumps off my arms at the cool breeze from the sea. "Can we go now? I'm not really feeling this."

"Aww, okay." Keely pouts but hooks her arm to mine, then Miles's. "Come on, Miles, you're stuck with us."

Relief washes through me as we leave the beach. The last thing I wanted was to go back to that party, I'm not in the right headspace to meet everyone again.

A fenced path leads us to the suburbs. Coral Park connects us to Keely's neighborhood, so we follow the curved pavement until we reach a field surrounded by the backs of houses. Stars slice through the sky, and ropes dangle off the wooden posts of the playground, bathed in the navy hue of night. Miles, Keely, and I used to climb to the very top of the jungle gym and feel like we were on top of the world. Looking at it now, it's barely taller than me.

West slinks back into my mind. Right over there, behind the set of slowly creaking swings, is the last place we spoke before my fall. He was thirteen with his friends, I was eleven and by myself. He'd been ignoring me for a while, but I was a brave, persistent child. Nothing like who I am now. Under the afternoon sun, I'd jogged over to him and asked if I could play soccer with them until Miles showed up. The other guys laughed, and West just said, "Go away, Olive. You can't hang out with us."

His friends laughed. Anger, embarrassment, and confusion

cluttered my mind. I called him a jerk and stormed away, vowing I would never talk to him again.

That was a lie, of course, because I attempted to follow him on Instagram a year later.

"Hey, Earth to Olivia, are you there?" Miles says, and I snap from my reverie. His eyes burn a hole through me.

"Sorry, what's up?"

"It's nothing," Miles mutters. "I was just trying to ask you about New York. Isn't living in the city crazy?"

"Define crazy?"

"That winter lantern festival looks amazing. Ever been?"

"No, I haven't. But it is really pretty."

Dana and her friends went last year. Their profiles were illuminated with pictures of the lantern animals while I was taking a homework break in my room. Maybe Miles was expecting me to become some city girl with a super exciting life, like Dana Long and her penthouse apartment with an indoor pool, but I'm not like that at all. I don't even have friends, not real ones. Just girls who talk to me because we're on the same volleyball team. Miles needs to know the truth, but Keely saves me by shouting a *WOO* at the top of her lungs, so loud birds flock from a tree nearby. She spins in a circle with her hands in the air.

"Look at all this *space!*"

"She's really drunk," I tell Miles.

He laughs and puts his hands in his pockets. "Yep, that's Keely Myers for you."

"She does this a lot?"

"Oh yeah. Officer Myers's daughter is one of the biggest drinkers in town and he has no idea about it. Isn't that hilarious?"

"No? Not really."

"I don't mean she's a joke or anything!" Miles saves. "Not at all! Keely's great."

"Okay . . ."

We're halfway through the park, on the path that snakes through the grass. Sidewalk chalk hopscotch has been drawn on the concrete, and it reminds me of when Miles, Keely, and I got in trouble for scribbling stick figures because you aren't supposed to vandalize public parks, even if it'll wash away with the rain.

A high-pitched scream erupts. Up ahead, Keely falls into the grass and scurries back on the heels of her hands.

"Keely!" I run at her, Miles beside me, but we stop in our tracks. A rotten, putrid smell permeates the air, so pungent it oozes into my nostrils like some kind of chemical. I know that smell. Rats get killed in the city a lot, and their tiny bodies create enough stink to fill an entire alleyway when they roast in the sun all day.

Torn-up, fluffy lumps of flesh are scattered at the leg of the bench beneath a flickering street lamp. Broken bones, shreds of skin, bloodied fur.

Squirrel carcasses.

Three of them have been mutilated, like they'd been dissected in Science class. Their chests were sliced open, rib cages pulled apart, tiny organs splayed onto the ground. It's way too clinical to have been done by another animal—no, this has a human touch, exactly like the report my mom had worried about. Some pieces of skin are uneven, like the person who did it messed up partway through. Maybe got angry.

"*They say that's how serial killers start out,*" Mom says in the back of my mind.

Miles helps Keely to her feet, and she balances herself on yellow Converse. It's like the drunk has been slapped right out of her. "God, that scared the shit out of me," she says. "What kind of freak would leave this here?"

"My parents and I saw something about this on Caldwell's news site before we came," I say.

"It's happened a bunch of times now." Keely shivers. "But like, closer to downtown—like in town hall and at church."

"I don't think it's happened in the neighborhoods," Miles adds.

"We should call your dad, Keel," I say.

"Wait—no, we can't. He'll know I was drinking!"

"Liv's right, Keely," Miles says. "We should call your dad."

Keely chews on her bottom lip. "No. He can't find out I'm drunk. Let's leave it for someone else to find, they'll call it in.

"What, like a little kid?" Miles says. "Come on, that's not right. Here, have a piece of gum to cover the smell."

Miles and I stare at her expectantly. At least he's on my side about this. After a beat, Keely groans and snatches the gum. "Fine, but you guys better cover for me if my dad knows something's up."

o o o

The swing set creaks against the silence as we wait for Roger to get here. The rusty chains are cold in my hands, and my feet swipe against the earth each time they touch the ground. We're far enough away from the carcasses that the visuals are unclear, but the queasy feeling remains.

"Do you think they were in pain?" I ask absentmindedly. Miles and Keely look at me.

"Probably," Keely says. "That looks pretty bad."

"Nothing deserves to go like that."

"They're just squirrels, Liv," Miles says. "Don't worry about it."

"I know they're *just squirrels*, Miles, but I can't stop imagining what they went through."

"Maybe the person killed them before they tore them apart."

"Or maybe they tortured them."

Silence. Darkness drenches us, but light from the waning moon perforates the clouds. When two police cruisers pull alongside the curb, I skid to a halt and hop off the swing, relieved. Roger hurries out of one car, another cop from the other, and they meet us at the edge of the playground. As one of three cops in Caldwell, Roger has sporadic hours despite being the police chief.

"You kids okay?" Roger asks, huffing as he jogs toward us.

"We're fine, Dad," Keely says. "It's just like what happened before."

"Where are the carcasses?"

Keely nods toward the park bench but avoids her dad's gaze. Roger's lips purse in a grim line, and he nods at the other cop, a red-headed woman in her twenties. I recognize her as Maggie Jones. She was a senior in high school when I was in the sixth grade. Popular too. The beautiful lifeguard type, but I doubt she ever knew I existed. When she turns on her flashlight and points it at the bench, the beam overpowers the weak light of the street lamp.

Roger gets down on one knee and observes the carcasses for a long moment. The squirrels' lifeless, beady eyes gleam against the flash-light. Roger straightens up and hooks his hand to his belt. "We should call the state troopers on this one," he mutters to Maggie before he faces us, his police chief's badge reflecting. "Okay, you kids get out of here. We've got this."

There are police officers all over New York City, but Caldwell is small and sleepy—a state trooper wasn't ever called in the entire time I lived here. Not that I remember, anyway.

"But Dad, what's going on?" Keely says. "This is so gross!"

"It's nothing to worry about, Keely. We've got it all under control."

If they had it under control, it wouldn't keep happening. This is creeping me out way too much.

"I'm just glad we found it, and not some little kid," Miles says.

"You did the right thing by calling me." Roger turns to Keely, and the serious look on his face becomes the expression of a concerned father. I know both sides of him well. Keely looks scared when he steps closer to her, but he doesn't seem to notice her smell. "You just head on home now, okay? You kids stick together and get home fast. Miles, have your parents pick you up from our house."

With that, we hurry away. I take one last glance at the trees surrounding the park. If someone had wanted to watch this, it would be easy to hide behind the leaves of an oak, up in the branches where no one can see.

o o o

The porch light clicks on when we get to Keely's house. It's a single story, ranch-style home with beige brick and black shingles. In the garden of red and pink roses, a cement stepping stone of Keely's handprint is displayed. We made some together in kindergarten, but my parents lost mine in the move. Facing us on the cobblestone path that leads to the front door, Keely sighs.

"Whew, I think I'm off the hook. My dad didn't notice I was drunk at all."

"You're good now," Miles says. "Honestly, I don't even feel it anymore."

"Tell me about it. I really wanted to keep partying, but that was the biggest buzzkill. Let's just call it a night. Pick it back up tomorrow?"

Miles nudges Keely's shoulder with his fist. "You got it."

Awkwardness spikes, so I shift away when Miles looks at me. He outstretches his arms, and before I can process it, he's hugging me. I hesitantly hug him back. The citrusy smell on his shirt is so foreign—Miles never smelled anything like this before. It was always spring laundry, and he was warm. Now his skin is cold on mine, and his frame is so much bigger. His shark tooth necklace digs into my cheek. Somehow, it's like I'm not hugging Miles Hendricks at all. He's a completely different person.

Disappointment weighs on me. Of course Miles is different—

people change when they grow up. I've changed, too, but unlike everyone else around me, I've regressed; they all grew up and got into drinking and partying, but I stayed a little kid, attached to my stuffed animals and watching movies in my apartment with my parents. My friends all left the nest, but I never did.

"It was awesome seeing you again, Liv," Miles whispers into my hair, and honestly, it makes me feel a little weird. I'm relieved when he breaks away and walks down the driveway.

"But Miles, wait!" I say. "Roger said you should call your parents for a ride!"

"Don't worry, I'll be fine. I'm not scared of some animal killer." Miles grins over his shoulder before he disappears into the night.

4

Sunlight pours through the blinds of the Myerses' guest room. My body is heavy and my head throbs, because the last thing I remember is falling asleep to orange streaks of dawn coming through the window. Now the clock reads half past ten. Dammit, I didn't even sleep for four hours.

On the plus side, I didn't dream. The events of the night spun around my mind like a violent whirlpool until I drifted into a state somewhere between sleep and consciousness. Honestly, I prefer it—better to feel like crap all day from a lack of sleep than to see horrors of my nightmares, to feel the anxiety brought on by visions that always feel so real.

My hands drop into the plush, brand-new bedspread. The guest room is tidy and impersonal, with slate-gray walls, seashells, and fake coral on the nightstand. A canvas print of a beach hangs above the dresser. I saw the same one in IKEA with my parents.

Someone pounds on the door, and I jolt upright. Keely bursts inside.

"Rise and shine, sleepyhead!"

"How are you not hungover?"

She laughs, hair in a tangled bun atop her head with powder-yellow pajamas on her thin frame. "Trust me, I feel like shit. But if I *act* like I don't, sometimes I can trick my brain into really believing it. Don't rain on my parade and come get some breakfast."

Keely Myers has an admirable ability to adapt to anything. I'm sick at the thought of what we saw last night, but she's already moved on.

"We should spend some time together today." Keely elbows me as we head out of the spare room. "*Real* time, like the old days."

I let out a relieved laugh. "Movie night?"

"You read my mind."

We weave through the familiar, striped-wallpapered halls of Keely's house. Roger has a turntable set up in the living room next to a bookshelf filled with records. Afghans are spread over the arms of the living room couches. We pass a watercolor painting Keely's mom did of a hibiscus syriacus, the national flower of South Korea, and photos of their family. The smell of rosemary and tomatoes soaks the air as we enter the kitchen. At the stove, Sun wears a black blouse adorned with maroon roses and stirs a pot. She's a kindergarten teacher, so she has the summer off.

"What're you making, Ma?" Keely asks, and we sit at the table.

"Tomato soup," Sun says.

"For breakfast?" Keely grumbles. "I want pancakes. Or waffles."

"*Twelve thirty* is not breakfast time, Keely. Have a bowl of cereal."

Keely drags herself to the pantry. "Lucky Charms okay, Liv?"

"Sure, anything's fine."

"Afternoon, everyone." Roger walks in wearing his full uniform. I want to ask him what happened after we left last night, but he goes to the counter and greets Sun. Keely has told me the story of how they met—how Roger grew up in Caldwell Beach with his father, and Sun traveled here from Korea to take a trip across the US. She had never planned on staying—not until she met him.

A heaping bowl of Lucky Charms appears under my nose. Keely shovels a spoonful in her mouth and takes out her phone. The milk transforms the marshmallows into gooey blobs, one of them vaguely squirrel-shaped.

Sliding the bowl on the table away from me, I whisper, "So I ran into West last night."

Keely drops her phone. "Wait, you saw West? Why didn't you tell me?"

"I don't know. I didn't want to upset Miles, then things got a little crazy."

"Did he say anything? About ignoring you for *literally* years?"

"Does it matter? I probably just imagined we were closer than we were. I mean, Miles was my best friend."

"I don't know, you spent a lot of time with West too."

"Do you know what happened? With him and Miles?"

"Not a thing. You know how it is here, everyone talks about everyone. But who knows what's true? Miles and Faye say that West got kicked out and that's that. There've been tons of other rumors about him over the years."

"Okay, tell me. Please, you're killing me."

She picks up her spoon and licks it clean before dipping it back in the bowl. "The rumors range from everything to drug dealer, to serial killer, to not even being related to the Hendrickses at all."

"Of course they're related. They have the same eyes. And dimples."

"Hey, I didn't say I believed it. That's just what people say."

"And *serial killer*? Really? People need to get a life."

"I can see it. Well, I can't *not* see it. I mean, the guy comes from one of the richest families in Caldwell—like literal millionaires—yet he works at the body shop. It's a little weird. Plus, he's so quiet and closed off. He doesn't hang out with any of the guys he used to in high school."

"That doesn't make him a friggin' serial killer, Keely. He was 'disowned,' remember? He must work so he can like, pay for his life."

"Whatever, Liv. What's with all the *West, West, West*? I thought you liked Miles? Especially after that hug last night."

My cheeks flush. "Miles and I are just friends."

This is causing major déjà vu. One time in the fifth grade, Keely and I were having a sleepover in her room when we snuck out past midnight to use the Easy Bake Oven in this very kitchen. Keely poured chocolate batter into the tiny pan in my hands when she asked for the first time, "So do you like Miles?"

"Obviously," I said, oblivious, and once the batter was all in, I set it on the counter and dotted it in silver sprinkles.

"My mom and dad think you two are going to get married." Keely slid the pan into the tiny oven.

"What? Gross! I don't like him like *that*. He's just my best guy friend."

"Yeah, that is gross," she eventually agreed. "I mean, if I had to pick any of the boys, I would definitely pick Carter. He has the longest eyelashes."

"Carter's cute," I admitted, even though at that age, none of us really knew what it meant to actually like a boy. All I knew was that it wasn't Carter I liked. Or Miles, or anyone else in our grade. Keely and I used to tell each other everything, but this one I kept a secret, like a locket around my neck. I'd known it—maybe even for years—but it didn't start to make sense until I got older. Keely must have forgotten that I've never claimed to like Miles as more than a friend. He probably doesn't like me that way either.

I hope not, anyway.

When someone knocks at the front door, my body jolts and knocks the table. Milk spills everywhere, and I quickly dab it with a paper towel.

"Jeez, you okay?" Keely asks. "It's just the door."

"Who's here?" I don't know why my voice trembles.

"Don't know, let's find out." She runs out of the room, and seconds later, "Miles!"

Crap, I didn't expect him here so early. I'm still in grubby gray sweats and a volleyball T-shirt. Miles was practically a brother to me when we were younger, but it's weird now for him to see me like this. Keely's pajamas are cute, while I look like a hobo, so of course she invites him inside.

"You're here early," she chimes, "but come on in."

Miles walks through the archway to the kitchen wearing a sleeveless shirt that shows off the lean muscles on his arms.

"Hi," I peep.

"How's it going?" He sits in front of me and smiles.

"Mr. Hendricks." Roger walks over. "I'm seeing a lot of you in the last twenty-four hours. How are your folks?"

"Hi again, Chief Myers. They're good, I'll tell them you said hi." He pauses. "Sorry to ask, but did you guys find anything else out about what happened last night?"

At least Miles had the guts to ask what I couldn't.

"Sorry, son. Nothing yet."

"Damn, that's too bad," Miles says. "Anyway, I actually came over to ask you something else. Since it's sort of a special occasion that Liv's back in town, I asked my parents if we could hang out at our family's cabin for a couple days. But I wanted to make sure it was okay if I invited Keely and Liv to come."

The Hendrickses' cabin was Miles's favorite place to go when we were kids, but it's outside of town, so we only went when his parents brought us. It was the one place where Miles felt like a king; West was never there, and I wasn't bossy, so we played whatever games Miles wanted and swam in the lake nearby. As much as I'd love to see it again, the request catches me off guard. It's only my second day here, and I haven't even adjusted to Keely's house yet. Besides, movie night with Keely sounded just like old times.

Roger's brows furrow. "I don't know . . ." He looks at Keely. "Do *you* want to go, Lemon?"

Keely glances at me, then to her dad. "I mean, hell yeah, of course I do!"

"Olivia?"

Everyone's eyes fall on me, and I tense up.

"Sure," I say. I don't want to become The Grinch of Summer, I just hope I can catch some sleep, because the irritated, dry sensation in my brain really sucks.

Sun sets a bowl on the table, and steam rises from the orangey-red liquid. "Will anyone else be going, Miles?"

"Nope, just us. And maybe my sister."

Faye. I was bound to see her eventually but was hoping to put it off for a while longer.

"I don't see a problem with it," Roger says. "As long as you girls keep your phones on in case we need you. And it goes without saying: no drinking, no sex, no—"

"Dad!" Keely exclaims. "It's just Miles. We're not doing any of that."

It's both impressive and scary how good Keely is at lying. Roger eats it up like a bowl of ice cream, even pats her head with a warm smile.

"I know, Lemon. You're the responsible one."

"I'll call your parents, Olivia," Sun says. "Just to let them know the plan."

"Okay, so we're good?" Miles stands. "My dad's going to let me borrow his Jag, so after you guys get packed, come to my place, and we'll drive over."

Keely shouts, "Yes! Can't wait!"

I'm probably going to regret this.

o o o

A giraffe-shaped tree looms over our heads as Keely and I walk the cobblestone path to the Hendricks estate, our backpacks thrown over our shoulders, the afternoon sun hot and sticky. English ivy intertwines on the reddish-brown brick of the mansion that towers three stories above us. Keely knocks on a mahogany door that looks like it's built to accommodate seven-foot tall giants. An iron hanger shaped like a snarling lion's head is mounted to the center of it, and when no one answers, Keely bangs that too. Birds flock from a cherry blossom nearby.

"Okeydokey, no one's getting the door," she grumbles. "Maybe he's around back." Keely adjusts her crop top. "Want to go check? I'll keep on knock, knock, knocking."

"I guess."

Leaving Keely at the front door, I crunch across the gravel of the driveway to the side of the house. This excessively huge estate has been in the Hendricks family for generations. Miles's great-grandfather, Barron Hendricks, sold gunpowder in the early 1900s, which made him a millionaire. Since then, the estate has been passed down to the eldest son. If that's their family tradition, then it should go to West next . . . but considering he's "disowned," I'm sure Miles will be the one to inherit this property. Personally, I never understood why anyone would want to live here, anyway—there's too much space, and it intimidates me.

I'm hidden behind the hedges when I hear voices.

"Look, the money's not for me. It's for Amelia." *West.* I didn't even see his car, but the parking lot does extend along the other side of their house.

"Amelia isn't here, is she?" That baritone voice belongs to Brian Hendricks, West's father. "Weston, if you ever hope to become a part of this family again, you'd better clean your goddamn act up."

"Fuck off, seriously? I work harder than Miles and Faye could ever imagine. Forget it, I don't want to be part of your messed-up, narcissistic family."

My feet are frozen in the grass, my back pressed to the wall, and the thorns prick my skin through my blue tank top. If I get caught, West will think—

"Olivia?"

Crap.

West appears in front of me, his eyebrows pulled together. "Were you eavesdropping on us?"

"No, I was just, I was—"

"What did you hear?"

"Nothing," I lie.

"Whatever, bye."

I jog in front of him, stopping him. "West, wait."

With our bodies so close, his face changes—his anger fades, and a flicker of something I don't recognize takes over. I take a step back, embarrassed by my rashness. Where did I get the guts to stop him?

"What?" he asks.

"Are you all right?"

West rubs his eye with the palm of his left hand, just like he did when he was a little kid. "Yeah, I'm fine. Just frustrated with my dad. Look, sorry I snapped just now. I didn't mean to."

"It's okay."

I open my mouth to say something—anything—but then Miles appears at the side of the house.

"West," he growls. "What are you doing here?"

West pushes past Miles and says, "Leaving," before he vanishes around the corner.

"What an ass." Miles scoffs. "Anyway, forget him. I've got my car packed. Where's Keely?"

It takes me a second to regain my composure. "Banging down your front door," I say. "Let's go."

By the time Miles and I reach the front of the house, West's car is zooming away from the estate.

o o o

"I can't believe your dad lets you drive this thing," Keely says as we get into Miles's dad's black Jaguar. I hop into the passenger side, swallowed by the smell of pine and cough drops, as Miles gets behind the wheel.

"This isn't even his best car, honestly," Miles says in a way that is somehow not braggy, but his voice has a sharp edge, likely still annoyed from encountering West. Miles puts on a pair of Ray-Bans and says, "I don't know about you guys, but I'm ready to hide away for the rest of the weekend."

"Totally agree," Keely says.

It takes ten minutes to drive from the estate to downtown, and then we're reaching the outskirts. We pull up to Caldwell's final stoplight before the countryside. After all these years, it still takes forever to turn green.

My arm rests outside the open window, and the sun beats down on my skin. On my right, an old man hobbles up to a convenience store and grabs one of the newspapers from the rack. Though the weather in Maine is hot in July, he wears a dark green raincoat and a bucket hat, a scraggly beard covering his face.

Old Man Jenkens. When I was about five, he was the first—and only—person to ever show me how to hook a worm at his fisherman's supply shop. I didn't like fishing too much because I always viewed fish as my friends. (Yes, *Finding Nemo* was my favorite movie.) Mr. Jenkens had laughed when I said that, a short, gruff laugh. But I thought I must have been pretty special, because I had never seen anyone else make him smile. Everyone else at school was scared of Mr. Jenkens; they said he kept bodies in his basement, or that he was actually a ghost who came out of the fog to haunt us. The years haven't been kind, and his beard is three shades whiter than the last time I saw him. But he's never scared me.

A rusty silver minivan pulls up beside us with an unnecessary rev of its engine. Dean Bowman is in the driver's seat with his arm thrown over the wheel, Faye Hendricks on the passenger side with her feet on the dash. I almost want to hide my face, but if Faye recognizes me, she doesn't acknowledge it. The back windows are tinted, but I can make out another figure through them, probably Shawn.

"Yo, Hendricks!" Dean shouts, and his aviators reflect the sun, Miles, and me.

Miles leans over, and I shrink beneath his weight. The blond hairs of his arm tickle my cheek. "Hey! Race you to the cabin!"

"Yeah right, you rich asshole." Dean revs his engine again.

"Wait, what?" I whisper to Miles. "You said it was only going to be us."

Miles opens his mouth to reply, but he's interrupted by Dean honking his horn over and over again while he looks in the direction of the convenience store. With a huge grin, Dean yells, "Hey, Jenkens, you goofed any kids yet today? Old creep!"

This isn't right. The light turns green, and Dean rockets ahead. Mr. Jenkens, still clutching his newspaper, spits on the ground with a disgruntled scowl. His eyes lock with mine before Miles flies us past him.

o o o

The cabin is more of a single-story house, with terracotta-stained logs lining the exterior to create a "natural" look. The air in the woods is dense with earth and moss, and the sun barely peeks through the cracks in the canopy of leaves above our heads. We're completely remote out here—Miles's family owns the whole lake and rents out some of the other cabins in the area, but there isn't another property within shouting distance. Dean's minivan is already parked outside, and laughter echoes from behind the cabin.

"I just don't get why you didn't tell us Dean and Shawn were coming too," I say and slam the car door behind me. "You said just Faye might come. You lied to us, Miles."

Keely slings her backpack over her shoulder and gets out of the backseat. "What's with you, Liv? Who cares! Obviously we weren't going to tell my parents there'd be other guys here."

"Sorry, Liv." Miles ruffles his hair. "I wasn't trying to trick you."

Suddenly I feel dramatic, like I'm totally overreacting. "No worries," I say, trying to keep my tone light. "Sorry, guys. I don't mean to be so on edge, I'm just overwhelmed by . . . everything." I plaster a smile on my face. "No more moping, I promise! I can be fun too." *Maybe.*

"I know you can," Miles says.

When we get around to the back, Faye Hendricks is standing around a daytime campfire. She passes through a cloud of smoke on her way to us.

"Did you guys get lost on the way or something?"

White-blond waves reach below her ribs, and freckles stipple her cheeks. Her legs are long and willowy as she moves with the same whimsical, ballet-dancer grace she's always had. Miles and Faye are twins, but their faces look nothing alike. Their similarities are their blondness and paleness and susceptibility to sunburns. The skin beside Faye's pink spaghetti straps and Miles's cheeks below his sunglasses are a matching shade of red. I feel bad for thinking all her photos were Facetuned because she really is *that pretty.*

"Wow, Olivia. You look amazing." Faye's lips curve, but her voice is hostile. There was a time when I blamed my accident on her. I'd think, *if Faye never taunted me, I never would have been on that cliff.* But Dr. Levy helped me understand that Faye never made me do anything. I chose to be on the cliff that night. Blaming her will only redirect negativity and stunt my healing process.

"Thanks," I say.

"Seriously, I didn't expect you to be so tall."

I'm not tall. I'm five foot six.

Dean appears behind her and slings a limp arm over her shoulder, wearing the same white shirt he was in at the boat party, only now a leather jacket is thrown over it. I wonder if he's washed it since, or maybe he just has a bunch of the same shirt. He kisses the side of Faye's head, but he's looking at me the whole time.

Gross. Why is Faye with this guy? I guess beneath his sliminess, there is something decent-looking about Dean, but his slit-like brown eyes and long nose are serpentine.

I never cared about "adult gossip" when I was a kid, but I do remember my parents talking about how Dean's dad yelled at his wife all the time. Sometimes when I biked around the block, I'd see her smoking cigarettes at the curb of their house, looking thin and sad. But despite how close our houses were growing up, Dean and I never had a single playdate. He only ever hung out with Shawn, so I'm not surprised to see he's here too.

Unlike Dean, I can see why Shawn is appealing. Though he and Dean are paternal cousins, most of Shawn's genetics came from his mother's side. He has tawny skin and an athletic frame under that Nike jersey. Keely practically levitates to him, and I get the feeling she's liked him for a long time. How did I not know this? I guess being away from Caldwell for so long made me less privy even to my best friend's secrets.

We go to the fire, and I sit on an empty lawn chair. Dark smoke pillars into the afternoon sky, shielded by the forest, and a pile of firewood is stacked carelessly next to the pit. Faye is about to drop onto a log when Dean stops her.

"No, babe. Not there. Over here, beside me."

I want Faye to tell him to go fuck himself, but she obeys without question. Wow, the Faye Hendricks I knew wouldn't let anyone tell her what to do, not even teachers. The only person in the world she listened to was her mom. *People change.* Maybe this new Faye won't be as mean as the old one.

Dean opens a cooler full of ice and beer and passes some to Shawn.

"Where do you guys keep getting all this booze?" I ask.

"I got my brother to pick all this up," Shawn says and hands Keely a bottle. She pops off the tab.

We're lying to Sun and Roger about so many things . . .

"Your cop dad okay with you being here?" Dean asks Keely.

"Yeah, obviously," Keely mumbles against the lip of her beer, then nods at Miles. "What about *your* parents? They're not going to show up, are they?"

"They don't care about anything we do." Miles pokes at the fire. Cinders float into the air, and orange sparks pop against the sunset. The effect is hypnotizing, and before I know it, the sun is gone, and relaxation flows through me. I lean back in the chair and stare at the deep sea of stars through the leaves above. I'd forgotten how beautiful the sky is out here. No light pollution, just nature. But as the last shred of sun bleeds from the sky, the fog rolls in. Goosebumps rise on my skin, so I focus on the conversation, even though I haven't said a word.

"Man, Webster is the worst," Shawn says. "As soon as a chick graduates, he adds her on Facebook. I swear half his friends list are girls from school."

"Definitely," Miles agrees. "Guy's a creep."

"Yeah, he weirds me out too," Faye says. "I saw him lurking downtown once and he couldn't even make eye contact with me."

"And he liked one of my posts!" Keely says. "He totally creeps us!"

"Mr. Webster?" I ask. "Didn't he used to be really nice?"

Dean chuckles. "Are you high? You must be thinking of Mr. Weber from the third grade. We're talking about *Mr. Webster*, our asshole Science teacher, Olivia."

"Right . . . totally."

"Get with the times, Liv," Faye says and smiles against her bottle.

How am I supposed to relate with them when I'm so oblivious to their lives now? We were all supposed to grow up together, but now I'm disconnected and detached, a severed artery. I don't know how to speak or laugh effortlessly like they do, and silence is better than making a fool of myself.

Faye stands and claps her hands together. "Everyone, listen up. I think it's time we all decide who's crashing where."

Keely and I should definitely share a room, but she and Shawn are sitting next to each other on a log, and their shoulders brush as they drunkenly sway. *Oh no . . .*

"There are only three bedrooms," Faye says. "Dean and I are sharing the master, but that means there are two left—who's sleeping where?"

Across the circle, Miles stares at me. A small shudder of discomfort moves up my spine.

"You can crash with me, Keely," Shawn says. "I've got dibs on the room closest to the kitchen."

"Yeah? I'll think about it."

Judging by that mischievous look on her face, she's into this. But if Keely crashes with Shawn, that would leave me with Miles. I've never slept in the same bed as a guy, and maybe I'm not exactly experienced— but I know myself well enough to know this doesn't feel right. Miles is my friend and everything, but I don't want to share a freaking bed with him after being back for only a day. The couch is an option, but Miles might get offended. I check my phone. It's already 10:00 p.m., and I have zero bars of service, only a weak Wi-Fi connection from the cabin. Sweating, I glance into the darkness of the trees surrounding us. They close around me, suffocate me.

I stand. "Hey, I'm going to grab a glass of water. Anyone want anything?"

"Cooler's empty," Dean says, "just grab a round."

"Come with me, Keel." I nudge her. "I need an extra pair of hands to carry everything."

Once inside, with the sliding door shut behind us, we're engulfed by the mustiness of the cabin. It's an open concept where the living room mirrors a kitchen with a bar. Hendricks family photos line the wooden walls. Brian and his wife, Beatrice. Miles and Faye as kids. Their grandparents. Even some horse on a ranch they must have visited.

Not a single photo of West.

The air conditioner blasts icy air at me. I turn around and a giant deer stares back at me.

I scream.

"What the hell!" I exhale, my hand over my heart. It's only a head mounted to the wall above the fireplace, but even its glass eyes look alive.

"You good?" Keely laughs.

"That thing is incredibly creepy."

"Right? Miles's dad is way too into hunting."

"I know, but this was never here when I was a kid. I think I'd remember it."

"Anyway, what's up? Because I know you're totally capable of carrying those bottles, so . . ."

I pass her to the kitchen. "I'm okay, it's just . . . you're not going to ditch me for Shawn, are you?" Keely's silence gets under my skin. I reach into the fridge and take out four beers, a cooler for Faye, and a water bottle for me. "Keely, come on."

"You don't want to share a room with Miles?"

"No! Are you kidding?"

"I thought you were cool with him!"

"I am, but not like that. I don't know. It's too soon."

"But I really, really like Shawn."

"Keely, please don't make me share a room with Miles." I shove a few of the beers in her hands. "I'm not doing it. I'll sleep on the couch if I have to, but that'll make it so weird. And what ever happened to us spending *real time* together?"

Maybe I'm being self-centered for wanting her to drop her plans for me, but right now, my own best friend is a stranger. We've always had each other's backs. Even in the fifth grade, when Faye told everyone I was so weird because I'd been dropped on my head as a baby (which was untrue), Keely defended me. Miles didn't. That was the defining split between them as my best friends: Keely was always there, while Miles often took the side of his bully of a twin. I can't blame him for that; Faye is literally his other half. But it drove me nuts when we were kids.

"The thing is," Keely finally says, "Shawn just told me he brought condoms."

"Seriously? Keely, you're . . ." She's a virgin, I'm about to say. I stop myself. Whether Keely wants to have sex or not is her decision, but why does it have to leave me in a room with Miles? "Then I'll sleep on the couch," I say, unable to hide the irritation in my voice. As I'm about to slide open the door, Keely sighs.

"Liv, wait."

"Yeah?"

She kicks at the bear-shaped rug. "Me and you will crash together tonight, okay? You're right, tonight was supposed to be about us. Besides, I shouldn't rush into it with Shawn. I shouldn't do anything with him while I'm drunk."

"Thanks, Keel."

Back outside, Miles stands by the fire, the flames contorting his face. "I'm telling a spooky story, so get comfy, ladies." Miles might dress like a surfer, but he was always a theater geek. Something dramatic is about to happen. I sit on the log, and Keely heads back to Shawn.

Miles takes a deep breath. "This is the tale of old Mr. Jenkens, and how he became . . . the Caldwell Animal Slasher!"

You too, Miles?

"No, he isn't," I say, even though I have no idea if that's true. But seeing Dean yell at Mr. Jenkens earlier was awful, and something tells me he doesn't deserve that treatment.

"Oh, but he is!" Miles points his finger in the air. "Legend has it, Old Man Jenkens once had a pet squirrel. He was the best squirrel in the world, and they were best friends."

Keely shivers before she scoots closer to Shawn, and he wraps his arm around her. Dean drinks his beer while Faye checks her phone, totally bored. Miles's movements are animated and theatrical as he speaks.

"Jenkens came home from fishing one day to discover that his best friend, the squirrel, had run away. It destroyed him."

"Come on, Hendricks," Shawn mutters. "Where the hell are you taking this?"

Miles holds his finger up again. "Jenkens searched all over Caldwell for his squirrel, but he never found him. As the years went on, Jenkens became so encumbered with grief, that he . . . stopped shaving his beard. The once handsome, bushy-tailed young man was becoming angrier, and bitterer, until one day . . . he snapped!"

When Shawn grabs Keely's shoulders, she screams. Everyone—including Keely—laughs, and she playfully slaps Shawn's shoulder, shaking her head like she's embarrassed. But everyone's laughing *with* Keely, not at her. She melts back into the group easily, but none of that comes naturally to me. Not at home in New York, and apparently not here either.

"Anyway," Miles sings, "Jenkens, by this time an angry old man, discovered that the only way to cure his loneliness and resentment toward squirrels was to take their lives. Now, Jenkens roams forests—just like this one—in search of woodland creatures to tear apart. Limb. By. Limb."

Maybe this would be funny if we hadn't seen a maimed squirrel literally last night. Miles is weirding me out.

"For real, though," Dean says. "If anyone's slashing those animals, it's that old creep."

"He does have all that taxidermy in his shop," Faye says.

"Your dad has lots of that stuff too," I say without thinking, and everyone looks at me. Miles and Faye exchange a glance.

"You think my *dad* is the squirrel killer?" Faye snickers, but her face is flat. "Yeah, right. Do you have any idea how common trophy hunting is? I hate it, but my dad does what he does. Cute little squirrels aren't his style, but Old Man Jenkens has a stuffed squirrel behind his desk."

"He does?" Miles asks, still keeping his dramatic voice on. "I mean, of *course* he does! That's the body of his ex-best-squirrel-friend. He kept it as a trophy."

"I thought you said he never found that squirrel?" Keely says.

"I'm changing it. He did find the squirrel, but punishing it wasn't enough. He now enacts revenge on all of squirrel-kind."

Thankfully Miles lets his story end there. He sits next to me while everyone else continues with other conversations. It's weird for his tan shorts to brush my bare leg, and for me to smell the lime on his cologne. Maybe it's because I didn't sleep last night, but I can't think of what to say—all I know is that being next to Miles reminds me of West.

"Miles?" I take an uneasy sip of my water. "Maybe it isn't my place to ask, but who's Amelia?"

"Huh? Where'd you hear that name?"

"I accidentally overheard West and your dad talking today."

"Oh. Amelia is . . ." He shakes his head. "Nah, she doesn't matter. Trust me."

"But—"

"Hey, so I was thinking, maybe we could make plans to hang out alone sometime this week? Like after the trip's over, so we can catch up just you and me."

"Oh . . . sure." So, no Amelia questions. I guess it's none of my business, anyway. And it's nice Miles wants to catch up, just us.

"Evening, boys," someone says, and we all turn around to see a man standing in the shadows at the side of the cabin. "And girls," he adds.

The figure steps into the light of the fire, and my heart stops. It's West—and he has a girl on his arm.

Miles jumps to his feet. "What the fuck are you doing here, man?"

"West, come on, let's go." The girl tugs him back, her voice soft, angelic, her straight brown hair floating down her shoulders. She pulls on West's arm until he looks at her.

"Hey, it's okay," West says, almost like a coo, like he doesn't want us to hear.

"Let's just go," she says. "We should let the kids have their fun."

"Baby, come on."

Baby. He called her baby. It's cheesy, but there's something endearing when it comes from his raspy voice.

"I'll wait in the car." She doesn't look at us. "Hurry up, okay?"

"Okay."

He kisses her. It's nothing but a short peck, but it creates an unexplainable flare of jealousy in me. Of all the things I've seen West Hendricks do—from climbing to the top of the tallest tree to reeling in a massive sea bass—I've never seen him kiss a girl. Passing my feelings off as nonsense, I watch Amelia-or-whoever take off around the side of the cabin. West's eyes land right on me.

"West," I breathe out, but he looks past me to Miles.

Miles's glare deepens. "What are you doing here? You were going to break in, weren't you?"

"Didn't think you'd be here." West's face is almost cruel, predatory. He walks into the circle and gives off an intense aura, like we're on private property and he's holding a shotgun. Even though I'm here with everyone, it's like I'm not even part of the group—I'm floating above it, out of my body, watching it happen.

"You don't have permission to be here," Miles says.

"You really think I didn't get an extra key made? Sometimes I like a little vacation too, Miles. And do you have permission to have all these kids here?"

"Of course I do. Mom and Dad don't care, they just don't want you using the place for whatever sick shit you're up to."

"Maybe not." West nods at Dean, whose arm is draped over Faye. "But if they found out about *that,* don't you think it'd be a little different?"

Faye shoves Dean off her. "You better not tell, Weston."

"Maybe I won't. Or maybe I will."

A pause thickens the air and accentuates the sounds of the forest around us: mosquitoes buzzing and crickets chirping. We've been dropped into the middle of a dysfunctional family war zone, and every word loosens the pin on a grenade.

"Fine, West," Miles says. "What do you want?"

"Next weekend, I want the cabin." West slides his hands in the pockets of his dark denim jacket. "Don't tell Dad."

"Fine. Now will you leave?"

West looks at me once before he takes off. It's only when he's gone that I realize I've been clutching this water bottle with trembling hands. Without the drunken chatter in the air, West's engine clearly revs out front.

"Yo," Dean slurs, "your brother wheels the hottest girls."

"Shut the hell up," Miles and Faye spit.

"Seriously, Miles," Dean goes on, laughing, "you didn't get his game at all."

Shawn chuckles like an idiot with him, before a palpable silence pours in. The fire dies as the embers fizzle to ash.

Miles bounces to his feet. "Anyone need a drink?"

Everyone nods. Faye doesn't carry the same fake joy—her thumbs tap erratically at her phone. I don't blame her. Apparently, she isn't allowed to date. Or maybe she isn't allowed to date Dean. From what I remember of her parents, anyone who isn't a billionaire's son isn't good enough for her, and Dean's family is on the low end of middle class like mine.

"That was so weird," Keely whispers to me. "With West, I mean."

"Yeah. Do you know that girl?"

"Not at all. I didn't even know West had a girl. Then again, I guess he has a lot of girls. She's definitely not from Caldwell." She leans closer to me so no one else can hear. "You know what else I noticed about her?"

"What?"

"She looks like you."

But she isn't me.

My chest sparks a *pop* and *fizz* of jealousy. Childish emotions I thought I could keep buried. I can't believe I'm jealous over a girl I don't know dating a guy I have nothing to do with. So, West grew up to be hot. It doesn't matter. Miles is hot too. But I've never felt the same surge of energy for Miles as I always have for West.

Even right after Miles and I became friends, Miles's nature was always tepid, easy to be around. I was never nervous near him—not until I met his older brother for the first time.

Miles and I had been playing in the sandbox in the backyard when West emerged from the forest in his Boy Scout uniform: a tan button-up with a sash covered in patches. Apparently he'd been tracking a deer to test out the skills he'd been learning. West's dad was a hunter, but West would tell me later that he'd never kill anything with legs—he just liked to track animals. Maybe just to prove he could.

When West came into the sandbox, Miles told him to go away, and West kicked over his sandcastle. I said something along the lines of, "You're mean!" and tried to shove him, but West didn't budge.

"Who are you, anyway?" he asked, and I focused on my feet, intimidated by his size.

"Olivia . . ."

"What kind of name is Olive?"

I puffed up. "It's *Olivia*."

"Sounds like Olive to me."

In that moment, I hated it. But West never stopped calling me Olive, and somewhere along the line, it blurred into something I silently adored; something only he said.

Coming back to Caldwell was supposed to help me move on— but I should have known all it would do is make me relive the past.

5

A few hours later, everyone's voices become drunk gibberish in my ears. No one even notices when I sneak into the cabin to call it a night. When I get into the room I'm sharing with Keely, I shut the door behind me and press my back to it. Cackles sound through the windows, but they're muted enough that I have a moment to breathe.

The double bed takes up most of the room, and a fox skin hangs on the wall across from the window. Not looking at it, I change into a pair of plaid pajamas and crawl under the soft linen sheets. A photo frame with a picture of Miles and his dad on a golf course sits on a nightstand. Shutting off the lamp, I sink into the pillow, well aware I won't be sleeping much tonight, even though I'm exhausted.

Light from the full moon seeps through the window, and the shadows of tree branches sway like fingers behind the glass. Just as I'm drifting away, everything goes quiet. I open my eyes to the wooden, knotty ceiling. Everyone must have passed out, because all I can hear are insects trilling and the AC rumbling. Suddenly wide awake, I peer out the window. Embers smolder in the firepit, and a thin stream of smoke curls into the night. The seats are empty.

If they came inside, Keely should be here with me. I go to the living room. The light from a digital clock illuminates the deer head in red, and I shudder away from it.

"Hey, is anyone in here?"

Silence. Goosebumps rise on my arms. The thought of moving through this dark, quiet cabin freaks me out, but there's no way I'm sleeping alone tonight. Keely has to be around here somewhere.

Outside, the air is colder than I remember. A round moon glows blood orange through the trees, dimmed by the fog. Mesmerized, I follow the light until I'm halfway into the woods.

"Keely?" I call out. "Miles? Hello? Where are you guys?"

A twig snaps and my breath catches. I spin around, but I'm surrounded by nothing but trees. Footsteps move through the underbrush. They grow louder. Faster.

Someone—*something*—is charging at me.

Heart thudding, I rip through the trees. Branches slice my arms and legs. When my foot catches on a root, my knees skid into damp, cold mud, and slide right into the shore of the lake. I scream and try to get away, but the mud is too thick. My feet sink deeper. Something grabs me from behind and forces me under water. Hands grip at my throat, and only one thought ripples through my mind: *I'm going to die.*

All at once, air fills my lungs. I gasp and jolt upright. Drenched in sweat, it takes me a moment to process the fact that I'm still in the bed at the cabin. Streams of sunlight pour through the curtains, and the spot beside me is untouched. Keely never came to bed.

A nightmare. I grab at my throat, as if to make sure the hands aren't really there. The taste of lake water is still strong on my tongue, and the sensation of my airways being clogged is heavy. I breathe in. Out. In. Out. Remember what Dr. Levy said: it's all in my head. As long as I can breathe, I'm alive.

It's been so long since I've had a nice dream, like floating on clouds, or even something random and nonsensical, like people who have different faces than they do in real life. No, my dreams are always terrifying, and always recurring. Normally the one about being held under water takes place in a bathtub or a pool. It's never happened in a lake before.

Shivering, I pull myself out of bed and put on a clean tank top and a pair of shorts. In the kitchen, the granite island is littered with plates and half-empty cups of orange juice. A tray of bacon, eggs, and hash browns sits on the table, no longer steaming. It must be for me. I sit down and dig in, but end up poking at my food more than actually eating it.

Minutes tick by, and I cram a bite of crunchy, overcooked bacon into my mouth. Still no sign of the others. When Keely doesn't reply to my text, I head outside. The sun is warm and the air is filled with bark and earth, exactly as it was in my dream. I snap the elastic against my wrist.

Ouch. Okay, definitely awake.

Laughter and splashing echo through the forest. From memory, I follow a short path through the trees until I reach the murky green lake. It's shallow along the shoreline, but gets deeper and darker farther out. The surface stretches at least a few yards to the pine trees on the other side. Keely and Shawn jump off a short cliff into the water, hand in hand. Faye and Dean splash each other while Miles does laps. I used to love swimming here with Miles, but now—especially after last night's dream—the earthy smell makes me nauseated.

Keely spots me. "Liv—you're awake!" she stammers, and everyone stops to look at me.

"You guys left me," I mumble.

"You were passed out, and we wanted to go swimming . . . and you can't, you know. . ."

Of course they'd have to leave me behind to swim, but Keely's words still sting. "You could have at least told me where you were going," I say.

"Chill out, Olivia," Faye says and sends a spray of water in my direction. The moment the cold touches my skin, I let out a scream. Everyone but Keely laughs.

"Don't do that!" I shout. "What the hell is your problem, Faye?"

"What? It was an accident!"

"No, it wasn't!"

"Guys, stop," Keely says.

Dean chuckles. "Come on, Olivia. Why don't you just come in the water? It's not so bad."

"Yeah, it's nice in here," Shawn agrees.

Miles steps toward the shore, and I step back. He reaches his hand out. "C'mon, Liv. Come in."

"No," I say. I can't believe him.

"Buzzkill," Faye mutters. When she splashes at me again, my feet slip in the grass and I almost fall but manage to catch my balance.

"Stop it, Faye!"

"That's not helping." Miles shoves himself in front of her. "Come on, it'll be okay, Liv." He extends his hand farther. Water dribbles from his hair and onto his cheeks, and his eyes match the forest and body of water behind him. "You trust me, don't you? It's just a lake— you can't drown out here, I won't let you."

"No!"

"Like I said, buzzkill," Faye says. "Why are you even here, Olivia? It's the cabin, we *swim*."

My nails dig into my palms. She said *buzzkill*, but in my head I hear the words she said all those years ago.

Chicken.

The night I fell began at Bailey Pearson's end-of-the-year pool party with everyone in the sixth grade. My rivalry with Faye had been building up for years—she hated how close I was with Miles, and apparently West too. She taunted me every chance she got, and she always tried to distance me from her family. Most of my childhood was spent on the defense, but when we got older, I learned how to fight back.

Storm clouds were rolling over the sky from beyond Bailey's backyard, so the party would have to be brought inside soon. Everyone was still swimming, Faye in a white bikini. I envied how much confidence she had in her body. She was cool and hot, and it came off so authentically. I would never tell her how much I wanted to be like her, but I was uncomfortable with my body and sought attention in different ways. All I had was that I was daring. Daring, like West was. Maybe I couldn't be like Faye, but I could be like her older brother.

Miles and Keely helped me move Bailey's trampoline between the roof of the house and the pool. Some people cheered me, others gasped as I climbed the roof, jumped onto the trampoline, and bounced into the deep end of the pool. Everyone else started doing it, too, but Faye refused. Then, while I was crossing the pool deck, Faye pulled me aside from everyone else.

"Who are you trying to impress, Liv?" she said through gritted teeth. "My brother isn't here."

"He's right over—" I stopped myself, because of course she meant West, not Miles.

The embarrassment kicked in; West was my weak spot and Faye knew it, yet for whatever reason, she'd never started a rumor that I liked him. She just threw subtle jabs at me every now and then, normally when Miles wasn't around. Deciding not to engage, I walked away from her—but then Faye's voice rose loud enough for the whole party to hear.

"Real badass, Liv! But I bet you're still way too chicken to even attempt the cliff challenge."

The party stood still. Faye's boyfriend at the time was some grade eight guy, and his friends had done it five times, or so she said.

"I'm not stupid," I told her. "Only idiots go up there."

"Like I said, you're too chicken. I did it no problem."

All the attention turned on Faye, and everyone peppered her with questions about how she did it and if she almost fell. Faye basked in the attention like a celebrity photographed by the paparazzi.

Silently, I stood to the side of the party, my anger boiling. Miles's voice sounded from behind me.

"Don't worry about Faye, Liv." He awkwardly held his hands together. Miles was becoming taller and more gangly, but he hadn't hit his growth spurt yet and was about half an inch shorter than me. "She's just lying for attention."

He was probably right, but as Faye soaked up the attention, something in me snapped.

I took off, right then and there, determined to prove her wrong.

That's when everything changed. All because I couldn't stand the idea of Faye being viewed as stronger than me. All because I cared what people thought too much. Regret pools in, weakens my muscles as I tremble near the shore of the lake.

More than anything, I wish I could go back in time and make one different decision.

Don't go on that cliff. Put your pride behind you.

But nothing will ever change the past, and Keely's voice snaps me to the present.

"Can you guys shut up? She almost drowned when she was a kid, are you dumb?"

"It's just water." Faye looks at me. "Look, Liv. I'm standing right up. It would literally be impossible to drown out here."

Voice shaking, I say, "You guys don't get it. Faye, it was you who—" I stop myself. No. It isn't Faye's fault, it's my own. I never should have let her get in my head again. I can't blame them for not understanding—to them, I'm being oversensitive and dramatic about something normal people enjoy.

Faye's right. I am a buzzkill.

Turning away, I dive into the forest, crashing like a wave as I storm back into the cabin and find my way to the bedroom. Tears sting my eyes. This isn't what I wanted from this trip. I wanted to reconnect with my old life, to blend back in with Caldwell, to somehow pick up where I left off before I fell. How stupid and naive was I to think that? It's been five years. *Everything* has changed.

Most of all, me.

The daring little girl who used to love playing in the water with Miles is gone, and maybe he doesn't get that, and that's why he tried to get me in that lake. Deep down, I know he's just trying to help.

Stuffing my things into my backpack, the zipper catches, and I can't stop crying. Just as I fall onto the bed, someone knocks on the door.

"It's just me." Keely leans against the door frame, guilt on her face. "The others are still out at the lake."

"I'm so humiliated, Keely."

"Don't be. It's cool, Liv . . . they understand."

"No, they don't. Miles means well, but Faye's taunting me and Shawn and Dean are laughing their asses off. I don't even want to be here anymore. I feel like I don't know any of you."

"What? You know *me*, Liv."

"Barely. You didn't even come to bed last night." And I don't want to tell her about last night's dream because she might judge me. None of this is right.

"Sorry . . . we all passed out in the living room." Keely sits beside me on the bed, a towel wrapped around her torso, her hair in wet straggles over her shoulders. "And of course you know me, Liv."

"Not really. This trip isn't turning out how I hoped at all."

"But it's only just starting. I know the others are being dicks, but they're not trying to be mean . . . they're just sort of like that, you know? Sometimes I get poked at too; we all do."

"If they're 'just sort of like that' then why are you even friends with them?" When Keely says nothing, I ask, "Can I please just call your parents for a ride?"

"Wait, *what*? You actually want to leave?"

"I'm not having a good time, Keely."

"But . . . my parents won't let me stay if you go."

Shit. I take a breath and rub my eyes with my palms. Whatever happened to proving I can be "fun"? If I call Keely's parents, it will ruin her whole trip.

"Fine," I say, frustrated, "but I'm staying in here for a while."

Keely's quiet for a moment. "I know we're off to a bit of a bumpy start, but we'll spend lots of time together after this weekend is over, I promise."

"Okay."

She apologizes again and exits the room. With the door shut, the silence blankets me. Lying back on the bed and wiping what's left of my tears, I take out my iPhone, the only distraction I have in this place. There's a follow request on Instagram in my notification center. I open it, and I almost can't believe what I'm seeing.

West followed me. At about eight o'clock this morning.

I press accept and request to follow him back since he ignored my old request. I hold my phone to my chest and take a deep breath. When it buzzes, West accepts. For the first time ever, I have access to his social media. I wait a couple of minutes, partly hoping he'll direct message me since there's a green bubble next to his name, but he doesn't, so I take a deep breath and message him first.

Wow, you followed me. I'm shocked

Lol, well you proved me wrong. I thought I'd
never see you again. Now I'm seeing you
everywhere. Sorry if I killed your vibe last
night.

You didn't! Did your night go okay?

Meh

Meh?

Meh.

Okayyy lol

He reads it but doesn't reply. Five minutes later, he goes offline.

Hint taken. But that's okay. It's probably stupid, but having West add me has been the best thing to happen since coming back to Caldwell Beach.

For the rest of the weekend, I find myself thinking of him to distract myself from how awkward it is hanging out with everybody. I spend most of the time in the bedroom reading, scrolling through my phone, and I don't let my guard down until we're driving back to town in Miles's car.

6

The rest of the week trickles away faster than I expected, and by the time Friday rolls around, I've mostly recovered from the disaster that was the cabin.

"Okay, you have to get this dress," Keely says, standing beside me in the reflection of Sea Breeze's dressing room mirror. "Liv, it makes your eyes look so blue."

There aren't many clothing stores in Caldwell, but even when we were kids, Sea Breeze was the place to be. All the cool teenagers shopped here, but we were more loiterers than anything since we were too young to wear half the clothes. But now I'm older and actually have money from working at my parents' shop. And this dress really does make my eyes look blue.

I search the azure fabric for the tag. "Eighty dollars, yikes."

Keely adjusts the straps of her dress, which, as always, is yellow. "You're on vacation. You're allowed to buy a dress."

"You know my family, Keel. Thrift shop owners. Everything I wear is hand-me-down."

"It's one dress, and you look so pretty. Besides, you're going to Miles's place on Sunday, right? To hang out alone?"

"Keely, I already told you. Miles is just my friend. I don't like him like that."

"*Okay*, point taken. You don't like Miles, I'll stop pushing it. The only reason I wanted you two together is so you can double date with Shawn and me."

"Can't I just be your third wheel?"

"You don't mind?"

"Not really."

Keely smiles, her cheeks rosy from the cream blush I watched her apply this morning. "Good. Because I really like him, and I want you two to be friends."

Shawn's all right. From what I remember of him from elementary school, he was a sporty kid, always playing kickball on the playground or swinging from the monkey bars like it was no problem. We didn't talk much at the cabin last weekend, and I haven't seen him since— Keely kept her promise about us spending real time together. Every day has been movies and staying up late on the internet, laughing at videos and creeping people's social media profiles like we used to.

"Why do you like Shawn so much, anyway?" I ask.

Keely's face lights up with a big smile. "Okay, so get this. Shawn *never* dates anyone. Like girls will try to get with him because he's so hot, but within a week, he ghosts them. But we've been talking for like, two whole weeks, and he even wanted to sleep together."

I pause. "He's not just trying to use you, is he?"

"I don't think so. He's never slept with any of the other girls. Shawn's a virgin, just like I am. And I know because nothing stays a secret in this town. If he'd slept with someone, it would've gotten out. Besides, I'm having fun with him right now—it's not like I'm totally invested yet."

Keely's never had a real boyfriend, but she has a long history of falling too hard, too fast. This is exactly like it was when she had a crush on Carter in the fifth grade, even though he kept rejecting her. When it comes to boys, Keely's always been all heart.

But I say, "Fair enough. It is summer, after all."

"Plus, Shawn barely even has any friends, period. Like he parties and stuff, but the only person he *ever* hangs out with is Dean. But ever since Dean started dating Faye, it seems like Shawn's trying to be more social too. So yeah, I feel special."

"Then I'm happy for you."

After we change back into our regular clothes, we duck under the fake boat hanging between the dressing room and the store and head for the cash register. Nets and oars decorate the counter. Once we pay, we tuck our new dresses into our backpacks and step into the warm, sticky evening.

Keely wants to walk past Shawn's house, so we head down Pinewood Avenue to the low-roofed bungalow at the end of the street that thumps with trap music. The sun is still up, but I guess it isn't too early to be drinking. On the porch, Shawn holds a can of beer while Dean lights a cigarette. The door to the house is open, and people are draped over the living room furniture inside.

"Olivia, Keely," Dean says. "Get over here!"

I'm not stoked about it but meet them on the rickety wooden porch.

"What's up, Keely?" Shawn smiles and hugs her, and Keely's knees almost buckle. So, maybe this is a bit more intense than her old crush on Carter. Shawn doesn't strike me as the most trustworthy guy, but he's not the worst either. Besides, the bright smile on Keely's face warms my heart.

"You girls staying?" Dean asks. "Party's just getting started."

Both social situations I've been in so far have been disasters. "I'm not really feeling it, but thanks for the invite."

"Yeah, we'll see you guys later, though," Keely says.

"Just because Olivia doesn't want to stay doesn't mean you can't." Dean smirks against his cigarette. "C'mon, it's a party, Keely. Hang out with us."

"Sorry, guys, I can't . . ." Keely looks at me with big, guilty brown eyes, like she's waiting for my approval. I want to stop being that clingy best friend, especially because of the way they're all looking at me right now.

"It's okay, Keel," I say. "You should stay."

"You sure?"

I nudge her with a grin. "We've hung out every day this week. Besides, I could use some time alone to wander." I want to see if my favorite tree is still around, but I don't say it out loud because Dean would probably rip on me.

"Really? Seriously, I can come if you want," Keely says.

"No, don't worry about it, really. Have fun."

"Okay, tell my mom and dad I'll be home before midnight."

"No problem." I head down the driveway, thankful to have some time to explore by myself.

o o o

The beach is a short walk from downtown. Salt carries on the ocean air, and the sun's position, slowly sinking toward the horizon, reminds me of so many evenings spent here. Shadows reach through the golden rays that paint the sand. Keeping my distance from the shoreline, I move along the overgrowth until the beech tree appears ahead. Even in the full bloom of summer, sparse leaves sprout from the thick, sturdy branches.

It's still here.

Hot sand hisses beneath my feet as I run to the tree. But stopping at the trunk, my nerves fray—this wouldn't have even been up for discussion when I was a kid; I would have just started climbing. But now the tree towers over me like it could be fifty feet high. One wrong move and a branch could snap and my leg could break. Or worse.

None of this is right. The old Olivia would never be scared. Shoving my fear aside, I take a deep breath and feel around for a sturdy branch to grab onto, then hoist myself up each one until reaching the strongest. I scoot my butt along the bark and get comfortable. This used to be my thinking place, my own personal Giving Tree. Not even Keely or Miles came with me, but one time, when I was ten and West was twelve, he found me crying here.

I'd been at an all-girls slumber party at Bailey's, but Keely was home with the flu and a full-raging fever. Her mom wouldn't let her go, no matter how hard she begged. Faye would be there, so I was nervous to go without Keely, but I did it anyway. Sure enough, when it came to truth or dare, Faye tried to force me to choose the former, digging for information about who I liked, whether it was Miles or someone else. But I always chose dare. Normally Faye would get me to do something gross like eat fish food, but instead, she told everyone that I didn't have a crush because I knew no one would ever like me back.

It's so stupid looking back on how upset I got, but she'd struck a chord. I got Bailey's parents to call mine to come pick me up early. When they arrived, I begged them to take me to the beach and let me be alone. They walked along the shore nearby while I came here and sat on this branch. The sea swallowed the sun the exact same way it does now.

West then appeared at the bottom of the tree. Without saying a word, he climbed up and sat next to me. We remained in silence, listening to the waves lap against the shore, until I finally said, "Your sister's mean, West. She hates me."

He kicked his dangling feet. West was getting bigger, and the hair on his legs had darkened, his muscles becoming pronounced. "Faye makes my life hell too," he said. "She and Miles."

"I just don't understand why she hates me so much."

"Faye doesn't like having her toys taken away. You spend too much time with my brother."

"But he's my friend." I couldn't stop crying. I didn't expect it, but West wrapped his arm around my shoulder and rested his cheek against my head. He had never been affectionate with me before. Miles and I hugged sometimes, but never West—so feeling his warmth turned me to stone.

"Don't cry, Olive," was all he'd said. He held me until my tears dried. My heart thrummed against my ribcage, because by this time, I was old enough to understand why West always had such an impact on me. He was my crush. Not Miles. *West*.

But I never told Keely or anyone else, because Faye was right: he would never like me back. West was older, so much cooler. And the only way to keep a part of him to myself was to hide the fact that I liked him. Fool myself that we could go on being the friends we all were. And that day seven years ago was the only time he ever touched me like that.

Right now, he's probably touching that other girl. At the cabin, maybe in the bed I slept in while I was there. It's pathetic that, after all these years, the thought of him still makes my heart sore.

The sky transforms into nautical twilight, a sea of navy and violet. The waves move with the rhythm of the wind. I begin to climb down the tree.

o o o

By the time I'm back in the suburbs, the moon is a silvery crescent against a near-black sky. Mosquitoes nip me through the thin fabric of my gray zip-up.

Walking alone at night is never fun. It wasn't a problem when I lived here before because Caldwell is so safe—the jail's holding cell has mostly been used as a drunk tank over the years. Besides, I always felt good knowing Keely's dad was patrolling the streets. But nighttime in the city was way different, way more dangerous. I'm used to keeping my head down, but as I turn onto Oak Crescent, a bush jostles. I look over my shoulder, into the obscurity between the trees that separate the properties. A bird hoos, insects buzz—and when a twig breaks, I jump and walk faster.

The street is totally empty. My phone shows 9:33 p.m., but it feels so late. The lights in most of the houses on this street aren't even on.

Another twig snaps.

My pulse jerks into my throat, and I pick up the pace. *Calm down, you're being crazy.* I close my eyes and snap the elastic.

But then I hear *clap, clap, clap* behind me. Footsteps.

Gasping, I check over my shoulder. The street is deserted. My blood pumps faster than a coursing river and thuds against the back of my skull. Screw walking—I'm running. My shoes pound the road as I book it. My imagination races faster than my legs move. Kidnapping, rape, *murder.*

The animal killer.

When I slam straight into a body, I scream.

"Jesus, Olivia?"

West stands in front of me—all six-foot-something of him—with a Rottweiler at the end of the leash in his hand. Every tide in me calms.

"What's up?" he asks. "You good?"

"I don't know." Hugging myself, my teeth chatter. "I felt like someone was following me, but—"

The way West steps closer and looks over my shoulder makes me feel safe. "What do you mean? Did you hear someone?"

"Maybe, no, I just . . ." I brush my hair behind my ear. "It was just a weird feeling. Forget I said anything?"

He half smiles. "Okay. You want to walk with us?"

"Oh, right!" My anxiety was so high, I didn't even say hi to the puppy. I pat his too-big-for-his-body head, and his flappy pink tongue hangs from his mouth in a panting dog smile.

"This is Oscar," West says. "Come on, boy, let's walk Olive home."

"Hi, Oscar."

Oscar woofs.

As I fall into step beside them, my jitters vanish, like they were never even there at all. Thank God West can't read my mind and know how much I've been thinking about him over the past week because it's beyond embarrassing.

"So," West says, "last weekend. Awkward, huh?"

"Yeah . . . I wasn't expecting you to show up."

"Likewise. I should've known Miles was going to be there."

"Why aren't you there now? With your girlfriend?"

"We broke up."

Okay, heart. Stop leaping. We pause as Oscar raises his leg at a tree.

"How come?" I ask. "You seemed . . . close."

"Yeah, I don't know." The corners of his eyes crinkle. "I don't like it when people say one thing but mean something totally different. Melissa was really bad for that."

Wait, *Melissa*? So that wasn't Amelia?

West puts his free hand in the pocket of his jacket. "She was all pissed off I couldn't get the cabin last week when I said I could, but then she pretended like everything was fine for the whole weekend. Then when I went to drive her home—she lives a few towns over—she started tripping on me. Shit like that was pretty much a weekly occurrence with her, so I just dropped her off and said it's over. She didn't care." His voice lifts near the end in a subtle way I'm sure he doesn't want me to hear. I do hear it, though. It's the slightest crackle of pain.

"I'm sorry," I say.

"Thanks. I'm not that upset about it. I guess I feel free more than anything."

"Free to do what?"

We pass under a street lamp, then dip back into the night. West's aquamarine eyes meet with the clear sky, his free hand tucked into his jacket, and the offshore wind breathes through the leaves of the aspen tree on someone's lawn. The lights in their house are out, and the *ting ting* of their wind chimes tinkles through the air.

"Anything," West eventually says. "I can walk around with you like this and not have to worry whether Melissa will be pissed or not. She didn't like me hanging out with girls, which caused a lot of problems since my roommate is a girl."

I can't blame her, considering West is drop-dead gorgeous, but he probably didn't appreciate being told what to do. I've never been in a relationship, but I wouldn't want to be with someone like that, someone who would try to control me.

We pass by a stretch of grass occupied by a single willow. Not knowing what else to talk about, I say, "I didn't know you had a dog."

"Yeah, he's a good boy. A girl I was seeing last year brought me to this shelter, and I wasn't planning on leaving with a puppy, but hey, here I am. Can you believe he's only a year old?"

"Wow, he's really big."

Oscar lifts his leg at another tree. When we continue walking, West says, "You should come see me sometime."

The answer is yes—five million times, yes—but I bite my lip and play it cool. "And do what?"

He smiles and shows the dimples in his cheeks, accentuating the attractive stubble that lines his jaw. "I don't know, catch up, whatever. You can tell me what it's like in the big city. I can tell you how nothing's changed here."

"It feels like everything's changed."

"I don't know about that. But you've definitely changed."

Fizzing soda pops throughout my body as he stares at me, and I don't know what to do about it, so I look away. "I should get back. Keely's parents might wonder where I am."

"Yeah, let's go."

We continue up the street, toward Keely's neighborhood. I pet Oscar and pretend to be occupied by him, but in reality, my mind plays questions on repeat. West is incredibly attractive. And he's single now.

Stop.

The last time I allowed myself to feel anything for him, he ended up hurting me more than anyone ever has. I still don't understand why he was so mean to me in Coral Park, only a year after holding me for the first and only time.

If this summer is about facing my past, I need to face him too.

"West, can I ask you something?"

"Okay."

"What happened before I left? I thought we were friends, then you started acting weird. Sure, you were always a little distant with me, but that day in Coral Park, when you told me to go away . . . you really hurt my feelings." My laugh sounds pathetic. "Maybe you don't even remember it."

The stretch of silence is too long. Our feet scrape against the road.

"I do remember," West says. "And you were my friend. I didn't mean what I said to you, I didn't want you to go away. The guys had been teasing me for spending time with you and Miles, and I just . . ."

"Was that all it was? Because they teased you?"

He rakes his hand through his hair. "I had other issues too, Olive.

Issues at home. But none of that shit is an excuse. I was a brat, plain and simple. I'm sorry."

God, the number of times I've imagined him saying those two words—I'm sorry—but I never thought he would. It's surreal.

"Thank you," I whisper. "I just wish you hadn't let me think I'd done something wrong all these years."

"For what it's worth, I really am sorry."

The sound of bubbling water fills the night. Since Caldwell is built up the side of a cliff, there's a bridge that cuts through the middle of town, separated by a rapid river with a small waterfall that leads into the ocean. The drop isn't that high, but by memory, I know there are rocks frothing with the current. A tall metal railing bars in both sides of the bridge to prevent people from falling. Billows of mist engulf it, but something else is there. It takes me a moment to realize what I'm looking at, and I instinctively grab West's arm.

"Oh my God, West, look!"

A man stands on the railing of the bridge, and it looks like he's about to jump.

"Holy shit." West's voice is low, and we both turn to ice. We're close enough to the man that he'll hear us if we speak too loud, so West whispers, "We can't spook him. Here, I need you to hold the dog and stay here."

"But—do I call the cops?"

"Not yet, we can't freak him out. I know him, he's my friend. Let me handle it." West shoves the leash into my hand. "Oscar's a good dog, but he'll bark if he senses something's off. Stay here, keep him occupied. I'm going to try to talk him down."

"Okay. Okay, I can do that." My mouth is as dry as sand. I grip the leather leash like my life depends on it.

On the bridge, the man's body wobbles, and I squint to make out the side profile of his face through the darkness. That grizzled beard, that hunched back—it's Old Man Jenkens.

When I think of people who want to throw themselves off bridges, I think of troubled teens or people who are stressed out in their middle age. Not disgruntled men in their sixties. But of course, there's no age limit to something like this. It's hard to imagine Jenkens in any other form, like he's always been old, cantankerous, and ready to jump off a bridge. But he hasn't always been that way, I know that. He was once young like us. With dreams. Aspirations.

West raises his hands. The water below crashes loudly and muffles out their voices, so I step closer in order to hear West shouting, "Hey, Jenkens! It's me. Don't be scared, I'm heading down your way, okay? Just want to talk."

"Weston. Damn, didn't expect to see you. Get out of here, boy."

"I have a better idea, why don't you come down here?"

Jenkens looks down and laughs. Then he glances back over his shoulder and finds me and Oscar.

"Shit," Jenkens says, "you brought company."

"Yeah, that's Olivia Cathart. You remember the Catharts, right? They used to live here."

"Of course I remember the Catharts. Jesus, boy, I'm old, not senile." The teasing nature of his voice unsettles me, considering how close he is to death.

"Jenkens, come on, man. Come down and talk to us."

"Dammit, I can't tell you how many times I thought about jumping off this thing, and this is the closest I ever came to it, and now you . . ."

"Don't do this, man."

"Why not? There's nothing left for me here."

Mist from the waterfall envelops them. West is quiet, like he's desperately thinking of something to say. I want to help, but my knees are Jell-O. West said no cops, but Roger would know what to do. I dig into my pocket for my phone.

But of course, it's dead.

My bones shake. On the bridge, West has inched closer to Mr. Jenkens. Oscar paws impatiently at the grass, and the wind picks up, rustles through the leaves. I tie the dog to a tree then step closer to the bridge until their voices are clearer.

"Sure there is," West says. "And I mean, if you go like this, you're going to traumatize us forever. Do you really want to carry that?"

This gets Jenkens cackling. "I admire your honesty, Weston. That's something your rotten old dad doesn't have. But fuck if I care, I'll be dead!"

"There's no guarantee of that, you might wash up down at the beach all clogged up with algae." West holds his arms out like he's ready to grab Jenkens if he jumps. Another burst of wind blows in, harder this time, and battles the back of Jenkens's windbreaker. "Besides, who's going to look after your shop?" West asks.

"No one. That's the whole point. There's no one."

West subtly waves me over. I'm seized with fear, but only for a moment. *Get it together—I have to help!* On shaky legs, I approach them, terrified that one wrong move will cause Jenkens to jump. I carefully step onto the bridge.

"Hey, Jenkens," West says, "Olive's here."

Jenkens's withered eyes find mine. He's broken in ways I can't fathom. For a man with such deep ridges on his skin to be looking into a willing death—it's haunting. And if he jumps, it will follow me forever.

"Hey," I say. "Hey, I remember you. I remember your shop."

"I remember you too, kid. You look just the same."

He laughs at me, and I flinch. More wind pushes against him. This time, in our direction. West almost grabs him but stops when Jenkens catches his balance with a post. Oscar barks.

"I'm sixty-eight years old." Jenkens coughs. "I should be allowed to decide my time. Get out of here, you don't have to see this."

"What's going on, man?" West asks. "Do you have cancer? You dying?"

"No, I'm not dying."

"Then come on down, you don't have to do this. Please?"

After a long, heated moment, Jenkens sighs. "Not going anywhere, are you?"

"I can't just let you do this. Come down, we can talk about it, get you some help."

The wind dies. Time on the bridge stands still. But then it restarts, and Jenkens eases himself off the ledge, saying, "Really thought I'd do it this time. Guess I'll save you kids the trauma. Bridge'll be here tomorrow."

West dives forward to grab him, but Jenkens swats him away. "Fuck off me, boy."

Jenkens lands safely on the bridge, and relief flows through me. "Dammit," he mumbles. "What're you kids doing over here, anyway? This part of town's always dead after nine p.m."

"Why were you trying to kill yourself?" West asks.

"I'm sick of all this shit. Sick of this town. Can't afford to leave it, got nowhere else to go."

"Did something happen?"

Jenkens's features harden as he hides his face beneath straggles of straw-like hair. "Some kids vandalized my property again."

Again?

"What?" West says. "What the hell did they do this time?"

"About two hours ago I stepped out for a damn coffee and they graffitied some bullshit all over my newly painted garage." He spits on the bridge. "Calling me a serial killer and a goof. Guess this is what I get for living out in the woods; assholes aren't afraid to go after me in broad daylight with no neighbors around to give a shit."

"That's bullshit," West says. "You know who did it?"

"Some teenagers, no doubt. Who knows which ones."

A cold awareness creeps through me. Miles, Faye, Dean, and Shawn. They all thought Mr. Jenkens could be the animal killer. I could see the others doing this, but Miles? The Miles I knew would never do such a thing. But even if Miles wasn't involved, he could be guilty by proxy for telling that stupid squirrel story. He joked about a man who was going through a difficult time, riled up the others just to get a laugh. He could have cost Mr. Jenkens his life.

"Let's tell the cops, Jenkens," West says, his tone softer. "Maybe they'll look into it. But you've got to let me get you some help, man. Let me drive you to the hospital. If you need help with bills, I can figure something out. But I can't trust you to not throw yourself over as soon as I'm gone."

Jenkens laughs and protests, but there must still be fight left in him. Because he agrees.

o o o

West's apartment is in a basement unit under the fish 'n' chips shop, and though the restaurant is long closed, the smell of fried grease permeates the parking lot behind the building. The stench reminds me of the chicken shack beneath my apartment back in the city.

Jenkens and I shuffle our feet, shifting around under a buzzing street light as we wait for West to return without the dog. Jenkens asks about my parents, and I tell him about their store, and he talks about the slow business at his, and we chitchat like he didn't just try to commit suicide. When West comes back out, he presses a button on his keychain, and a silver Dodge pickup truck lights up.

"Roommate's ride," he says to me. "The 'vette's a two-seater."

"I can just walk home from here, it's not too far—"

"You're not walking alone. We'll drop you off before we head to the hospital."

I hesitate, then go to the passenger side. It's one of those huge trucks with four doors, and the hot, stuffy interior smells like air freshener. West jumps in the driver's seat, Jenkens in the back. Various keychains dangle from the rear-view mirror. I'm in some random girl's pickup truck under Hello Kitty and Nintendo keychains, and my childhood best friend's (hot-as-hell) brother is driving, and there's a suicidal old man in the backseat. What is my life?

When West starts the car, "Call Me Maybe" blasts from the speakers and shatters my eardrums. He flicks it off. "Damn it, Sandy."

West and I lock gazes before I catch my haggard reflection in the window—buggy blue eyes, unkempt brown hair—then snatch a glimpse at Jenkens, who hides his face. The truck grumbles as it starts, and West drives in the direction of Keely's house. West's driving is slow and steady, a contrast to my buzzing thoughts. So much happened in such a short time, I can hardly swallow it.

All I have to say is, I'm really, really glad we were on that bridge.

Though I doubt West and Keely have ever hung out, he knows exactly where she lives. Caldwell is small like that. It's one of the things I miss: the tight-knit sense of community that I didn't have in New York. West pulls up to the Myerses', where the TV in the living room flashes blurred images through the curtains. Keely probably isn't home yet, and Sun will be absorbed in a television drama while Roger is at work.

"Thanks for the ride," I say to West.

He gives me a crooked smile. "Goodnight, Olive."

"I hope you feel better, Mr. Jenkens." I hop out of the truck.

"Thanks," he says. "I'm glad you're home, it's nice to see you with Weston."

As the truck drives down the street, I'm convinced there's no way the animal killer is Mr. Jenkens. Only a person with no soul could dismember bodies like that, even those of small animals like squirrels. And if the eyes are an open window to the human soul, then I saw Mr. Jenkens's, and he's not capable of that kind of evil.

The concrete stairs on Keely's front stoop are still warm from the summer sun. Taking a moment before going in, I sit and call Miles.

"Liv?" The sound of bassy music and voices from the party almost drown him out.

"Miles," I say. "Did you vandalize Mr. Jenkens's house?"

"What?" He must've gone to a different room, because the background noise fades. "What are you talking about? Why would I do that?"

"Somebody vandalized his house, Miles. You were telling that weird story at the cabin last weekend."

"Yeah, but that was a joke, Liv. Did you even see Jenkens's house?"

"No, but—"

"It wasn't me." His tone becomes harsh, defensive. "People have tagged his house before, this isn't even the first time. And I've never had anything to do with it. Do you really think I could do that?"

The Miles I used to know *would* never do that. He was always the good kid, the well-behaved rich boy who followed me everywhere I went.

But maybe I don't know the new Miles.

"Maybe," I say. "I don't know."

"Look, are you still coming over tomorrow? We can talk about it then."

"I'm not sure if I want to anymore."

"Is that Liv?" Keely says, followed by some muffling. "Liv!" Keely shouts into the phone. "What's up? Are you coming back over here? Where are you?"

"I'm already at your house. Are Dean and Shawn there?"

"Somewhere around here, yeah."

"Were they out earlier?"

"Hmm, maybe they got food or something, but nope they've pretty much been here. Why, what's up?"

"I'll tell you later. Has Miles been at the party all night?"

"Hundred percent, I ran into him after you left. What's this about? You're killing me with suspense!"

"Thanks, I'll talk to you later."

"Liv!"

I hang up.

If Miles was there all night, he couldn't have vandalized Mr. Jenkens's property. Still, something smells off about this.

Not even thirty seconds later, a text pops up from Miles.

I didn't do anything, Liv. But I'll try to find out who did, okay?

Leaving him on Read, I go back inside and hide in my room, ready to put this night behind me.

7

When the sun rises the next morning, I contemplate avoiding Miles, but I won't be able to believe he had nothing to do with Mr. Jenkens until I see him face-to-face. I arrive at the Hendricks estate midday, the sound of the ocean in the distance overpowered by the song-birds cheeping, dipping their blue feathers in a garden bath between two rosebushes. *Setophaga cerulea*, otherwise known as the cerulean warbler. Their melodies harmonize as I knock on the door of the mansion and smooth the fabric of the blue dress over my thighs. Moments later, someone opens the door—and I shrink beneath the icy gaze of Miles's mom, Beatrice Hendricks.

A floral silk robe hangs off her thin frame, and her silver-platinum hair is in a tight bun. Beatrice was never particularly *mean* to me when I was a kid, but it was the look on her face that made the hairs on the back of my neck stand up. The wrinkles around her fuchsia-painted lips have deepened; she must still smoke those long, thin cigarettes on the second-floor balcony.

"Yes?" Beatrice asks, voice clipped.

"I'm here to see Miles?"

Her eyes trail down my dress. "Right. How could I not recognize you? You're the Catharts' child."

"Olivia."

"Right. Olivia. Please, come in."

I step into the cold house and immediately feel like an ant. The ceiling is so high and creepy old black-and-white photos hang on the red-and-gold wallpaper, the smell of cleaning products and paper in the air. Of course it's beautiful, with the winding staircase that leads to the second floor and the multitude of hallways that branch from the foyer, but what do people do with this much space? Not much, apparently, because when we were kids, I remember most of the rooms in the house being occupied by nothing but extravagant, over-priced furniture. Sleeping here is probably like sleeping in a crypt.

"Miles is showering right now so you'll have to forgive his tardiness," Beatrice says. "You're welcome to wait for him here."

Beatrice's slippers clap against the floor as she leaves, and the foyer becomes dead silent. Not knowing what to do with myself, I step over the pearl-and-burgundy checkered tile and check out the pictures on the wall. As I look at the portrait of Miles's grandfather when he was young, I realize I'm next to the hallway that leads to his dad's office.

Brian Hendricks, like Beatrice, always intimidated me. But there was one time in particular he really freaked me out. I'd been waiting for Miles in this exact spot, and I could hear Brian yelling at some-one, but I didn't understand what it was about. I crept up to the door to his office, where Brian sat on a leather armchair and spat into a phone, his face twisted in a menacing rage. My breath caught, and I went to run away—but my feet tripped over themselves, crashing me into the wall. Brian's footsteps had thundered against the floor, rattling the chandelier and pictures on the wall. He'd stomped so loud, I thought of him as the giant from *Jack and the Beanstalk*.

I braced myself—for what, I'm not sure—but the thumping stopped. When I opened my eyes, Brian looked down on me like I was a timid animal. "I apologize, Olivia," he said. "I thought you were Weston, up to no good again."

Brian left without another word. I've always wondered what he would have done if I *had* been West.

The other side of the foyer leads to another hall. A shrill voice sounds from a room where the door is slightly ajar—Faye's dance studio. They converted it from a family room when Faye took up ballet. Inside, Faye and Beatrice oppose each other. I shouldn't spy on them, but the chill in Beatrice's voice freezes me.

"This is unacceptable, Faye," Beatrice snaps, oblivious to her daughter's tears. "Your aunts are coming all the way from England to see your performance. We didn't pay all that money for your lessons so you could recklessly hurt yourself. You should know how to manage your injuries by now."

The room is lined with mirrors and railings, and Faye wears a pink leotard. Red streaks the dance studio floor next to a bloody pointe shoe.

"Mom, it's not my fault," Faye sputters. "I was rehearsing the choreography exactly as I was taught, I—"

"It's *Swan Lake*, Faye. You need to be elegant, you can't be stumbling around on stage with a broken toe."

"It's fine. I can still dance. It's fine."

"No, you can't. You're going to embarrass our entire family if you pull a stunt like this on a stage in front of hundreds of people. We're taking you to the hospital to get an x-ray on it. If that toe is really broken, you aren't performing."

Beatrice leaves through another doorway and slams it behind her.

"Damn it!" Faye screeches, before she stomps over to the shoe and crams it back on her foot. Faye attempts to pirouette, only to have her foot crumple beneath her. As soon as she collapses, I rush to her side.

"Hey, maybe you shouldn't be on that," I say.

"What the hell, Olivia? Stalker much?"

Grunting in frustration, Faye roughly undoes the ribbons on her shoe, kicks it off, and peels off her tights. Once she has all the layers off, she carefully unwraps a bandage to reveal a black, pussing big toe with a busted nail. I try not to gag.

"Lovely, isn't it?" Faye says. "If you're going to gawk at my disgusting feet, at least make yourself useful and grab my bandages."

After hurrying over to the first aid kit in the corner of the room, I hesitantly hand it to Faye. She doesn't tell me to leave, so I sit on the floor across from her as she rips into the bag and tears out a package of white gauze.

"Are you okay?" I ask.

"Can you fuck off, please?"

I scowl at her. "I'm just trying to help. I haven't been here for years, why do you still hate me so much?"

"Don't flatter yourself. Hate is a strong word." She laughs and wraps the bandage around her toe, trembling as it makes contact with her flesh. "It's not like you're my biggest fan either."

"Because you were always mean to me."

"As if you were the nicest to me." Faye focuses on her feet. Her hair is tied back in a tight bun. Rosacea splotches her paper-white cheeks; Miles has it too. She sighs. "Look, I don't *hate* you. And for the record, I shouldn't have splashed you at the cabin last week."

"Is there an apology somewhere in there?"

"Yeah, right," she says, but there's a smirk on her lips. I almost smile too.

"It's fine," I say. "Thanks, for . . . sort of saying sorry."

We fall quiet. And it's the strangest thing, but for the first time in my life, I don't feel any hostility between us. Maybe I could even talk to her.

"But seriously," I say, "I never figured out why you had it in for me when we were kids."

She adjusts the tape around her toe. After a moment, she shrugs and meets my stare. "Honestly? I'm Miles's twin sister, yet when we were kids, he cared more about hanging out with you than me. I wasn't *jealous*, it was just annoying, because you cared more about hanging out with West. It was painful watching him chase you."

"What? I hung out with Miles way more than West."

"Don't play dumb, Liv. It's not cute. You clearly used Miles to get to West."

"Is that what you think?"

"It's true, isn't it?"

"No!" It really isn't. I liked West, but Miles was my best friend. I had no idea Faye thought that. "I never used Miles," I say. "Honestly, I'm a little hurt you'd think so low of me. But I don't know why I'm even surprised."

"Don't take it so personally. I call things how I see them, but maybe I was wrong."

As Faye slides the pointe shoe back on her foot and redoes the ribbons, a mark on the inside of her arm catches my eye. It's a yellowing bubble, shaped almost like a horseshoe—a burn, maybe—but it doesn't look like any burn I've ever seen.

"What happened to your arm, Faye?"

She slaps her hand over it. "It's just a smiley. Haven't you ever gotten a smiley?"

"No . . . what's a smiley?"

Faye rolls her eyes like it's no big deal, then shows me her arm. "It's when you get a Bic lighter really hot and press it to your skin until it makes a scar. See? It looks kind of like a smiley face. Dean showed me."

"Dean did that to you?"

"Only because I wanted him to."

Faye focuses on her shoe, and I study her face. There's no way she would *want* him to burn her like that . . . right?

"Anyway, I need to practice," Faye says. "Our theater performance isn't for a few weeks. My toe is fine—I've had worse and still danced."

She tries to stand but topples over. I get up in time to catch her. Faye shoves me away and balances herself, but winces in pain.

"I can't believe I'm saying this," I tell her, "but I think your mom is right—you should get an x-ray on that before you keep dancing."

"Ugh. Fine, I'll figure it out. Just leave me alone, okay?"

I want to tell her to be more careful—with dancing, and with Dean—but my welcome is already overstayed. Just as I leave the studio, Miles comes down the stairs to the lobby.

"Liv, there you are." He wears a curious smile on his face. The clean smell of his body wash reaches my nose. "Come on, I have somewhere to take you."

When he touches the small of my back, I resist a squirm to avoid being rude and allow his fingers to brush me as he leads me outside.

o o o

The forest stretches for acres behind the estate, and the afternoon sun creates prismatic shards of light on Miles's face as it peeks through the leaves. As I tell him about what happened with Mr. Jenkens, I search for any sign of deceit on his face, but Miles just nods thoughtfully with his hands in the pockets of his shorts.

"So Jenkens was just going to jump?" Miles asks. "That's screwed up."

"That's one way to put it."

"But you know I had nothing to do with it, right?"

Something still doesn't feel right, but if Miles is lying, he's really good at making his eyes look honest.

"You were at the party all night," I say. "There's no way you could have done it. But you're not going to tell that stupid squirrel story anymore, right?"

"Of course not."

"Okay. I'm just glad I ran into West. He handled everything. It was scary."

"Right. West." Miles cranes his neck back and focuses on the sky, then me. "You didn't say why you were with him."

"I just ran into him."

"Huh."

In the calm breeze, my dress flows behind me like a mermaid's tail. I love the way this dress looks on me, but suddenly I feel naked with Miles, like this thing is made of plastic wrap.

"We're almost there." Miles leads me through an opening in the forest. White balls of dandelion fluff bounce off the grassy knoll, and in the center of the hill is a blanket with a picnic basket and cooler beside it.

"Miles, what is this?"

"This is my way of saying sorry."

"For Mr. Jenkens?"

"No . . . for the cabin. For trying to get you to swim. Keely made me realize it was wrong. I'm so sorry."

This is way too much like a date for my liking. Still, it's the sweetest thing a guy has ever done for me. It must have taken him a while to set up.

"C'mon, sit with me!" Miles plops down on the blanket cross-legged.

Smiling tightly, I flatten my dress and join him, but there's an unsettled awkwardness between us. Alone with him, on this hill, feels secluded. No, *confining*.

When Miles hands me an egg salad sandwich, I shake those thoughts away. Miles is my childhood best friend, it's good to be here with him. I take a tiny bite, and my senses are overwhelmed by the deliciousness of egg, green onion, celery, and some fancy Dijon taste. Miles grins, all dimples.

"What's high school been like for you, anyway?" he asks. "You still killing it with your grades?"

"I guess I am. Math, not so much. But I've always been good at Science. What's Caldwell High like?" I laugh a little. "We used to be so jealous of the high school kids. West and his friends, they were so cool. I always looked forward to going there."

"Honestly, you're not missing much. Other than that, I'm the head of the Drama Department, so I totally pick the coolest plays."

"I knew you'd be a drama geek."

"Some things don't change."

"But some things do."

"Yeah. Some things do." His stare lingers on my face a little too long. "You probably have a boyfriend or something back home."

"A boyfriend? No, I've never had a boyfriend. Like, I've been asked for a few school dances, but I've never said yes."

"You didn't like those guys?"

"Not really. Wow, that sounds mean."

"No, I get it. I've never had a girlfriend either." He bites into his sandwich, swallows, and pats his lips with a napkin. "Figured I'd know when the right girl comes along." He winks at me, and suddenly I wish I had a shell to hide in. He can't be hitting on me, can he? He never did when we were kids. And I really don't want him to.

Thankfully, Miles changes the subject. "Tell me about the big city," he says.

The big city. West called it the same thing the other night. Miles's voice is a lot different than West's. More twangy. West's is like tires crunching over stones.

"What do you want to know?"

"Tell me what it's like! Dude, I've always lived in this stupid town. Sure, I've traveled the world with my parents and shit, but tell me about New York."

"The streets get pretty hectic, especially during the day. I take the train anywhere I can't walk, but these huge rats come out at night, and it's becoming a pretty big problem for the city."

"Gross. Well, what're your friends like?"

"They're pretty into sports, I guess. I'm on the volleyball team."

"You're a sporty girl now, huh?"

"No, not really. I'm just kind of random." The people who know me in New York City would never imagine how much I once loved the sea. Before the accident, I was Mermaid Girl, the girl who loved to swim, who wanted to be a fish.

Now I'm just blah. I wish Miles wouldn't ask me to talk about the city; it makes me feel boring.

After we eat, Miles tosses our garbage into the basket and asks me to come back to the house with him.

"Shouldn't we clean this up?" I ask.

"Nah, I've already asked the housekeepers to deal with it."

Right, housekeepers. Maybe they were the ones to set this whole thing up while Miles was showering. We take a manmade path through the forest back to the wide yard of the estate.

"It's so weird," I tell Miles. "I've always known you live like this, but I've been away for so long, so it's strange seeing it again."

"Live like what?"

"Like, you know . . . super rich."

Miles runs his fingers through his blond curls. "I guess I don't really think about it."

"It's just such a contrast. From West too. I mean, he's living under a fish 'n' chips shop and—"

"You went to West's apartment?"

"Not inside. Just waited out front last night with Jenkens."

"Oh."

When we reach one of the many doorways that lead into the estate, Miles holds it open for me and smiles. I duck under his arm and find myself in the kitchen, where their personal chefs knead dough and chop vegetables at the massive marble island. My mouth waters at the smell of onions and baked bread. A woman in a chef's hat zips to one of the three stoves and pulls out the biggest turkey I've ever seen.

"Throwing a banquet?" I ask Miles with an uneasy laugh.

"My dad's having a few guests over, some business thing. It's not important. Come on, let's go to my room."

We move through the house, past the library, walls of imitations of Renaissance art and creepy photos of Miles's dead family members, until we get to the winding staircase. The carpet is soft under my feet, but every step increases the nervousness in my veins. At the top level, I take a deep breath. The door at the end of the hallway used to be West's room. I only ever went in there once, when Miles and I were trying to find out if he had any cool stuff we could steal. We got caught, of course, and West was mad at us for weeks. But I remember he had one of those car beds. And I remember he had less stuff than Miles did, so I didn't understand why Miles wanted to steal from him at all.

I wonder if that room is empty now, or if they left West's furniture when they "disowned" him. Every corner of this estate is haunted by something. Then again, West has haunted me since I moved away.

"Liv, c'mon," Miles says, and I follow him into his room.

Miles's walls are the same shade of seafoam they always were, and dark blue curtains sway with the draft from the open window. It's all so familiar, but especially the smell: laundry detergent mixed with something sweeter. Memories leak through my mind—we built Lego castles and played with toy cars on this very hardwood floor. But

Miles used to have cartoon posters all over his walls, and now there's nothing. Just plain walls. He was a messy kid, crayons everywhere, and now his bed is made up like it belongs in a showroom.

This is the first time I've actually been alone in a guy's room since I became a teenager. The walls close in as Miles sits on his bed. It would be even more awkward to just stand here, so I join him but keep my distance.

"What do you feel like doing?" I ask.

"I don't know. What do you want to do?"

"Not sure . . ."

We're quiet for several moments, and I bump my knees together. When Miles's finger pokes me in the side, I flinch.

"What was that for?" I rub the spot.

"Sorry." He grins and ruffles his hair. "I'm awkward."

The silence sets me on edge. Shakespeare plays are stacked on the nightstand, and I'm about to grab *Macbeth* when Miles takes my wrist.

"Hey, so listen." His touch lowers to my bare knee, his fingers grazing me. Dread stabs me. I want to tell him to stop, but my body is stone. A boy has never touched me like this. This isn't what I envisioned the first time being like—the first time wasn't supposed to happen today at all.

"Do you remember what everyone said about us?" Miles asks. "When we were kids?"

With every inch he gets closer to me, my face gets hotter, my body stiffer. A warm wind through the window floods me with his scent.

"Miles?" I stammer. "Can you please—"

Before I can say *stop*, Miles climbs on top of me, and I become harshly aware of how small I am. I was always bigger than Miles when we were kids. Taller. Stronger. But now he's a six-foot tall guy, and I've barely grown. Backing into his pillow, I try to escape him, but he has me blocked in with both his arms.

"Miles? What—what are you doing?"

His eyes flutter over my face, and he tries to kiss me. I shove my hands into his shoulders. He's too heavy to move.

"What's wrong?" He tries to kiss me again, but I force him off me with all my might. Miles's weight lifts, giving me a chance to slip away.

"What the hell are you doing?" I slowly back toward the exit, and Miles's face is bewildered.

"Liv, I'm confused . . ."

"You can't just—you can't just *kiss* me like that! You didn't ask me, you didn't make sure I was okay with it. What the hell, Miles?"

"Look, I'm sorry." He gets up. "I just thought, because when we were kids, we—"

"I haven't seen you since we were twelve. We're just getting to know each other again. I thought we were *friends*, Miles." I put my hand on my forehead. "I don't think we should hang out for a while. I'll let myself out."

I storm through the door, but fingers grip my wrist and pull back so hard I almost topple over. Pain shoots up my arm, because his hand is wrapped around the wrist my elastic is on. His skin is like sandpaper scraping against me, and I wince, but Miles doesn't let go.

"Wait," Miles says, voice pleading. "Don't leave, Liv. Can we talk about this?"

"My wrist—you're hurting me!"

"What?" He glances at his hand before he drops it. "Shit, Liv, I'm sorry, I didn't—"

I bolt toward the stairs. Miles chases after me.

"Liv, wait!"

"Stay away from me, Miles!" I race down the stairs and nearly slip across the marble floor of the foyer before I'm out the front door.

o o o

I'm holding back tears the entire thirty-minute walk back to Keely's house. This isn't how things with Miles were supposed to turn out—I never pictured him capable of being so aggressive. I shouldn't have even worn this stupid dress. It was supposed to make me happy, but now Miles's touch is attached to it, his lips nauseatingly close to mine. To make things worse, he's been blowing up my phone since I left.

Liv, I'm sorry, I didn't mean to upset you.
I'd never hurt you. I only wanted you to stay.
Can we talk, Liv? Just answer the phone.
Please let me know that you know I'd never
hurt you.

But I don't know that. I didn't know that when he was cornering me on his bed, and I didn't know it when his fingers were so tight around my wrist I couldn't move.

Kicking my shoes onto the mat by the front door, I storm toward my room. Keely's in the hallway. She tugs her earbuds out, and I can hear pop music playing from them. "Whoa, hey, I thought you were at Miles's?"

"I left."

"What happened?"

When I don't answer, she pulls me into her room and shuts the door. I collapse on the stool by her vanity. Keely's bedroom is the same sunflower yellow it's always been, but instead of the Polly Pockets she'd had lining her dresser, there are bottles of foundation and golden highlighters. Keely sits on her bed next to a giant Tweety Bird plush.

"Did Miles do something?" she asks, stepping over her words.

"Yeah. Sort of."

I want to say I trust Keely more than anything, but she said it herself: I've been gone for a long time. She might think I'm overreacting. She might take Miles's side, since she's been around him way more than me over the past five years. My wrist is sore from where he grabbed me, so when I snap the elastic against it, the pain is magnified.

Even if Keely takes Miles's side, I have to tell her, starting from the picnic and ending with the texts he won't stop sending. Keely looks shocked, and I nervously anticipate her reply.

"Holy shit," she finally says. "Did you feel like, threatened?"

"A little," I say. "I was shocked, mostly. Now he won't stop texting me saying he's sorry. I'm not replying to any of it."

"Wow, that's so awkward and terrible. Guess he got the wrong idea from you guys staying in touch all these years. But don't feel bad, Liv—you did the right thing by getting out of there. No guy should make a move if you don't want him to."

"Really?" I laugh, relieved. "I was a little worried you'd take his side."

"Are you kidding? He tried to force a kiss on you—*twice*—and grabbed you. That's not okay. My dad would be pissed if a guy did that to me."

"Let's not tell Roger, please. Maybe forget this ever happened." I crawl onto the bed with Keely and bury my face in her pillow.

"Forgetting sounds good." Keely pulls out her laptop, which is covered in smiley face stickers, and opens it. "Let's watch Netflix?"

"Sure."

I curl into a ball as Keely scrolls through the movie selection, but the sick feeling inside me won't go away. I would expect something like this from a slimeball, from someone who gives me the creeps. But never Miles. Never my childhood best friend. Sadness weighs on me, and I'm starting to think my mom was right.

Maybe this trip was a bad idea, after all.

8

The world beyond the window of my room is obsidian, darkness so thick and opaque I can't see anything past the branches that scratch and poke the glass. I'm frozen under the blankets of my bed. My breathing comes out weak, grating, but I'll die if I don't inhale soon. When I try to scream, only a weak sound comes from behind my closed lips. Moving is like wading through the heaviest quicksand.

Wake up. I need to wake up.

I have a 360-degree view of the room. Bubbles fizzle beyond the glass and algae scrapes the window. At three knocks, I freeze. A man floats outside and looks in on me. The top half of his face is obscured by shadows, but his smile is luminescent. Bright white teeth, a wide grin, a fist that taps slowly. Foam festers from his lips as he mouths something at me. He waves his hand. Back and forth, back and forth, before he opens the window. Water comes rushing in and fills my airways with the taste of seaweed and raw fish.

"Liv! *Liv!*"

I wake up drenched in sweat.

Keely is above me. Her hands are firm on my shoulders, worry all over her face. Half-buttoned pajamas hang off her thin frame. Remnants of glow-in-the-dark star stickers remain on the ceiling from when this was Keely's playroom. Low, brassy thunder rumbles outside, and raindrops pound the window. A flash of lightning flickers before everything goes dark again. The green digital clock reads 5:08 a.m.

"Keely." I put my hand on my sweaty forehead.

"Liv, you were screaming."

"I was? I . . ."

My thoughts race, trip over each other, and fall down. I can't keep up with reality. That dream had been so real that the pain of drowning still reverberates through my lungs.

"I'm okay," I lie. "I'm good."

Keely fidgets with her bracelet. I can smell alcohol on her; she was partying again last night while I stayed home. It's been a week since what happened with Miles, and I've managed to avoid him, but my nightmares are getting worse.

"I don't think you are," Keely says. "This is the third night I've woken up to you screaming. If my parents hear you—"

"They'll call my parents. I know. But they're just night terrors, they happen at home too. It's not a big deal."

"If you say so," Keely says, unsure. "You going back to sleep? Because I think I'm up for good now. I'm still a little tipsy, so the hangover hasn't started yet, but I can feel it coming."

"Yeah." I swing my legs off the bed. "Let's just stay up."

Through the windows, the dark blue sky is brightening, and a gentle rain falls. The lights in the halls are dim but the coffeemaker crackles from the kitchen, along with the strong smell of espresso. When Keely and I reach the corner of the hall, she halts.

"What?" I whisper.

"Shh!"

Roger and Sun are talking in the kitchen.

"It makes me sick, Sun," Roger says. "This whole thing doesn't sit right."

We peek around the corner. Sun's arms are crossed over her lilac housecoat while Roger is already dressed for work. There's an ill air between them.

"And you really have no idea who could be doing it?" Sun asks, voice hushed.

"There are no leads. No DNA. We got an expert in and she says she's seen this behavior before—called it potential *zoosadism*."

"But what does that mean?"

"It means that these crimes, the way this person is splaying out these animals, is possibly sexual."

Keely and exchange a horrified glance. We shouldn't be hearing this. When I go to leave, to head back to my room, I knock a console table. *Shit.*

"Keely?" Sun calls out. "Are you over there?"

Caught in the act, Keely and I step from behind the wall.

"You girls are up early." Roger throws back his coffee and kisses the side of Sun's head. "I better head to work. Have a good day, girls."

He leaves, and the house rattles as he shuts the front door behind him. With a grim expression, Sun moves to the kitchen counter. "Are you two hungry? Did you want breakfast?"

"I'm okay, Mom," Keely mumbles. "Maybe I'll have cereal in a bit."

"Same," I say.

"Okay." She forces a smile. "I'm going to go get ready for the day then."

Once Sun is gone, Keely focuses on me.

"Holy crap," she whispers. "This animal shit is still going on."

"I know." A shiver moves through my spine. "It really freaks me out, Keel."

"Ditto."

We don't see Sun for the rest of the morning. By the time it's light outside, Keely and I are watching TV in the living room. I'm curled on the La-Z-Boy, still in my pajamas, while Keely shovels Lucky Charms into her mouth and flips through the channels. She lands on MTV, where a rerun of *Jersey Shore* plays.

"Ugh, can't we have anything new?" she says and flips the station.

Through the curtains, the front yard is gray. The rain has been on and off all morning, and right now it sprinkles against the glass. Last night's nightmare weighs on my mind. I don't know who that man was, or what he wanted from me. But the feeling that he wanted to harm me is all-consuming. Goosebumps raise the hairs on my arms, and I rub them out. How can someone so imaginary feel so real?

"Liv, Cindy Huang is having a party next week," Keely says and scrolls through her phone. "You in?"

"Sure." I can't avoid every party, and maybe another week will be enough time to recover from what happened with Miles, but when my phone buzzes in my hand, I nearly spill my cereal.

It's him. He's sent me dozens of messages over the past week.

Can we talk please?
You can't ignore me forever
Just give me a chance to explain.
Liv, I'm so sorry if I upset you.
Can we just talk?

God, just leave me alone, Miles. But it's true—I can't ignore him forever, not in this small town. I'm typing up a reply when Keely says, "Oh my God, my dad's on TV!"

Dropping my phone, I turn my attention to the TV, where a woman with glossy brown hair holds an umbrella and a microphone as the wind whips around her. Behind her, Roger and other cops crowd around town hall. Caution tape barricades the steps.

"Another desecrated animal carcass has been found downtown, this time, right on the steps of town hall," the woman says. "I will warn you—the following imagery is graphic, and highly disturbing."

The camera cuts to a faraway shot of town hall's steps. It zooms in. The image is slightly blurred, but I can still make out the mangled carcass of a deer strewn over the steps, its throat slit, its head hanging back with its tongue out, barely connected to the trachea. The image is only on the screen for a few seconds before Roger's concerned face appears, and the reporter holds a microphone to him.

"We live in a very small community, so this type of behavior is being closely monitored," Roger says. "We're taking it seriously."

"Would you say residents should be worried?" the reporter asks.

"Right now, we have no reason to believe there is any real danger. That said, I would still advise everyone to keep their pets inside. Lock your doors and windows at night, and err on the side of caution when it comes to traveling alone at night."

"Do you think Caldwell citizens are in danger?"

"The victims have only been woodland animals so far, and we have no evidence to suggest anything else—or any*one* else—could be targeted."

"Does there appear to be a motive behind these killings?"

"It's unclear. But we're urging everyone—please, if you've seen anything suspicious, come down to the station and give a statement. Any small detail can help us put an end to this vandalism."

"Thank you, Officer Myers."

Keely shuts off the TV. "Oh my God. I know my dad can't say much on TV, but I seriously think this is getting weird, and . . ."

I tune out Keely's words, lost in a haze of images of torn-up animals and last night's dream. My phone buzzes in my hand and startles me. It's Miles, and his words make my heart drop.

I'm outside.

Keely doesn't notice me zip out of the room to the front door. With bated breath, I peek out the window. Lightning flickers. The rain picks up, slams hard from the cloudy sky, and ricochets off the puddled concrete. Miles stands at the end of the driveway, his hair and clothes soaking wet.

My hands shake as I type a message to him.

Please go away, Miles. I'm not ready to talk.

Just give me a chance.

No. Please leave.

I dare to look out the window again. Miles stares down at his phone with a pensive expression on his face, and when he glances at the house, I duck behind the door. When I look back outside, Miles is gone.

o o o

The storm clears up by the late afternoon. Keely has a date with Shawn that I didn't want to intrude on, so I go for a walk. Even though being near the beach is still difficult, I want to check on Mr. Jenkens's shop. Waves crash all around me as I take the boardwalk to the shore. Warm, damp sand touches my feet through my flip-flops, and though the sky is clear, the post-storm smell of rain hangs in the air.

Mr. Jenkens's fisherman's supply shop is down by the shore, but it's more of a shack with fishing net thrown over it. Mr. Jenkens hunches over a box that reads LIVE BAIT. It's been more than a week since the bridge incident. West told me on Instagram that Jenkens had been committed to the hospital's psychiatric ward for overnight observation.

"Mr. Jenkens!"

He shields his eyes from the sun with his hand and waves when he recognizes me. The rubbery smell of worms and fish surrounds me, and the ocean behind the shop stretches into oblivion.

"How are you?" I ask.

Mr. Jenkens ties up a plastic bag filled with a goopy glob of dirt and worms. "Okay."

Out of pleasantries, I rock on my heels. "Do you want some help getting that garage cleaned up?"

"Oh . . . that. Weston dealt with it." His speech is mumbly, so I have to really listen to understand. "Good kid. keep him."

"Keep him? Oh no. I don't think he's mine to keep."

He nods his head at the shop. "In there."

"Pardon?"

Just as I finish my sentence, West comes out of the shop with a fishing rod over his shoulder. "Olive! What are you doing here?"

I avert my stare, heat flushing through me. "I came to see how Mr. Jenkens is doing. Keely's out with Shawn."

"Right on. The water's calmed down since the storm, so I'm going fishing. Want to come with?"

The last time I went on a boat, I threw up. Maybe not the best idea. "I don't know, West. Me on a boat is a recipe for disaster."

"No pressure," he says. "But it's safe, I promise."

"Ain't she the kid who fell off that cliff?" Jenkens asks West.

"Yeah," West says, "she's scared of the water. You don't have to do anything you don't want to, Olive. But you said before that you want to get over it, so . . . one step at a time, right? I won't let you fall in."

West's presence is like lying in a dim room surrounded by candles.

Safe, comfortable, warm. I like the way he makes me feel. But I can't go out on that water, not even with him. I'll freak out, cry, panic, or worse: puke my guts out. Totally not cute.

At my silence, West says, "No worries . . . see you later, okay?"

The deck creaks beneath his boots as he heads down to the docks. I don't want him to go—this is my shot to spend time alone with him.

"West, wait!"

With a grin, he gestures for me to follow.

A ball of anxiety grows inside me as we reach a rusty silver motorboat that already has some boxes in it. West gets in first. It rocks beneath him, and once he catches his balance, he offers me his hand. I stare at it.

"Just to warn you," I say, "That night we met by the lighthouse, I totally threw up on the houseboat. I might freak again."

West grabs a bright orange life jacket and gets out of the boat. He steadies himself on the dock in front of me, and his smell of earth and sea reaches my nose. When he holds open the life jacket, I turn my back to him and slide my arms through before we're eye to eye again. His firm hands grip both sides of the vest, and he clicks the buckles over my clothes before he fastens the straps.

"Too tight?" he asks.

Face burning, I shake my head.

"Good. You're not going under water in this." West hops back into the boat and reoffers me his hand. His calluses are rough against my skin, and when my feet thump onto the boat, I immediately crash into the seat.

"You good?" West asks.

"Yeah. Yeah, I'm good." My eyes clamp shut. The boat shifts, and oh God, this was a bad idea. But this is the closest I've come to facing my fears, so I snap the elastic and open my eyes to a world of blue as West revs the engine and rockets the boat forward. The sea pulses beneath us.

West says, "I was surprised to see you over here. For someone who's scared of water, you seem pretty drawn to it. I figured you'd be off somewhere with my brother."

"We aren't really hanging out right now."

"What, like in general, or just today?"

"In general, sort of . . ."

"Okay, I'll bite. Why?"

Immediately, I'm back in Miles's room with him on top of me, his lips nauseatingly close. "He tried to kiss me."

"Oh. Don't know what to say to that." West's silence makes me regret everything, but then he says, "Did you kiss him back?"

"No! He *tried* to kiss me. I didn't want him to."

"Brutal." He pauses. "So to be perfectly clear, you don't have a thing for my brother?"

"No." *I have a thing for you.*

"Good to know."

I watch him, study him. He's focused on the waves around us, and the muscles on his arms flex as he directs the boat. The shoreline grows smaller as we soar farther out. I need to keep talking to him—I need to stay distracted, because it's too late to turn back.

"Why is that good to know?" I shout over the sound of the engine.

"No reason. I don't get along with Miles, if you haven't noticed."

"He sort of grabbed my wrist," I blurt.

"What?"

"He wanted me to stay. But I get really anxious sometimes, so I snap this elastic band against my wrist. The skin is always sore, so when Miles grabbed it, it really hurt. I've been avoiding him ever since, even though he's apologized to me a million times, and he says he didn't mean to hurt me."

West glances at my wrist and pauses. "If he hurt you, you're right to stay away from him, Olive. He's my brother, but I'm not going to defend him."

"But do you think I should forgive him?"

"I can't make that call for you."

I'm quiet. West is right, only I can decide. But right now, staying away from Miles sounds good.

West stops the boat. When it sloshes around, I grab onto the sides and take a deep breath.

"You good?" West asks and sets up a fishing pole.

"Y-yeah."

Water ebbs around us in every direction, and the coast is small and picturesque, like a postcard.

"I won't pretend to understand why Miles does the shit he does," West goes on. "I know he's my half brother, but sometimes I wonder if we're even related, period."

"Wait, half brother?"

"Did you not know that?"

"No . . ."

West reaches into the pocket of his jeans, opens up his wallet, and tosses a picture to me. It flutters in the air and I catch it. It's of a young woman with black hair and olive-toned skin. She's on a bridge, and behind her is clearly Athens. I recognize the Parthenon in the distance.

"That's my mom." He takes the picture back and puts his wallet away. "She's the reason I look like this, and they look like that."

It makes sense. As a kid, I never questioned why West didn't look anything like his siblings or their mom. Genetics can be weird; West's dark features could have come from a distant relative or something.

"Why didn't you guys ever tell me?" I ask.

"I was pretty ashamed of it when I was a kid. Not because of who my mom was, but because I was 'the bastard child.' Pretty sixteenth century, I know, but it's how my dad and Beatrice viewed me. My dad even made me promise not to tell Miles and Faye. They only found out when they were like ten, and by then they were too ashamed to tell anyone I was their half brother too. Not much of a secret anymore, though."

I think back to that day Beatrice had dragged West away too roughly by his arm, and it's even more awful with this new information. "Well, what happened to your mom?"

"Died during childbirth."

"I'm sorry."

"It's okay. I never knew her, so. My dad met her on a vacation in Greece. It was just a fling, but his moral code made him feel obligated to raise me, even though my mom's parents wanted to."

"I'm sorry . . . that's awful. But Miles still said you were—" I stop myself.

"He said I was what?"

I take a deep breath and pray he won't get mad at me for asking. "Miles said you were disowned."

West laughs. "He's dramatic. I wasn't disowned, I left. Beatrice always hated my guts, and my dad's always been a prick. I bailed when I was sixteen."

"But don't you—" I bite my tongue. "Sorry. I'm asking too many questions."

"It's cool. Don't I what?"

"It's just that most people would try to stick around, at least for the money."

"The big house wasn't doing shit for my happiness. But my dad did buy me my Corvette. He helps me out sometimes."

Like with Amelia.

"What was your mom's name?"

"Penelope."

I scan our surroundings and shield my vision from the glare above us with my hand.

"Oh jeez," I say, "we're really far from shore."

West puts a worm on his fishing hook. "You want me to take you back?"

"No. It's okay, I'm okay." *Snap.*

He throws his line out. I stare at West's back, at the crisp black T-shirt that clings to his toned shoulders, the skin of his neck bronzed from the sun. Inhaling in a deep, clean breath of ocean air, I shut my eyes and allow my body to melt into the seat. The boat rocks and lulls. Seagulls squawk over our heads. Maybe this isn't so bad, after all.

"Got a bite." West flexes as he reels in the line, and a scaly black sea bass pops out of the water. West takes it off the hook. When it drops on the boat's floor, I scream. "What?" West picks it up, and it wiggles and flaps in his hands. "What did you think I was going to do with it?"

"I don't know! Put it back?"

"The city turned you into a punk, Olive. You've got to reconnect with your roots. Here, hold this fish."

"No!"

He throws it at me. I scream and fall back. My foot slips and sends me tumbling right over the edge of the boat. I brace myself for impact.

Dark water. The current jerks me back and forth.

Sturdy hands grip my arms and pull me back into the boat. It rocks like crazy beneath us. My heart pounds, but I'm dry—and when my bearings return, I realize West is holding me, and my legs are awkwardly tangled in his.

"You good?" he asks with an uncomfortable laugh. Mortified, I go to roll off him, but the boat is too narrow.

"Sorry!"

West pulls me firmly onto my seat. "No, I'm sorry. I shouldn't have thrown the fish. That was out of line. Looks like the sucker got away anyway."

I'm safe, but the terror of almost falling in paralyzes me. "West, I need to go back," I squeak out. "Please."

As West starts the motor and directs us to land, I grip the sides of the boat. My teeth chatter, even with the sun beating down. When West docks the boat, he helps me off and steadies me by taking both of my hands. I'm too numb to even process his touch on my skin. West unbuckles my life jacket and throws it on the boat, then places his hand on the small of my back.

"Olive, you good?"

On autopilot, I nod. People walk up the beach while a group of other fishermen waits to get by us. Quickly as he can, West ties up his boat, then directs me off the dock, and as soon as the sand touches my feet, I can breathe again.

"Shit, what do they want," West mutters, and my head snaps to the side.

Miles and Faye are coming up the beach toward us. *Oh no, not here, not now.* I don't even realize I've ducked behind West until Miles and Faye are right in front of us.

"I thought I might find you out here, Weston," Faye says, not glancing at me. "Dad's looking for you. I think he wants to talk to you alone about Amelia or something. You've been avoiding his calls."

"Why doesn't he come see me himself? It's not like I'm hiding."

"I don't know, but he's trying to care. Can't you see that?"

"It's not your job to tell me this shit, Faye. He can come say it to my face."

"Can you please just go see him so he'll shut up about it? He said he changed his mind about helping with Amelia."

West grunts. "Fuck's sake, fine, I'll go see him." He faces me. "I've got to go, Olive. You need a ride?"

I can feel Miles staring at me. "I'll walk," I say.

"All right, see you." West half smiles and thaws my still-frozen state. He slaps Miles's shoulder hard enough to knock him back before he takes off, leaving me alone with his siblings. Faye's anger radiates. I know her well enough to tell when she's mad at me.

"So you can go on little boat dates with Weston, but you can't sacrifice five minutes of your day to talk to Miles?"

"I . . ." Of course this is what it's about. Did Miles even tell Faye the full story? That he tried to kiss me—twice—without my consent before he grabbed me? Maybe she wouldn't even care if she knew the full truth. I manage to say, "I have my reasons, Faye."

Miles's cheeks are splotchy and red, focused on the shoreline beside us. "Stop it, Faye," he mutters. "Let's just go. She doesn't have to talk to me."

"She's being a stuck-up bitch, Miles."

"Stop." He tugs at her arm. "We're leaving."

My lips are zipped shut, but there's nothing to say anyway. I don't forgive Miles, and I won't pretend to. Faye starts ranting at Miles as they take off down the beach, but thank God they actually leave. Miles glances at me once over his shoulder, and our eyes lock as the sea crashes behind me.

The realization hits me like a tidal wave. The man in my dream last night was Miles.

9

I'm starting to think that I maybe, sort of, totally hate parties. Spasmodic pop music pounds my head, and bass reverberates through the walls. Feet thump on the hardwood floor as bodies crash into bodies, drinks spilling on their shoes. It's *chaos*.

Dr. Levy has taught me ways to compartmentalize my anxieties, but with people crowding around me and yelling, not even my elastic comforts me. At least this one isn't on a boat—Cindy Huang's house is a lot more leveled. It isn't as huge as the Hendricks estate, but still a massive, three-story Victorian-style home on the waterfront.

Apparently there's safety on the couch of a party, because I've been sitting here with my phone for two hours and only a few people have bothered drunkenly talking to me. I've found my corner to hide, to try to calm my breathing, but I really have to pee, and someone might take my spot if I move, or worse—I could run into Miles.

Even though I haven't seen him, his sneakers are on the mat by the door, so he's here somewhere. My eyes keep flitting through the crowd, searching for any sign of his face.

Faye and Dean are on the other couch, and my peripherals catch his hand slipping up her shirt. She grabs his wrist. His hand goes farther up anyway, and I can't help but stare now, hoping Dean will back off if he notices there's an audience. Faye grabs him, but he only shoves his hand higher. When she digs her pink-painted nails into his forearm, he stops. The music muffles their voices. She mouths something at him with a scowl. Dean's features harden before he shrugs with an insincere smile and leaves the couch, disappearing into the crowded house.

Faye looks over just in time to catch me watching. I turn away, but she slides beside me on the couch. Purple and green lights from the disco ball flash in her half-lidded eyes, framed by wintry lashes—no mascara.

"Enjoy the show?" she asks. Faye wears her usual apathetic face, but her cheeks are flushed. Her rosacea has always deepened when she's upset.

"Are you okay?" I ask.

"Why wouldn't I be okay?"

It isn't my place to say anything. Faye is her own person, and I've been gone for five years. But it's an itch I apparently can't control, because I say, "Dean seemed sort of grabby."

"Am I supposed to be mad my boyfriend can't keep his hands off me?" Faye laughs, but it's empty. "Anyway, the real question here is, are you fucking my brother?"

It's obvious which brother she's talking about. "No."

"Really? Because you two seemed real cozy on that boat the other day."

Where is Keely when I need her? My hands shake, but I hold my ground. "I'm not doing anything wrong by hanging out with West, Faye."

"He's a player, you know that, right?"

Player. The word bounces around in my head and gets lost somewhere. Keely told me West has had a lot of girlfriends over the years—but he would never try to *play* me.

"He'll break your heart," Faye goes on, "which is something Miles would never do. Why don't you at least give Miles a chance?"

"Why would I give him a chance when I already know I don't like him like that?"

"Okay then. I hope you've told *him* that."

"He knows."

Now he does, anyway. Maybe I should have clarified sooner. But even if Miles got the wrong idea, that doesn't excuse him putting that much pressure on me, and not stopping immediately when I shoved him away the first time. And he definitely had no good reason to grab my wrist as hard as he did.

"Okay," Faye says. "Don't say I didn't warn you about Weston."

"West is a good guy. Besides, like I said, we aren't together."

"But you like him."

I've never told anyone about my feelings for West—not even Keely has figured it out. But Faye sees through me in a way no one ever has.

"Even if I do," I mumble, "that doesn't mean he'd like me back."

"He would, but probably not for long. None of the other girls lasted."

What she really means is *you're nothing special, Liv*, and that's what I've feared all along.

Faye ties her long hair back in a ponytail. "If you don't believe me, why don't you try asking him about Amelia? I wonder if he'll be honest. Doubt it." She leaves the couch and vanishes into the party, limping ever so slightly on her injured foot.

The conversation leaves a sour taste on my tongue. I take out my phone and squint at the light. West's profile picture on Instagram is his Corvette—not him, just the car. He has one of those Car Guy profiles, where every picture is some engine or a bunch of tools I know nothing about. There's one of him, though, where he's standing in front of the ocean at sunset, his skin drenched in orange, his black hair disheveled. He looks beautiful, and I wonder where he goes on Friday nights, or if he ever thinks anything of me at all. I want to message him, but stop myself, afraid it would come off as annoying and desperate.

Maybe someday I'll work up the courage to ask him about Amelia. Until then, screw this couch—I need to pee. The first floor of the house is a zoo, so I zip around the banister to the upper level. Someone's elbow slams into my rib as we cross paths on the second floor.

"Sorry, I—"

The distinct smell of citrus reaches my nose. *Miles.*

My feet almost slip on the white carpet, but I balance myself. It's dark up here, too, save for the light that comes from the open bathroom door. The party thumps beneath us, yet somehow, we become the only two people in the world. Visions of how he looked in my nightmare sweep into my mind, soaking wet and foaming at the lips.

"Liv," Miles says, his face drooped in a sad expression as he tugs at his shark tooth necklace.

"I was just leaving."

He lets me duck past him toward the bathroom door but follows after.

"How long are you going to pretend I don't exist?"

Clenching my teeth, I face him. "I don't know what to say, Miles. You made me really uncomfortable. You were way too pushy, and you hurt me."

"Nothing was supposed to go like that. I'd give anything to go back in time and just ask you before trying to kiss you. It was a mistake, I didn't know what I was doing."

When Miles takes a step closer, I jolt back and crash into the wall, knocking a picture of Cindy Huang's father. Miles holds his hands up as a sign of peace while I regain my composure. A couple of drunk girls giggle as they run up the stairs, shove past us, and take over the bathroom. Great, so much for peeing.

"Can we talk now?" Miles says.

"About what?"

"Please, just let me give you this."

As I eye him suspiciously, he reaches into the pocket of his shorts and holds out his hand. Three opaque stones tinted with turquoise land in my palm. I rub my thumb along their smooth, glossy surface.

"Sea glass," I say.

"Yeah. When I saw them, I thought, the color is just like your eyes."

The guilt is immediate. For a moment I see the Miles I knew as a kid. That little boy was nothing like the Miles I saw in my sleep. I've heard dreams are a way for the subconscious to show what our waking minds can't see—our third eye. But Dr. Levy said they can be senseless too. They can mean nothing, and I don't know how to tell the difference. Maybe that nightmare I had about Miles didn't mean anything. Maybe he really didn't mean to hurt me that day, and it wouldn't be such a crime to accept his apology and move on.

"Thanks, Miles." I tuck the stones into the front pouch of my purse. "This is sweet."

"You're welcome. I understand if you can't forgive me. I just can't stand us not being in each other's lives after we were apart for so long. Can we be friends again?"

"I don't know." Sadness takes over his face and melts me a little more. I add, "But it's a start."

Miles smiles tightly before he goes back downstairs. I wait to use the bathroom before going down, too, but as I'm reaching the first floor, shouts come from the kitchen.

"Turn the music off! An ambulance, we need an ambulance!" Cindy shoves through the crowd and the music goes quiet. The lights go up, and everyone stares at each other with clueless looks on their faces. Shawn barrels down the hall, Keely draped in his arms. Her shirt is covered—and I mean *covered*—in bright green vomit. It's fluorescent, like toxic waste.

I don't think twice, I just run. Shouldering people out of my way, I yell, "Keely! Get out of my way—Keely, are you okay?" I reach Shawn's side. "What happened to her?"

His normally tanned skin is sickly pale. "I don't know, we were taking shots, and I don't know, man, she must've drunk too much. Fuck, she needs help."

"Call an ambulance!" Cindy yells to no one in particular.

"Shit, cops are coming?" someone shouts.

The whole room panics. I'm shoved into a wall as people flood the hallway and elbow each other to get to their shoes and out the front door. Frustration explodes inside of me—I need to call for help, but someone knocks my phone out of my hand, and it gets lost in the stampede of feet.

"Stop!" I say. "Get out of my way!"

But I'm pushed back again. My butt lands with a thud on the staircase. The chaos doesn't cease until the room clears, the front door left open. Outside, the last few people from the party hop Cindy's front fence.

My phone is on the floor with a crack in it, but it turns on when I snatch it. Shawn and Keely are nowhere in sight, so I call 911 and stumble to the front porch, relieved to see they're lying on the grass. I blabber Cindy's address to the operator and beg them to hurry. Caldwell is too small to have its own hospital, but there's one just outside of town that surrounding towns use too. The operator talks me through, and I relay the information to Shawn: "Keep her on her side so she doesn't choke on her puke. They'll be at least ten minutes."

Shawn kneels over her as she sputters up more vomit. Cindy places her hand on her forehead beneath her black, pin-straight bangs.

"Are the cops coming?" she says. "Oh my God, I can't have a girl die at my house!"

"She's not dying!" I say, but my heart is pounding. If the alcohol doesn't kill Keely—her parents will.

Lights flash up the long driveway of Cindy's property. I pray it's the ambulance, but it's a cop car that rips up to the house and squeals to a halt.

Roger.

I tell the operator the police have arrived and hang up the phone. Of course I gave them Keely's name, so Roger must have heard about it. Horror is all over his face when he tears out of his cruiser and is at Keely's side in seconds. Roger presses two fingers to her neck to check her pulse. Keely shivers in the fetal position. Roger sighs, smooths down her hair, and glances back at us.

I'm totally helpless. I don't know what to do but stare.

More flashing lights up the driveway. Another cop car, followed by the ambulance, and the front lawn becomes swarmed with officers and paramedics. Roger stays by Keely as they lift her onto a gurney, and I chase them when they wheel her to the ambulance, feeling like I'm out of my body.

"She's going to be okay, right?" My voice shakes.

"Stay back, Olivia," Roger says. "Please."

I do. Cindy and Shawn are already being interrogated as Keely is placed in the ambulance. Roger exchanges a few words with them before they drive away, and then he's back on me.

"Olivia. What happened?"

"I'm sorry," I stutter, "we lost each other . . . I don't know, I don't know what happened. Last time I saw her she was fine, then she was with Shawn."

Another officer talks to a drunk, blubbering Shawn, and another to Cindy. Roger glares at them, and he twitches like he's on the verge of an eruption. But he says, "I'll deal with them later. I need to make sure my daughter is okay. Come on, Olivia. You're riding with me."

o o o

Keely has to get her stomach pumped. That's all the nurses tell me before I'm forced to stay in the waiting room alone. Minutes tick into an agonizingly long hour as I sit with my pounding head gripped between my hands.

Please let Keely be okay.

There's a mural of fish on the wall, and the movie *Up* plays on a tiny flat-screen TV. I haven't been in this hospital since my fall. All of those memories are dreamlike and hazy now. I remember waking up and thinking I was dead, and my parents were hovering over me. There were doctors, but their faces are blurry. Miles, Keely, and Roger were sent in once I was stabilized, and Miles cried because he blamed himself.

But whatever happened after that is blank. I must have gone home, and soon after, my parents and I were packing up our lives.

"How much did she have to drink?" Sun's voice sounds from up the hall, and I stand at attention. Still wearing her robe from home, Sun enters the waiting room with Roger. They both look exhausted.

"They say it must have been a lot," Roger says, calmer than he was before.

"Is Keely okay?" I dare to ask.

Roger nods. "It's alcohol poisoning. She'll pull through, but we need to have a word with you, Olivia. Come here, please."

Sun stands back and watches as Roger and I sit. My throat knots up. Roger's still in his uniform from work; he might as well have put me in an interrogation room.

"Olivia, how long has she been drinking like this?"

I tug at my elastic. I'm terrified for Keely, and it'd be for her own good if I spilled everything right here, right now. But that would be totally betraying her.

Roger senses my hesitance. "Listen, Olivia. I've always trusted Keely. Now I'm learning the hard way that I can't. I know what I'm asking you to do, but we could really use your help on this one. I can tell you haven't been drinking."

"I haven't been," I murmur. "Honestly, Keely took off at the party and I couldn't find her. I had no idea how much she was drinking . . ."

"Keely isn't the first teenager to get her stomach pumped in this hospital, but she's the last one I ever expected to see. I need to know how long this has been going on. How long has my kid been drinking under my nose?"

Tell them. It's the right thing to do.

But I can't do that to Keely. I just can't.

"I don't know . . . I'm sorry."

With a disappointed sigh, Roger turns away. "You girls have a curfew from now on. Ten p.m. sharp every night. No exceptions."

I nod obediently. Roger goes to Sun, and guilt twists the knife in my gut. For the first time, I feel homesick for my bedroom in Hell's Kitchen, for my spot at my parents' little round kitchen table, for our balcony that faces the brick walls of another apartment building. Leaving Sun and Roger behind in the waiting room, I head outside into the cool night. Insects buzz around the faint lights. Plopping down on the concrete edge of a garden, beneath a tall glowing sign of an H, I take out my phone and call my mom.

"Livvie?" she answers, and I sigh in relief.

"Mom. Hi."

"Are you okay?"

When I fill her in about what happened, she bombards me with questions about *my* safety and if *I'm* okay.

"I'm good," I tell her for the fiftieth time. "Mom, I didn't drink anything, I promise."

"Good. Poor Sun and Roger, I can't imagine what they're going through."

"I promise I won't make you find out. What's Dad doing?"

"Sleeping. Long day at work."

"How's the shop?"

Mom pauses. She's probably at home, legs crossed on our couch with the TV muted in the background. "I won't lie, things have been a little rough. The air conditioner broke down, so we'll have to come up with the money to repair it, but don't worry about us, sweetie."

"Okay. Tell Dad I said hi?"

"Will do. I'm so worried about Keely. I'll have to call Sun and Roger in the morning."

"Sure. I'm going to go back in, though, okay? I love you."

"I love you too. Be careful."

"Don't worry about me."

Before she can express more concern for my well-being, I hang up. Dark clouds sail overhead and shield the moon and stars.

All my childhood friends are so different now. If I never moved away, I wonder who I would have become. Maybe Faye and her friends would have thought I was cool, and maybe I never would have been called a buzzkill. Or maybe I would be the one getting my stomach pumped inside.

I reach into my purse and touch the sea glass Miles gave me. Their cool, round shapes calm the impending storm in my head, and for a moment, I feel okay again. The summer isn't even half over. There's still time for me to reconnect with my old life—and if Keely stops drinking so much, maybe things will get easier.

When I get back inside, Sun and Roger are gone, the waiting

room filled with the faces of strangers anticipating good or bad news. Sitting alone in a corner, I spend the rest of the night parachuting between reality, nightmares about drowning, and dreams of kissing West.

10

My foot creaks against the floorboard as I sneak through the hall of Keely's house. The night startled me awake again, but this time, the dream has dissolved behind the fog of my mind; it exists only in fragments.

Running. The lighthouse. A man.

I shudder away from the images, from the terror that still lingers. The house is dark and the air conditioner rumbles through the walls, its icy breath raising the hairs on my arms. Roger's snoring softly sounds. Keely's bedroom door is closed, but she's sound asleep in there, still recovering from when she got her stomach pumped last week. Since then, she's been beyond grounded, and we haven't hung out with anyone. No Miles, Shawn, Dean, or Faye.

No West.

And honestly, I've liked spending the week with just Keely, but being cooped up in the house is making me claustrophobic. I didn't think it would be so hard to sleep away from my own bed. That's why I'm up in the middle of the night, only a few hours before Roger has to get up for work. No one will notice me at this hour.

Maybe a shower will wash this anxiety away.

In the bathroom at the end of the hall, I lock myself in and turn on the light. The room is small and narrow, with blue-and-gray accent towels and a soft carpet shower mat, and the sound of the fan comforts me. A deep breath, and my shaky hands turn the knob of the shower until streams of water pound the bathtub.

Waves crash all around me. The ocean rushes into my lungs.

I snap the elastic and force myself to stay in the present.

Billows of steam swallow me as I step inside, and hot water pelts my back. The seashelled tiles of the stall kaleidoscope when I zone in on them for too long, so I blink myself out of a trance and lather pear-scented shampoo into my hair.

An opaque window is built into the wall of the shower. It distorts the dark world behind it and only allows the vague shape of a tree to be seen. I've been dreaming a lot about windows, about someone watching me through them.

Something knocks on the glass. Startled, I get soapy water all over my face. I take a deep breath. It's nothing. I'm imagining things. I'm safe.

Just as I'm thinking it was a bird, a light-colored shape appears behind the window, only touching the sill.

A hand.

Screaming, I scramble out of the tub and fall into the shower curtain. It tears off the hooks and gets caught between my legs. Moments later, someone knocks at the door.

"Liv?" It's Keely. "Liv! Are you okay?"

I look back at the window, and of course, nothing is there.

"Roger, I swear, there was someone outside."

We've been in front of the computer in the living room for half an hour. Roger's face is illuminated by the black-and-white images on the screen, while Sun and Keely stand back and watch, their expressions grim.

"Olivia, we've gone through every second of footage." Roger opens the camera to the driveway. Nothing but blackness and the trees swaying in the wind. "There's no one out there. No one's been out there since I got home from work."

"But . . ." I hug myself and shiver. My cold, wet hair has dampened the shoulders of my T-shirt. "I swear I saw someone. They tried to grab the windowsill."

"The camera caught no one, and I didn't see any prints when I went outside." Roger sighs and spins on the desk chair. Reading glasses slide to the tip of his long nose. "Look, Olivia. Don't take this the wrong way, but have you been taking your medication?"

Embarrassment and anger stab me. His eyes say *you imagined it*, and I consider getting mad—but I have no way to prove what I saw was real.

"Yes, I have been," I say. "I know what I saw. What if the person slipped by the cameras?"

"It's unlikely. This security system is state of the art."

"But there's no camera that points exactly to the shower window."

"That's true, but . . ."

"Liv," Keely says, "you *have* been having those nightmares—"

"I know the difference between reality and nightmares," I snap, even though I'm not a hundred percent sure that's true. For the past week, my brain has felt swollen, tight against my skull. But this felt different—it felt real. It *had* to be real.

Right?

"Nightmares?" Roger clasps his hands together. "Are you okay, Olivia?"

"I'm fine!" They all flinch. When they look at me like I'm a wounded animal, I mumble, "I'm sorry, everyone. Maybe I did imagine it. I'll just go to bed."

"Liv, wait!" Keely says, but I brush her off and go to my room, closing the door behind me and shutting the blinds so not even a sliver of moonlight can get in.

What I saw was real. I'm not crazy.

But the proof was right there, on Roger's security tapes. There's no way I'm sleeping anytime soon, so I take out my phone. It's after 3:00 a.m. now, and twenty minutes ago, West texted me. I open it right away. He's never messaged me this late before.

Hey, you up?

Hey, yeah unfortunately

What's wrong?

It's nothing. I just can't sleep. Anxious. :(

Same. I'm bored. We should hang out soon.

I'd like that a lot

:) Well I'm going for a drive, talk to you later.

Take me?

I could come pick you up right now.

Not a single part of me wants to go outside even for a second, but it'd be worth it to see West. Maybe he could even help me make sense of everything that just happened, because I'm lost. I'm desperate. When we were kids, West always knew what to do. One time, while playing down at the beach, I broke my favorite toy boat and it wouldn't sail anymore. I panicked and tried to shove the little wooden mast back into the hull, but it was destroyed. Then West came over, and he told me he could fix it—so we went back to the

Hendricks estate, and he made me wait outside of his room until he came out with my boat, good as new. We went back to the shore, and it sailed better than it ever did before.

But my mind is not a toy. West can't piece me back together with hot glue, but I still want to see him.

Okay, Olivia, slow down.

Sneaking out would mean betraying Sun and Roger, and they've been so good to me. At the same time, the darkness in this room is deafening, and the thought of being in here alone terrifies me. Wondering whether what I saw was real or not will drive me in circles.

So when sleep settles over the house again, I creep down the hallway and sneak out the side door.

o o o

The Corvette waits for me at the corner of the street. Running to it, I slide into the passenger side. The smell of leather, motor oil, and West's earthy cologne overwhelms my senses.

"You look cute," he says.

My cheeks flush. "I'm basically in pajamas." Sweats and a T-shirt, but still. I wanted to look decent for West but wasn't about to do my hair and makeup at three in the morning, so I'm barefaced and still damp from my shower. But I like the way he looks at me. It almost makes me forget what happened at the house—almost.

"Doesn't matter," West says. "I like you in pajamas."

"Thanks."

West tells me that his car is a tangible piece of history, a fragment of the 1960s. It's pretty cool. The seats are low, and the long, curved nose of the electric-blue vehicle stretches before us, illuminated by the moonlight. West drives down Keely's street, and soon we cross through downtown, by the park with the fountain, past his apartment. Only our shared silence fills the air, but it isn't uncomfortable. Intervals of street lights brighten his face as we get near the outskirts of town. Within five minutes, we exit through a narrow road lined by the forest. The strong scent of evergreen leaks into the car. The farther from town we get, the hazier my memory of what happened in the shower becomes.

"Are you going to tell me what you're so anxious about?" West eventually asks.

"Well, I'm fine right now." In fact, the calm rumble of the car lulls me. If I fell asleep here, I bet I wouldn't dream of anything bad at all.

"But before you weren't," West says.

"No, but I'm not sure I'm ready to talk about it. You go first?"

"Okay." His hand is draped over the steering wheel, the other on the stick as he drives. "It's just life. My job. I'm worried about money, and my dad's getting cheap when it comes to helping me out."

"I'm sorry. That sucks."

"Yeah. Your turn."

"I've been having a hard time sleeping lately. Really bad dreams. And even when I'm awake, sometimes I . . ."

"Sometimes you what?"

Keely doesn't even know the full extent. That these nightmares happen so often, they make me feel like I'm not human, and I'm scared of what she'll think if she knew. But as we drive down the empty road, I feel safe. Unjudged. Like West will accept me.

"Do you ever feel like something's there, even though there maybe isn't?" I ask.

"I'm not following."

I huff, frustrated with myself. "Forget it. You're going to think I'm out of my mind. It's impossible to explain."

"Olive, I'm right here listening. Try me."

"It's just—sometimes I have these really vivid dreams that someone is chasing me or watching me or wants to hurt me, and when I wake up it can be hard to remember what's real and what isn't. Does that make sense?"

West is quiet for a moment, his eyes on the road. "Can't trust everything you think. You went through something rough when you were a kid. Being back here is probably triggering some bad shit."

Like seeing things in windows that aren't really there. "I was diagnosed with PTSD," I say, "but it's never affected me like this before. I've been having night terrors since my fall, but now that I'm here, it's like they've magnified times a thousand. I'm getting better at being near water, yet somehow I don't feel like I'm recovering at all."

"Maybe you should start there, focus on one thing. You said you came back here to get over your fear of the water, right? Maybe if you work on that, you'll get over this other thing too."

"Maybe . . ."

"What do you think? Ready to take a dip yet?"

"You mean actually get in the water?"

"Yeah. If you get in and get out unscathed—which you will if you're with me—then you might see that it's all in your head, and that the water can't hurt you. And hey, if you do freak out, I won't tell anyone."

My lips are dry. "If I'm with you?"

"Did I say that?"

I can't help but grin. I'm not ready to get in the water, not even with West. But something old resurfaces in me; the part of me that wanted to take risks, to challenge myself.

We're far from town now. The area is so dead at this hour, and we've only passed two other vehicles. The entire state of Maine is ninety percent forest, so no matter how far we go, more trees surround us.

Running my hands along the worn leather of the seat, I say, "I really like your car."

"Thanks." He gives me a quick smirk, like I've inflated his ego. Even West isn't impervious to compliments, I guess.

"I bet it goes really fast."

"It does."

"You should show me."

"You want to see how fast it goes?"

I nod. Slowly.

West presses down on the gas pedal. The engine growls, and the car whips forward. Adrenaline strikes. It's a good adrenaline, though; not like the crippling fear in my everyday life. It's tingly and euphoric, a roller coaster ride. I'm not the type to chase cheap thrills; I learned that lesson five years ago. But being with West makes me want to live again, like I did when I was a kid. When I'm with him, I never fell off that cliff.

"Faster," I whisper.

Our eyes meet again, and he accelerates more. When I don't protest, he goes faster, and faster, until all I feel is the car shaking and my heart beating. The frame wobbles like it's going to explode into pieces—and then silence. Smooth, perfect sailing, like we've broken through a barrier. West's knuckles turn white as he grips the wheel. The rumble of the engine is sleek and silky and stable. The thumping of my pulse is supersonic and *alive*. The world outside is nothing but a blur of black, blue, and green, and it's exhilarating. I want to soar as far away as we can, beyond those clouds, into the stars above, straight to the moon.

"Oh my God!" I shout.

"You okay?"

"I'm good!"

"Okay, okay, I've got to slow it down—I don't want to get in shit." Steadily, the speed drops until we stabilize. West's pupils are saucers. "You always were a thrill junkie, but I didn't think you were like that anymore."

"Trust me, I'm not. I don't know what came over me."

"Me neither. But I've always liked this side of you."

We drive around for a long time and listen to the classic rock station on the old-school dial radio, talking about everything and nothing. I tell him that Keely and I binged Ryan Gosling movies the other day. He tells me *Drive* is his favorite. We talk about being kids and how much we both miss the time when things were simple. Eventually, West starts yawning. He directs the car toward Caldwell Beach. Even though I don't want this night to end, I'm feeling heavy, too, and it's nearly 5:00 a.m. Roger gets up for work at six, and he already lost sleep when I woke him up over nothing.

West idles the car at the corner of Keely's street as rain drums the roof, metallic and poppy. My breath stops when he reaches across the seat and grazes my cheek with his callused finger, evoking a shiver.

"You're going back to New York at the end of the summer, aren't you?"

I press my cheek to his warm hand. "I don't want to think about that."

He brushes my hair behind my ear, then takes his hand away and leaves a trail of fire beneath his fingers. *He just touched me.* But now he silently focuses on the street behind the windows. The air in the car is humid, and my hair sticks to my sweaty skin.

"What's wrong?" I squeak out, still in disbelief.

"Nothing."

Whatever just happened with us wasn't nothing. Him touching me wasn't nothing. Why did he stop?

"West."

Finally, he looks at me, and it's a defibrillator to my chest. Because his eyes are hooded and his lips are slightly parted, an expression I'm sure I mirror. *Desire.*

But he turns away. "My brother tried to kiss you."

Oh. The heat of his touch remains, but the moment has fizzled out and died like a campfire drenched in water.

"I didn't want him to kiss me," I whisper. *I wanted you to.*

My heart clenches. I could tell him, right here, right now, how I've always felt about him. But the fear of rejection is too strong. Part of me does feel bad that this might hurt Miles, but a bigger part would do anything to be with West.

"Miles and I are just friends," I say, throat tight. "I made that clear to him."

"But he likes you." A pause, and West scans my face; memorizes it. "Do you think it's fucked up I don't care?"

"Maybe, but . . . you two aren't even close."

"No, we aren't." He laughs a little. "Hell, most of the time I can't stand the kid."

"But not all of the time."

"He's my little brother."

"Of course . . . I couldn't ask you to hurt someone you love, West."

Still, the hope that somehow, someway, this conversation will turn back to where it was when he touched me tinges me with frustration, because I never asked Miles to kiss me. All of my childish dreams about West are coming to life, so close they're at my fingertips, yet still too far away. It doesn't feel fair. Maybe that's selfish—they're family, and I'm just a girl who used to live here.

"That's the thing." West wipes his palms on his faded black jeans. "It doesn't bother me, because he doesn't own you."

"No, he doesn't."

"Like you said, we aren't close," he says, quietly this time.

The relief is enough to overflow the guilt. Nothing can stop the trembling in my arm as I reach for him, for his hand. Our fingers interlock. Intoxicated, I watch him bring the back of my hand to his lips, and with a tectonic shift, he kisses my skin.

"I'm glad you're here," he says and drops my hand. I tuck it over my lap. Even after the kiss—which I'm still processing—West's hesitancy is written all over his face, and outside, sunrise has started to peek over the horizon.

"I have to go," I mumble, even though this whole thing has confused me. Are we something now? Should I back off?

"Yeah, okay," West says. "Hey, if you're not hanging out with Keely tomorrow, why don't you come up to the cabin with me? Bring a bathing suit, just in case."

"Are you sure? My curfew is ten p.m."

"Just for the day, then."

"Okay. I'd like that."

"All right. Night, Olive."

"Goodnight, West."

When I get out of the car, he nods at me, then drives off. His taillights fade into the early-morning fog, beams of yellow consumed by murky gray. My fingers graze over my left hand, right where West's lips were.

I can't believe it. He likes me back. All the making out I've been doing with him in my head might actually become a reality.

Back in through the side door, I slowly creep through the dark halls of Keely's house. The bathroom door is slightly ajar, and tingles of fear return—but I'm able to shove them away.

What I saw wasn't real. It's like West said: I've been going through a lot. I just need more sleep.

One step at a time, right?

11

The next day, I sit on the front porch with my backpack and wait for West to pick me up, the noon sun warm on my skin. When the door opens behind me, Keely steps out in her pajamas. I dodge her curious stare, the same way I've avoided her all morning. She tried talking to me over our bowls of cereal, but I mostly gave one-word answers. It's hard not to be mad at her for telling her parents about my nightmares.

"Hey, there you are," Keely says, and when I don't reply, she joins me on the concrete ledge of the porch. "Shawn invited me to the beach, but I told him I can't go because I'm still grounded. They're all partying later too. I feel so left out."

"That sucks," is all I can think to say. I'm sad for Keely and everything, but still annoyed she was so quick to assume what I saw last night wasn't real—even if it wasn't.

We fall silent for a few moments before Keely says, "Look, about last night—"

"You didn't have to tell your parents about me having nightmares. Your mom's going to call mine, and my phone is going to blow up with worried texts from my parents."

"*I* was really worried about you."

"So was I when you got alcohol poisoning, but I still didn't tell your dad how long you've been drinking."

Keely's shoulders drop. "*Okay*, point taken. I'm sorry. But for the record, I asked my parents not to call yours. I insisted that you're totally fine."

Fine probably doesn't fit my description, but I can't have Mom freaking out. Whatever's going on in my head, I can handle. I'm doing the work. Facing my issues.

That's why my bathing suit is under my clothes.

"All right," I say. "I've pretty much concluded that what I saw was a bird or something, anyway."

"I mean, it must have been, right? What else could it be?" We fall quiet. My backpack is on the ground beside me, and Keely nods at it. "You going somewhere?"

"West is picking me up. We're going to the cabin for the day."

"You're hanging out with West? Alone?" Keely's nose scrunches. "Wait, do you like him?"

Face hot, I avert my stare.

"Holy shit," Keely says. "*Of course* you like West. How could I never see it before? Why didn't you ever tell me?"

"I don't know. It's not that I didn't trust you, I just didn't want anyone to know."

"Every girl has her secrets. But hey, I totally support you. A summer fling with West would be super cute."

Summer fling. Is that all we would be?

"But as your best friend," Keely continues, "it's my duty to tell you that West totally has a reputation as a player. I can't vouch for that personally, but he's had a million girlfriends over the years, all of them from out of town. Be careful, okay?"

"Faye said the same thing, but he's different with me." I can still feel his skin on mine, his lips on my hand.

It's naive, I know that. West has hurt me before, but everything in my heart screams to be near him. That has to mean something.

Keely snorts a little. "Sure, every girl thinks that, Liv. Not that you aren't special—you totally are. Just be careful. And not just with your heart, okay?"

I tug at the string of my jean shorts until it rips off. "I will."

Keely heaves out a sigh and rests her chin on her palms. "I'm so jealous you actually get to see the guy you like."

Her playful demeanor cracks, her lips curved down. This is a horrible thing to suggest, but I don't want Keely to be sad. Shawn's nothing special to me, but it seems like he's the only thing that makes her happy.

I nudge her. "Hey, when has not being allowed ever stopped you?"

She grins. "Good point."

Roger's cruiser pulls into the driveway. Keely and I stand.

"Hi, girls." Roger yawns and walks up the driveway in full uniform.

"Hey, Dad," Keely says. "What are you doing home?"

"Just came for some early lunch, I'm starving." The sun reflects off his sunglasses, but he takes them off and tucks them into his shirt pocket before he looks at me. "Olivia, about last night . . . I apologize for what I said about your meds. It wasn't my place. Thing is, I want you to feel safe here. Caldwell's still a good town, and we haven't had a violent event in God knows how long. Well, aside from this damn animal killer . . ."

"Thank you, Roger," I say. "Did something else happen?"

He smooths his thumb along his belt and stops at the holster of his gun, his brown skin wrinkled into a grimace. "No point in drawing it out, I suppose. You girls will hear about this eventually. Yesterday, someone killed a dog."

The hairs on my neck raise.

"A *dog*?" Keely says. "Oh my God, no! That's a bigger deal than a squirrel or a deer, right?"

"Yep. Horrific sight. Do I ever feel for Mrs. Daly, waking up to that, her poor pet drowned to death and then left on her lawn."

Drowned.

The word echoes through the caverns of my mind.

Roger clears his throat. "Sorry, girls. I'm exhausted. I shouldn't be telling you this stuff. Come inside, Lemon. And Olivia, that ten p.m. curfew is law. No slipups."

I quickly agree, not wanting to get on Roger's bad side. West's Corvette pulls to a stop out front.

Roger shields his eyes from the sun with his hand. "I thought it was Miles you two were friends with."

"I'm friends with West too." I slip past him. "I'll be back before ten, okay?"

He shrugs and waves me off. Keely yells bye as I hurry over to West's car and slide into the passenger seat.

"Hey, you good?" he asks. "Chief Myers is looking pretty serious."

"Yeah, I don't know," I tell him, unsure if I should be repeating things Roger says to me. "It's about the animal killer, but Roger isn't saying much. He's just really serious about my curfew."

"I'll get you home on time." West shifts the gear out of park, and we drive away in silence. Anxiety claws through me at the thought of being in that cabin again—but for different reasons than last time. The entire way there, I glance at West's hand on the stick shift, remembering when it was clasped to mine.

o o o

West tosses his keys on a console table and flicks on a light. The overhead fan spins and casts cool wind on my arms, which eases the musky humidity in the cabin. It's so quiet in here without Faye and them running around wasted.

"Damn, it's stuffy in here," West says. "But if I turn the AC on, my dad'll notice the electrical bill. You good?"

"I'm okay." As okay as I can be alone in a house with him.

I follow him into the kitchen and drop my backpack on a stool by the bar. West inspects the fridge, his black T-shirt tight against his frame, and somehow I'm only now noticing he's in blue swim trunks. My aqua bikini is underneath my tank top and shorts. I picture myself floating on the lake, the water so dark beneath me; my feet are gone, and the room spins.

I can't do it. There's no way.

But this is my chance to try.

To distract myself from the budding panic, I run my finger along the smooth surface of the bar while West digs through the cupboards. On the wall is a photo of Brian, Miles, and Faye in front of the lake. Miles is on Brian's shoulder while Faye holds onto his leg, the sun high behind them. They look happy.

"Why aren't you in any of these?" I ask.

"Huh?" West keeps rifling. "Don't know, you'd have to ask my dad that. Probably because Beatrice doesn't want my face on the walls of her precious vacation spot. Not that I care."

"But where were you when this was taken?"

"Probably with a nanny."

"They'd just leave you alone?"

"Yep." West shrugs, hands hooked to the handles of the cupboards. "I came here a few times, but my dad and Beatrice stopped bringing me because I'd always end up pissing off Miles and Faye. They wanted 'peace,' so it was easier to leave me at home."

"That's terrible."

"Whatever. I got to play video games and sports without my annoying siblings, can't complain about that."

"But didn't it get lonely too?"

"At first, maybe. But I got over it pretty quick."

In the photo, the lake looks just the same as it did when I went last time. We could go there and swim in it now. West wouldn't let me drown. My knees shake, because I can't really be thinking of doing it, can I?

"Guess I should've brought food," West mutters and closes the cupboards. "I can always drive and grab us something."

Tucking my hands behind my back, I face him. "I'm not really thinking about food."

"What are you thinking about then?"

I glance at his shorts. "You're wearing your bathing suit . . ." With a tug on the strap of my bikini, I reveal mine to him.

"No shit." He smiles wide. "So does that mean you're down to swim?"

"I don't know. Maybe we can just go sit by the lake?"

"Yeah. C'mon, let's go."

West offers his hand, and I take it.

The woods are hot and dry as we make our way to the lake. Even with the film of sweat on our palms, we don't let go of each other, and I don't think I'll ever get used to touching him. Elation washes over me as West holds up a branch and allows me to pass under. Once we reach the lake, we sit back in the grass, a fair distance from the muddy shore. The water ripples and shines with bits of sunlight, and the breeze is cool under the shade of the tree.

Pulling my knees to my chest, I descend into the memory of the last time I was here. Beside me, West sits cross-legged and shreds a leaf.

"The last time I was here," I say, "Miles tried to get me into the water. Faye kept calling me a buzzkill."

"Sounds like my siblings." He laughs once. "They're both assholes."

I pluck a flat rock out of the dirt and try to skip it over the lake, but it just plops in. "Miles is really different from when we were kids. I don't know how I feel about him." The sea glass he gave me is still in the front pouch of my purse, which I left back at Keely's. Despite everything that happened with Miles, sometimes I touch them and feel okay again. They were a thoughtful gift. A gift that reminds me of who we used to be. What West said last night was true—Miles doesn't own me. But the thought of his face twisting in betrayal upon seeing us together makes me sick with guilt.

"People change." West leans back so his forearm grazes the small of my back. Our eyes meet. "Not gonna lie, you grew up to be really beautiful."

"Oh, wow. Thank you."

God, everything he says is so effortless. Like he's said it to a lot of girls, to be honest.

"West, can I ask you something?"

He nods. "Shoot."

"Are you a player?"

When he laughs, it's almost like he expected the question. "No. But I'm guessing someone told you I am."

"Sort of."

"Do you think I'm trying to play you?" Biting my lip, I shake my head. "Good, because I'm not."

"Will you tell me about Amelia?"

Now he tenses. His stare drifts across the lake before he reaches into his pocket and pulls out a frayed wallet. He removes a photo and glances at it before he hands it to me. A toddler with olive skin and blue-green eyes sits with her fist in her mouth, surrounded by pink blankets, and a bow is tied to her wispy brown hair.

The Amelia theories had ranged from secret girlfriend to long lost sister to great-grandma—but not this.

"I was going to tell you," West says, "but the thing is, no one in Caldwell really knows, because it's none of their business. My family likes keeping their secrets buried, so Miles and Faye don't even gossip about it, even though they hate me enough to."

He's speaking, but a broken record in my head repeats *West has a kid West has a kid West has a kid.* He takes back the photo.

"Faye told me to ask you about Amelia," I say. "She said you'd lie."

"I normally would. If I'm dating a girl, I'll tell her about my kid, but I never date Caldwell girls, so word hasn't gotten out."

"Why is it such a secret?"

"My dad's ashamed I knocked someone up at sixteen and couldn't even get her to stay with me. And I don't need everyone in this town talking about what's my business alone, so I never told anyone about it. Don't spread it around, okay? Not even to Keely."

"I won't, I promise." It's like I've been punched in the throat from shock, but I can keep a secret. I would never betray West after he trusted me with this information. Information he gives to no one else. Does that make me special?

"All right," he says. "Anyway, that's part of the reason I left home. And why Miles and Faye like to act like I was disowned. In a way, I guess I was. My dad thinks I'm a huge fuck-up." He tosses the leaf. "Whatever."

"I don't think you're a fuck-up." Teen parent and fuck-up aren't synonymous—shit happens. But there is one question heavy on my mind: who the heck is the mom?

"I'm doing okay," West says. "I visit my kid when I can. I pay child support with my own money."

"That's a lot of responsibility. I can't even imagine." Yikes, sometimes I can't even take care of myself. And West is only two years older than me. To carry all that at nineteen . . .

"If you think differently of me now, I get it," he says.

"No, I still—" I stop myself. Though it's obvious at this point that I *like-like* him, saying it out loud is so exposing.

"Some girls run off," he goes on. "I don't want you to go any-where."

"I'm not going to. But why isn't Amelia with you?"

"She's better off with her mom. I visit whenever I can, but . . . that's what's best for her." The dejected tone of his voice contradicts the words he says. Without thinking, I reach for his hand. West inter-laces our fingers and smooths his thumb along the curve of my palm, and my head rests against his shoulder. We sit like that for a long time, listening to the lake as the wind whistles through the trees.

It's a lot to take in, but I don't care if West has a kid with another girl. It just sucks I've missed out on so many years of his life. But maybe things were supposed to turn out this way. Maybe now that we're older and more mature, we can be together.

The sun shifts to its peak and beats down on my bare arms and legs. West suddenly reaches out and grabs something.

"What are you doing?" I ask.

"Check it out." His hands are clasped to create a dome, and he moves his thumb so I can see inside. A pair of eyes stare back at me.

"A frog!"

"You still like them, right?"

"Yes!"

West laughs as he slips the cold, slimy frog into my hands. I gen-tly hold it, and its little heartbeat pounds against me.

"It's a pickerel frog," I say and observe the squareish brown spots on its back.

"Why am I not surprised you know that?" West says. "You still into all that wildlife stuff?"

"Not really. I kept some of my textbooks, but reading them just reminded me of what happened here, so I sort of got out of it."

"Too bad. You used to love identifying species. Guess you haven't forgotten everything."

"There are a lot of things I can't forget about my life here."

When the frog ribbits, I open my hands and allow it to jump away and hop into the lake. The water ripples, entrances me. A shaky breath fills my lungs, and I shut my eyes to block out how it felt when they were inflated with ocean water.

"He's got the right idea," West says and stands, peeling off his shirt.

Before I can react, he runs and dives into the lake before he emerges and threads his hand through his dark hair. He stands easily—the lake isn't deep near the shore. But it's still hard to picture myself going in that water and not drowning, even though logically, I know I'll be okay. West wouldn't just let me float there and die. Maybe if I do it, all of this could go away: the flashbacks, the dreams. No more fear, no more nightmares. The sounds of the forest fade behind the thundering of my heart against my eardrums.

Droplets of water race each other down West's shoulders and arms. His lips don't move, but his voice resounds in my head. *You'll be okay. You'll be okay.*

On wobbly knees, I take off my shirt, then drop my shorts. Fear coils through me. Sharp, barbed wire constricts my heart. The water ebbs with every movement of his body, and West's words in my head are a siren's call. *You'll be okay. You'll be okay.*

"Whoa."

I snap from my trance. He's standing again, and his eyes trail all the way to my legs.

"Damn, are you trying to kill me?"

"What does that mean?" I stammer.

"It means you look good."

"Oh. Thanks."

Don't get me wrong, I want him to find me attractive. But now isn't the time. I must be insane—there's no way I'm getting in that water.

"Never mind." I grab my shirt. "I can't."

"If you're not ready, you're not ready. But you'll be okay," West says, out loud this time, and it's surreal, but I believe him. So I drop my shirt back on the grass and kick off my flip-flops. West's smile widens. "Atta girl. You can do it."

My feet sink into the silt. I touch my toes to the surface of the lake and yank my leg back like it's been electrocuted. But it isn't as freezing as it was on the night I fell. This water feels different. It's murky, chalky with microorganisms and algae, and when my foot descends into the silt again, there are plants between my toes. This isn't the ocean. It's not the same. I can swim here. West holds out his hand, so I take it. He walks me into the water, and oh God, it's so cold, and the earth is so slimy, but I keep going, one step at a time, until I'm half under.

"Oh God, West, I can't." My teeth chatter and my body trembles. I need to get back, but West squeezes my hand, keeps me grounded.

"You can," he says. "Come on, you're already halfway there. I've got you."

"Please don't let go."

"I won't, I promise."

Keeping my eyes closed, I step farther into the water. When my feet raise from the ground, my legs know to kick. I flip onto my back and float, and when I open my eyes, a great blue heron flies past the clouds rimmed with the silver lining of the sun. West is still standing, his hands firm on my back to help me stay afloat.

"There, see?" His smile reaches his eyes. "You're okay."

"I can't believe this." I roll onto my stomach and kick again, hurling myself forward, but West keeps his hands on me at all times. A sense of freedom surges through me as I adjust to the temperature of the water.

"See, you got it," West says.

We both laugh as I straighten up, and he grips the curve of my torso. When he pulls me to him, adrenaline slams into me, so I wrap my legs around his hips and grab onto his shoulders. Water drips from his dark eyelashes onto his cheeks. I'm close enough to feel his breath on my lips. The coldness fades until all I can feel is his skin on mine.

Just as West is closing the gap between us, I see something move out of the corner of my eye. We look up and Miles is standing on the shoreline.

"What the fuck are you doing here?" West shouts.

I slip behind West, holding onto his back, and he stands in front of me. Miles looks at West and me, and I want to shrivel up and die. As if I'm not horrified enough, two other people appear from the forest.

Oh *shit*.

Miles's dad looks exactly the same—thin brown hair, an expression that looks like he has a permanent pickle stuck up his ass. Beatrice stalks up from behind him. And here I am, practically naked, latched onto West like a damn leech. West uses his body to shield me from their sight, and I keep piggybacking him.

"What the hell?" West yells. "Get out of here!"

"You want *us* to get out of here?" Brian's voice booms. "This cabin—this whole goddamn lake—is my property, Weston. What do you think you're doing here?"

Beatrice grabs a fistful of Brian's black golf shirt and whispers, "This is what he does, Brian. He brings all these promiscuous girls up here right under your nose. You're going to end up with another grandchild you can never see."

I'm not *promiscuous*; I haven't even had my first kiss yet.

The water rises around me as the pressure increases. What had just felt freeing is quickly becoming a cage, and the euphoria from being so close to West disappears as reality crashes back in. Terror pumps through my veins, so intense I'll explode if I don't get to land.

"West, I need out," I manage to say.

"It's okay," he says before he focuses on his dad. "Seriously, please leave. She literally just got in the water, you guys are messing everything up."

"Oh no, we're having a conversation. After I helped you with Amelia, this is how you repay me?" Brian points his finger at us. "Get your damn clothes on and meet me back at the cabin."

Brian and Beatrice disappear into the forest, but Miles remains, his eyes full of both anger and hurt, before he follows after them. This is bad, really bad. West carries me out of the water. With my feet on the land, I scramble farther away from the shore with my heart still pounding. I can't believe I actually swam for the first time in five years, yet somehow, all I can think about is this Hendricks drama. Water drips from the ends of my hair and slicks down my goosebump-covered body in tiny rivers. When a towel wraps around my shoulders, I sink into the warmth.

"You're okay," West says.

"I know. Thank you."

"That was intense." West puts his shirt back on. "I'm sorry. Not sure losing my temper with them was the best idea."

After drying off, I pull up my shorts. "It's not your fault. You weren't expecting anyone, especially your parents. What are they doing here?"

"No idea. But I have a strong feeling Miles had something to do with it."

"He couldn't have known we were up here."

Once we're dressed, we hurry through the forest. My wet bathing suit soaks my clothing, gross and soggy against my skin. West and I take the short walk back to the cabin, where we find Brian, Beatrice, and Miles waiting for us by the firepit. I try to make apologetic eye contact with Miles, but now he's the one who refuses to look at me. That was a horrible way for him to find out about me and West.

"Weston." Brian breaks away from the others and slides his hands in the pockets of his tan shorts. His gaze lands on me, and I tense up. "And you're Miles's friend. Interesting."

Perfect, now Brian Hendricks is unimpressed with me. It doesn't matter what he thinks—especially since he and West don't get along—but I've always hated being disliked. Even by someone *I* dislike.

"Well," Brian says to West, "I'm sure you can imagine my surprise, coming up to my cabin to find this, Weston."

"Bullshit, Miles told you to come here, didn't he?"

"It doesn't matter. Hand over the key."

West growls, but digs his keychain from his pocket and shoves it in Brian's hand.

"Is this the only one you have? Don't lie to me."

"Yes. That's it, seriously. I don't know why I can't just have it. I don't wreck the place, I don't even have parties."

Brian looks at me, then back at West. "You know why."

"Do you think that matters? I have my own apartment; I can do whatever I want."

"I certainly don't want to provide you with alternative places to impregnate girls."

"Dad, what the fuck."

Face burning, I look at the chipped blue paint on my toenails. Can somebody kill me now, please?

"Do you have belongings inside?" Brian asks.

"Yeah." West takes my hand. "I'll grab my stuff, and then trust me, you won't see me for a long time."

We enter the cabin in silence, and I snatch my backpack off the bar stool as West gathers his keys.

"You got everything?" West asks tensely. I nod and throw my backpack over my shoulders. "I think I dropped my wallet somewhere," he says. "Follow me out back."

Through the back doors, we end up at the firepit again, but

the rest of West's family has moved to the front of the cabin. West searches the grass. A click sounds from the sliding glass doors, and I turn to see Brian watching us with his hand on the lock, his face shadowed. After a moment, he disappears into the cabin, probably to lock up the other doors so we can't get back in. Something about him is even more terrifying than when we were kids.

"There you are," someone says.

Miles rounds the side of the house, just as West tucks his wallet into the pocket of his swim trunks.

"Miles," I begin, "I can explain—"

But I'm cut off by West storming toward him, and Miles squirms as West shoves him into the wall of the cabin by his chest.

"If you ever do anything like this again, I'll fucking kill you," West says. "You might have Dad fooled, but not me. Are you so jealous you had to ruin everything for us?"

"Are you kidding?" Miles shouts. "You come out here with *my* best friend, and you're giving me shit for showing up?"

West slams him again, and Miles yelps in a way that makes me feel terrible. This type of violence freaks me out.

"Stop!" I say. "Let him go, West. Please."

West's eyebrows are stitched with rage, but he releases the pressure on Miles's chest. Miles regains his composure and adjusts his shirt.

"So what, was this your plan all along?" Miles asks West, voice dripping with hatred. "Hook up with my best friend the moment she comes home to see me?"

West laughs, but it's sarcastic. "See, that kind of fucked, entitled attitude is exactly why you'll always be a brat. She came back to recover, not just for *you*, Miles."

"Not just for you, either, asshole."

"Stop it," I cut in. "If you're going to fight with each other, please don't make it about me."

"But it is about you," Miles says.

"I don't want it to be."

Both Miles and West are staring at me now, and I hate it, I hate being the center of attention. This day can't get any worse. Miles needs to know the truth about me and West, but there's so much betrayal on his face. I'm shaking so hard I need to lean against the side of the cabin to catch my balance.

"West," I say, "give us a moment alone, please."

"What?"

"Please."

"Whatever." He takes off around the side of the house, leaving me out back with Miles. Hesitantly, our eyes lock. He's going to hate me for this.

"Miles, did you know we were going to be up here?" I ask.

"Nope," he says, clearly pissed.

I look over my shoulder for his parents or West, but voices come from the front of the house—probably Brian yelling at West again. I face Miles. "Listen, I'm sorry you had to find out like this, but West and I are—"

"I know what you are," he snaps. "Save it, Olivia. Have you always liked him?" When I'm silent, Miles scoffs. "So when everyone said we'd get married when we were kids, you already knew you liked him instead of me?"

"What was I supposed to say, Miles? I was a kid! I didn't think you actually liked me back then, you never said anything!"

Miles is silent, and I am sick to my stomach. Suddenly everything we've ever done together needs to be reanalyzed. The way he'd sometimes touch my wrists, or how he'd always follow me around—to me, it was always platonic. But to him, maybe all of it was sewn together with the hope I'd like him as more than a friend. The same way I always hoped, deep down, that West would like me.

"You were always my friend first," Miles says. "Guess we're not even that anymore."

"Why? Because of West? We can still be friends."

Miles starts walking away. "I don't want to be friends with you if you're with him."

"Are you serious?" I chase after him. "So what, that's it? If I don't like you back, you don't want anything to do with me?"

"You already wanted nothing to do with me, anyway. Just piss off, Olivia, you're the shittiest friend I've ever had."

Before I can stop him, Miles takes off. I stand there, trembling with anger and guilt and so much confusion.

Maybe it's better Miles and I don't talk anymore. After what he did to me, isn't that what I wanted?

I don't know anymore.

West appears again and says, "What a little prick. I should've kicked his ass."

"He's your brother, you would really hit him?"

"Of course I would. Olivia, I get how that must've looked for you, but you have no idea what Miles is like. He brought my dad here on purpose to get me in trouble."

"How is violence any better? He was terrified of you."

West actually laughs. "He wasn't terrified, trust me. He just wants you to feel sorry for him."

"You're way bigger than him, West. I don't like violence. Can you just take me home please?"

"Seriously? Come on, we were supposed to spend the day together."

"This is too much for me. I just want to go home, please."

With a sigh, West wraps his arm around my shoulder. "Okay, let's go." I lean into him, but my mind still plays what Miles said on repeat. Maybe I am a shitty friend. Maybe I deserve to be hated by him.

We head around to the front of the house, where the Corvette is parked. Miles and his parents watch us get into the car and drive away. Through the back window, I catch sight of Miles glaring at me until we can't see each other anymore.

12

The radio fills the silence between West and me on the drive back to town. We're passing the population sign when evening falls. My phone buzzes in my hand: a text from Keely. I had filled her in on what happened at the cabin, hoping that telling my best friend would help ease my mind, but it didn't.

OMG I'm so sorry! I told Miles you guys were there, but I had no idea he would do that. I'm sorry, please don't be mad at me!!

I reread the text five times before anger singes through me. West pulls up to a red light as we reach downtown.

"Wow," I say.

"What?" West asks, hand draped over the steering wheel. He doesn't look at me.

"You were right. Miles knew we were there. He told on us."

West says nothing.

"I can't believe him," I go on. "That's so petty. I can't believe I even thought about being his friend again."

The light turns green, and West keeps driving, taking a left toward Keely's neighborhood. "I just wanted to spend the day with you," he says, his voice tired. "I don't want Miles to ruin what we had going. You swam, Olivia. You did really well."

My heart pulls at the memory; I wanted to spend the day with him too. And I still can't believe I swam. But images of West shoving Miles into the cabin drown out the positives. I don't even know if I should be mad at him. I'm more worried, really.

"I don't like it when you're violent, West," I say quietly. "I have to be able to trust you."

"I get it, and neither do I. Honestly, I lost my cool. I'm sorry you had to see it."

"I'm mad at Miles, too, but the way you talked to him was messed up."

"I know."

"You were mean to him when we were kids too."

"Yeah. I was."

"Well? Why? Because you don't talk to me like that. Or anyone else, I hope."

We pull up to a stop sign. Within three minutes, we'll be at Keely's house, but the road behind us is empty, so West throws the car into park and stays put.

"Miles is my brother. There's a lot about us you don't know." He laughs and rubs his eye. "That kid can be a nightmare."

A *nightmare*. The dream sweeps into my mind. Miles floating outside my window, waving back and forth before letting all the water in, condemning me to death. It was just a dream. But what wasn't a dream was when Miles grabbed me. The pressure of his fingers on my wrist echoes still—I can't let myself forget that. I had been confused about whether our friendship should really end earlier, but now I'm certain.

We're too different now. Whatever we had as kids is clearly gone.

But this, with West—it's real. So as the car idles, my hand inches toward him, tempted to touch him again. He leans toward me, too, but just says, "You know, I always liked this about you."

"Liked what?"

His eyes crinkle, and he averts his stare, almost like he's shy. "You always told me how it was. I mean, you were the sweetest kid, but when it came down to it . . . you always told me how it was."

"I didn't even realize I was like that."

"You were. You still are."

I wring my thumb along my elastic and laugh a little. "I didn't even think you liked me much when we were kids."

"Are you kidding? I always thought you were cool, Olive. Life at home sucked, but you always wanted to hang out, and—"

"Go on," I say, smiling.

"You're making me sound like a sap."

"No, I love it. Keep going. Please." I don't even care if I sound desperate. It's like I'm finally reaching land.

West says, "You always had this smile, like, you could light up any room. When my dad was real mad at me and my stepmom hated me, being around you made me feel like I wasn't so hated. Even when you were getting mad at me for being mean to Miles."

"Oh, wow. Just FYI, you didn't act like you liked me much at all. You were a little mean. And intimidating."

"Yeah, well, I was a dumb kid. Trust me, I liked you. I didn't come around to hang out with Miles—I could see him at home. I came to hang out with you."

We fall quiet, still at the stop sign, but we haven't seen a single other car. I could go back to Keely's, spend the night alone in my room like I had planned. But I don't want to anymore.

"I don't want our day to end here," I say.

"It doesn't have to. Come home with me. I'll get you home before ten."

My mouth is dry. "Promise?"

With a smile, he nods. "Scout's honor."

○ ○ ○

At West's apartment, he leads me through a door to a cramped, humid staircase. The smell of fish 'n' chips from upstairs is overpowered by a distinct basement smell, like concrete and wood. I like it. It's more like home than the wide property of the Hendricks estate. A place like this suits West more than that lonely mansion ever did.

Inside, shoes litter the mat by the door and voices come from around the corner. A buttery popcorn scent hangs in the air, and a tall, skinny girl with ginger hair and huge glasses zips into the den.

"West! There you are!"

"Sandy," he says, just as Oscar paws his way toward us, his tail wagging. He nudges me with his head until I pet him.

"You're still fixing that little hole in my room, right?" Sandy asks.

"Yeah, tomorrow cool?" He kicks his boots off.

"Totally, whenever you have time, no rush!" Sandy's hazel eyes fall on me. "And you must be Olivia!"

"Hi, yes, I am," I say. *West talked about me to his roommate*?

"You have no idea how useful West is to have around, girl," Sandy says. "Punch a hole in the wall? He'll fix it. Hungry? This boy will literally go out on a boat and catch freakin' dinner. He is everything."

Awkwardly, I laugh. Sandy is really nice, but I'm not good at meeting new people.

"Yes, Sandy. I'm a handyman," West says. "We get it."

Her giggle is contagious. "Are you ever."

Sandy isn't the type of person I would ever expect West to be friends with, let alone live with. But considering there are Nintendo posters all over the walls and not a single piece of West anywhere, this must be Sandy's place, and he's just renting a room.

"I've got Jen and Davies over," Sandy says. "Come hang with us!"

The living room is divided from the kitchen by a sectional couch, where a guy in a *Walking Dead* T-shirt sits with a black-haired girl watching TV. I've never seen either of them before. West and I scrunch together on the leather armchair while the others are on the couch. We both fidget. They end up putting on *Sixteen Candles*, a movie I totally love, but I can't focus on it with West sitting so close to me.

Partway through the movie, West whispers into my hair, "We should probably shower. I think they're noticing we stink like a lake. You want to go first?"

"No, you go," I say. Sitting on the couch, watching this movie with these strangers is somehow a good distraction from how overwhelmed I am. I need to catch my breath before using West's freaking shower. But my hair is definitely crusty with lake water, so it needs to happen eventually.

"Be right back," West says.

Fifteen minutes later, he returns to the living room, and he smells really nice. He waves for me to follow him. As I grab my backpack, Sandy and her friends don't notice me leave. At the end of the hall, the bathroom is still steaming from West's shower. He hands me a dry towel.

"You got a change of clothes?"

"Yeah, in my backpack," I say.

"My bedroom's right here." He points to a closed door. "Just come in when you're done, okay?"

"Okay, thanks."

I slip into the bathroom, enveloped by the humidity, and press my back to the closed door. It smells like clean body wash and West. This is all happening so fast it makes my head spin, but we aren't going to have sex or anything—he hasn't even kissed me yet. Maybe I want to, a little, but I'm a virgin. Oh God, I haven't even told him that. *Slow down.* We haven't kissed. And there's no pressure with West. But all of this—being in his apartment and using his shower—is very real. Still, I get into the water, comforted by the warmth and the fact that his shower stall has no window in it.

After I'm done, I get changed into my clean clothes and brush my hair, smelling like aloe and cucumber instead of the lake. Everything I needed was packed in my backpack in case I showered at the cabin.

I leave the bathroom, get to West's door, and take a deep breath before opening it. West is lying on the bed but he stands when he sees me, eyes wide. I close the door behind us. West wipes his palms on his jeans, and my backpack drops on the floor. The others laugh outside, but the silence between us is louder.

"So," he says, "this is the only room in the house that actually looks like mine."

A rustic ship's wheel hangs on the blue-gray wall beside his bed, where the sheets are messy and the pillows are scattered. Random knickknacks litter his desk: pens, a pocketknife, a wrench. A notebook with some numbers written on it is open next to a pile of stones. When I spot a little wood carving of a boat, I pick it up and smooth my finger along its matte surface.

"I remember this," I say. "You made it."

"Yeah," he says. "We were out at the docks."

"And you had a little carving knife."

"My dad lost his shit when he found out I had that. Pretty sure he threw it right in the trash. I was destroyed. I loved that thing."

West reaches over me and takes the boat. It looks so tiny in his big fingers, but I remember when his hand was small, and mine was too. When West puts down the boat, I face him. My breath hitches as he traps me in with his arms, and I scoot onto the desk.

"Is this okay?" he asks. His eyes, half-lidded under his long lashes, glance at my lips. I nod, but a tidal wave slams my chest and sloshes with different emotions: desire, longing, fear. If we kiss, it could change everything between us forever. But I want that change. I touch the neck of his shirt and breathe in his earthy musk. He leans his weight onto me.

"West, I—"

My phone vibrates in my back pocket and rattles against the desk. I go to touch it, but West grabs my wrist.

"Don't," he rasps. "Not now."

The intensity in his voice captures me. I slap my phone on the desk, and he positions himself between my parted legs. His fingertips graze my outer thighs, and I'm suddenly very thankful I shaved everything.

My phone buzzes again. I quickly check it.

"It's Sun," I say. "I—I have to answer it."

West groans, but backs off. I mouth *sorry* at him and press accept. "Hello?"

"Olivia?" Sun says. "Where are you? Is Keely with you?"

"No, I'm with West."

"Did you see the time? It's after ten."

Oh crap. She's right—it's 10:03 p.m. "Sun, I'm sorry, I—"

"Please get back as soon as you can. Keely snuck out of her bedroom and she isn't answering our calls. This isn't like her, so we're getting worried."

I lock eyes with West, whose face drops with disappointment. I don't want to leave—I want to stay right here, on this desk, and find out what West would have done if Sun never called. But I can't disobey her, especially if Keely took off.

So I tell Sun that West will drive me home right away, and we hurry out of the apartment, leaving our possibilities to echo in his room.

13

When I close the Myerses' front door behind me, my voice echoes through the empty hall. "Sun? Are you home?" Dim lights shimmer off the hardwood floor as I kick my Vans onto the shoe mat. Keely's yellow Converse are missing.

"Olivia? Is Keely with you?" Sun appears at the end of the hallway, pale with her arms wrapped over her housecoat. "Have you heard from her?"

"No, I tried calling, but she didn't pick up for me either."

Sun places her hand on her forehead and paces. "This isn't like her at all. She always keeps in touch. Always. Roger is going around and checking parties, but we still haven't found her."

When I reminded Keely earlier that the rules have never stopped her from getting what she wanted, I didn't mean for her to sneak out and get in trouble *today*. I meant more that she could still talk to Shawn. Oh God—I'm such an idiot.

Sun calls Roger with the house phone connected to the wall. "Yes, Olivia is here now . . . Keely isn't there? Where else could she be?" She sucks in a breath. "Okay, I'll try to stay calm. Just get her home safe, Roger. Please."

By the time Sun hangs up, her eyes—dark brown, just like Keely's—are glassy with tears. I want to tell her Keely's okay, that she must have just snuck out with Shawn, because there's nothing else she would have done. But Sun looks genuinely scared.

"Keely is still grounded," Sun says, "so when we saw she wasn't in her room, we got very worried. It isn't like her to sneak out. She didn't tell you anything at all about where she was going?"

Kicking at the floor, I hold my hands behind my back. I can't lie to Sun, but if I tell her the whole truth about what *I* said, she'll be so mad at me. "Keely mentioned she was upset she couldn't hang out with Shawn anymore, and she did mention something about a party, so . . . maybe she's with him?"

"Maybe. Roger has a call out for Shawn."

"I'm sure Keely's okay," I say, and I mean it. She's probably at the docks, drinking Smirnoff Ice with Shawn, leaning into him with a flirtatious smile. But saying those words to Sun feels so fake, and it would offer her no comfort.

I follow her into the kitchen. With a sigh, Sun picks up a steaming pot of tea, and the sweet smell of chamomile breezes with the draft from the open window. Awkwardness pricks my arms, and my hands cross behind my back like a guilty little kid.

"Maybe you should go to bed, Olivia."

"But Keely—"

"Roger and I will deal with it. Having you up won't help. We can talk about you being late for curfew after we find our daughter."

My shoulders are heavy as I go to my room, shut the door, and press my back to it. Engulfed by the silence, I crawl under the covers of my bed, which, after all these days, has started to smell a little like home.

When I manage to fall asleep, I dream of being held under water until my airways fill with seaweed and raw fish.

o o o

Footsteps pacing outside my room startle me awake. Golden sunlight pours through the blinds. Roger's voice booms through the walls, and recollections of last night clap into my head like thunder. Keely must be getting yelled at for sneaking out. I tear out of bed and into the hallway.

"Hey, is Keely back?" I say, but as soon as I'm in the living room, the answer stares back at me. Tears stain Sun's cheeks, Roger is still in his uniform—and several other cops are flooding in through the front door. They move through the living room in a row, like worker ants. A female officer ducks into Keely's room, followed by Officer Jones holding a yellow notebook with sunflowers on it. *Keely's journal.*

"Olivia, come here," Roger says. I've never seen him look so scared.

"What's happening? Where's Keely?" My voice shakes. Gently, Roger pulls me into the living room with him and Sun.

"Olivia, if you know anything about where Keely could be or who she could be with, now is the time to tell us. Please, no secrets."

"But why? Where's Keely? Is she okay?"

"They never found her," Sun says, voice strained. "She's missing."

The room spins. "But . . . no, she can't be missing. She has to be with Shawn. There's no one else."

Roger's composure cracks; his shoulders tremble, and the cop demeanor can't mask the fact that he's a terrified father right now. "I've already spoken to Shawn, Miles, and all of Keely's usual friends. They were at a party at the Garcias' house, and according to everyone—including Shawn Watters—Keely just disappeared. No one knows where she is."

Pressure builds behind my eyes like an overflow of water in my brain; I want to say something, *anything* that could help them find her, but I have nothing. Nothing but Shawn. The sudden urge to call my mom pokes at me, but worrying her all the way in New York City won't help find Keely here, now.

When Officer Jones comes over and taps Roger's shoulder, he snaps out of it. "Sir, we reviewed her journal and we can't find anything helpful other than her interest in Shawn Watters."

"Damn it," Roger says. "Thank you, Jones. Please put it back where you found it. Olivia, is there *anything* else you know? Anything about where Keely might go or who she could be with?"

"I'm sorry, I—I don't know."

Sun grabs Roger's arm. "Roger, you have to go look for her now, please."

"You're right. You stay here in case she comes home." He nods at the other cops. "Come on, everyone, let's move!"

Before I can offer my help, the other cops follow Roger, their footsteps thundering over the hardwood until the last person slams the door closed. The silence they leave behind is suffocating. That image I have of Keely drinking Smirnoff Ice with Shawn at the docks is replaced by my worst nightmares: her body, gutted and mutilated, blood seeped into the earth, throat cut. Exactly like the way the animal killer left the squirrels and deer.

"I'm going to go look for her too, okay?" I say.

Sun doesn't reply, just goes into the kitchen, her body shaking. Clearly, she's too worried to care what I'm doing. Running to my room, I grab my phone off the nightstand and text West to pick me up. Even though I want nothing to do with Miles, he'll know where

Shawn is. I frown at our messages, because there's an unread text in my inbox sent at 3:58 a.m.

I'm really sorry for what I said, I didn't mean
it. I still want to be friends. I just can't believe
you'd go swimming with him, but not me :(

My skin crawls. For Keely's sake, I ignore the weird feeling and text Miles back.

Are you with Shawn?

Yeah, you heard about Keely?

Where are you?

Shawn's place.

Stay there, I'm coming over.

o o o

The AMBER alert for Keely blared from my phone shortly after Roger left, and it made this all too real. West drove us here in a hurry. Now we're at Shawn's house, and Shawn cradles his head in his hands and sits on his living room couch while I stand over him.

"I swear, I don't know where she is," he says.

"But she was with you last night, right?" I ask.

"Yeah, but . . ."

"Come on, Olivia," Dean drones from his spot beside Shawn. His arm rests over the back of the floral couch while he picks at a loose string. "We already told the cops everything. Why are you playing detective?"

Faye leans against Miles on the love seat, a bottle of Gatorade loosely clutched in her hand. Miles hasn't looked at me or West once since we got here. Apparently Shawn's parents have already joined the search effort to find Keely. West leans against the wall by the front door and silently watches.

"I'm worried about my best friend." My eyes sting, but I try to keep it together. "Shawn, please, what happened to her?"

"I don't know! She was at the party and then she was just gone!"

"Relax, cousin," Dean says. "You have an alibi. We all saw you."

Shawn's shoulders shake, and his light brown eyes meet mine, desperate and pleading. "Look, I'm worried about her too, okay? But I swear, I don't know anything. I'll tell you exactly what I told her dad: we were all wasted, hanging out in Emma's living room, then Keely went to the bathroom and never came back. Emma said Keely went into the backyard to pee because the line for the bathroom was huge. You know Keely, she's always doing crazy shit like that."

Shawn could be telling the truth, or he could be lying, but the fear on his face is evident. Either way, I don't trust him.

Faye limply stands like this situation is boring her. "Okay, my head is killing me, I feel like death, and this isn't helping anyone. Shawn doesn't know anything, Liv, so are you going to do something about Keely or just keep wasting time?"

"We should look for her," I say.

West stands from his position against the wall. "I agree."

"The cops are already searching the woods," Miles says and flashes his phone screen. "It's all over the news and the Caldwell Police's Facebook page. The adults are saying they don't want kids involved, they're worried more of us will get lost or something."

"You're going to sit here and do nothing, Miles?" I say. "This is *Keely* we're talking about."

Dean laughs. "That girl was *wasted*, Olivia. Like always. They're going to find her passed out on the side of the road somewhere."

"Don't you guys get it? She could be hurt! Some sick person is murdering animals in town, and now my best friend is missing, and—"

When West's arm wraps around me, I suck in a breath and hold in my tears. "Hey, we're going to find her, whether they help us or not," he says, and his voice is the only comfort in this strange place. We share a quick, shy smile, reminding me of what almost happened last night—but now is not the time. I can feel Miles glaring at us.

Out of the four of them, Faye is the only one still standing. "Olivia is right," she finally says. "The least we can do is look for Keely."

"You serious?" Dean says. "Babe, you saw how drunk Keely was. She's probably fine. The cops will find her."

"You don't have to come, Dean."

"I want you to stay," Dean says.

Faye avoids his gaze but keeps her posture strong. "We should start at Emma's house."

"That's where the cops started," West says and smooths his hand over my shoulder. "It'd make more sense to start farther out and move in. We should split into groups to cover more ground. Keep your phones on you so we can stay in contact and know whether they found her or not. Agreed?"

Everyone is quiet as they exchange uneasy glances.

"We can't do anything the police can't do," Miles says.

"But it's better than nothing, Miles," I say.

After a moment, Miles nods, unsure. "Okay, I'll help."

Dean lets out an annoyed sigh. "Fine, looks like we're all going. Shawn, get your shit together."

○ ○ ○

We split into three groups: me and West, Miles and Shawn, and Dean and Faye. We began on the outskirts of town, but now West and I are deep in the forest. West marks an X on every few trees we pass, as he's done for the past two hours we've waded through the trees. The deeper we get, the hotter it becomes, the more terrified I am for Keely's safety. The sun reaches its peak, bleeds through the leaves, and blinds me. When something stings my leg, I slap it, and a black fly buzzes around me. I wag my arms in a useless attempt to scare off all these terrible bugs.

"You okay?" West asks from in front of me.

"Fine," I mutter, "let's just keep going."

I take his hand and he hoists me over a fallen tree. I hop over the other side but stop to catch my breath, dizzy from being in the heat for so long. Dehydration creates a dry, sandy sensation on my tongue. A canteen materializes in my hand, and I immediately twist off the cap and chug some water back.

"Didn't realize you were so thirsty," West says. "Sorry."

"Thank you." I wipe my mouth and give him back the canteen. "You're always prepared for everything."

"Yeah, I was a serious Scout. Becoming an Eagle was the proudest moment of my life."

"I remember."

"I wanted to say sorry, by the way."

"For what?"

"'Scout's honor.' I messed up. I didn't get you home on time."

"It's okay. I just want to find Keely."

"Yeah, you're right." West gets down on one knee and scans the ground.

"What are you looking for?" I ask.

He grabs a handful of brushwood and throws it to the side. "A trail. I thought I had something, but it could've been a deer. Come on, let's keep moving."

The emergency signals on both our phones blare from our pockets again, cutting into the sounds of the forest. I take mine out, and it's another AMBER alert for Keely. She hasn't been found. It's already noon.

"Hey, hold up." West gets down on one knee. "Looks like something cut through this way. These branches have been stepped on."

He brushes twigs away from the dirt. "This part of the forest is really wet. Check this out."

It's barely visible, but there's a partial shape of a footprint. That diamond pattern belongs to a Converse.

"That could be Keely's shoe!" I exclaim. "I have to text Roger!"

"Yeah, and tell him we'll keep going. We're onto something."

I text Roger and send him our GPS location, hoping it will be enough to guide him. West moves more sticks out of the way.

"There's too much shit in the way, but I think I've got a trail." He holds up a branch and allows me to pass. "Come on, this way."

After climbing over the thin trunk of a fallen down aspen, my feet get caught in nettles that scratch at my ankles. I duck beneath a spiderweb as birds squawk above us. More fallen-down trees and thick, unruly foliage, and then we find ourselves in a sparse area of trees. West is focused on the ground the whole time.

"Shit," he says.

"What is it?"

Pressed into the dirt is another footprint, but this one is way bigger than the last. Bloodcurdling images of Keely being attacked make their way into my mind, but I snap my elastic to keep them out.

West takes a picture with his phone. "Looks like the trail splits. Bigfoot took off over there, but Keely's footprints go that way."

"Does that mean she's okay? If there was a man here, he didn't hurt her?"

"I don't know." West marks an X on a tree and circles it. "But we can't stop now. It'll rain soon, I can feel it. I swear this is the rainiest summer I've ever seen in my life."

West is right. Before long, dark gray clouds roll in as the wind brushes the tips of the trees. The smell of rain drifts into the air.

Up ahead, there's a pointed roof of a structure between the trees. I think it's an old fort or something, until we reach a rough trail that leads into a clearing.

A log cabin. Not one like the Hendrickses'—this one's a real cabin made out of stacked, decaying logs. The door is topped by a set of antlers, and a window is on each side—no glass, but they lead into the pitch darkness of the cabin like two inky eyes. Leaves and branches cover the ramshackle roof, and the wood rots at the joints so the structure half collapses into itself.

"What is this place?" I ask.

"An old hunting cabin, by the looks of it." West squints into the light. "There's lots of abandoned shit in these woods. Hey, Keely, you in there?"

A distant caw from a crow resounds through the woods and rustles through the trees. Other than that, dead silence. The cabin's obscure gaze traps me. Part of me wants to see what's inside. A bigger part is too terrified to budge, scared something will crawl out of those pitch-black eyes if I make a wrong move.

But Keely could be in there. I take a step toward it, only to be gently pulled back on by West.

"Olive, don't. It could collapse on you."

"But we have to check. We saw Keely's footprint, West. She could be in there."

His jaw tightens, but he nods. "Then let me do it."

West moves toward the cabin. Just as he's about to turn the flashlight on his phone to peek in the windows, something flutters in the corner of my eye. It's a monarch butterfly—but on the ground near it is another footprint.

"West, look!"

He hurries over. "Fuck, she has to be here somewhere. I think they go that way. Come on, let's go."

We wind over roots and crunch over twigs. I now have a crosshatch of cuts all up my legs, and the fully gray sky casts a shadow over the entire forest. When the sound of trickling water reaches my ears, I stop.

"Wait," I say. A distant memory flows in, something I haven't thought about it years: when we were kids, Keely and I loved roaming the forest, but Roger always told us that if we ever got lost, there was an easy way to get back to town. "The river leads to the ocean," I say.

"What are you talking about?"

"It's something Roger used to say when we were kids. He said that if we ever got lost in the woods, we can follow the river, because the river always leads to the ocean."

We're running now, and rain begins to splatter my arms. The trickling gets louder. I reach the river and skid to a halt. Upstream, beneath a tree, I see her: legs bent, yellow dress barely covering her body.

All the hope I had stops, settles over me the same way the wind calms and leaves the forest in a quiet, solidified state.

She isn't moving.

I run, trip over my own feet, and skid on my knees until I'm beside her. Her legs are sliced up from sticks, and bug bites have created fat red hives all up her arms. Mud splotches her skin and her eyes are shut peacefully.

"Keely, oh God, no, no, no." I hover my hand over her cheek, too afraid to touch. "West, she's dead, she's—"

West gets down on his knees. Gently, he presses his fingers to her neck. My brain throbs, and I snap my elastic over and over again, wishing I won't feel anything, wishing this is nothing more than another one of my fucked-up nightmares.

"She's dead. Oh God, West, she's dead."

"Olivia, calm down. She isn't dead."

West smooths Keely's hair from her face. She grumbles as he lightly shakes her shoulders, and her head falls to the side.

"Keely!" I say.

"Huh? Liv? West?"

The relief is enough to cripple me. "Keely, you're okay."

Her eyes lull into her head. "Guys, I was so thirsty I drank river water, and now I feel really sick . . ."

"Here." West pulls the canteen to Keely's lips, and she slowly drinks. "There, you're all right. Who did this to you?"

"I don't know, I just woke up in the woods." She relaxes, but her brows pinch in pain. "I really don't feel good. I want to go home."

"Everyone's looking for you, Keel," I say. "We were so worried."

But Keely doesn't reply, just falls back asleep. So I do the only thing I can: I call Roger and tell him to follow the river to us.

o o o

I've never been the type of person to hate hospitals, maybe because there's something sobering about being surrounded by life-saving medicine and machines. After my fall, I remember feeling safe waking up to white lights and my friends and family.

But right now, I hate it. Because the anticipation of finding out what happened to Keely has me caught in a time loop—it's only been three hours, but it feels like ten. This is the second time Keely's been in the hospital, but I'm even more worried now than I was before.

Rain slams against the windows of the waiting room, and West returns with a bag of chips and a soda from the vending machine. He sits next to me. Just as West is opening the chips, Roger emerges from the hall. We both jump to our feet as he comes over, thumbs hooked to his belt, his face drawn with exhaustion.

"How is she?" I ask.

Roger is quiet. "I can't tell you how grateful I am that you found her," he eventually says. "Keely doesn't remember anything about who took her or why, just that she woke up confused in the middle of the forest and kept walking until she found the river." Roger places his hand on West's shoulder. "Taking a picture of that footprint was smart thinking, West. It could be anyone's shoe, but it's the only lead we've got. The team is still investigating for evidence in the woods, but the rain's almost surely washed it all away."

"I just hope you find who did this to her," Wests says.

"We will. Nothing like this has ever happened here, not in my thirty years on the force."

"Can I go see her now?" I ask, and Roger nods. Sun is talking to a nurse in the hall when I slip into Keely's room. She sits upright on her bed, surrounded by white sheets. The nurses have combed the sticks out of her hair and tied it into a ponytail. I want to hug her, but hold myself back when I see the tears dried on her cheeks.

"Hey, Keel," I say delicately.

She wipes her eyes with the sleeve of her hospital gown. "Hey."

"How are you holding up?"

"I don't know. I feel like shit."

Taking a seat in the vinyl chair beside her bed, I can't stop fidgeting.

"Come on, Liv, please don't look like that," Keely says with a groan. "It was super uncomfortable, but the doctors, like . . . checked me out. Nobody *did* anything to me. I'm actually fine."

"Trust me, I'm really glad about that, but I still don't understand what did happen."

"Honestly? Me neither. I was at the party, then everything went black, and suddenly I was wandering through the middle of the woods, totally confused."

"Did someone drug your drink or something?"

"Apparently not, they ran tests and I just had a lot of alcohol in my system. Which is kind of weird because I only had a few mixed drinks. Guess they were stronger than I thought."

"Well, what's the very last thing you remember?"

"God, it's all so foggy. But I remember being at Emma's party with Shawn and them. Then I ended up losing them. I went to the bathroom, but I remember it being occupied for like, ever. Pretty sure people were doing coke inside, so Emma told me to just go to the bathroom in the backyard, which is so gross, but I did it because I was dying. The last thing I remember is looking for a place to pee."

"And that's when you could have gotten lost."

"That's what people are telling me."

"But we found you so deep inside the forest, and when West was tracking you, he found a guy's footprint."

"Yeah, my dad showed me. But if some guy took me out in the woods, why wouldn't he, like, *do* anything to me? As messed up as this sounds, I'm almost more freaked out that he'd drop me in the woods and just do nothing."

"That is really weird. Maybe he wanted to, but chickened out."

"I don't know, or maybe the footprint was totally unrelated. Either way, crisis averted." She holds up her phone. "To make everything worse, stupid Shawn just texted me and said we're done hanging out. Apparently, I'm too much drama."

Anger soaks up some of my anxiety. "He's such a dick."

"I know!" Tears gloss over her eyes. "But honestly, he's right. I am too much drama. My freaking cop dad questioned the guy I like over all of this and when I got alcohol poisoning. Drama literally follows me."

"Screw him, Keely. You're worth so much more than some idiot guy who disappears at the first sign of trouble."

"Yeah, I know. But I still really like him. How dumb is that?"

"It's not."

Someone knocks at the door, and we turn to see Roger and two younger cops.

"Lemon, we need to get an official statement from you now, if you feel up to it."

Keely sighs. "Fine."

After telling Keely I'm glad she's okay again, I leave the room and meet West in the hall, and we walk together past the vending machines to a vacant part of the hall.

"Don't you think it's weird?" I say to West.

"Yeah, there's a lot of that going on here lately."

"But before I came here, things were normal, weren't they? Someone had been killing squirrels, but after I arrived, it was a deer, and then a dog—and then all of a sudden Keely gets dropped in the forest?"

"Yeah, it's fucked up, but what does it have to do with you?"

A nurse rolls an elderly man on a gurney past us, and I keep quiet until we're alone again. I hesitate. I don't fully understand what I'm thinking—maybe I shouldn't say it at all. "I . . . I don't know. Forget it."

West scans my face, like he's trying to read me, before he pulls me into a hug. I melt against him, and he smooths my hair down.

"You've been through a lot, Olive. You should get some sleep."

"Yeah, maybe you're right."

But something tells me sleep won't take this feeling away.

Strange things have been happening in this town. And I can't help but feel like I'm the cause of it.

14

Because I helped get Keely home safe, Roger and Sun didn't ground me for missing my curfew. But I don't leave the house for three days anyway. Now Roger is at work, still trying to make sense of what happened to Keely, while Sun has taken her out shopping for the first time since she was discharged from the hospital. The house is too quiet, so I step out for an evening run.

Pink and blue sweeps over the sky like a watercolor painting. My lungs heave as I suck in breaths of ocean air and jog down the quiet road, past houses and stretches of trees. I'm sweaty under my volleyball hoodie and acoustic music blasts from the headphones in my ears. Back in New York, jogging alone around the park was one of my favorite things to do. It's much more peaceful here. There's a tree on every lawn, and children draw hopscotch on the road with sidewalk chalk. I catch my breath outside of a single-story house with white paneling and a green roof.

My old house.

I've been avoiding visiting it, because the memories are as painful as they are nostalgic. I've missed it here so much. Everything is the same, yet so completely different. I remember azaleas, white curtains, and a butterfly-shaped lawn ornament—but I see tulips, purple curtains, and a concrete birdbath. Instead of my mom walking around in paint-splattered overalls, an old woman hobbles from the side of the house with a watering can. She catches me staring. Not wanting to be a weirdo, I wave politely and keep running.

So many days of my life passed by on this street. Sometimes when I think about the time before the fall, it's like looking through a cracked mirror, an outsider viewing home movies of a girl I don't know with friends I don't recognize.

My phone buzzes in my pocket, and West's name appears on the screen. I'm glad, even after five years apart, we at least found our way back to each other.

When can I see you next?

Since I've been staying home and West has been busy with work, we haven't had a chance to continue what almost happened when I went to his apartment. My face tingles at the thought of him wanting to see me. Wanting to finish what we started.

I text him back and say we should meet soon, just as someone shouts over the sound of music in my ears. I tug out my headphones. A familiar chuckle makes my hair stand on end.

"Olivia! You in there?"

Dean, Shawn, and Faye sit under the awning of a panel house. An American flag hangs over the living room window, and a pile of garbage bags sits at the end of the broken-up driveway.

Right, the Bowmans live here. Another thing about living on this street was that I always saw Dean and Shawn attempting to skateboard or hogging the road with their street hockey. Now, they're draped over chipped wicker furniture on the porch with cans of beer in their hands. They ditch the beers and walk across the lawn. I don't want to see them, but we meet on the driveway anyway.

"Where's Keely at?" Dean lights a cigarette. He wears a faded leather jacket. "Or did she get lost again?"

He and Shawn laugh. I ball my fists. Maybe it's just some joke to these two, but they aren't the ones who hear Keely's quiet sobs through the walls at night.

"That isn't funny," I say. "What's wrong with you, Shawn? Keely's traumatized, she could have used your support."

Blanching, he stuffs his hands in the pockets of his basketball shorts.

Dean speaks up before Shawn has a chance to answer. "She might be your friend but, man, that chick is *annoying*. We walked through the forest hungover as fuck looking for her, total waste of time. What kind of idiot gets themselves lost trying to piss? You better be done with her for real, Shawn."

"Yeah, totally," Shawn says. "Fuck Keely."

"How can you say that about her?" I say. "You guys realize she's my best friend, right?"

"Come on, Olivia," Dean dials back. "We're just joking."

Faye avoids my gaze as I quickly check her arm. A new red mark has bubbled up from her skin, but she slips her hand over it when she catches me staring.

"You want a beer?" Dean offers.

"No, I'm fine," I say.

"What, too good for us now?"

I don't care what Dean thinks, but negative confrontation of any kind freaks me out. "Aren't your parents home? Won't they get mad about you drinking?"

"Where do you think I got the booze?" Dean laughs. "My dad's passed out like an old drunk in the basement."

"What about your mom?"

Dean's features harden. He glares at me for a long moment before he says, "Whatever, Olivia, don't drink with us. Hey Shawn, give me a bit, okay?" He grabs Faye's hips and grinds into her ass. She wriggles under him but keeps quiet as he leads her into the house and slams the door behind him. If I wasn't sure of it before, I am now: something isn't right with Dean and Faye's relationship.

"What was that about?" I ask Shawn.

"My Aunt Helga—I mean, Dean's mom—died."

"Oh God, I'm . . ."

Wow, I'm an idiot. I had no way of knowing what happened to her, but I feel awful for bringing it up. Dean isn't great, but no one deserves to lose a parent so young. I'd be devastated without Mom and Dad. I love them both on their own, but it's them *together* that completes me.

"I didn't know," I say.

"Yeah, it was a while ago now, but . . . anyway, can you maybe not tell Keely what I said about her? I didn't mean it."

"Then why are you being such a dick?"

"I like Keely, but her dad's a cop. Dean's right, dating her isn't exactly fun. She brings the heat." He laughs and rubs the back of his neck. "And she does stuff like gets too drunk and lost in the woods. It's fucked up. So she should just stay away from me."

"Whatever. Goodbye, Shawn."

Just as I'm about to keep jogging, Miles appears at the end of the driveway with a plastic bag with a bottle of Coke in it. We stare at each other, both caught off guard.

"Liv," he says.

"Miles . . . hey."

Even though Miles tried to help find Keely, I don't like the way I feel when he looks at me, like I'm plunging into an underwater abyss and he's the one dragging me deeper.

"Can we talk?" he asks.

"Maybe some other time. I have to go."

"But wait—"

I put my headphones in and jog home.

o o o

"Keely? You home yet?"

"In here, Liv."

Peeling off my hoodie, I enter the kitchen, where Keely sits at the table and flips through a magazine over a bowl of cereal. The warm lights accentuate the auburn undertones in her hair. Shawn and Dean don't deserve to have her in their stupid lives.

"You feeling okay?" I sit across from her.

Keely doesn't look up. "A little. Shopping with my mom sort of helped, but I still feel horrible about what happened."

"That's better, at least." I pause. "I ran into Shawn and them while I was out."

She slams the magazine shut. "Did they say anything about me? I feel so shitty everyone was looking for me, it's so embarrassing."

"Well . . ."

Dark brown eyes blink at me expectantly. If I tell Keely what they said, she'll probably cry. Even though she has a right to know, now isn't the time—she's still recovering from what happened. "Not really," I say. "Honestly, I don't know why you even care what they think. They're assholes."

"You don't really get it, Liv. You were gone for a long time. A lot changed. I didn't want to say anything, because I don't want you to like, feel bad. But being real, after you moved away, I had pretty much no one. Miles was always more your friend than mine, and I wasn't close with anyone else. Then when we started high school, everyone was drinking, and no one wanted to hang out with me because my dad's the chief of police. I had to try extra hard just to get invited to parties, to get in with Faye. I've been trying to prove I'm cool for years, and in the end I still get ditched. I'm such a loser."

"No, you're not. I'm sorry I moved away. And I had no idea you felt that way."

"You had to go. I get that." She shrugs halfheartedly. "But yeah, things have been pretty lonely over here. I guess finally being accepted into Dean's group made me feel cool. Even though I know they can be dicks."

"Trust me, you're way cooler than them. You want to do something? Watch a movie?"

"Nah, sorry. I'm pretty bummed out, kind of just want to be alone. That cool?"

"Yeah, of course."

Keely drags herself from the table and disappears down the hall. Without her in the room with me, the sounds of the house reverberate: the fridge rumbling, the air conditioner flowing. Crickets trill outside the windows. I wring my thumb around my elastic band. My life wasn't the only one that changed the night I fell. Keely's Instagram posts made me think she was happy without me, but I'd forgotten how easy it is to fabricate a life on social media.

Something has been bothering me since I left Dean's earlier. I open the Instagram app and hover over the search bar before typing Faye's username. She has three thousand followers. Almost all of her posts are selfies, and I'm a little jealous of her ability to look so effortlessly pretty with no makeup and no filters. I don't wear much, either, but I also don't take many pictures. Scrolling down Faye's page, there are a few photos of her and Dean, but they only started three months ago. They obviously haven't been dating for long.

Whether it's with clothing, the angle, or her hand, the burns on her arm are always hidden. If Faye thinks they're so normal, why is she hiding them on Instagram?

The sick feeling gnaws at me. I can't trust Miles with anything—he hangs out with Dean all the time. If something is going on, Miles must not see it. Or maybe he doesn't care.

West. Even though he and Faye aren't close, there's no way he'd be okay with this.

I have to tell him.

o o o

Everyone is in bed by eleven, so I sneak out the side door. The waxing moon bleeds through the overcast sky and leaves a cold feeling on my skin.

My lungs are tight from anxiety. As my feet clap the sidewalk, I try to ignore the feelings of paranoia that materialize behind me, making me tempted to glance over my shoulder into what I know is a dark and empty street. After only a minute of walking, I spot West's Corvette idling at the end of the street, and the engine grumbles through the otherwise dead night. I get into his car, and System of a Down plays through the speakers. He turns it down as I buckle my seatbelt.

"Hey," he says. "How's Keely?"

"She's good. You should come see her sometime."

"Yeah, I'm glad she's all right." West wipes his palms on his jeans. "You said you wanted to talk to me about something. What is it?"

Silence, the calm rumble of the car idling. The song switches to a quieter one, more melodic.

"It's about Faye."

"What about her?"

"Don't you think her relationship with Dean is a bit weird?"

"I don't like the guy, but Faye and I aren't close. Her boyfriend is her business."

"But . . ." I suck in a breath. "What if he was hurting her?"

"Hurting her how?"

"It's just, she has these burns all over her forearms, and she said they're called 'smileys.' She said she wanted him to do it to her, but . . . it's really weird. I'm worried about her."

West pauses, his face expressionless for a moment as he digests the information. Then, his nostril twitches. "You're sure?"

I nod. West starts driving.

"Wait, where are we going?"

"Dean's house. Being an asshole boyfriend to my sister is one thing. Hurting her is another."

"West, hold on. I just think you should talk to Faye in private, make sure she's okay."

"That's not how I do things. Sorry, Olive."

Before I can protest more, we're rocketing toward Dean's street. We get there in less than five minutes. West parks outside of the house with the American flag in the window, gets out, and storms up the driveway. I nearly trip over myself as I chase after him.

"What are you going to do, West?"

"Just going to have a word with my sister. And Dean, if I have to."

"Wait! I don't want violence, that isn't why I told you."

"I'm not going to get violent. But if she's in trouble, I'm getting her out of here."

West bangs his fist on the front door until Shawn whips it open. He frowns, then finds me over West's shoulder. "What are you guys doing here?"

"Faye, you in there?" West shouts.

After some muttering, Faye skitters to the front door in one of Dean's T-shirts, legs pale and twiggy beneath it. The smell of tobacco and weed sizzles from inside the house. In the living room, Dean is sprawled over the plaid couch with his feet on a coffee table cluttered with ashtrays and beer bottles, NASCAR on the TV. Faye's eyes bulge, and she shoves Shawn out of the way as she hisses, "Weston, what the *hell* are you doing here?"

"The fuck's going on?" Dean says, but doesn't leave the couch.

West leans closer to Faye. "We need to talk."

"Seriously? If this is about Dad, this is not the time. You can't just randomly show up at my boyfriend's house, Weston." She glares at me. "And what is *she* doing here?"

Before I can squeak out a reply, Miles takes Shawn's place beside Faye. His gaze turns sour on us.

"Let me see your arm," West says to Faye, and the rouge on her cheeks deepens.

"What? No! Get out of here!"

"You guys need to go," Miles says, but West ignores him. He grabs Faye's wrist and holds her for long enough to catch a glimpse of her scarred forearm. In a quick blur, he's inside Dean's house.

Faye shouts in protest. I stumble in after West, just as he and Dean get in each other's faces. Dean's a few inches shorter than West and way skinnier, but his posture doesn't waver as West backs him into the wall.

"What did you do to my sister?"

"What, you going to kick my ass in my own house?" Dean laughs. "I didn't do anything to Faye. If she wants to leave, she can go."

"Dean, no," Faye sputters. "I didn't know he was coming, I swear. I don't want to go anywhere."

Part of me knew something like this could happen, but I guess I didn't think too far ahead, blinded by what I thought was the right thing to do. West and Dean keep spitting in each other's faces while Faye starts crying, and Shawn watches. When Miles lightly pushes my shoulder, I snap out of it.

"What is this, Olivia? Why did you bring him here?"

"I just—I told him about Faye, and—"

"What *about* Faye?"

When I look back over at West and Dean, West has backed off and is now observing Faye's arm. His tense shoulders relax and his features soften. "Faye, let me get you out of here. Come on, I'll drive you home."

"No!" Tears fall down her cheeks. "You're embarrassing me! Please, just get out of here. I'm fine, West. Nothing is happening."

Dean saunters away from them and swipes a beer off the table. "The fuck is this, Olivia? What'd you tell this psycho?"

"You burned her, Dean."

"She mostly did those to herself, idiot—"

"It's none of your business," Miles cuts in. There's something in his eyes I've never seen directed at me, not from him. Anger embers through the blue-green like a forest fire. He leans close to me, so close that the sickening smell of his cologne fills my nostrils. "Don't you get it, Liv? You make *everything* worse. If we wanted West in our lives, we would talk to him. But we don't. Why? Because he's a controlling dick, and *I'm* handling things. Now he's stressing my sister out when she has her performance in a couple of days. What's the point of bringing all this up now? Oh, right, you love the drama, don't you, Olivia?"

"No! I didn't want this, I—"

West and Faye come over. West says, "Come on, Olive, let's go."

"I only wanted to help," I say, crying.

But everyone is looking at me like they blame me. West takes my hand and drags me toward the front door.

"Touch my sister and you're dead," West says to Dean before we both leave.

o o o

A tense silence surrounds West and me as we drive toward the beach. Though my tears have stopped, everything replays over and over again, and I wish I had never opened my stupid mouth. West is too quiet. I wonder if he blames me for saying something, or if he's just worried about his sister. I would understand either way.

There's a dirt parking lot near the beach for visitors, positioned at the bottom of the cliff and the lighthouse. West parks there. Not far beside us, waves foam against the shore. On the other side, the cliff extends over the ocean, and the lighthouse cuts through the night.

"You feel safe here?" West asks. "I've got to pop up to the lighthouse and check on something and I might as well do it while I'm out."

"It's fine," I mumble. "I can handle being near the beach now. You found me here at the beginning of summer, remember?"

"Yeah. I guess a lot has happened since then."

More silence, thick and palpable. West's features are darkened by the night, but moonlight leaks through the car window like molten silver.

"I shouldn't have overreacted," West says and runs his hands over the steering wheel. "Fuck, I'm too hotheaded."

"It was my fault for even bringing it up," I say. "I should have talked to Faye myself first."

"No, she's my sister. I'm glad you told me. Just wish I'd handled it better. The thought of that greaseball hurting her made me so furious, I couldn't see anything but red." He shakes his head. "Now she hates me even more than she already did."

"I don't understand why your family is so against you." My voice comes out quiet. "You're good, West. You don't deserve it."

"Thanks, but it doesn't matter what I deserve. They don't have to like me just because we're blood."

His words have a weight to them. It's strange, the things we notice as kids, but don't fully understand at all, like the time Beatrice grabbed West and dragged him away. I knew West's parents were mean to him, but I never understood what that really meant. That he was being neglected. Maybe even abused.

THE SUMMER I DROWNED ° 191

"I remember the way your dad treated you when we were kids," I say. "He was mean. Beatrice too."

"Family's complicated. I want to be there for my kid so she never has to feel like she can't trust me. But I can't go around acting the way I did with Dean just now. That kind of shit is exactly why Sophie has sole custody of Amelia. I gave it up willingly when we were younger because it was best for Amelia, but still."

"Is Sophie your ex?"

"Yeah. We were young and stupid when we got together, not right for each other at all. But we're on a better path now. We both want what's right for Amelia."

"I know." My throat tightens. "That's what I like about you, West. You try to do the right thing." I go to touch his hand, but he pulls away. "What's wrong?"

Hesitance, and a sad smile touches his lips. "I like the way you look at me, Olive. Like I've never done anything wrong in my life."

With the radio off, we can hear the ocean crashing outside the car, like we're under water. And it's warm, too warm.

"But you're going to leave," West says.

I can't explain why his words hurt, but they sting so bad, like being zapped by a jellyfish.

"I don't want to think about leaving," I say. "I'm here now with you."

"My life used to always be about living in the now. But with Amelia in the picture, I have to think about the future."

"Of course you do, but what are you saying? Do you not want to hang out with me anymore?" I haven't even kissed him yet—if he bails now, it will kill me.

"That's not what I mean. You're all I think about."

"Then what's this all about?"

"I don't know. Sorry, I'm in a messed-up place right now. I need air."

West gets out of the car, and I follow after. Fog rolls over the coastline. The ocean air is cool on my skin; nights in Maine are never too hot. I always liked that about this place.

"I've got to check on the lighthouse," West says. "Stay here, okay?"

West wanders off into the dark. Leaning against the still-warm hood of the car, I worry he's having second thoughts. We still have an entire month before I leave, but if it already hurts this much, maybe West would rather avoid being with me at all.

He needs to think about the future. Maybe his future can't involve a girl who can't stay.

To distract myself from my thoughts, I walk, watching my feet squish against the grass. The sound of the water grows louder. I freeze when I look up, because the lighthouse is right in front of me. Its bright red paint shines under the moonlight, and its height towers endlessly into the hazy sky. Beyond it, on the edge of the cliff, is a short wooden fence connected by ropes that sway in the wind. The hinges creak and scrape against my ears.

This is where it happened. Where everything changed.

It's scary to think people have really died down there. Like Samwell Ellis, the boy who cracked his skull when I was in kindergarten. He didn't have the chance to recover, to move away from Caldwell and get better. He just hit his head and never woke up. This rope isn't enough—kids can easily slip under it. So can adults. So can I.

The wind picks up, coils around my wrists, carries me to the edge of the cliff.

If getting over my fears means facing them head-on, I should look down. So I do. Then I'm over the rope. It's exactly as it was five years ago—the rocks, jagged like teeth, and the water, sloshing in a violent rage. This is where the nightmares take place. Where I've spent so many of my days, only in memory.

A gust pushes against my back. The waves overlap and swallow one another. I picture myself falling into it. The current jerking me back and forth. The bubbles fizzing around me. The taste of the ocean.

Someone is calling my name, but his voice is distant, like he's yelling through glass. There aren't many times when this thought has slithered out from dark crevices of my mind—but sometimes, I do wonder if I would have been better off if I'd died that day. My parents never would have had to pay for therapy. I never would have had to dream of death over and over again.

Someone yanks on my wrist and hurls me backward. I'm jerked out of my trance just in time to see that my right foot has extended over the edge of the cliff. I scream as West pulls me away and locks me in his arms so I can't move. He drags me away from the cliff, and once we're halfway down the hill, he collapses on the ground and hugs me. I go limp against him. I can't feel anything—not my muscles, not my heartbeat. My memories since I got out of the car are as blurry as the clouds that creep over the moon.

"What the fuck, Olivia?" West's fingers thread through my hair, and his pulse thuds against my head as he holds me to his chest. "I thought you were going to walk right off! Jesus Christ, what happened?"

"I—I don't know, I—"

"Why'd you go over there, huh? Fuck, I thought I was going to lose you."

"I . . . don't remember. I just wanted to look."

"You scared the shit out of me. If I hadn't run, you would've . . ."

He holds me tighter. I shut my eyes and slip into a comfortable darkness, balling the soft cotton fabric of his shirt in my fist. I can't wrap my head around what just happened, but I can focus on him. His erratic breathing. His smell of earth and sea. The way he presses his lips to the top of my head, but doesn't kiss me, and how it makes me feel achingly safe and numb all at once.

"You're okay," West says, over and over, until it sounds like he's trying to convince himself.

o o o

After West carried me away from the cliff, I lost my voice. By the time he gets me in the car, I'm still paralyzed, unsure if what just happened was real, a flashback, or a combination of the two. Maybe this is the place where nightmares and consciousness meet.

It doesn't take long for West to pull the Corvette up to Keely's street. When he parks, I shrink away from his concerned gaze. I want to be at home in my bed—not the Myerses' guest room bed, my own bed. With my blankets and pillows and stuffed animals and Aqua, who I really should have brought. With my mom, who always strokes my hair when I have panic attacks because she knows it calms me.

West drapes his hand over the steering wheel. "You going to tell me what that was back there?"

The silence is heavy. I don't want to push him away, but I can't explain what I don't understand myself. When I picture myself standing at the edge of the cliff, the car fills up with water. I lean against the headrest.

"Olive." West's voice keeps me grounded. "What's going on with you?"

"It's nothing," I lie. "I haven't been sleeping well, okay?"

"I could've sworn you were going to walk right off that cliff."

"I didn't know I was doing that."

West's jaw is tight, and his Adam's apple bobs as he looks away. I know he doesn't mean for the expression on his face to hurt me, but it does.

"You think I'm crazy," I say, and tears sting my eyes.

"Don't say shit like that about yourself. No, I don't think you're crazy. I'm just worried." West falls quiet. Outside, the world is still.

"Please don't look at me like that," I whisper.

"Like what?"

"Like I'm some sort of timid animal who needs to be handled with care. I get treated like that at home, sometimes by my parents, sometimes by teachers because my school knows about the problems I have. I'm trying to get better, so please don't treat me like I'm different."

"Okay."

"Thank you."

When more silence threatens us, West grunts and unbuckles his seatbelt so he can face me easier. "All right, look. Here's what I think: you need a break from this goddamn town. Why don't you come to Camden with me tomorrow? I want you to meet Amelia."

"Really?" I can't help but smile. Finally, West cracks one too.

"Yeah, really," he says. "What do you say?"

"I'd like that." I put my hand on the door handle. "But I should go. Goodnight, West."

"Night."

Leaving him is always the worst part. But as I'm halfway across the lawn, West's car door opens.

"Olive, wait."

He rounds the hood in one quick motion. Before I can even process it, I'm trapped in his arms. Even after everything that just happened, my knees go weak. He supports my weight.

"I thought I was going to lose you," he says against my forehead. "Fuck, I haven't been that scared in a while. Not since I heard about the last time you fell."

We pull away. His eyes are dark blue and pained under the midnight sky, splashed with more stars than I could ever dream of counting. I stare at his mouth, drunk on his scent and the heat of his body near mine. Everything around us fades. With his hands on each side of my face, West kisses my forehead, then his lips press against mine: soft, warm, and everything I've ever dreamed of. He inhales a sharp, ragged breath. I'm surprised at how fast my confidence rises, how easy it is to throw my arms around his neck and kiss him back. The feeling is hot and cold; his tongue grazes mine, but his stubble is rough against my skin.

"I was not expecting that," I whisper. I've never been so warm.

"Sorry," he says. "I was tired of waiting."

"Don't apologize. Please."

We kiss again. Everything urges me to stay with him—we could even go back to his place and sleep in his bed, and we wouldn't have to say goodbye so soon. But I can't. West must know it, too, because he bumps his forehead to mine and says, "I guess I should let you go."

"Okay. But tomorrow?"

"Tomorrow."

He holds my hand and grazes his finger along my palm as he pulls away. My heart is still pounding as he gets into his car. He waves to me once before he drives off, and the Corvette disappears into the darkness of the street.

○ ○ ○

Later that night, after tossing and turning in bed for hours, something scuffles outside my window. A hack and a cough scrape the silence of the night. I stare blankly at the ceiling and listen as the sound is strangled, like something is scarfing up its last breath. I'm too petrified to move, but convince myself I'm having another nightmare until I drift away again.

15

One of the things I miss most about living in Caldwell Beach is the mornings—waking up every day to dewy, cantaloupe-orange skies, caws of blue jays, and coos of mourning doves. When I wake up in the guest room, my recollection of last night returns in waves.

The good comes first. When I touch my lips, I can still feel West kissing me, even though it was dark outside the last time we were together.

But the bad comes back too. After what happened on the cliff, I need to call Dr. Levy. But she'll say it was an "episode," and then she'll tell my parents. They'll all want me to come home. I can't do that, not yet. Especially after I finally kissed West.

Pulling myself out of bed, I take my antidepressants and put on the blue dress so West can see me in it later. Like most mornings

I wake here, Sun and Roger are in the kitchen making coffee, and Keely is digging around in the cupboards for cereal. We all say our good mornings, and Roger asks me to grab the mail, so I step outside. The sun is hot on my sunscreened skin, but there's still a fresh, cold feeling in the air when it's this early. But as I walk across the front lawn to the mailbox, an off smell reaches my nose.

With a frown, I spin on my heels and scan the lawn. It's the exact same stench as the night Miles, Keely, and I found the dead squirrel: flesh mixed with the smell of grass and Caldwell's constant ocean air. Morbidly intrigued, I gravitate toward it.

Around the side of the house, right below my window, is an animal carcass.

The scream is instant. I fall back on the heels of my hands and skitter away, just as the front door flies open and Roger sprints outside. He's at my side in seconds, Keely behind him.

"Oh my God, Dad!" Keely says.

Roger hoists me to my feet, and I fall onto him. "You okay, Olivia? Here, stay back."

But I can't look away. Torn pink flesh clings to its bones with matted and bloodied gray fur and sharp little teeth. It's an opossum. Or, it was.

Keely tries to hold me back, but I stagger closer to the animal. Flies buzz around it.

"You girls get inside," Roger says, his voice serious. "I'll take care of this."

"What the hell happened?" Keely asks. "Why is this on our lawn, Dad?"

"The animal killer," I say, stunned. "It was him. It had to be him."

I picture a man—a faceless man—creep up to the house, peek through my blinds, and watch me sleep. He puts the carcass on the ground and smirks.

But *why?* Why me?

"There's no sign of foul play." Roger kneels next to the carcass and points at it. "If you look along the neckline, you can see teeth marks. Looks like he got in a fight with some other critter and wandered down here to die."

The hairs raise on my arms. I try to rub them out, but the feeling that I'm being watched doesn't fade.

"Why would it be at my window?" I ask. "There's been other stuff, too, like that night I thought I saw something in the shower. What if—I don't know, what if they're trying to send me a message?"

As soon as the words escape my lips, I realize how they sound.

Roger says, "I'm the police chief. If it was a message, it was more likely for me. Let's just go inside and check the cameras."

A few minutes later, we're huddled around the computer desk in the living room. Sun joins us with a coffee mug. When the screen loads to last night, a sudden realization turns me to stone: they're going to see I snuck out. But I'm right about the animal killer, I know I am. Maybe if I can prove it, the other things won't matter as much.

On the screen, the different camera angles show the Myerses' house late at night. Roger fast-forwards through the footage. Tugging on my elastic, I brace myself for the timestamp to get past 11:00 p.m. Two minutes after, we see me sneak out the side door.

"What the—" Roger pauses, and his angered eyes fall on me. "Olivia, you'd better have a damn good explanation for this."

"Please, I'll explain after you see what happened with the animal."

Roger exhales through his nose but continues the footage. Like last time, nothing out of the ordinary shows up on the screen. Trees sway with the wind, and the odd squirrel or rabbit hops over the lawn. Then we see me return with my arms crossed, a smile on my face because I'd just kissed West.

On the screen that shows the guest room window, the light goes on inside—me, getting ready for bed—and then it turns off. Shortly after, a shadow moves across the screen.

"Hold on." Roger zooms in. At the top corner, an opossum limps onto the property.

Alone.

I wait for a man to follow it. To appear and strategically place it to mess with me, but no one ever comes. There's no animal killer. No man. Just a poor, maimed animal, and it falls to its death right outside of my window.

"See?" Roger says. "Just the opossum. No one is sending you messages, Olivia."

"But . . ."

Roger lets out a long, heavy sigh. I've heard it before—he always exhales like this when he's about to say something that will disappoint Keely. But he's locked on me.

"Olivia, I'm sorry, but we're calling your parents and having them pick you up as soon as possible. Either tomorrow or the day after, most likely."

"W-what?"

"Mom, Dad, no!" Keely exclaims.

"Lemon, we've been thinking about it since you went missing." Roger focuses back on me. "We'll always be grateful you helped bring Keely home, Olivia, but the truth is, being responsible for you and our own daughter is becoming a little too much. Especially if you're going to break the rules and sneak out at night."

"It was stupid—it won't happen again, I promise. Please don't make me go back to New York. I'm sorry I snuck out, but I had a good reason—"

"What reason could you have to break the rules, Olivia?" Roger says. "What's more important than us being able to trust you?"

Sun places a gentle hand on my arm. "I'm sorry, Olivia. It's best for everyone if you're with your family."

The truth is, I understand why they don't want me around anymore, but I try to hold in my tears.

"This isn't fair, Dad," Keely whines. "She snuck out one time, big deal!"

"It isn't just about that, Lemon," Roger says.

Sun gently squeezes my arm. "We're sorry, Olivia. This decision is final."

I see the looks on their faces. It's about more than me sneaking out; this is about my mental state.

"It's okay. Really, I get it." I back away so they won't see me cry, but my voice comes out strained. "Can I please go spend the day with West?"

Roger and Sun share an uneasy look, before Roger says, "All right, go ahead. But be back early, please. Before dark."

Keely keeps nagging her parents as I slam the door behind me and collapse on the front porch. Maybe it's stupid to be so upset—I'm not their kid, they don't owe me anything. Their reasons are logical: I broke the rules, and I understand they have a lot on their plate, and they probably think I'm losing my mind. But it still hurts to be thrown out, and I'm not ready to leave Caldwell Beach. I've been anchored to this place since the day I left. This town isn't done with me yet.

When West's Corvette pulls outside, I wipe my eyes with my bare wrists, but it only makes them wet and slippery. He parks and jogs to the porch.

"Whoa, what's going on?"

This is exactly what he worried about, but I have to tell him. "I'm leaving early, West. Tomorrow or the day after, probably. Keely's parents know I snuck out last night."

"Oh . . . shit."

The tears keep coming. West eases himself onto the porch beside me and leans so his arm brushes the small of my back.

"No changing their minds?" he asks.

"I don't think so. Even if I could, I'd feel horrible trying. They're clearly not comfortable with me being here."

"Brutal. I'd say you could stay with me, but I doubt your parents would go for it."

"Really?"

"Yeah."

"You're right." I laugh. "My parents would never go for that. But it's a nice idea."

West stands and offers me his hand. "Don't worry, at least we've still got another day together. Come on, let's make it count."

o o o

Acres of trees stretch beyond the long, narrow road, topped by a cerulean sky. West talks about Oscar, Sandy, his job at the body shop. A little bit about his dad. The calm rumble of the car lulls me into a state of comfort. I lean back on the headrest, and my eyes flutter shut with the warmth of the sun on my face. I listen to his words, his gritty voice. No nightmares, no bad thoughts.

Mom texted me and said she and Dad will be here tomorrow to take me home. I didn't reply—if West and I only have so much time left together, I'm not wasting it. Amelia is adorable in the picture, and I bet she's even cuter in person.

Camden, like Caldwell, is heavily populated with trees, but unlike my hometown, there's a constant stream of cars driving in and out. We arrive at a farmers' market where the parking lot is packed full. A toddler is in the arms of a girl standing next to a tall guy wearing aviators. That must be Amelia with Sophie and her boyfriend. When West and I get out of the car, Sophie approaches us. She has brown hair and matching dark eyes. Amelia looks more like West. Like in the picture, her olive skin glows so much it spar-kles. She wears a lime-green dress and her hair is in curls. Her gaze wanders all over the place, like she can't decide if I'm more interest-ing than West, or if the tree behind us wins.

Sophie shakes my hand with a tight but not unfriendly smile. She and West exchange awkward eye contact before she heaves Amelia into his arms. He takes her with ease, like her tiny frame was made to fit his.

"Remember that she needs to eat at one," Sophie says, "and not too much ice cream, or she'll barf all over you and poop all over me later. There are snacks in the bag."

"Thanks, Soph. I know."

"See you at four." Sophie kisses Amelia's head before she goes back over to the other guy, who touches her back before they walk away and get in their car. They drive off, and West uses Amelia's tiny arm to wave goodbye.

"Hey, kiddo," West says.

"Hi, Daddy," she mumbles.

"She can talk!" I say.

"Yeah, she's three, so she talks a lot. But she's shy around new people. This is Olive, Amelia. She's one of my best friends from when I was as big as you. Can you say Olivia?"

Amelia smiles at me, then says something that sounds more like *Wivia* than Olivia. It's adorable.

"Come on," West says, "let's get ice cream."

Since West's Corvette has only two seats, neither of which seem toddler appropriate, we walk downtown, West carrying Amelia. It's way livelier than Caldwell, with twice as many gift shops and convenience stores. The ice cream parlor has a fluorescent pink sign, and the smell of baked waffle cones makes my mouth water. West gets rocky road, I get cookies and cream, and Amelia gets a small cup of vanilla.

"I get to do this with her once a month," West says, pushing through the door and holding it for me. "Sometimes twice."

I take a bite of my ice cream before the sun can melt it too much. "How come not more?"

"It's what Sophie wants. We're on good terms now, but it wasn't always like this. When Amelia was first born, I wasn't the greatest dad. Not right away. It was a lot to take in, and I was sixteen and stupid. Sophie was a lot more mature than me. But now that I'm cleaned up a bit, she's starting to let me see her more. When Amelia's a little bigger, and I have my own place, she'll probably be spending every weekend with me."

"That would be good, right?"

"Yeah." He shifts Amelia up. "Anyway, I think it's sandbox time, isn't it, kid?"

She lets out a musical giggle. We go to a park with a wooden jungle gym surrounded by grass. There's a rustic charm to it, like it's been loved by generations. West plops Amelia in the sandbox and hands her some tools from the bag Sophie gave him. West and I sit on the edge of the square, and he stretches out his long, denim-clad legs. A warm breeze touches my skin; the air tastes different here. More like sugar, less like death. I lean on West's shoulder, and he wraps his arm around me.

"It sucks that you're leaving tomorrow," he says. "When you left Caldwell last time, I wanted to say bye to you. Even got you a present."

"What was it?"

"These little blue stones. Sea glass."

Sea glass. The words are electric with familiarity.

"The moment I saw them," West says, "I thought the color was just like your eyes. Fu"—he stops himself from swearing—"sappy, I know. I was a sappier kid than I wanted anyone to know about."

West keeps talking, but his voice becomes muted. His words make me dizzy. I'm suddenly back in Cindy Huang's upstairs hallway with Miles, accepting the three pretty stones he gave me. The sea glass that looked just like my eyes. After Miles ratted on West and me to his parents, I tucked them in the small pocket of my suitcase—banished them, because they don't bring me comfort anymore.

"What happened to the sea glass?" I ask.

West shrugs. "Lost them, then I got cold feet and didn't come to say bye to you because I didn't have a good present. I felt like an idiot. Regretted it ever since."

I don't know how it's possible for West and Miles to have had the exact same thought about me and gotten the same gift.

Or maybe they didn't.

"What's wrong?" West asks.

Confusion clutters my mind, makes me dizzy. "It's just . . . Miles, he—"

"He what?"

I'm unable to say it, because Miles is still West's brother.

"Nothing," I say. "It's just really sweet, that's all."

West laughs. "Would've been sweeter if I'd actually given them to you."

He wraps his arm around me, so I push this whole thing away and focus on spending time with Amelia. It's not like it's a big deal, anyway. Just some stupid rocks.

16

After we say goodbye to Amelia, it takes an hour to get back to Caldwell Beach. We still have time to kill before I have to be at Keely's, so we head to West's place.

"Looks like Sandy's out," West says and locks the door behind us. Oscar trots over from a dog bed in the living room and nudges West's leg until he pets him, then does the same to me.

It's strange to walk into the living room and not see Sandy with her friends. The apartment is dead quiet. Oscar goes back to his bed and curls into a ball while West and I make eye contact that doesn't break.

The air becomes heavy with the unspoken possibility of what we could do here. We're completely alone. Not even Oscar will try to stop us.

I'm as overwhelmed as I am excited. West must sense it, because he wipes his palms on his jeans and says, "Do you want anything? Water?"

"Sure."

He leads me into the kitchen. There's barely any room between the stove and the off-white counter, and the microwave looks like it was made in the '70s. There's some splatter on the stove—pasta sauce, probably—and photos of Sandy and her friends are stuck to the fridge with big magnets. West is in some of them too.

Right now, Miles is probably in his huge estate with his personal chefs and more space than anyone could know what to do with. It's hard to believe West grew up in that same house, but he was never spoiled like his siblings. Besides, I like it better here. It feels more like a home.

West hands me some tap water in a black Batman mug. My mouth is dry, so I chug it back. When I set the mug down, he's staring at me.

"Uh . . ." He hooks his hand to the back of his neck. Face red, he steps closer to me. "Look, if you're really leaving soon, there's something I want you to know."

My lower back touches the counter as he backs me into it. "What is it?"

West stares at me for a long moment before he grunts in exasperation. I gasp as he picks me up like I'm made of nothing and scoots me onto the counter so we're at eye level. He rests his hands on my knees, and his heat radiates through me. I really should be focused, but it's hard when his body is so close to mine.

"I lied before," he says. "About why I didn't follow you on Instagram."

That gets my attention. "What do you mean?"

"Honestly? I was mad you left." He shakes his head, black hair in pieces over his forehead. "Not mad at you, just . . . mad. At myself, mostly. I know I stopped hanging around you and Miles before you fell, but I always wanted to talk to you again. I just didn't know how. Then when I found out you were leaving, I didn't even have the balls to ask if you were okay, or say goodbye, or give you a stupid present. So when you followed me, I didn't accept because seeing you online just reminded me of how much I regretted fucking things up with you. I was a stupid kid. But I cared about you far more than I let on."

All that time I'd thought he just didn't like me anymore, but that reality has been shattered in the best way possible. I scan his face, captivated by how beautiful he grew up to be.

"I cared about you too, West. I thought you were the coolest person in the world. I still do. More than ever. I tried to move on in New York. I tried to make friends, but it was so hard for me to fit in. And honestly, I think I wasn't able to open myself up to anyone there because so much of me still lived here. So much of me still thought of you."

"I never should've shut you out of my life." West touches my cheek. "One of the biggest mistakes I ever made. I'm sorry if I hurt you."

"You didn't. Okay, you did—but it doesn't matter now."

"Just—let me make it up to you." He presses himself between my legs.

"West, I—"

Before I can speak, his warm lips are on mine. I drink him in, his smell that swallows me like a stone in the sea. My breath catches as his fingers brush beneath my dress, and *oh God*, I'm getting dizzy.

"Is this okay?" he asks.

I nod a bunch of times because it is more than okay. West doesn't know I'm a virgin—I have to tell him somehow, but I don't want to ruin the moment. He picks me up and hitches my legs to his hips. He kisses me and carries me down the hall. Then we're in his room, and the door shuts behind us, and I'm in his bed. He slowly climbs on top of me, eyes locked on mine the whole time. My tense muscles relax, and everything in me becomes light and free as my head meets his pillow. He positions himself between my legs and lowers his weight onto me.

"I don't want you to go," he whispers against my lips. "This was never just for the summer for me."

I'm tingling from the hollow of my thighs all the way to my cheeks, and it's enough to make me float away. "I don't want to go either. You were my first crush." I stare at his mouth. "And my first kiss."

He kisses me and says, "I can be your first everything, if you want me to be."

Oh man . . . I'm done. I don't want to think about how I'll feel when I'm gone, or what will happen between us. I just want to be close to him. "I do want that."

He smiles wide, then his lips are on mine again. He easily slides off my dress, but I don't feel exposed. The way he stares at me makes me feel like I'm the only thing in the world. Nothing has ever made me feel so special. So *seen*.

"You sure about this?" he asks, his breaths labored as he reaches around the side of his bed. I hear cardboard opening, plastic crumpling, and everything gets real. I nod.

When our bodies connect, I don't think about who I am outside of this room. Who I was before, or who I'll be tomorrow. The pain is searing at first, but then the feeling becomes hot water rushing through me, a tide that swells over my head—but this time, it doesn't drown me.

o o o

When West pulls into the driveway of Keely's house, the sunset casts golden hues over the black roof. I'm not about to forget the feeling of being with him, and I can tell by the way he looks at me that he's thinking the same thing.

"I'm going to miss you," I say. "I hope that isn't weird."

He laughs. "Of course it isn't weird. I'm going to miss you too. You blew my mind."

"Your mind, huh?"

West's face goes red, and we both laugh. "Think you can try to get your parents to let you stay for a few more days? Get a motel or something?"

"I doubt they'd go for that, but maybe."

"New York's not that far, but I might only be able to visit you once in a while."

"You would visit me?"

The mood shifts so fast it shocks me. West straightens his back in the seat. I blink at him until it hits me: he's being serious. Long distance didn't even cross my mind—in fact, I didn't think much of anything that would happen later.

"I mean . . ." He clears his throat. "Yeah. If you wanted to like, stay together."

"You would really do that?"

"Would you?"

I nod, and he cracks a smile.

"Thank God. I was about to feel like a huge idiot." He pauses. "It just sucks. I never got to take you on a real date."

"There's always next time?"

"Definitely next time. I promise."

"I'll hold you to that. But I better go in. I'll text you. Maybe we can meet up again tomorrow and you can say hi to my parents?" I laugh awkwardly. "They're going to be a little surprised I'm dating you, just as a warning."

"Yeah? That's okay. I'd like to see them."

We quickly kiss, and it feels like only the beginning. I get out of the car and watch West drive off, waving the whole time. This is how things are supposed to feel. Happy and fun and elevated and nostalgic. This is what I wanted from this summer, even if I didn't fully realize it until now.

I go to the front door, but as soon as my hand touches the handle, voices sound from the other side. I carefully open the door, and everything—everyone—goes quiet.

Sprawled over the living room couches are Keely, Shawn, Dean, Faye—and Miles.

"There she is," Dean says.

Keely hops to her feet. "Liv! Hey . . ."

Having them all here, especially after what happened last night, feels like an attack. "What are you guys doing here?" Suspicion leaks from my tone.

"They sort of just showed up," Keely says.

"I didn't realize you guys were talking again." My eyes are on Shawn now, because I'm thinking about what he said yesterday, which was definitely "Fuck Keely."

"I texted her last night to apologize," Shawn says. "Then Keely said you were leaving in a day or two, so we stopped by."

"But it sounds like you don't want us here," Faye says, but as always, there's a hint of aggression in her voice. "We haven't seen you in five years and now you're about to leave again. We're saying goodbye, Liv."

"It's fine, I guess. But I thought you'd be mad about last night."

Dean shrugs, his arm slung over Faye's shoulder. "Water under the bridge."

Roger comes into the room and puts his hands on his hips. It's been a while since I've seen him without his uniform; he wears a plaid shirt tucked into a pair of dad jeans. "Oh, Olivia, you're home," he says. "Lemon asked if your friends can stay for a bit to say goodbye."

My friends? I'm not even sure they're Keely's friends, especially after what she said about them hating on her for being a cop's daughter.

"Thank you, Roger," I peep.

"I'll be in the basement with your mother, Keely. But if I catch a drop of alcohol in this house, don't think I won't arrest any of you."

Once Roger is gone, everyone's focus is on me. I tug on my elastic and force a small smile. Maybe giving them a chance isn't such a bad idea. If tonight really is my last night in Caldwell, I may never see these people again. But Miles still intimidates me. Our memories together are sour now, and I wasn't sure if I wanted to see him before I left. Now that choice has been ripped away.

Plus, I just lost my virginity to his brother. This is so weird.

Sitting on the armchair, I bump my knees together. Miles pulls up a stool and leans on it while the others squeeze on the couch.

"So," Faye says, "heard you were out with West today."

Everyone looks at me.

"Yeah, we went for a drive," I say.

"Are you guys are like, dating?" Dean asks.

I nod. Shawn laughs and smacks Miles in the arm. "Tough loss, buddy."

Miles's nostrils flare. "I'm going to the bathroom." He storms out. Shawn and Dean laugh. Faye texts while Keely exchanges an apologetic look with me, so I take out my phone and message her.

> Why did you let them in? It's so awkward with Miles :(

I'm sorry! They honestly just showed up, and he said he'd be cool!

> Do you really forgive Shawn for being so shitty with you?

Idk. I'm def not dating him, but I felt weird turning them away...

> Just don't let him hurt you again.

When Miles returns, I tuck my phone under my leg so he won't think I'm texting West about him. Keely turns on the TV, and some jazzy pop song floods the room.

Everyone starts talking and laughing, but I'm insulated from it all, trapped inside a fish tank. The grandfather clock ticks and I count the songs that play. After seven, Shawn, Miles, Keely, and Faye are caught up in a conversation about Carter Bonnet, who apparently spends a lot of time with Cindy Huang. It's rumored they both have syphilis, but unclear who gave who what, and I can't help but think of the conversation as dumb and untrue.

Someone touches my shoulder, and I jump. Miles stands over me with a stiff smile. I'd been so zoned out I didn't even notice him.

"Oh . . . Miles. You scared me."

"Can we talk? Come into the kitchen with me, away from the others."

It's confining, but everyone else's voices remind me I'm safe, so I follow him to the kitchen. Miles leans against the wooden countertop and tucks his hands in the pockets of his shorts. The silence is uncomfortable, so I fill a cup of water and sip from it. He's still being quiet and it makes my hair stand on end.

"What did you want to talk about, Miles?" I take another sip of the lukewarm water.

Miles hooks his hand to the back of his neck, where the skin is lobster red. "You're leaving tomorrow. It doesn't feel right to see you off on bad terms."

"Miles, why did you bring your parents to the cabin that day?"

"I wanted to protect you, Liv. From West."

"Why would I need to be protected from West?"

"You don't know him as well as you think you do."

I set down my cup. "I do know him. He's a good guy, and he's a good dad to his kid. I like the way he treats me, and I like the way he makes me feel. Why would you want to ruin that?"

"That's what all the girls say."

214 · TAYLOR HALE

"What does that mean?"

"It means he has a track record, Liv."

"Maybe I'm not just some girl to him. Maybe to him, I'm actually someone special. Or did you not even consider that?"

Miles sighs. "Whatever, you're not going to believe me. Just forget it. Can we stop fighting now?"

We fall quiet. Keely's laughter sounds over the music. Downstairs, Roger and Sun's TV program emits muffled voices.

Maybe it is pointless to hold onto these negative feelings about Miles. He did try to help find Keely when she disappeared, and he had a right to be mad at me last night for telling West about a situation with Faye I knew nothing about. Dr. Levy would probably say I don't have to *like* Miles, but it'd be better for me to leave on good terms with him. That would be the healthy thing to do.

"Okay," I say, and Miles's hopeful eyes meet mine.

"Yeah?"

"You're right. Leaving on bad terms doesn't feel good. What we were when we were kids meant something."

Before I have a moment to react, Miles wraps his arms around me. He's strangely cold, but I hug him back, only because I'm leaving tomorrow.

"You were my best friend, Liv," he says. "I was so excited to reconnect with you this summer."

"I'm sorry it didn't go great. We're just different people now."

Miles frees me from his arms. His blond hair looks fluffy under the yellow kitchen lights. "Do you think you accomplished what you came here to do? The whole scared-of-the-water thing, I mean."

"No . . . I failed hard."

"Then you know what I think?" A sudden smile plasters his face. "I think you should stay."

"What?"

"Stay in Caldwell. Just for a few more days."

"I can't. My parents are getting me."

"Then convince them to stay. There's a motel, cottage rentals. Your parents obviously know the area."

I laugh, not because it's funny, but because West had suggested something similar. The sea glass creeps back into my mind.

"Liv?"

I snap out of it. "My parents probably won't go for that."

"You came here to conquer your fears, right?"

Miles places a firm hand on my shoulder, and that bad taste returns to my mouth. But his eyes are kind, and his smile is gentle, and there are good memories. Miles and I playing in the water and meeting up every day after school. Being partners on a class project in the third grade. Picking leaves out of his curly hair.

"Stay a little longer," he says. "Conquer your fears. You can do it, Liv."

Miles leaves the room, and I lean against the kitchen counter.

Maybe he has a point. Maybe it would be possible to try again, but with my parents' support this time. Maybe they should have been here all along, and then I wouldn't have felt so unsafe and scared here.

In fact, I think Miles is right: I'm not ready to leave yet. I want to stay.

17

The next day, I wait on the front porch for my parents with Keely, my suitcase packed beside me. Mom texts that they're five minutes away.

"I can't believe you're going." Keely's eyes fall to the freshly mowed grass. "This summer was such a disaster."

"It wasn't all bad." I nudge her. "We had some fun. Like watching movies and stuff. And I'm glad you made me buy that dress."

Keely laughs, but there's a sadness in it. "Yeah, I guess. But this is all my fault for drinking so much. I should've just hung out with you instead of trying to impress those stupid guys. I'm sorry, Liv."

"It's okay. It's more my fault for sneaking out. Are you still going to hang out with Shawn and them?"

"I don't know." She tugs at a loose string on her yellow sundress. "I'll still chill with them, but I'm so done with Shawn."

I know Keely well enough to see when she's not telling the truth—somewhere inside her, for reasons that I don't get, she still likes Shawn.

"I'm sorry, Keel," I say. "But who needs boys, anyway? You totally don't."

She shoulders me with a grin. "Easy for you to say when *West* is in love with you. Have you guys done it yet?" My face is instantly aflame, and Keely slaps my arm with a huge laugh. "Oh my God, your face! Chill out, I won't bug you too much about it. But be honest: was it good?"

My lips twitch into a grin. "It was good."

We both sigh and look up as sparrows flock from an oak into the clear afternoon sky. Roger and Sun come outside, just as my parents' rental sedan pulls up the avenue. Even though I don't want to go, I'm relieved at the sight of my parents getting out of the car. I hug Mom first—she doesn't give me a choice—then Dad, and feel at home for a fleeting moment.

"Are you okay, sweetheart?" Mom grabs my face.

"Mom, I'm fine," I grumble.

She smothers me in another hug. Dad shakes Roger's hand and says, "Thank you for everything, Rog. We can't tell you how much we appreciate it."

"It was no problem. Keely loved having Olivia here." Roger places his hand on Dad's back and leads him away. "But there are some things we should talk about before you go."

They all go and talk by the birdbath.

"Yikes." Keely rocks on her heels. "Think you're going to be in trouble?"

"I don't know. It's more the disappointment that makes me feel horrible."

"Bigger yikes."

Mom and Dad are giving me *the look* when they come back over with Keely's parents. Roger told them some of what happened on the phone, but I imagine he just filled in any remaining blanks.

"Time to go, Olivia," Dad says.

With a nod, I face Sun and Roger and hold my hands together. "Thank you so much. I really appreciate you putting up with me."

Despite everything, Sun's smile is warm. "You're welcome, Olivia."

I hug her, then Roger.

"Maybe next time, you girls can have the summer you wanted," Roger says.

"I hope so. Thanks, Roger."

My parents and I walk away. I catch Keely's eyes once more before I get into the back of the rental car and shove my suitcase to the other side. It has that new car smell, unfamiliar and neutral. Dad gets behind the wheel while Mom takes the passenger side.

"Oh honey," Mom says. "What were we thinking sending you here without us?"

"Mom, I'm fine."

Dad rubs his eye beneath his glasses. "You're not fine, Olivia. I was wrong about everything, we never should've left you here." He looks at Mom and mutters, "She broke all of Roger's rules, and some of our own."

And there it is, the crushing disappointment. Before the accident, letting them down wasn't as big of a deal; I was always worrying them when I was a kid by swimming too far out into the sea and climbing trees. But now it's different.

"It's her mental health we need to worry about," Mom whispers as if I can't hear them.

"Then let's get her back to Dr. Levy so she can do her job."

"We need to be a support system for her right now."

"So what, we just don't punish her for sneaking around at night?"

"I don't know, Allen."

Their back and forth raises the frustration in me until I snap. "Guys, stop!"

"Don't speak to us like that," Dad warns.

I sink into the seat. "Sorry, it's just—I can hear you. So please stop talking about me like I'm not right here."

My parents sigh and stare out the window at the sunny day.

"I know it was stupid to sneak out," I say, "but I had my reasons."

"And was a boy involved in those reasons?" Dad asks without looking at me.

"Maybe, but that's not the point. The point is, being here has been hard, but it's also been totally amazing." A smile spreads across my face at the good memories. "I mean, I swam. For the first time since I was twelve, I actually swam. It was only one time, but still. I can actually walk along the beach now and not be scared. I went on a boat and everything."

They share a concerned look.

"So please don't make me go yet," I say. "I've come so close to being able to cope with my fear. And I have friends here, I have a life. Can't we stay for just a bit longer? Rent a place?"

"You want us to *stay*?" Dad laughs sarcastically. "Olivia, you've got to be kidding me."

"I'm serious." I focus on Mom. She's always been easier to deal with than Dad, and even though he hates to admit it, she's the one who makes the final decisions. I take a page from Keely's book and bat my eyes. "Please? I *swam*, Mom . . . you can't say that isn't big for me."

Sighing, Mom touches Dad's arm. "We do have Greg watching the shop. We could afford to stay somewhere for a couple of days."

Dad catches me in the rear-view mirror. "Who's the boy?"

I draw a breath. "West."

"*West*? You mean Miles's brother, West."

To my parents, West is just "Miles's brother." Miles used to come around the house all the time, but West and I were only ever together at the beach or the Hendricks estate. To them, Miles is still my childhood best friend. A jolt of guilt zaps me.

"Well, this is a surprise," Mom says. "I always thought you would end up with Miles, if anyone from Caldwell at all."

"Yeah, and Miles was a way nicer kid," Dad mutters.

"West is different now, Dad. He's good."

Red dots Dad's cheeks. I've never had a boyfriend, period, so I have no idea how he's going to react.

"If you don't believe me," I say, "let's find somewhere to stay tonight and have West over for dinner."

"I don't think it's a good idea, but I'll leave this one up to you, Carrie."

Mom fidgets with her long brown hair before she groans. "I hate when you two put me on the spot. We'll stay for one more night, two at most. Okay?"

"Deal," I say. Dad grumbles.

Relief flows through me as we drive toward downtown. My summer isn't over yet, after all. I still have time to swim again—but next time, I want to do it in the ocean, all on my own.

o o o

There wasn't much available on such short notice with Airbnb, but Mom found a cottage along the water with a wraparound porch surrounded by the sea. The wind blows through my hair from the deck, my elbows propped on the railing. Seagulls squawk and the waves lap against the sand as the sun descends into the ocean, making the horizon a swollen ball of light.

Inside, my parents are setting up the pizza boxes Dad ordered from Sergio's. It was his favorite place to eat when we lived here. They bought some clothing and supplies while we were downtown, but only enough for a couple of days, and they told only Keely's family where we would be.

When West's Corvette revs nearby, I run to him as he parks

alongside the pastel-blue cottage. As soon as he gets out of his car, I'm in his arms.

"Hey." He lifts me into a hug and smooths his hand over my hair. "You're really staying?"

"Not for long, but still." I smile wide when he sets me down. "We can be together for a couple days at least."

West kisses me, just as Dad clears his throat behind us, standing in the doorway, and scratches behind his ear. He says, "You coming in for pizza or what?" and lets the door shut behind him. We follow, but West stops me by pulling on my hand.

"Wait. He's not going to bite my head off, is he? Angry dads are not my specialty. Guess I'm not always the ideal choice for their daughters."

"Well . . ." A look of horror flashes across West's face. I laugh. "Don't worry. My dad's harmless, he's just not used to me having a guy around. But once he sees how great you are, he'll come around."

We go inside. The cottage is dinky and humid, but it has two bedrooms and a wooden round table that's only a little wobbly. Board games are stacked onto the shelves in the living room next to an old box TV, and everything has that cabin smell—musty, but something about it feels like home. And it's close to the water, which is surprisingly fine.

West shakes Dad's hand with a nervous smile. Dad returns it with too much aggression for my liking, but West holds his ground. When he goes for Mom's hand, she surprises him with a short hug.

"The last time I saw you, you were up to my shoulder." Her smile touches her eyes. "How are you, West?"

"I'm okay, thanks."

"Hope you like pepperoni," Dad says.

"That sounds awesome."

We all sit and grab slices. I slick my socks against the bumpy linoleum floor and glance around the table. I've never seen West so nervous, his face damp with sweat.

"Olivia told us you were really there for her this summer," Dad says. "I suppose we should thank you."

West swallows his pizza before he speaks. "She was there for me a lot too."

Mom rests her chin on her hands, where she has multiple rings stacked on each finger. "This town has brought us a lot of bad luck, but we're glad Liv had you to rely on."

"How's your family these days?" Dad asks. West and I stiffen—crap, I forgot to tell him not to bring them up.

"They're all right," West says. "I'm not actually living with them anymore."

"That's a surprise. Any particular reason?"

West looks even more nervous, so I chime in and say, "West is a mechanic, Dad. He works at the body shop."

Dad's eyes flare the same way they always do when someone brings up cars. "A Hendricks kid working as a mechanic? You're full of surprises."

"Only an apprentice," West says, "but I'm on my way up."

I can tell Dad's trying to be that protective father, but the facade is sliding off. "I like cars myself, but I had to sell my '75 Mustang when we moved away from Caldwell Beach. Not much point having a car like that in New York City, and where parking's criminally expensive at that."

"Sorry, that sucks. Did you see mine out there?"

"Must've missed it while you were—never mind."

"It's a '68 Corvette."

Dad's shoulders square. "Might need you to give me a tour of that one."

"Sure, I could show you right now if you want."

They both set their slices down and are out the front door in seconds. Mom and I look at each other, dumbfounded, before we both laugh.

"Looks like they have something in common, after all," Mom says.

"Yep."

Mom's smile melts, concern taking over her face. "Are sure you're okay, Livvie?"

"Yeah, I'm fine," I say, because I really am fine. I always am when West is near. If I'm stranded out at sea, he's the island over the horizon and the lifeboat that carries me home. Will I be lost without him?

Mom and I are done eating by the time Dad returns with West, laughing like old buddies. Dad was bound to be swayed eventually—at least the awkward part is over now.

Dad ropes us into a game of Settlers of Catan, even though Mom and I hate board games. He and West spend most of the time talking about cars, and Dad tells him long-winded stories about his early twenties when he dreamed of being a race car driver. Dad narrowly beats West at the end of the game, but I suspect West let him win.

"Well, it's getting late," Dad says. The clock above the stove reads 11:43 p.m.

West stands. "I better go."

He shakes Dad's hand and hugs Mom before I walk him to the door. I tell my parents to give me a minute and follow West into the humid summer night, shutting the door behind us. Finally, with a moment to breathe, I jump into West's arms. He hugs me back.

"That went better than I thought." He sets me down, but I keep my hands on his shoulders as he holds the curve of my torso.

"I knew they'd love you."

"You give me too much credit."

We fall quiet. The wind has picked up, and the waves roar now. I crane my neck back and look at the band of the Milky Way that spreads across the entire night sky. Soon, I won't have any of the three things I love in front of me: the stars, the ocean, and West.

The ocean. I never realized it until right now, but I do still love it. I always did. Even if the thought of being under water still terrifies me.

"Hey, so I wanted to give you this." West reaches into his pocket and slides something cold into my hand. "I know a pocketknife is a shitty gift to give your girlfriend, but I know you feel unsafe sometimes, and I don't know." He laughs. "Maybe don't tell your parents that I gave you a knife, but I wanted you to have it."

I smooth my finger along the surface of the knife's sheath. A pattern of waves is engraved into it. I press a button, and the knife pops out.

"Whoa, okay." West closes it and encases my fingers around it. "Don't go flashing it around, okay? It's just to help you feel safe. Carry it in your purse or something."

I totally do not need a knife, but I love that he's giving me a present. "Thanks, West. I like it."

He grins. My skin goes up in flames when he grabs my hips beneath my shirt and backs me into the wall. "Wish you could come home with me," he whispers, pressing into me, and I stare at his mouth.

"I wish I could too. But if I sneak away from my parents, they'll get pretty mad."

"I know, and I'm not going to make your parents hate me already." He kisses me. "But hey, if you're staying for a few days, you should come up to the estate for a barbeque. My dad called me earlier. We're still not on the best terms, but he's throwing a big party for the whole town the day after tomorrow, and sometimes he likes to have me around for show, even though Beatrice would rather keep me buried. You should come with me."

I don't think I'll ever get used to that look on his face, like I'm the only thing he can see, even with so many stars above us. "Sure," I say. "If I can convince my parents, I'd love to be there with you."

"Cool. Goodnight, Olive." He places another electric kiss on my lips. I don't want to be away from him, not even for a minute, let alone for months and months and months. But we have a little more time together. Worrying is a waste of it.

West and I are still kissing when headlights flash in my peripherals. The cottage isn't far from downtown, but only the Myerses and West know we're here. Roger's cruiser pulls into the driveway. My parents must have seen him through the window, because they hurry onto the porch. That same panic I felt when Keely went missing in the woods resurfaces. Roger exits the car holding a black fabric briefcase.

"What's going on, Rog?" Dad says.

Roger walks up the steps to the porch. "Evening. Sorry to intrude on you folks like this, but I felt it was better to do this in person."

"Why?" I ask. "Is Keely okay?"

"She's fine. Don't worry, that's not what this is about."

I let out a breath of relief, but another fear takes over: if it's not about Keely, I don't know what other reason he could have to be here.

"Can I come in?" Roger asks.

"Yeah, of course," Dad says. "Hey West, maybe it's better if you take off."

West looks at me. "But—"

"Dad, no," I say.

"Sorry, but I agree," Roger says. "You mind, West?"

He nods. I tell him I'll text him and then he's gone. Anxiety fastens around my throat as we go back inside. Roger unzips the bag and takes out a laptop, placing it on the kitchen table.

"I need to show Olivia something and get her opinion." Roger looks at me. "That night, when you thought you saw something in the shower window. Are you still sure of what you saw?"

Completely caught off guard, I picture that night—the hand I knew was there—and everyone looking at me like I was insane. Frustration throbs through my brain as I try to materialize the images in my head. "I'm sure of what I saw, but not if it was real. All of you seemed to think I was imagining things. I'm sorry, but why are you bringing this up?"

Roger pauses, opens the laptop, and types. He says, "We caught someone sneaking around our property, trying to see in the windows. On camera this time, Olivia. I saw him with my own eyes."

This has to be a joke. I can't help the exasperation that comes out of my voice. "You all said I hallucinated, Roger. Are you telling me it really happened now?"

"It's possible. For that to happen to you, and for this to happen now—it's too coincidental. He could've snuck by the cameras the last time."

That's exactly what I said before. I dig my nails into my palms. I knew it. I knew what I saw that night was real. "You didn't believe me," I say, unable to hide the anger and betrayal in my voice.

The room goes silent. Guilt fills Roger's eyes, and he reluctantly meets mine. "You're right, and I really am sorry, Olivia. I shouldn't have been so quick to dismiss you."

Hugging myself, I turn away. "You shouldn't have." Pause. "When did it happen?"

"About an hour ago, but he got away. My officers are over there searching the area, but nothing yet. You thought you saw a hand, correct?"

"I *know* I saw a hand. Like someone was trying to grab onto the ledge and peek into the window. You said there weren't any prints."

"There weren't, but—but maybe they just didn't touch the glass. Maybe I didn't look hard enough."

I say nothing else, though I'm still steaming, still trying to process this.

"Here." Roger shows us the screen. Dad wraps his arm around Mom's shoulder, and I lean my palms onto the table to get a better view of the screen.

It starts with the guest room window, which up until today,

was my room. A hooded man sneaks up to the windows and peeks inside, but his face is completely hidden. I've seen this before, but somewhere in a dream. The man's face in the window.

Miles?

"Do you recognize him?" Roger asks.

He has a thin frame—maybe athletic—but I can't tell. Processing the picture is like drilling nails into my brain. Mentioning Miles would be a *serious* accusation. Just because I dreamt of him doesn't mean he was ever really there.

"I . . . can't tell."

"Here's another angle." Roger switches the camera to the front of the house, where the man sneaks along the wall with his head low.

"I don't know," I say. Mom rubs my back to calm me down.

"You can tell by his posture that he's a younger man," Roger says. "My best guess would be someone trying to get to know the layout of the place in order to break in and steal. But it's also possible someone was trying to spy on one of us."

Or on me.

Miles knew I was leaving, but I never told him if it was today. For all he knows, I could still be at the Myerses' house.

"I've already talked to Keely," Roger says. "She insists there aren't any boys in her life who might want to spy on her, but what do you think? Could Keely be hiding something else?"

"She's only dated Shawn."

"I plan on having a word with him." Roger squints at me. "What about *you*, Olivia? Is there anyone you might suspect would want to spy on Keely? Or yourself, even?"

"Well . . . I made Miles pretty mad when I started dating West." *Please don't let this be a mistake.*

"Livvie, not Miles—" Mom puts her hand over her mouth.

Even Roger looks surprised. "Really? You think Miles is capable of this? I thought he was your friend."

"I really don't know. Please don't tell him I said his name. It's—it's not like I can prove it, but I upset him a lot this summer. But we had a good talk yesterday when they all dropped by your house. Things seemed better, but—"

My mind is being jerked back and forth on a fair ride like the Zipper. I see the sweet Miles I knew as a kid, the civil Miles I spoke to last night, and then the one who was livid with me for being with West.

"Thanks, Olivia," Roger says. "I'll take a look at Miles. The motive is there. And again, for what it's worth—I really am sorry I didn't believe you. I've got to get back to work, but I'll keep you updated."

Dad questions Roger as he packs up his stuff, but my head drifts out into the sea. I blink, still in shock, still unsure if giving Miles's name was the right thing to do or the biggest betrayal of my life.

When I snap out of my daze, Roger is gone.

"Livvie, get some sleep," Mom says. "We're leaving first thing tomorrow."

"No!" My parents flinch. When I realize I've snapped, I say, "I'm sorry. But please, don't make me leave town yet. I'm not ready."

"Olivia," Dad says, "if there's some kind of lunatic in this town, it's best if we head home. Especially if you think it's someone you know."

"I'm not leaving yet."

Storming to my room, I crawl into bed. Static fuzz in my brain makes it hard to think. It isn't a coincidence that guy is suddenly creeping around Keely's house right after I came to town. Maybe it isn't Miles, but whoever he is, he must have gone there looking for me. And when Keely went missing—maybe this is all connected. Maybe whoever is following me was trying to get to me by getting to her first. I don't know. But I feel responsible for everything that's going on.

I stare at the ceiling for hours, my mind on high alert.

When a shadow moves behind the window, my breath halts.

Something scuffles outside. On rickety bones, I move to the window. My trembling hand extends to the edge of the polyester curtain, and I rip it so hard it almost tears from its hooks. Behind the glass, wooden posts hold up the roof. There's a spruce tree and a dark, narrow street. Clouds canvas a moon rimmed with yellow. This side of the house faces away from the water, into the street, and there's distance between every cottage on this road, so whatever the sound is can't be a neighbor. I take a wary step closer.

On the ground, below my window, is a pool of crimson. My pulse pounds as I follow the trail until it lands on the mutilated carcass of a deer. Its throat is slit the exact same way it had been splayed out at town hall.

The man outside Keely's house. The animal killer. *They're the same person.*

And he found me.

My brain throbs. Anger, thick and oozing. I blink and I'm outside. Stones dig into my bare soles, and the cottage is now several feet behind me. I don't know how I got here. Moments ago, I was in my room, but now a cold air swallows me. I can't remember anything. I can't think. Blue and red lights flash all around, and the world turns sideways. Suddenly I'm on the ground and holding the knife above me. Two police officers shine flashlights in my face.

"Miss, what happened?" one of them asks. I can't see his face, only the silhouette of his hat over that bright, bright light.

"Michaels, turn that thing off," the other says.

The street goes dark again. I scuffle back.

"We're going to need you to put down the weapon," a man says.

"Are you hurt?" the other asks. "Where'd you get that knife?"

"I don't know," I say, "I don't know, I don't know, I don't know!"

Someone grabs me. I fling the knife. My right cheek is pressed into the gravel, and everything goes black.

18

Blinding white light surrounds me. Voices murmur beneath the steady sound of beeping.

"What happened to her? Is it because of her medication?"

My vision is trapped in a fish-eye lens: the ceiling, the corners of the room, a bag of fluid hanging next to me. Flashes of blue and red flicker in my memory. My hands were bound. The back of a car.

The animal killer.

No, more than that. People in white lab coats, muttering words.

Psychosis. Schizophrenia. A result of her PTSD.

My reality is fragmented. Disjointed, stained-glass memories. They feel as real as my nightmares. I try to look around the room, but a sharp pain jabs my neck when I move. Fear takes over my body, just as my parents rush to my side and hover over me, their faces as pale as the ceiling above their heads.

"What's going on?" I say drowsily.

My skull throbs, and I pull myself up in the bed. A gangly tube sticks out from my hand like a piece of spaghetti. I scream and rip it out. Pain fires up my arm and blood pumps from the wound. Mom gasps. A woman in blue scrubs appears and presses a cotton pad onto my skin, but I shove her away.

"What are you putting in me? Why am I in the hospital?"

The room spirals. My parents are replaced by two other nurses, and their faces glitch in and out of my vision. I kick and scream until someone binds me. A pinprick, and the IV is back in my other hand. My limbs become numb, and my body is being weighed down by sand.

All at once, everything slows. I black out—I'm not sure for how long, but when I come to, the beeping is calm. Steady, like the ebb and flow of the ocean. If I listen hard enough, I can hear waves. It reminds me of when Miles and I were kids and we'd press seashells to our ears, even with the sea right in front of us. I close my eyes and I'm on the beach.

"Liv, you have to listen to me practice," Miles says.

I stretch my legs out on the white sand. The sun glares above us. I'm building a paper boat like the one West showed me while Miles holds out his copy of The Secret Garden.

"I don't get why you're so obsessed with it," I say. "Everyone has to read it and perform in groups. It's not like we're even doing it as an actual play."

"But Mr. Burton said we could organize a real play if enough people care."

A beach ball appears at my feet. I look up, and my face heats because West is running over. I pick up the ball, still stunned when West appears in front of me. I blink at him, my voice caught in my throat.

"What are you looking at, Olive? Can I have it back?"

"S-sorry."

West takes it and runs off. I look at Miles, but he's storming away with his fists balled at his sides.

"Miles, wait!" I chase after him.

I used to always chase after him.

"She's awake," someone says.

Cold tears wet my cheeks. The hospital room materializes around me again, and I'm dizzy. This time, I don't have the strength to rip the IV out, but I'm conscious enough to understand where I am. Whatever they're putting in me must be a sedative, because I'm so, so heavy. Mom places a warm hand on my cheek.

"Did they catch him?" I murmur.

"Catch who, sweetie?" Her voice is desperate, like she's already asked the question a hundred times.

"The animal killer. He found me. There was a deer."

"You're certain it was a deer?" That voice belongs to someone I don't know. My vision adjusts to a woman who stands next to me and observes me like I'm some sort of science experiment. She has full eyebrows and a long black ponytail, and she's young for a doctor, maybe thirty.

"Who are you?" My voice comes out grainy, full of distrust.

"Olivia, I'm Dr. Reddy." She extends her hand, but I don't shake it, so she holds her clipboard to her white lab coat. "I work in the emergency ward here at the hospital. I'd like to talk to you about what happened last night. What do you remember?"

It hurts to think—to remember—but images flicker through my mind like damaged film. "There was someone outside, they put a dead deer on the ground for me to find. I remember getting really angry, but then . . . I don't know." I cover my mouth as the memory returns. "Oh my God, I went outside. Did I chase him? Why would I do that?"

Even the thought of it chills me to the bone. I wasn't myself last night; someone else took control of my body.

"And there were cops," I say. "Did they catch him?"

Dr. Reddy's lips are in a tight smile. "No one has been arrested. Do you remember trying to harm a police officer, Olivia?"

"I wouldn't do that. It was him, the animal killer."

"The police officer said it was you, but it was an accident. Why do you think it was the animal killer?"

"Because . . . he was there."

"But I don't think the officer would have any reason to lie. Do you?"

"Hold on," Mom cuts in. "Doctor, we really appreciate everything you've done, but Olivia has a psychiatrist back in New York. We should get her home right away."

"Yes, that's a good idea. Though I wouldn't recommend traveling until we know she's stable."

I hate the way they're talking about me like I'm not even here. "I'm not going anywhere."

"Olivia, we need to get you home," Mom says.

"*No!*"

"Carrie," Dad says, "can we step back and let the doctor do her job?" He puts his arms around her shoulders and leads her to the other side of the room. Dr. Reddy pulls up a stool and examines her clipboard. I shift as far away as I can.

"Olivia, your parents updated me on your past, and we were able to get some information faxed to us from your doctor's office in Manhattan. You were diagnosed with PTSD—"

"Can you just tell me what's going on?"

"Sure. You're here because it appears you had an episode last night. Do you understand what that means?"

"Of course I do. I've been dealing with flashbacks since I was twelve."

"That's not quite what I'm talking about." Her face softens. "When I say you had an episode, I mean that you lost touch with reality for a little bit. Does that make sense?" She's stepping on eggshells. When I don't answer, she taps her pen on the clipboard. "Last night, you claimed there was someone after you. That someone put a deceased animal outside of your window. Can you describe what you saw?"

Images of blood strobe through my mind. "It was a deer, and it was bleeding everywhere. Its throat was slit just like the deer the animal killer left at town hall."

"You've seen that exact deer before?"

"No, it was laid out differently."

"Olivia, this might be difficult for you to hear, but the police didn't find anything like that outside your window."

"That's impossible. If they couldn't find anything, then the killer must have come back and moved it."

"Why do you think he would he do that?"

"To mess with me."

"Do you think he messes with other people?"

"Maybe . . . I don't know."

"The officers went back and checked, and there was no sign of any animal, or any evidence of blood."

She's lying. She has to be. I know what I saw. I feel like I'm being tested and filmed, like they're shoving me into a corner. The walls close around me—my airways close up, and my vision goes white.

"How have you been sleeping lately?" Dr. Reddy asks.

"Terribly," I squeak.

"A lack of sleep can be damaging to the psyche. It can even cause hallucinations."

Every click of her pen amplifies the throbbing in my head, and when I process what she's saying, frustration rockets to my cheeks. "I know what I saw. My friend's dad thought I was crazy before when

I thought someone was outside the house, but then we caught video evidence of him. I'm not crazy."

"No, no one thinks you're crazy. We're just trying to get to the bottom of why you saw what you did."

"I saw it because it was *there.*" The feeling of water swells above my head. "I want to go. I can't breathe. Mom, I can't breathe."

"Livvie, you're okay."

Mom is at my side again. I grab onto her arms and beg her to get me out. I don't trust Dr. Reddy. I hate the way that nurse looks at me like I'm feral. My pulse hammers my eardrums as the panic returns—I try to thrash, but I'm strapped to the bed. The nurse comes over and puts something else in the IV bag. My head becomes featherlight. Mom and Dad are yelling, but I can't hear them anymore.

I try to fight it, but I slip away.

o o o

Weightlessly, I dream of floating like a buoy on calm, frothy water, clouds above my head and blue everywhere. For the first time in years, when my eyelids flutter open, I don't want the dream to end.

I wake up slowly. This time, I'm not surrounded by white lights; I'm bathed in a syrupy-orange glow. The sun sets through the window of my room in the cottage.

"Livvie, can you hear me?" Mom hovers over me with a smile. I sit up and clutch my throbbing head.

"Mom? What happened?"

She hands me a glass of water, and I chug some back before she sets it on the nightstand. "We discharged you from the hospital, sweetie. Those doctors were doing their best, but we need to get you home to Dr. Levy."

I rub my eyes. I don't remember putting these pajamas on. I don't remember much of anything, really, other than leaving the hospital in a blur. Voices sound through the walls—Dad talking to someone else.

Mom must sense what I'm thinking, because she says, "West came to see you."

Even though my body is cold, my heart warms. I try to stand, but my knees wobble. Mom holds me up.

"Take it easy, Livvie. They put far too much medication in you."

That explains why my head is still spinning. Mom helps me out of the room, into the bathroom. My skin is so pale, my dark hair almost black in contrast. I don't recognize my own reflection. Still, I brush my teeth, wash my face, and tie my hair back in a ponytail. Slightly more awake, I go into the kitchen. As soon as Dad sees me, he rushes over, but I'm looking past him at West, who stands beside the kitchen table. He wears the same torn-up look as them.

"Jesus, Carrie, should she be walking around?" Dad asks.

"I'm okay, Dad," I say and move past him to West. Though most of my body still feels like it's been numbed by a dentist, I'm slowly beginning to thaw. The clouds in my head part to reveal opaque memories.

The doctor said I hallucinated everything. That can't be true, but I can tell by the way everyone's looking at me that they believe it. I'm a burden to all of them, but somewhere in this town, the man who caused this is alive. I wonder if he enjoys terrifying people. Maybe that's what made me the perfect target for him; the girl who jumps at the sight of her own shadow. The perfect girl to torment.

I know I should be scared, and when the sedatives wear off, I probably will be. I should want to get far away from Caldwell, but I don't—because there are still things for me to overcome. I want to prove to everyone that I can be strong. I want to look the killer in the eyes when the police find him. I want to show him that he *lost*.

"Hey," West says hesitantly. "I got worried when you didn't text me. Your parents told me what happened. Well, some of it."

With nothing to say, I wrap my arms around him and place my ear against his beating heart. He hugs me back and presses his lips to the top of my head.

Before I saw the deer, my memories of last night are crystal clear; I remember West leaving, Roger coming over, and the image of the man creeping on the laptop. I also remember telling Roger I suspect Miles.

West has to know the truth. Maybe he'll even know something about Miles that we don't, so I grab his hand and lead him toward my room.

"Sweetheart, keep that door open," Dad says.

I leave it open a crack and sit on the bed. West waits a beat before he joins me. I open my mouth to tell him about Miles but get choked up—because West might get upset with me for suspecting his brother. He and Miles have issues, but they're still family.

"I told your parents about what happened on the cliff," West says and fidgets with his hands. "I'm sorry, but I think they had to know."

"I understand."

"What happened to you, Olive?"

The last thing I want is to push West away, so I take a deep breath and tell him the truth about the deer. My truth, anyway. When I'm done, the first thing he does is check outside the window. He comes back over with confusion on his face.

"You're sure you saw a dead thing out there?"

"It was as real as you are now."

"But the cops wouldn't lie about it not being there, Olive."

"I know."

"Were you drunk or something?"

"No! You know I don't drink." Overwhelmed, tears fall from my eyes, and I try to wipe them away. "Besides, they checked my blood and I was sober."

"What else do they think it could be?"

We both lie on the bed, and West pulls me to his chest. His skin is warm through his shirt.

"It's all right." He runs his fingers through my hair. "You don't have to tell me what's going on in your head, but whatever it is, it's not going to change how I feel about you."

I hold him tighter. "That's the thing, we don't know what it was. They think I imagined it. But what if the animal killer planned all of this? What if he came back and moved the carcass? What if he took Keely as a distraction? What if he's been killing animals for me? Because he knew I was coming back to town." West is silent. "I know how it sounds. My parents don't believe me either."

"Hey, don't worry." He wipes one of my tears with his thumb. "You've been through a lot. I bet when you leave this place and get home to the city, you'll look back on all this and wonder why you were even upset. You'll go totally back to normal."

"But I wasn't normal in New York either." I pull away. "I'm weird at school, my friends only talk to me because we're on the same sports team, and I'm so jumpy that people actually used to make games out of scaring me."

He pauses. "You never told me that last part."

"It's the truth. Being back here has been messing with my head, but if I leave now, I'll just be going back to being that scared, jumpy girl in New York. How is that better?"

"But maybe Caldwell isn't the place you're going to heal, Olive. Don't get me wrong; I'd love for you to stay. But not if this place is making you feel like shit." His words make sense, but I'm just too stubborn to accept them.

I sit upright in the bed. I have to tell him about Miles, but I don't know how. "Who do you think the killer is, West?"

"How should I know?"

"Last night, when Roger came over, it was because he wanted to show me footage of someone lurking around his house at night." I say, "Peeking into windows, including the window of the room I was sleeping in."

"What, someone was *spying* on them?"

"I think he was there for me." When West doesn't reply, I blurt, "I told him I suspect Miles, West."

His eyes flit over my face, but I can't tell if it's confusion or concern that crosses his features. "You think Miles was spying on them, or you think he's the animal killer?"

"Both, maybe. I don't know."

West shakes his head and looks away.

"Please don't be mad at me," I choke out. "It's just—I made him so upset this summer by being with you. I thought if anyone would try to spy on me, it had to be Miles."

He leans forward and holds his hands together. Grunting in frustration, West runs his fingers through his dark hair. "Jesus, Olivia. I'm not mad at you, but I wish you'd talked to me before the cops. I've got my issues with my brother, but I wouldn't accuse him of that. He might be a freak, but he's not a killer. Remember how upset he got when we were kids and my dad was always killing shit? Miles cried at every bit of roadkill until he was like, thirteen."

It's horrible, but somehow, what West is saying doesn't ease my suspicions. "I only told Roger I thought Miles was the one looking in the windows."

West is quiet for too long, but I don't have it in me to break the silence. Finally, he says, "Maybe I could see him doing that."

"Wait, really?"

"I don't know. Maybe. He was always a bit weird, he used to creep through my room when I wasn't home all the time. But we'll both see him at the barbeque tomorrow, if you're still coming. I'll try to see how he acts."

"I'm still coming. I need something that makes me feel normal."

West opens his mouth to respond, just as Dad shouts, "Guys, come out here—they're saying something on the radio."

We go into the kitchen, where plates of reheated pizza and cups of grape juice wait for us on the table. West and I sit down, and I immediately cram a bite of pizza into my mouth. I didn't even realize how hungry I was. Dad turns up an old school antenna radio. The voice of a reporter crackles into the room.

"*We're getting reports that a suspect has been taken into custody regarding the case of the Caldwell Animal Killer. At this time, the evidence is being withheld, but police have identified the suspect as sixty-eight-year-old Robert Jenkens.*"

I drop my pizza.

"What?" West scowls. "That's not right."

"*Jenkens, known for his position as owner of the fisherman's supply shop along the shore, hasn't had a known criminal charge since the '80s, when he was charged with kidnapping his own daughter from his ex-wife. The daughter was eventually returned unharmed, but a restraining order was filed against Jenkens.*"

I don't know what happened with Mr. Jenkens's daughter, but it was decades ago. Surely he's changed. He isn't the animal killer—I feel as strongly about it as I did when Miles told his stupid story. But if they have him in custody, they must have something on him, and I'm not sure how to feel about that.

"*As of right now, no charges have been laid. We'll keep you updated as the story unfolds.*"

Mom turns off the radio. "Oh, that's just awful. I can't believe old Mr. Jenkens would do that."

"It isn't him," I blurt. "It can't be."

"Agreed," West says.

"How could you kids know?" Dad asks.

"We . . . just do," I say. "Mr. Jenkens is innocent."

"The police don't seem to think so."

"There's only one way to find out." West looks at me. "We've got to go see him."

Dad laughs. "The only way you're getting out of this house is if I'm driving."

o o o

We arrive outside of Caldwell's police station downtown, and it's strangely cold tonight, the sky totally clear. I'm wearing sweatpants and a hoodie, and my reflection in the rear-view mirror is ghoulish, but I don't care; I'm still numb. But I have to find out what happened to Mr. Jenkens.

Dad stops in the parking lot at the side of the building, and I ask him to wait for us there. He's irritated but allows West and I to rush out alone. The lights from downtown blot out the moon and stars. Just as we reach the station, with its concrete brick walls, we notice there are vans parked on the road and reporters crowding off to the side of the entrance.

"What the hell," West mutters.

We go into the police station, just as Jenkens storms out of a room. He adjusts his jacket with a gruff grunt.

"Jenkens!" West shouts.

We hurry over to him. He looks equal parts angry and dejected, but it's a good sign he's being released.

"What are you doing here?" he asks us.

"We didn't believe what we heard," I blurt. "And you're out now, so it can't be true, right?"

Jenkens is quiet. Behind the counter, a receptionist glares at us, so we step off to the side. West says, "Come on, man. Talk to us. What's going on?

"I found the dog," Jenkens says, so low I almost can't hear. "The dog that drowned."

My spine crawls. That was the one kill Roger said didn't match the animal killer's regular MO.

"Was already dead inside the water," Jenkens says. "Must've fallen in, but I knew right away it was the Dalys'. Didn't want to get involved, so I just put it on their lawn. Days later, I found the collar caught in one of my nets, knew how it'd look if I came forward with it, so I just kept my mouth shut. It's what I'm good at." He pauses. "But I don't kill nothing but fish."

I let out a breath of relief. "But why are you here now? Why did they arrest you?"

"Didn't hide the collar well. Some kid found it in my shop and played with it like it was a toy. Their parent saw it, and that's how all this shit began."

"But you're innocent," West says. "That's why they let you go, right?"

"I am innocent. But they only let me go because they didn't have enough to keep me. I'm still under suspicion. They made that much clear to me."

"They'll know you're innocent for sure when they find the real killer," I say.

Jenkens coughs into his forearm. "See how well my shop does till then, kid. Those reporters were talking the moment I got taken in. The damage is done."

Poor Mr. Jenkens. My summer has been rough, but his has been catastrophic.

"Well, where are you going now?" West asks him. "You need company? You can't go out there, there are reporters everywhere." When Jenkens doesn't reply, West says, "Come on, man. You know sometimes you were more like a second father to me than my own dad, right? You were the only adult who listened."

A pause, and Jenkens mumbles, "Can't stop you from following me, Weston."

West gently touches my arm. "I'm going to stay with him, okay? We'll sneak out back before those reporters see. I can come by your cottage later and grab my car. That cool?"

"Of course," I say. "I'll go home with my dad."

We quickly kiss, before I tell Mr. Jenkens I hope he's okay and go back to the parking lot, where Dad waits for me. As we drive back to the cottage, I think about how I told Roger about Miles; he must be questioning him soon, if he hasn't already.

I know West was doubtful, but Miles has been giving me bad vibes all summer, and with everything that happened to Jenkens, it all points to him. There has to be a reason for that.

19

The savory smell of grilled hot dogs permeates the backyard air of the Hendricks estate. A cloud of smoke billows from the barbeque as a caterer in a white uniform pokes food on the grill, but I'm too queasy to think about eating.

Since I slept all day yesterday, I didn't get much last night. Ever since I woke up, I've been worrying about so many things— Mr. Jenkens's well-being, and when I inevitably see Miles today.

My parents are beside me, but Dad keeps checking his watch and Mom is anxiously fidgeting with her hair. They agreed to come today only so I would be quiet and let them take me back to New York in peace. They're definitely uncomfortable with it, but I've insisted that I feel fine. Which is only a half lie. I flatten my skirt and scan the yard. Dean, Shawn, Faye, and Keely are sitting at a picnic table under the shade of a willow tree. When the guys see me, they laugh. Keely says something to them, and I get the grim sense that they're talking about me. I search for any sign of Miles, but he isn't there.

Feeling small, I look for West. Crowds of adults stand in casual circles, holding paper plates of potato salad and bottles of beer. A sprinkler cascades sheets of water in the air and gleams against the afternoon sun. A trail of little kids, tripping and falling over their own tiny feet, snakes through the yard.

"I should go find West," I tell my parents.

"Don't wander off too far, Olivia," Dad says.

I'm rounding the side of the estate when West's car pulls into the driveway. He gets out, and I run at him with a hug.

"Hey, I'm glad you're here." West is dressed nicer than usual, in a pair of dark jeans and a white T-shirt, opposed to his usual black. He squints at the sun and scans the backyard. "You seen Miles yet?"

"No, not yet."

"Me neither, but he's here somewhere. Let's get some food." West takes my hand and leads me toward the barbeque tent. Keely and the others watch from under the willow tree, and I realize this is the first time West and I are out publicly in Caldwell as a couple. It gains some looks—mostly from the adults. I look at my feet, but then a baritone voice booms from across the yard.

"Weston!" It's Brian. He stands under the wooden gazebo and waves to us, Beatrice and my parents next to him.

"Oh great," West mutters to me. "Since we're in public, he's putting on the Father-of-the-Year act."

Still, we awkwardly join them anyway. Brian places a firm hand on West's shoulder and squeezes.

"Did you get something to eat, darling?" Beatrice asks me, a pleasant smile on her raspberry lips. Her platinum hair is pinned back by clips and she's sweating beneath her foundation; I can see it threatening to melt away.

"No." It's blunt, but I'm not about to forget the way she treated me the last time we saw each other. I ignore the quizzical look from my mom.

"Anyway, Weston," Brian says, "I was just telling Allen and Carrie about your apprenticeship and how well it's going." It's like Brian has put on an entirely new face—he wears the same pinkish-red skin, leathery wrinkles, and golf shirt, but he's acting differently. *Fake.*

West is talking about his work when I spot movement out of the corner of my eye. Keely waves to me, beckoning for me to come over. I slip my hand out of West's grasp, and when he doesn't notice, I step away.

The shade of the tree is safe from the sweltering heat of the sun, and dots of fluff from dandelions float over the grass. Keely pulls me away from the others, who are still draped over the furniture. Miles is there now, too, and a sense of unease crawls from my spine all the way to the back of my skull. I focus on Keely as she hugs me.

"Oh my God, my dad told me you were in the hospital—are you okay?"

"I'm okay," I say. I love Keely, but if I tell her what really happened, she'll look at me the same way everyone in the hospital did.

"You know what happened at our house, right?" Keely shivers. "*So* creepy. But Liv, my dad questioned Miles. *Miles.* Why would he think it was him?"

I gulp. "Who knows who it could have been? Did Miles have an alibi?"

"Apparently he was in the forest behind his estate, but no one can actually vouch for him. But there's no way it was someone we know, right? I mean, I've been hanging out with Miles and he seems totally normal. Personally I think it was just some random creep."

Miles and the others walk toward us. I peek over my shoulder, where West is still lost in a conversation with his dad.

"You and West look cute," Faye says. She wears a long-sleeved pink blazer and shorts, scars completely hidden. "Whatever happened to you leaving town?"

"I'll be gone tomorrow," I say. "How are your feet?"

"Just peachy. My recital went perfectly, of course." There are still silver sparkles on her cheeks. The performance was yesterday and she must not have gotten all the costume makeup off.

"You hear what happened with Old Man Jenkens?" Shawn asks.

Behind Shawn, Miles's blue-green eyes drill into me, and I can't help but cower away from his gaze. I picture the hooded man from the security tape unveiling himself to be Miles with a sinister smile.

"Mr. Jenkens is innocent," I say. "The police let him go."

"No way." Miles crosses his arms and shakes his head. "He has to be guilty. I've been saying it since the beginning. Didn't your dad tell you what happened, Keely?"

"Not really, he doesn't tell me much."

"That stupid story you told was never funny, Miles," I say, anger taking over my trepidation about him. "It's because of you that some jerks vandalized his home, and it really affected him."

"I already told you that wasn't me, Liv," Miles says.

Shawn kicks at the grass. Dean shoves his hands in the pockets of his jacket and rummages for something, probably cigarettes. I narrow my eyes, before it hits me: I've been so stupid and blind.

"It was you two, wasn't it?"

Shawn opens his mouth to respond, but he just stutters our gibberish.

"Obviously it wasn't us." Dean laughs and glances at Miles. "At least it wasn't us *alone*."

Miles's face goes red.

"What are they talking about?" I ask. "Miles? You *did* vandalize his house, didn't you?"

"No!"

"He actually didn't," Keely says. "He was with me at the party all night."

"He might not have been with us," Dean says, "but he sure as hell had no problem helping us cover it up."

Damn it. I knew Miles had something to do with this, but I chose to believe in him. If I'd known the truth back then, the whole day he tried to kiss me could have been avoided. I could have avoided everything that had to do with him.

"You lied to me, Miles. You said you didn't know."

"Liv, I—" He reaches out, and as soon as his fingertips graze my arms, I jolt away.

"Don't touch me!"

"Just give me a chance to explain myself!"

But I'm already hurrying away. No one tries to stop me, not even Keely.

If there's one thing I have to look forward to when I leave Caldwell Beach, it's never having to see Dean, Shawn, or Miles ever again.

o o o

The next several hours are spent at my parents' side while West is busy with his family. By the time the sun sets, I leave Mom and Dad to walk alone around the property. A banditry of chickadees cheeps and picks sunflower seeds out of the grass, but they scatter when I move along the side of the house. This place is practically a castle grounds, a maze of hedges and fountains. With everything that's happened this summer, it's hard to believe Miles, West, and I ever played together here.

I follow the path between two bushes shaped like flamingos, where a cast-iron bench is placed in front of a colorful garden. I text West and tell him to meet me here, and he replies moments later saying he'll be a few minutes.

Taking a deep breath, I stretch out my legs, just as footsteps squish over the grass behind me. I stand, expecting to see West. But it's Miles. We're trapped in by bushes. I'm completely alone with him.

"Hey, Liv," he says like everything is normal. Fear freezes over me as he sits on the bench. "Can we talk now?"

West will be here any minute. If Miles tries anything, he'll be there to stop it—so I sit down, too, a good distance away. Miles leans his elbows on his knees and shreds a leaf apart, just like West always does.

Miles sighs. "All right, I knew Shawn and Dean had left the party. I knew Dean had a history of pestering Jenkens, so it wasn't hard to put two and two together. But when they told me the truth, they begged me not to tell anyone. I need you to understand that at that time, they were my only guy friends. I felt obligated to keep the secret."

"But didn't you feel any kind of guilt about Mr. Jenkens?"

"Sort of? I don't know. The old man's always given me the creeps."

"That doesn't give people the right to harass him."

"They were just messing around."

I think back to that night we found Jenkens on the bridge, how close he was to death, and it infuriates me.

"You're unbelievable, Miles. A man almost lost his life and got in trouble with the police, and you're passing it off as 'just messing around'?"

Miles stands, and instinctively, I do, too, but back away from him. The anger is back in his eyes, so I try to duck past him, but he blocks me off.

"Don't walk away," he says. "Listen, I'm done protecting other people. I need you to talk to me. There's something important I want to tell you. As I'm sure you know, Keely's dad questioned me about the guy outside of their house."

I stagger back again.

It was you, wasn't it, Miles?

"I think I know something about it," he says, "but I don't know what to do, because someone I care about could be in serious danger."

Something about the way he said that feels like a threat. I try to run past him, but he blocks me off again, just as West's voice reaches my ears.

"Hey, what are you doing?" West puts himself between Miles and I.

"Oh great," Miles says. "Of course you're here."

"You're freaking her out, man," West says. "What's your problem?"

"I'm trying to talk to Liv, West. Mind your own business."

"It's my business if you're making her feel unsafe. She doesn't want to talk to you, Miles. Back off."

"Unsafe?" Anger contorts Miles's face. "She was my best friend. You didn't even wait five minutes before you pounced on her and turned her against me!"

"You turned yourself against her. She's not your property, you selfish brat."

"You're my brother—you're supposed to have my *back*." Miles pushes West's shoulder. West regains his balance, his nostrils flared and his fists balled.

"Do that again, Miles," he warns.

Miles pushes him. West shoves him back so hard he trips and falls into the grass. Miles scrambles to his feet and dives at West, but West dodges his fist. West grabs Miles's shirt and throws him on the ground. West kicks Miles in the gut and causes him to retch in pain.

"Stay the fuck down," West says.

I hate seeing them like this. In this moment, I hate everything that we've become.

"West, stop." I tug at his arm as he kicks Miles again. "Please, stop hurting him."

I pull on West harder, and his eyes snap to me. It's like he isn't even in there—the West I know is gone, but only for a moment. When I beg him to stop again, he looks down in horror at what he's done.

"Oh shit. Miles, I'm sorry. I didn't mean to hit you that hard."

"Get away from me, West," Miles spits.

West tries to help Miles up, but he shoves him away, so West holds up his hands in peace and backs off. I'm paralyzed as Miles struggles to get up, but falls back down again. Looking at him now, as a crying mess on the grass, I can't help but wonder if Miles is even capable of the things I've accused him of.

"Miles," I squeak out and try to lift him by his elbow, but he shoves me away. Once Miles balances himself on his feet, he clutches his torso as he storms off, leaving me alone with West.

"Why did you do that, West?" I say. "You're way bigger than him, you didn't need to kick him!"

"I just wanted to put him in his place. I didn't mean to hurt him that bad."

"You were completely out of control!"

He wrings his hand along the back of his neck. "I don't know what to say. I lost my temper."

My phone buzzes in my purse, and I take it out. Mom texted me. "I have to go find my parents," I say.

West chases after me. "Olive, wait. Why are you mad at me? You don't even like Miles."

"Because it's about more than Miles. I don't like this side of you that thinks it's okay to hurt people."

"Seriously? Come on, guys fight sometimes. We're brothers, you think that's the first time we've gone at it?"

"You kicked him while he was down!"

"Yeah, it got out of hand, but I do feel like shit about it."

He looks at me like I'm ridiculous, but I can't just tell him it's fine because he's my boyfriend, or because he feels bad now.

So when I keep walking, and he stops following, I don't care anymore—I just want to be alone.

20

Darkness takes over the world through the window of my room. I'm lying in bed, the smell of the barbeque still embedded in my clothing. Before West showed up, Miles said he knew something about the guy outside of the window, but . . . part of me still believes *he* was the one who did it. If Miles was guilty, it would make sense for him to try to distract me and point the finger at someone else.

But who?

When my phone chimes, I check it right away. It's just Keely.

Hey, I heard what happened at the BBQ. It's
messed up that West hits his own brother.

I know. Things got way out of hand.

Can we meet up?

What for?

Talk about things one more time? I feel like I don't know anything that's going on with you.

It's true; I've hidden more from Keely this summer than ever before. Besides, we need to talk one-on-one, without Miles watching us. I sneak over to the bedroom door and peek through it. My parents are sound asleep on the couch, even though it's only 9:00 p.m. I hurry back over to my phone and text Keely.

Okay, but can you meet me here?

Yup, be there soon!

The floorboards creak as I move through the living room and scribble a quick note—*BRB, meeting Keely*—and leave it next to my parents. They'll be upset I left without telling them first, but they'll try to make me stay if I do. Mom's head rests on Dad's shoulder, and the magazine they were reading together has fallen to the floor. This entire trip is aging them.

Maybe I shouldn't go.

Keely texts and says she's outside.

I'll be right back, I remind myself. *Everything will be fine.*

Throwing my denim jacket on, I head out. The smell of rain hangs in the air. A storm brews over the horizon, thick black clouds that crawl across the dark sky as smoky wisps of fog waft over the coastline. The wind whips Keely's hair all over the place, and she hugs herself over her yellow dress and black jacket.

"I think we still have some time before the rain starts," she says. "Want to go for a walk? I'm seriously craving a soda right now."

The cottage isn't far from downtown, so a short walk leads to the gas station. Silence sweeps over us as we head down the street.

After a while, Keely says, "What really happened to you the other night? I was worried . . ."

"It's hard to explain, Keel. I'm pretty sure the animal killer found me and was messing with me, but everyone else is saying I imagined it."

"Whoa. Was it like, another one of your nightmares?"

"No, it was totally different. It was like he was really there."

"Oh."

More silence. A low thunder grumbles overhead, raising the hairs on my neck.

"I don't like this weather," I say. "Let's just grab sodas and get back to the cottage."

Keely picks up her pace. "Sounds like a plan to me." She pauses. "So hey, look, about Miles . . ." I stiffen. Keely goes on. "Covering for Shawn and Dean was wrong, but I get why he did it. I mean, this town is so small, we sort of have no one but each other. I don't blame Miles for wanting to keep his friendship with Dean and Shawn intact. I still hang out with them because I don't want to be alone either."

That makes sense, but I stay quiet for a few moments. "Why are you defending him, Keel?"

"Because I get where he's coming from. That's all."

As much as I don't agree with it, in a way I do understand why Miles would want to hold onto some of the only friendships he has, but still. "All right," I say.

"What are you going to do about West?"

"I don't know. He knows I don't like that side of him. It just sucks—I have to leave tomorrow, and I don't want to go on bad terms with him. Maybe he isn't perfect, but I really love him, Keely."

"Whoa, the L word? I didn't know you were that far gone." She laughs. I do, too, just as a crack of thunder explodes above our heads. Rain slams from the sky in an instant and drenches us. "Shit!" Keely shouts.

Up ahead, the gas station's fluorescent lights are blurry through the rain. "Come on," I yell, "this way!"

Our feet splash through puddles until we crash into the store. It's dry in here, but an oscillating fan sputters cold air at me, and the goosebumps on my skin are purple. The old man behind the counter looks up from this newspaper and gives us a funny, grumpy look. Keely and I share a laugh and run to the soda fridge as the storm lives on.

Just as we're paying for our drinks, a vehicle rolls outside of the gas station. Even through the heavy rain, I'd recognize Dean Bowman's van anywhere. Lightning flickers. Dean parks under the overhang and starts filling up his tank. There's no way Keely isn't going to notice him.

"Oh hey, it's Dean," Keely says as if she read my mind.

Outside, the rain pounds my shoulders like bullets. Keely and I take shelter under the overhang. Dean finishes pumping his gas as we walk up.

"What're you two doing walking around?" he asks. "Lovely storm, isn't it?"

Thunder booms and we both shiver from the cold. I cower farther under the overhang. *Please don't let me get hit by lightning.*

"Is this really the right time to be getting gas?" Keely shouts over the rain.

Dean glares at her. Sometimes, I swear there's hatred in Dean's eyes when he looks at Keely. Then again, he always looks like that. "My tank won't fill itself, Keely." A sudden, unnerving smile twitches at his lips. "Hey, you want a ride? Get in."

"You sure?" Keely asks.

"Yeah, it's no problem. You too, Olivia. In the van."

"No thanks," I say. "I'm staying not far from here. Come on, Keely, I'll wake my dad up and he'll drive you home."

"No way am I walking in this!"

Before I can protest, Keely gets into the van. Dean stares at me. "Well? You coming or what?"

This is giving me bad vibes, but I don't want to leave Keely alone with him. Miles is almost certainly in the van, too, but I can't see through the tinted windows. Everything in me screams *don't go*. I crawl in after Keely anyway. Sure enough, Faye's in the passenger seat, and Shawn and Miles are in the very back. I slide into the empty spot next to Keely in the middle row of chairs. As soon as the door traps me in the dusty, ketchup-smelling van, regret forms inside me. Dean gets in the driver's seat.

"Oh great. You." Faye looks back at me, her face malicious in the uneven light. "Did West kick your ass, too, or just his own brother's?"

Gulping, I glance back at Miles. He gazes out the window, into the empty parking lot. "West would never hurt me," I say and buckle my seatbelt.

"How do you know?" Faye says. "He hurts Miles."

"Has he ever hurt anyone else?"

Everyone is quiet, and Faye eventually says, "Probably."

"What West did wasn't okay no matter what," I say. "But to be fair—Miles, you did attack him first."

"Whatever, Liv," Miles mumbles. "Obviously you're taking his side. He's your boyfriend."

"I'm not taking anyone's side. What West did was awful, but I'm even more mad at all of you for what you did to Mr. Jenkens."

Dean scoffs and starts driving through the storm. Rain pounds on the windshield, and the sky is almost a shade of green. "This again? It was weeks ago, Olivia. And he's the animal killer. Why do you care?"

"He isn't the animal killer, they let him go."

"Why do you defend him so much?" Dean asks.

Faye juts out her bottom lip. "We all know Olivia likes to fix battered, broken things. Like my piece of shit brother." She clicks her tongue and sings, "You picked the wrong one, Liv."

"Shut up, Faye!" Miles snaps. Everyone flinches.

"Whoa, Hendricks." Shawn shifts away from him. "Calm down, man."

Keely and I exchange an uncomfortable-as-hell look. This is

weird. As we cruise down a dark street, my seatbelt grows heavy and constricts my ribcage.

"Where are we going?" I ask. "Keely's house is that way. Just drop us off there." I'll be in big trouble, but it's better than anyone knowing where the cottage is.

"You guys are zero fun," Dean says. More thunder and lightning. "We're heading to the cabin. Looks like you're stuck with us now."

"What?" My stomach drops. "No, I have to get back to my parents. I'll get in trouble. Forget this, just let me out."

Thunder cracks so loud, even Faye jumps. "Babe, maybe she's right," Faye whispers. "This weather is insane. Let's stop somewhere."

"My car, my rules."

Faye shuts up. The air cuts off from my lungs, but I try to practice the breathing that Dr. Levy taught me.

"Dean," I say calmly, "please let me out of the car."

"Don't stress so much. We're just cruising. You hungry?" He tosses back a paper bag. I peek into it to find fries with ketchup gushed all over them, and I kick it away.

"Okay, Dean, we don't want to go to the cabin," Keely says. "Seriously, drop us off."

We're already on the outskirts of town, passing by the population sign. The last time I drove out here, I was on my way to meet West's baby girl. The time before that, West and I were speeding so fast I felt like I was in a spaceship. That's probably the biggest thrill I've ever had since I fell. The accident made me timid, terrified to take risks. But West gave me the courage to try. I should be with him, not these people. But I'm trapped, and the deeper we drive into the forest, the more the water rises above my head. The raindrops on the windshield get lighter and the thunder dims. I shut my eyes. *Okay, everything's going to be fine. I'll just let him take me to the cabin, then I'll call Mom and Dad to pick me up.*

Dean nods at Faye. "Babe, pass me the booze."

She opens the glovebox and tosses him a silver flask.

"Are you seriously drinking and driving?" I ask.

"Calm down, city kid. Look, we're almost out of the storm." Dean laughs. "You might not be able to drink and drive back home, but it's cool down here. The roads are dead this time of night." Dean winks at me in the rear-view mirror.

Keely bites her lip. "Dean, wait . . . Liv is right. Drinking and driving is messed up."

"Did I ask you?" He glares at her, before he sighs and tosses the flask back at Faye. "Fine, have it your way. No drinking yet."

Everyone screams when Dean jerks the van to the side. He laughs as he steadies it.

"Dean, don't do that!" Keely shouts.

"You're all pussies," he says as he chuckles.

I need out of this car, but the van revs as Dean hurls us forward. If I try to jump out of a moving vehicle, I'll probably kill myself. An endless blur of trees speeds by the windows.

"Liv, are you okay?" Miles asks, but his voice alone is enough to freak me out.

"Leave me alone, Miles."

"Why are you such a stuck-up bitch?" Faye asks.

"She won't even talk to me," Miles says. "She always just runs away."

"Then make her talk now," Dean says. "She's not going anywhere."

"What I need to talk to her about is private."

Cornered, I sink into the seat. Maybe I should just jump out.

"Come on, Hendricks," Dean says. "Don't be a pussy. Tell her how you feel."

Miles is quiet for a long time before he says, "All right, Liv. Since you're here and you'll never talk to me alone, I want you to know that I wish things had been different between us. I thought what we had when we were kids was special."

"It—it was. But we were kids, Miles. We were friends. That's it."

"Everyone always said we'd get married, then you came back to town and you fell in love with—" Sighing, he stops himself. "Forget it. Wow, I sound so pathetic."

Panic rises like an ever-growing tide; it skyrockets over my head and swallows me whole.

"And now I don't know how to feel about you," Miles says. "I still love you, but I also hate you."

Hate. The word electrocutes me, and I think back to the footage of the man on the tape, then the dead deer outside my window. Even after everything, I never believed Miles could *hate* me.

"It was you, wasn't it, Miles?" I manage to ask.

"What?" he says.

"Outside of Keely's house, and the dead animals—it was all you, wasn't it?"

"Are you serious?"

My brain grinds against my skull, and I squint my eyes shut. I'm sinking. Suffocated. Trapped in this tiny space with these people I don't trust.

"Liv, what the hell?" Miles says. "This is what I was trying to say before, but you wouldn't listen . . ."

"Before what?" Anxiety overwhelms me, but right now, this is the only thing that makes sense. Miles did this. I know he did. If I'm trapped in this van with him, I want him to admit it.

"Yeah, before what, Hendricks?" Dean says.

"It isn't me, Liv," Miles says. "I know it isn't because—"

"Hendricks," Dean says through his teeth. "The fuck are you talking about?"

"Miles, seriously, shut up, man," Shawn whispers.

I don't understand any of this. We drive deeper into the darkness.

"No, I'm not taking the fall for this!" Miles says. "I know what happened! I know you guys lied about—"

The car lunges to the side. I scream. Metal crunches. Glass shatters. My body jerks forward, and the world turns red.

21

When I open my eyes, I feel seasick. My body sways like I'm on a rickety, wobbly boat. Pounding head, stiff neck, *excruciating* pain. My vision fades in and out of blackness. The van's headlights illuminate the kaleidoscope of glass scattered over the road. Why is everything upside down?

Strapped to the seat, my body is suspended, and blood throbs to my skull in waves. The seatbelt compresses my chest so hard my ribs might snap. Sucking in a breath, I unbuckle it and drop to the ground, which is now the roof of the upside-down van. More pain jolts through my neck, and shards of glass pierce my palms.

"Keely!" I say. She hangs over me, her black curls drooping like wilted flowers. I've never seen a more peaceful look on her face.

The silence in the van is deafening. Dean and Faye are strapped to their seats in the front like lifeless dummies. The back of the car is distorted, but I can make out Shawn with a stream of blood trickling down his cheek. I crank my neck back to check on Miles but wince when pain shoots up my spine. *I need to get help.*

My door is crumpled shut, so I squeeze through the broken window and yelp as tiny cuts howl over every inch of my skin. Once I haul myself out of the van, I stumble to my feet and cover my mouth with my cold, bloody hands. The entire back of the vehicle is caved into itself, the rumpled metal angular and pointed. It's like a movie prop. This isn't real.

The van's headlights brighten the empty road. An evergreen tree takes up the width of the street with broken bark and branches around it. The thick smell of motor oil and blood merges with wood, pine, and nature. Dusty clouds creep over the moon. The storm is gone.

The storm.

I back away from the vehicle. Before the crash, I freaked out at Miles. Even though Dean was acting like a maniac, I could have caused this.

Get it together. Digging my phone from my back pocket, I try to call 911, but there's no service. Nothing works. I scream everyone's names: Keely, Faye, Shawn—even Dean. But no one answers. Desperate for help, I sprint up the road, the asphalt pounding at the flimsy soles of my Vans, and *oh God*, it hurts. Everything hurts. The sound of my feet hammering the pavement evaporates until there's nothing but an insufferable ring in my ears. This winding road leads into emptiness and trees, but all I do is run, because I have to help them. I have to help Keely.

Tears wet my cheeks. My lungs heave, but I won't stop. At a mailbox up ahead, I dive toward it.

The Hendrickses' cabin.

We were so close. Hope swells through me, because light glimmers through the trees.

My legs are numb, but they carry me toward the cabin. A dim lantern illuminates the driveway, but everything else is doused in the darkness of the night. All I need is to get close enough to the Wi-Fi. Almost there.

When my foot catches on a root, my knees buckle. White-hot pain flashes through me when I collide with the sharp stones of the driveway. Every sensation in my body amplifies; the bruising on my legs, the cuts on the palms of my hands. My pocket is empty. Panicked, I pat down my clothes.

My phone is gone. I must have dropped it while I was running.

I don't even have the strength to cry.

Defeated, I roll on my back and stare up at the stars. They're so much brighter out here; millions of shimmery dots stipple the navy blue, and the tops of the trees extend like hands reaching for home.

Home. Where is home for me now? I have no idea, but I would give anything to see New York again, the crowded streets, the food carts. The girls on my volleyball team—I took them for granted. Everything in the city was safe, and only now do I understand how rare and precious it is to feel safe.

The sound of feet dragging on stone cuts into my daze. Ignoring the pain, I jump to my feet and tune into my surroundings. A voice resounds in the distance.

"*Olivia!*"

A cold chill comes over me. "Miles? Is that you?"

Dead silence. At the end of the driveway, a figure limps into the moonlight.

"Miles!" I run to him, but skid to a halt. Miles's shirt is torn open to reveal scarlet flesh, and his blond curls cloak his eyes. "You're— you're hurt."

When he falls toward me, I stagger back. "Olivia," he croaks out.

"Miles, we need to get help. Give me your phone."

"Leave them." He coughs and sprays blood all over me. I jump back, but he steps closer, eyes still veiled. "This is where you were supposed to be with me, Liv. This is where you chose *him*."

"Miles, stop." I step away and start crying. *Please don't let this be who he is.* I've never wanted to be more wrong about anything in my life. "Please, Miles, help me get to the others."

"I should kill you for what you did to me."

In this light, the image is clear: Miles in the black hood, peeking into the windows of Keely's house. The overwhelming fear—or *knowing*—that he wants to hurt me submerges my entire being.

Miles's hand extends toward me, but I vanish like smoke. Bolting to the cabin, I try to rip the door open. It's useless. I bang on the windows and move around the sound of the house. Maybe if I break one, I can use a piece of glass to defend myself. But Miles is right behind me—he tries to grab me, but the fabric of my skirt tears through his fingers.

Shit! Where am I supposed to go? There's nothing but trees, so I dive into the forest. My skirt shreds on a bush as thorns claw at my bare legs. I trip over my own feet and land face-first in a tangle of nettles, their barbed leaves slicing my cheeks.

"*Olivia!*" My name comes out harsh and full of hate. He rips through the underbrush, but I keep running. My throat hurts from screaming.

"Leave me alone, Miles! Just stay back! Why are you doing this?"

"I have to! Don't you get it? We were supposed to get married, Liv. That was our plan. But you chose West. You chose *West*. Do you have any idea how bad that makes me look? To lose you to West, like I've been losing to him all my life?"

"It doesn't matter right now! We have to get help. Don't you care about Faye?"

"You should really think more about helping yourself."

Oh God, he's going to kill me. This has to be a nightmare. Anything but the truth. Tangled up in the fingers of a dead tree, I stop and hold my breath. My pulse roars so loud I'm sure Miles will hear it if he gets too close. His feet crack over branches and dead leaves. He'll catch me if I run, so I sink to the ground, dried pine needles digging into my legs. Breathe. Just breathe. There's still hope.

Miles appears out of thin air and chases me deeper into the forest. Giving up isn't an option, but my heart stops when I splash into something cold and wet. The moon ripples off the lake surrounding me.

The water.

I've reached a dead end.

Swim. You have to swim.

But I *can't.*

Fear wraps around my throat as I take another step into the water. Just swim. I can do it. I have to. If I could do it with West, I can do it without him. But Miles is behind me, walking toward me, the grin on his face just like the one from my dream.

"There you are."

"Miles, stop—get back!"

He grabs me, and everything becomes cold and silent. Miles's face is contorted through the surface of the water, his strong hands pressed to my chest, holding me under. When he pulls me up, I gasp for air.

"Stop!" I scream. "Please, stop!"

"I can't." Miles pulls my face close to his, his breath sickeningly hot on my lips. "Nobody's even going to miss you. Do you think West will care? He won't. Your parents? They'll get over it. You're nothing special. I don't even know why I ever liked you."

I grip onto his wrist as he holds me by my shirt. "Miles, stop, please. You can still stop this. If you let me go, I won't tell anyone, I swear." I'm grasping at straws, but every moment above the water is invaluable. I just need to survive.

Miles says nothing as he dunks me into the water again. His strength is tremendous, and I'm as weak as a paper doll. My body betrays me; my kicks and flails do nothing. I should have trusted my instincts. My dreams warned me, my gut warned me. But my stupid, stupid mind convinced me to get into that van, and now I'm dead because of it.

As Miles's hands crush me like two mallets, my heart fills with despair. This will destroy my parents. I picture my mom in my dad's arms in that cottage, waiting for me to get back. And West—will he care? Is he even thinking about me right now? I wish he were here to save me. More than that, I wish I were strong enough to save myself.

I reach for something to grab, any kind of weapon, a rock to bash Miles's head in with, but everything is too small and sludgy. Bits of pebbles slip through my fingers as the strangest fog sweeps over me. *The calm.* It's familiar, cradles me like I'm a baby again, resting in my mother's arms. Nothing runs through my head anymore, no more fear. I just know it's too late.

I've always wondered what it would feel like to die, ever since I learned what dying really is. I guess it's just . . . peaceful.

22

I wake up in my grave. Lake water submerges half of my body, and the smell of algae and dirt circles me. Soaking wet and chilled to the core, I shoot up and suck in a breath. I'm on the shoreline. Soggy skin, scratched-up legs, shredded clothes sopping with mud.

I'm not dead?

Yelping, I inch away from the water until I'm on the grass. Sunlight peeks through the trees and sparkles off the water. A flutter of sparrows dances over the blue and salmon sky; a hummingbird pecks at a tree; a squirrel hops across the branches of two birches.

There's no sign of Miles anywhere. Carefully, I stand on wobbly legs. Just because I can't see him doesn't mean he's not here. He could be waiting for me to come out so he can torment me more. With daylight on my side, I pick up a branch sturdy enough to be a weapon.

"Miles?" I call out.

No reply.

"If you're out here, say something!"

I have no idea why he didn't kill me, but a thunderclap of memories hits me. Keely strapped to the seat. It all feels like a bad dream, but now that I'm awake and the sun has dawned, the evidence is still here. I have to get back to the road.

The trek through the forest is painful but easier to maneuver with the sun to guide me. Still with the branch in my hands, I keep glancing over my shoulder for Miles, but he never shows up. The thought of Keely's safety becomes my north star. I pass under canopies of leaves and dodge spiky bushes until I reach the road.

Free from the shade, the sun beats down on my waterlogged skin. I drag myself up the empty road. Something shines up ahead, so I run for it. My phone. It's still on and weakly connected to the cabin's Wi-Fi. Forty missed calls on Facebook, and the clock reads 6:00 a.m. Relief soaks me. Just as I go to call my parents, West's name appears on my screen. I answer immediately.

"West?"

"Olivia! Jesus Christ, you're alive. Where are you?"

"I'm—West, there was a crash—"

"I know. Where are you? They're trying to find you."

"Miles, he—"

"I know." West's voice breaks. "Olive, I know."

Miles tried to kill me. It still doesn't feel real.

"The cops found the van, but you're weren't in it," West says. "Where are you?"

"I'm on the road, near your parents' cabin."

"Someone will be there soon. Are you okay?"

"I don't know. What about Keely?"

"No idea, but I've got to call the cops and tell them where you are. Just stay put. Don't move."

He hangs up. I hug myself, feeling cold and empty and scared and so, so powerless. Holding my head between my hands, I try to block out the emotions. It's no use. As I lie on the dewy grass, I slowly turn to stone.

When I open my eyes, three vehicles are parked in front of me: a cop car, an ambulance, and my parents' rental sedan.

"Olivia!" Mom wails. She runs toward me but stops as I pull myself up. My parents wrap me in a tight hug.

"Guys, stop. It hurts."

They pull away, teary-eyed.

"We thought we lost you," Dad says. "Thank God you're okay."

"I'm okay." I grab Mom's hands. "Wait, Mom, Keely!"

"She's okay." Mom wipes her tears and smiles. "You're both okay."

I sigh in relief. "And the others?"

"We'll get to them."

Paramedics check me for injuries, but after a quick examination, confirm I'm physically fine other than the cuts. Still, they say I need to get to the hospital and get cleaned up to prevent an infection. But first, the cops say they need a statement. Mom and Dad keep their hands on my shoulders as I explain what happened. One officer, a stout man with a feather of hair on his head, keeps looking at me strangely. Then it hits me: he was the cop I apparently almost attacked the night I saw the dead deer outside my window. The thought is unnerving, so I focus on the other cop, Officer Maggie Jones. But when I tell her about Miles, even she avoids my eyes. I guess it isn't easy to listen to a girl recount being chased down and nearly drowned to death.

"So, wait," Officer Jones says, "you're saying *Miles Hendricks* chased you through the woods to the lake, where he then attempted to drown you?"

I've already explained it to her twice, but I nod again. "Yeah. It was Miles."

Mom's grip on my shoulder tightens. "Livvie, can you give your dad and me a moment alone with the officers?"

"Oh, okay . . . sure."

The cops eye me warily before they step aside with my parents and talk near their car. I look out into the forest, the mix of pine green and jade, the chestnut trunks of the trees, the overgrowth of weeds. It's not so menacing in the light of day.

"Come on, Olivia." Dad approaches me, and the cops get in their car. "The paramedics will take you to the hospital, we'll be right behind—"

"No, I want to stay with you," I insist.

With an exhausted breath, Dad mutters to a paramedic, "Think we can drive her? She's not seriously hurt, right?"

The man nods. Mom gives my arm a gentle squeeze and says, "Go on and get in the car, Livvie."

Something's off with my parents, but I slide into the backseat. My reflection in the mirror mortifies me—purple lips, blood all over my paper-white skin. I look like a living corpse, and these freezing wet clothes are going to make me sick for sure. Some of my cuts are yellow and bruising. My parents slip into the car and remain eerily silent as the drive begins.

"Are you sure you're okay?" Mom asks. "I can hear your teeth chattering."

"I just need a hot shower, and to see the others."

"About that . . ."

As we wind around the bend, more memories return to me. Up ahead, cop cars surround the wreckage of the van. Cops stand around and talk with their hands on their hips. The morose aura in the air is like thick pollution.

"Everyone's fine, right?" I ask.

Mom lets out a quiet sob. "Olivia, I'm sorry."

"Why? Did something happen?" At her silence, I scratch at my arms. "I don't understand. Mom, what's going on? Dad?"

Dad's eyes wither in the rear-view mirror, and he refuses my gaze. Mom turns back with tears dripping down her cheeks.

"Miles couldn't have done all that to you, Livvie. I'm sorry, it's impossible."

"What are you talking about?"

"Olivia, Miles is dead. The crash killed him."

23

My parents always watched the news. Both when we lived in Caldwell and after we moved to New York, our dinners were spent on the couch in front of the TV as reporters talked about politics and crime. I rarely listened—what was happening on my phone seemed far more important. But sometimes, when a story was particularly tragic, I would tune in and wonder what it'd be like to have the firsthand details of something like that. To be a part of it, not just a spectator through a screen.

Now I know. It's like floating outside of my body, wishing none of it was real.

The flat-screen TV above my hospital bed has been muted since I awoke, but when a grim-faced reporter appears on the screen, I turn it up. His voice bounces off the white walls around me.

"His body was impaled when the vehicle flipped into a ditch, the back of the vehicle colliding with a tree. His death was almost instant, and we think he suffered very little. That's the only comfort we can offer the friends and family of seventeen-year-old Miles Hendricks at this time.

"Miles's twin sister, Faye Hendricks, is in the hospital in critical condition, but we're being told she'll pull through. The other passengers, whose names are being withheld at the request of their guardians, seem to have escaped the tragedy with minor injuries.

"As for the nature of the collision, all we know now is that an eighteen-year-old male was the driver and that it's being investigated as an alcohol-related accident."

I shut off the TV and sink into the bed.

Miles died on impact. Nobody tried to drown me in the lake that night.

It's been almost two days since the crash, and no one has been in to see me except my parents, not even West. That's good, though. I don't want anyone to see me like this, and I don't know how I'll face him knowing his brother is dead and I accused him of so many things.

I went catatonic after Mom told me about Miles's death. My voice just isn't there, which leaves a lot of room for static noise in my head. And thought-loops. I've had a lot of those.

Miles died on impact. Nobody drowned me in the lake.

Dr. Levy once told me that sometimes when you experience something too traumatic for your brain to handle, your mind can trick you into thinking it wasn't real. Maybe you'll think, *This can't be happening. It has to be a dream.*

But what about when the opposite happens? When I dream of something so real that my mind convinces me it *is* real?

I can still feel him chasing me. Still hear the hatred in his voice as he bellowed my name through the forest. But I know now it was impossible. The police described to me the way Miles was found.

They used nice words like "twisted," "bent," and "with God," but what they meant was crunched, contorted, and slaughtered. It was evident on the faces of the men who pulled him out when they came to interview me: they had seen death. If I thought hard enough, I could picture Miles's mangled, bloody form burned into their retinas. I can almost see it myself now.

What did you want to tell me before the crash, Miles?

My sadness is chilled by the medication they pumped into me, but it's there, meshed with confusion and shame.

Mom knocks on the door before she pokes her head in. "Livvie?" When I don't reply, she steps in and holds out her phone. "It's Dr. Levy. Do you think you're up for a conversation yet?"

Only my parents and those two cops know what I thought I saw that night. The officers agreed to keep it a secret, and Mom said I can't tell anyone what happened. It would be disrespectful to Miles's family, and to his memory. She's right. The only person I can talk to is Dr. Levy, but my body is still numb.

With pursed lips, Mom hands me the phone and slips out of the room. Dr. Levy's face is on the screen with her office in the background. It's like looking into a world I know so well, but don't recognize anymore.

"Hi, Olivia," Dr. Levy says with a warm smile.

"Hi."

"Are you ready to talk now?"

I'll probably never be ready, but I nod.

My voice comes out weak, like rust scraping against metal, but I tell Dr. Levy everything. About the dreams of Miles. The animal killer. The lurker outside of Keely's house. Even West. I allow myself to be an open faucet, and by the time I'm done, Dr. Levy's eyes are full of a sadness I've never seen on her.

"I'm sorry you've had to go through all this, Olivia," she says. "You weren't ready to go back. I'm sorry."

"It isn't your fault. I wanted to be here, I really did. But Miles—" I lower my head in shame. "I don't understand why I saw what I did."

"We'll have to talk more once you return to New York, but it sounds as though you had a hyperrealistic night terror, Olivia. A combination of that and sleepwalking must have been how you ended up in the lake. And because Miles was with you the night you fell off the cliff, it's possible you subconsciously associated him with the event. Maybe that's why you started to view him as evil when you came back to Caldwell Beach."

So this thing with Miles—it was like the deer outside of my window at the cottage: not real.

I say, "But do you think Miles could really have been the guy outside Keely's house? Could he have been the animal killer? Or was he trying to warn me who it was before he died?"

"That's something I can't answer. You'll have to ask the police to keep you updated on the case. You don't have to tell them you suspected Miles, it won't do any good now. And if Miles was the one killing animals, the town will know if it stops happening. As for what he wanted to tell you before he died . . . unfortunately, only Miles knows that."

Images of Miles flicker through my mind. It's like I was blinded, clouded by his bad behavior until that was all I could see. Throughout the summer, every time I've thought of Miles, I thought of the time he tried to kiss me, and all the terrifying dreams I had of him, and how petty I thought he was.

But I never stopped once to empathize with him. To imagine what he was going through, watching me choose West over him.

"I'm a horrible person."

"Please don't say that, Olivia. You have a condition—you can't hate yourself for it."

"It's about more than my condition. I knew Miles was hurt but I completely ignored his feelings. Now he's dead, and the last conversation I had with him was in my head. It isn't fair to him. I had problems with him this summer, but I didn't want him to *die*."

Dr. Levy is quiet. "It's a horrible tragedy, but I need you to understand that it wasn't your fault."

She's only doing her job and trying to help me, but I don't want to talk anymore. "Thanks for calling me," I say. "I feel a little better."

"Call me if you need anything else. I've been in contact with your psychiatrist here in New York and we've talked to the doctors there. We all agree that maybe the medication you're on now isn't the right one for you. They're going to prescribe you with something to help you sleep until you get home. They'll also let you know how to start weaning off your current drugs. I'll see you when you get to the city."

"Thanks, Dr. Levy. Bye."

When Mom reappears, I update her on what Dr. Levy said, and even she is at a loss for words.

"Mom, how could I imagine something so real? I know Miles didn't do all that to me, but it feels like he did. And now I feel so guilty because he's dead, but I still—" I choke on a sob. "I remember him as a monster."

Mom holds my hands. "I don't know, sweetie. I wish I had more answers for you, but we'll work it all out once we get home, and everything's going to be okay, I promise."

"Okay." I don't believe it, but say it because it's what she needs to hear.

"Keely's here to see you. Do you want me to send her away?"

"No. I think I'm ready to face her."

Mom leaves, and moments later, Keely's arms are wrapped around my neck, her familiar smell surrounding me. "Liv, oh my God, you're okay!"

I want to say I'm glad she's not hurt, but the words aren't there, so I just hug her tightly. Keely pulls up a chair and sits. Bandages cover the cuts on her skin, and the pain of the crash is evident in her eyes.

"I'm so sorry, Liv, this is all my fault. I never should've gotten in that stupid van."

"You didn't make me do anything. None of this is your fault."

"And oh my God, Miles . . . I can't even believe he's dead. Like, I can't even process it."

"I know. I don't know what to think."

"What happened to you before the crash, Liv? You were freaking out."

"Can you just tell me one thing first? Did I cause the crash?"

"No! Last thing I remember, Dean was all pissed off at Miles, and then . . ." She shivers. "No, the crash wasn't your fault, Liv. No one thinks it was. It was Dean's fault for being reckless. He must've gotten distracted by whatever you and Miles were fighting about."

There's no way for sure to know whether I caused the crash or not, but I appreciate Keely not blaming me. Even if I still blame myself.

"What was that, anyway?" Keely asks. "Did you really think he was the animal killer?"

"I don't know. I was having a panic attack, Keel. They happen sometimes. It's because of my PTSD."

"Right, totally should've figured that." Keely plays with the brace-let on her wrist, our friendship bracelet. "But why did you accuse Miles of all those things?"

I swallow, unable to find the words.

"I know he upset you when he tried to kiss you, but I have to be hon-est, I could never picture him hurting anything. I mean, it's *Miles* . . ."

"I can't really explain it, Keel. I'm sorry."

"Guess it's over now, anyway. And I'm here for you no matter what. You're still my best friend. I know I was a crappy friend this summer, but I was just . . . I wanted Shawn to like me and for every-one to think I was cool. And now Miles is dead and everything is so screwed up."

"I know, but it's not your fault either. And I'm sorry too. I was the crappy friend."

"No, you weren't. West is somewhere in the hospital. He wants to see you. Should I go find him?"

"No, I should go to him."

West may not have gotten along with Miles, but I know him. He'll be destroyed over this. Talking to Keely has given me the strength to see him.

"Okay." Keely smiles. "Let's go together."

I move through the brightly lit halls, a walking corpse. Since we're under eighteen, we were put in the children's ward. The walls are painted with Care Bears and cartoon bees, murals of grassy hills and monarch butterflies. I've been fed nothing but chocolate parfaits and apple slices, because I can't stomach anything else.

As we're turning the corner, Dean's voice makes my hair stand on end. Even though he's newly eighteen, they must have just put him in with us. Keely and I turn to see him exiting a room in the jacket and jeans he wore during the crash, and he tugs at the hospital band around his wrist until it tears. He tosses it on the ground and stops when he sees us and frowns, like he wasn't expecting us to even be alive.

I'll always blame myself for what happened to Miles, but this is on Dean too.

"Olivia, Keely," Dean drones out. "Glad to see you two alive and well."

"How are they just letting you go?" I say.

"I wasn't drunk."

"But you crashed the van!"

"Don't know what to tell you. They found no booze in my blood, so I'm free to go." He tries to breeze past us, but I grab his arm. Dean slowly turns back. "What?"

"Miles is *dead*, Dean."

I don't know what I want from him. Maybe some hint of remorse, but he just scoffs once. "Don't act like you cared about Miles just because he's dead, Olivia."

His words are scathing and cruel, but they hurt the most because they're true. Dean adjusts his jacket before he disappears down the hall.

The interaction leaves a bad taste in my mouth, but we continue down the hall. Keely directs me toward Faye's room, where the door is open a crack.

"Faye, just listen to me, please," West says from the other side.

"No!" Faye shouts. "Get away from me, Weston. You're only making things worse."

"I want to change. Just give me a chance, please. I'm sorry I was such an ass. I'm sorry I didn't try to help you, or—"

"Don't you get it? I don't care what you have to say! You've been horrible to us our whole lives, and now suddenly you want to fix it because Miles is dead?"

"I know. I was selfish and shitty to both of you. But I'm so sorry. I thought we had more time to fix things. I thought—"

"It's too late. Go." Her voice is heartbroken. "Please, West. Go."

West comes out of the room, and he doesn't even see me before he disappears through the doors to outside. Keely and I stand there, stunned.

"Should I chase him?" I ask.

"I don't know, Liv . . ."

West should have a minute alone. I step in front of Faye's door while Keely stays behind. When Faye sees me, she stares blankly at the wall. Slowly, I enter the room. Her skin is paper white, and blood-soaked gauze is wrapped around her head and arms. The bags under her eyes are sunken so deep, they're almost purple. The look on her face is hollow.

"Oh great," she says. "Another one."

It doesn't carry the same usual annoyance; the tone of her voice is heavy, like she's putting all her energy into keeping it together. Maybe acting like her usual self is her way of coping. I don't know.

I can't even imagine what Faye is going through right now, but it's much bigger than what I am. Miles was her other half.

"Hey." I hold my hands behind my back. "I'm glad you're okay."

Faye blinks at me. "You know, it's funny. I think you and Weston are the only two people in the world that I hate equally. I look at you both and I just can't decide who's worse. I've barely been up for five hours and today has already been the shittiest day of my life. Now I'm being told that Miles's funeral is in two days. Not really sure what to think about that."

The funeral. It didn't even cross my mind.

"I see that look on your face," Faye utters. "After the way you hurt him, I don't want you anywhere near his funeral. But—" She looks away, tears streaming down her cheeks. "But as much as I've always hated it, Miles did love you. A lot more than you realized."

My eyes water. "I'm sorry, Faye. I didn't want any of this to happen."

She's quiet for a moment. "I know I have a messed-up way of expressing things sometimes, but I tried to get you to at least notice Miles this summer. I at least wanted you to talk to him. But instead you shunned him. I get he like, tried to kiss you, and did petty stuff, but what changed so much, Liv? When we were kids, nothing could keep you away from him. He tried to apologize to you for the way he acted."

I don't know how to explain to her that my negative feelings toward Miles were about so much more than the petty things he did. They were about more than the day he kissed me too. It's all too confusing; multiple versions of him exist in my head, and I have no idea which ones are real and which ones are a result of my own paranoia and nightmares.

"We just—he wasn't who I remembered him being," I say. "And I wasn't who he remembered me being. I think we both had expectations for each other that we couldn't live up to. And then—"

"And then you chose West."

"Yes. I chose West."

Faye looks at the wall. "I can't blame you for everything. I mean, Dean was my boyfriend." Her bottom lip trembles, and she cries harder. "Now my other half is dead because of my shitty choices. Jesus Christ. Have you seen Dean?"

"Did no one tell you? They let him go . . ."

"What? Is he here?"

"I don't know. We saw him take off."

"He should be arrested. I—I don't want him anywhere near me. He killed my brother, Olivia."

"Okay, we can tell a nurse not to let him in."

She lets out a breath. "Yes, I want that."

I glance down at her arms, covered in bandages. What's beneath is more than the evidence of the crash, but I already poked my nose too deep into her business once before. Faye catches me looking, though.

"You were right," she says, almost too low for me to hear.

I straighten up. "What?"

"You were right, Olivia. About Dean."

The air between us grows colder.

"He burned me," she whispers. "The first time, I thought it was just like—a joke. He told me it was normal to give people 'smileys,' and I thought it was okay because Shawn had some, too, but they were older than mine. But then he just never stopped."

"But Miles said you did them yourself."

"That's what I told him. I didn't want him to worry, and I didn't want to break up with Dean."

"Why? Dean was hurting you—why did you stay with him?"

"I don't know. Somehow, despite everything, I thought we were in love. He never hurt me any other way—it was just the burns. And they always came out of nowhere, even when he was in a good mood. I was so scared of upsetting him, but I can't forgive him for this. Ever since I found out Miles is dead, it's like I've woken up from some sort of twisted dream. I never want to see Dean Bowman again."

"Miles knew Dean was hurting you?"

Miles's voice rings in my ears, the words he told me at the barbeque: "*Someone I care about could be in serious danger.*"

"Yeah," Faye says. "He tried to get me to break up with him. He tried to protect me by always being there, but . . ."

My memories before the crash are fragmented, but I do remember Miles saying he knew someone had lied. But I don't know who he was talking about.

I shake my head. I'm too sedated to digest any of this right now.

"Don't mistake what I'm saying," Faye says. "I still hate you for how you made my brother feel, but you noticed something was up with Dean and me, and you tried to help, so thanks."

"Of course. I was worried about you."

She looks away. "You can go now. Please."

"I'll ask Keely to get a nurse to make sure Dean can't get in, okay?"

"Thanks."

Even though Faye and I have never liked each other, I've known her for as long as I've known Miles and West. She was always mean to me. Attention seeking. Yet I thought she was beautiful, and I envied her more than I cared to admit. And I think I now know, the real reason I crawled along the edge of that cliff five years ago. It wasn't because I wanted everyone to think I was cool or daring or badass. It was because I cared about Faye Hendricks's opinion. I never thought seeing her in this much pain would make me realize, for the first time in my life, that I care about her too.

o o o

I leave Faye's room feeling hollow. I have all the reasons in the world to feel guilty about loving West, but all I want is to make sure he's okay.

When I get outside, I find myself in the afterglow of sunset, on a concrete path lined with blue and pink hydrangeas. The late-August air is warm, but a cool breeze breathes through my cotton hospital gown. A distant memory unearths itself, blooms like a flower I had long forgotten about. Miles and I were seven, and he had fallen and scraped his knee, so I'd put leaves on his cut to work as a bandage because I didn't know any better. He thanked me anyway, even though he knew they weren't helping.

West is sitting on the ledge of one of the gardens and hides his face in his hands. It shatters me; I never thought I would see him cry.

"West?"

He wipes his tears with his wrists. "Olive. Fuck, sorry." I sit next to him, no words on my tongue. After several moments of sniffling, West says, "I'm sorry I didn't visit you sooner. I was going to after I talked to Faye."

"Don't apologize, it's okay. I talked to her too."

"She has every right to hate my guts. The last time I ever saw Miles, I hurt him."

"I'm so sorry, West."

Now we're both crying. He smooths his hands over his face and takes a deep breath. "I haven't been able to sleep at all. I can't stop thinking about him. All I can think about is how horribly I treated him, and then I feel even more fuckin' guilty because it isn't fair to suddenly feel bad now that he's dead. But I do. I just thought we had more time to change things."

"I'm sorry, West." It's so robotic, but I don't know what to say. We're on the same page, though. After all the things I thought about Miles this summer, it isn't fair to suddenly care about him now that he's gone.

But now everything is so *final*. When Miles was alive, there was drama, but somewhere in my mind, that drama had an end. Not like this. Not with death.

"When we were kids," West says, "my dad used to yell at me when I acted up, and it made me feel powerless. I hated it. More than that,

I hated the fact that Miles didn't get any of it. I didn't understand, you know? Why'd my dad hate me so much, but loved Miles and Faye? But I get it now. It's because he didn't give a shit about my mom, and he loves Beatrice. My dad never even wanted to have me, was just pushed into the role when my real mom died. And I guess the only way I could ever feel like I had any power in that house was to beat on Miles. Even just the other day, when I hit him—God, I never changed."

His words give me chills. "You took it out on him because it made you feel powerful?"

"Yeah. But once we got a little older, Miles started to realize he could outsmart me. He could manipulate my dad to get me into trouble. If I beat on Miles or pissed him off, it wouldn't be long before my dad would beat on me. But—can I blame him? He wanted me to pay for hurting him, and *fuck*." He crams his palms into his eyes and cries. "Fuck, Olivia, my little brother hated me, and he had every right to. For a while, I wanted to make things better with Miles, but my relationship with him was so fucked up, and he always had his guard up around me, so I never got anywhere with him. And I guess I gave up. So when you came back to town and we hit it off, I didn't care if he liked you. I went for you anyway, Olive. I can only imagine how much he hated me for that."

This conversation was bound to happen, but it still makes me nauseated with guilt. "Same here, but—" My voice breaks. "But I love you, West. And I never led Miles on. I didn't feel like we owed him anything."

He puts his hand on the back of my neck and gently squeezes. "We didn't. And I love you too." He pulls away. "But I'm going to need some time."

"I know. Me too."

"I'm going to take some anger management classes or something. Therapy. I think I need it."

"That could be good for you, West."

"Yeah." West collects himself and takes a deep breath. "What happened to you in the woods, anyway?"

I stiffen. In my head, Miles's phantom voice shouts my name.

"Olive?" West nudges me, and I snap out of it. "Your parents told me you ran off, and"—he points to my arms—"you're all scratched up."

"Yeah, I . . . I lost my phone, then I wanted to get help and . . ."

"Did something happen?"

Lying isn't an option, but I can't tell him the whole truth either. "Yeah. It was like that night again, when I went to the hospital after seeing the dead deer. I saw things again, but I can't tell you what, okay?"

"Okay, I get it. But are you good now?"

"For now. I need to get home to the city and see my psychologist, but not until the funeral." I pause. "Is it maybe okay if I come with you? Not as a couple, just—"

"Of course. You don't have to ask."

With a nod, I weakly smile. I don't know what we are now, but I'll need him with me. This thing that lives inside me wears Miles's skin like a cloak—it looks like him, talks like him, sounds like him. But it isn't him. It's me. And I'm terrified to go to his funeral and stand around the people who loved him and know that, even with his flaws, I didn't deserve to be friends with Miles Hendricks. He wasn't perfect, but he was far from evil. Maybe someday I can tell West exactly what I saw, but it's my secret. I'll spend a lot of time living with it.

I want to keep listening to West's voice, even if we just talk about nothing, but everything is different now. I check the time. "I have to get back to my room soon," I say.

We stand, looking at anything but each other. I try to keep it together, but when West pulls me to his chest, my knees go weak. I collapse in his arms and clutch at his black T-shirt, breathing in his achingly familiar smell. West kisses me on the side of the head.

"I'll see you soon, Olive."

And then he's gone.

24

The hospital discharges me the next day. Before I know it, I'm back at the cottage as if nothing ever happened, but instead of wallowing in bed, I sit with Mom in the living room and watch the VHS cassettes left behind. A sad collection of movies previous cottagers must have watched during their holiday—a few horror films mixed in with animated classics. Mom twirls my hair as I'm curled up on her lap, and *The Little Mermaid* plays on the old box television.

I try to focus on the movie, but my mind wanders. Dad had to drive home to check on the shop—seven hours to New York, seven hours back—but I know he won't miss Miles's funeral. I've never even been to one. All of my grandparents are alive and well, and I've never seen death firsthand, except my own near-death experience. I have to admit, it feels exactly how I imagined it would: empty.

The sky outside is dark, and a salty breeze leaks through the open window and sways the pale-blue curtains. The waves crash against the shore. Mom scrolls through her phone behind my head.

"Livvie?"

"Yeah?"

Mom picks up the remote and pauses the movie. "Maybe now isn't the best time, but . . . I thought you might want to look at some pictures. To prepare you for tomorrow."

When I sit up, Mom hands me the phone. An album she'd uploaded to Facebook years ago shows a reel of my childhood memories from before the accident. I barely use Facebook, so I didn't even know these were up.

My voice becomes lodged. With a somber smile, Mom taps on one of the photos, and it opens to a picture of Miles and me as kids on the beach—the same beach that roars outside of the window now. The ocean is alive, and even though it's night now, I know the sun blazes on the other side of the Earth. I'm alive, too, but one thing in this photo is gone forever. I still can't swallow that.

"I remember this day," Mom says.

"Me too." I can't help but laugh, even though tears drip down my cheeks. "Look, he's covered in sand. I buried him all the way to his neck, remember?"

"Like it was yesterday."

After this, we ran into the water, and I still remember the feeling of cold, crystal blue splashing up my bare legs. I feared nothing. Not the turbulence of the sea, not my own mind. Definitely not Miles. I've spent this whole summer trying to be that girl again, but instead, I descended into something I never imagined.

Overwhelmed, I say, "I need some air."

"Wait on the porch," Mom says. "I'll be there in a minute."

Outside, the sky is completely clear. I lean my elbows against the rickety wooden banister of the porch, and the chipped white paint digs into my skin.

I breathe in deeply. It wasn't the ocean that hurt me this summer; it was my own mind.

There's still one thing I haven't done yet. I don't want to be scared anymore. No, I *won't* be scared anymore.

Peeling off my shirt, I run toward the shore, just as Mom comes outside.

"Olivia, stop!" she screeches, but I've already kicked off my shorts. I walk into the icy water until my ankles are wet. Pebbly sand seeps between my toes. The waves push against my body, but I shut my eyes and listen. The *whoosh* is something I've known my whole life, the natural soundtrack to my existence.

It doesn't scare me anymore.

"Livvie, please," Mom begs. I look over my shoulder to see her crying, and she holds her arms out to grab me.

"Mom, it's okay. I have to do this."

Before she can protest, I reach into a part of my mind that had been buried under layers of sand for all these years. A sense of freedom surges through me as I point my arms into the air and dive under water. The dark blue, along with a freezing numbness, submerses me. When I kick, my body rockets forward, and so many memories flow into my mind.

There are things to be scared of in this world, but this isn't one of them. Because when the waves pull me under, all I have to do is kick. When the water gets too deep, I can swim to shore and stand again.

Air sweeps into my lungs when I emerge and smooth down my soaking wet hair. My breath catches, because a meteor shower slices through the night sky. There are so many shooting stars, I almost can't believe it. They pierce the darkness in a needle of light before they vanish.

"Mom, look!"

"I see them, sweetie," she says, laughing with me. Mom is already half in the water, her pajamas drenched. "Now come on back here, please!"

She's going to have a heart attack if I don't stop. I've done what I needed to do—I swam on my own, without West, without anyone. Smiling, I run back to the shore, into my mom's arms. We go back to the cottage together, but I take one more glance at the endless black and blue on the horizon.

I need to stop trying to fix the girl who fell, and focus on being the girl who survived.

25

When I pictured how Miles's funeral would go, I saw rain. A sky
blanketed in gray and the odd flicker of lightning over the mourners'
faces, because funerals are always gloomy on TV. But not today; the
sun shines the same way it does on any other summer day, and blue
jays caw as they swoop over the graveyard. Church bells chime and
overpower the quiet sobs of Miles's family and friends.

West and I arrived together but haven't touched out of respect for
Miles. He cries beside me now as the casket sinks into the earth. A
priest in a black vestment with maroon accents watches it solemnly,
along with a crowd composed of Caldwell citizens and Miles's family.
I resist the urge to reach out and take West's hand.

Miles's body is in that cherrywood box, and it sends ripples of
dread through me. It was closed for the viewing, because what was

left of Miles was not how his family wanted him to be remembered.

The air is saturated with grief, bitter like saltwater on my tongue. Across the circle, Faye wears a black dress that covers every inch of her skin. Beatrice keeps her composure, but tears stream through her makeup. Brian remains a statue, holding his hands firmly behind his back, but pain cracks the stoic veneer on his face. It feels wrong, like the natural order of the world has been flipped. I've heard the most difficult thing for a parent to do is to bury their child—it's supposed to go the other way around.

"*He was only seventeen.*"

I've heard that a lot today.

Once Miles is buried, the walk back to the funeral home is quiet. We pass fields of graves, some with wilted flowers adorning the headstones, others barren. I imagine Miles's will always have flowers on it. There are hundreds of people here, so many that I'm lost in a sea of solemn faces. Then I look back in the direction of the graves and see him.

Miles.

He stands in the parking lot, the wind blowing through his blood-soaked curls. His gaze is frozen on me, as if to say *you did this.* I clench my eyes shut, and when I open them, it's Dean Bowman who stands in Miles's place. I don't know which is worse.

Dean leans against a van eerily similar to the one Miles died in. When he catches me looking, he flicks his cigarette, gets into his new vehicle, and drives away. Part of me wants to tell West, but he's still wiping tears from his eyes with the sleeve of his black shirt. This day has been hard enough on him.

The reception room is brightly lit, with crystal chandeliers and ceiling-high windows. Across the room, my parents comfort sobbing relatives I didn't even know Miles had. West and I stand next to a table of appetizers and desserts. Not knowing what to do with myself, I pass a display of pictures of Miles. His last high school photo, with a big, dimpled smile and curly hair. Pictures of him as a kid in school plays, dressed in costumes of Shakespearean characters. Miles as a toddler in a diaper, and another of him on the first day of kindergarten.

"I remember that day," I say.

"Yeah, me too. Miles loved school. He loved the attention."

"Weston."

Brian. We turn around, and Brain's blue eyes have a film of tears over them, even though his expression is tight.

"Dad . . ."

Brian holds his hands together, but they shake. "How are you feeling?"

"Not great," West says. He looks over his dad's shoulder, where across the room, Beatrice watches us, then looks away coldly. As far as I know, she hasn't said a word to West about Miles's death. I won't pretend to understand her, but I wish she would put her personal feelings aside and be there for him, even a little. They both lost someone.

"Listen," Brian says, "I . . . I want you to know that—what I'm trying to say is, I want to see more of Amelia. She's my granddaughter. I want to be in her life, Weston."

"Okay." West's voice breaks. "I'm going to try to get her every weekend. Maybe see if Sophie will split custody with me."

"I would like that." Looking away, Brian squeezes West's shoulder. "You only ever have one family, son. It's easy to forget how to be grateful."

He walks away, and more tears fall down West's flushed cheeks. "Fuck, I can't do this."

My chest stings, but I follow West as he heads outside, into the warm day. Faye cries under the shade of a willow tree with Shawn and Keely comforting her. She and West haven't talked yet, but neither of them looks away when their gazes lock. We join them under the tree.

"Hey, guys," Keely says.

"Hi, Keel," I mumble.

West sniffles while Faye hugs herself and trembles.

"I can't believe he's really gone," Shawn says and adjusts his black tie. "Hendricks—I mean, Miles—was always around. I don't even know how the drama club is going to survive without him next year."

"He had so many plans," Faye says. "He had a whole stack of plays he wanted to put on next year."

"Well, maybe we can still do them?" Keely offers. "Like, to honor him."

Faye snorts out a laugh. "Except we all suck at acting."

We fall quiet. This is Miles's day, but I can't help but think about the huge gap between myself and everyone else. I won't be here for senior year, just like I wasn't here for the past five years. But this isn't about me, and now's probably a good time to tell them who I saw.

"Dean was here," I say, and everyone looks at me.

"Where?" Faye's nostrils flare.

"In the parking lot, but I think he left."

"That guy has balls showing his face around here today," West says through gritted teeth.

"I told him not to come," Shawn adds.

"Whatever," Faye says, voice shaky. "It doesn't matter anymore. What's done is done. Today is for Miles, and I don't want to think about the asshole who killed him."

A grim silence befalls us as a warm gust of wind blows plumes of dandelion fluff our way.

"Listen," Faye begins, "I wanted to have like, a memorial for him. Without parents. Without crying. Or, less crying." She laughs bitterly. "Really, I just want somewhere to drink in his name, but you know what I mean. I'm thinking we should all go to the cabin."

Images of Miles chasing me and drowning me flicker in my mind, so I wrap my arms over my chest and take comfort in my own embrace.

"I'm in," Shawn says. "Miles loved that place. But hey, let's just not invite Dean, that cool?"

"No shit, Shawn," Faye says. "What's with you?"

"I'm just like, as mad at him for crashing as you guys are, that's all."

He's acting suspiciously. Whatever Miles was going to say before the crash, Shawn didn't want him to, because he'd told him to shut up. But Shawn scans the graveyard like a terrified animal. There's no way he'd have the guts to be a killer, or even a stalker. He rolls up his sleeve just enough to show a faded "smiley" on his arm.

"You want me there too?" West asks.

"Yeah," Faye says. "You're a pretty good guard dog. Dean probably won't try to crash the party if you're there."

"All right. I wouldn't miss it."

"You too, Liv," Faye says, and my eyes snap to her. "Miles would want you to come. You should be there for him."

Pinpricks crawl up my arms. Miles wouldn't want me there if he knew how I really felt about him, and even the thought of returning to that place ties a knot in my throat. But I will go, because honoring him is the least I can do.

As sunset casts an orange glow over the sky, everyone talks about the good things they remember about Miles, but I find myself distant from it all. I don't believe in ghosts, but I can feel Miles looking at me in my peripheral vision, watching my every move. When I turn to him, he mouths something at me. His words whisper in the wind.

"*I tried to warn you it was him.*"

"Who?" I say, but don't realize I've said it out loud until everyone frowns at me. When I look back toward Miles, there are nothing but graves. I swallow hard. Maybe I have an idea of who, but I can't make another baseless accusation against someone after what happened last time.

26

We don't get to the cabin until after dark. West promised my parents he'd keep me safe, and they said it was okay if I stayed as long as I was with West the whole time, but they're almost certainly just out of fight. Watching my childhood best friend be buried wasn't easy on them either.

Draped over the living room furniture, everyone drinks and continues the ever-growing conversation about Miles. Even West has a beer. Despite being on a lower dose, I still can't drink while weaning off my meds. Besides, putting myself in any state of mind that might trigger me to see things is far from ideal. I'm already shaking on the couch and trying not to glance into the dark forest beyond the windows.

The truth is, I'll probably never have a "normal" life. But at least I still have a life.

"Do you remember that weird thing he used to do when we drove?" West asks Faye as he peels at the label of his bottle. "Every time Dad would take us out of town, Miles would read off every goddamn sign we passed, even if it was just for the speed limit."

"Trust me, I remember," Faye says. "It was annoying as fuck, which was one of the only things you and I ever agreed on. And we'd get pissed off when Dad would get us those big bags of hard candies, and Miles would leave all the gross banana ones."

West lets out a deep, throaty, genuine chuckle, but his smile fades moments later. "Yeah. What a kid."

Faye sits cross-legged on the couch and faces Keely on the other side. "Hey, can I ask you something? Why'd your dad interview Miles about the guy outside your house?"

"No idea," Keely says. "But I never thought it was Miles. No way."

"Yeah, he said he had no real alibi or whatever, like none of us actually *saw* him. But I know where he was that night. He had this place in the forest behind our house that he always went to think. Just some random spot of grass where he liked to watch the stars."

My heart falls. A spot in the middle of the woods—that could have been where he took me for the picnic. More guilt covers me. I sink into the tartan fabric of the couch. The memories of that day are even more horrible now that Miles is gone. West glances at me but says nothing.

"He liked to go there when he was upset, and I remember he was pretty torn up about—" Faye stops herself and glares at us. "You know what. Anyway, this has been the worst day of my life, second only to finding out Miles was dead in the first place. I think I'm going to pass out. Keely, share a bed with me?"

"Yeah, of course."

They stand, followed by Shawn.

"Guys, wait, what about me?" Shawn says.

"What about you?" Keely scowls.

"I dunno . . ." Shivering, Shawn rubs his arms and glances out the windows. "It's kind of freaky out here. I don't want to sleep alone."

"Really?" Faye scoffs. "You big baby. Fine, you can sleep on the floor next to us."

"Yes, on the *floor*," Keely says.

"Deal." Shawn chases after them to their room, leaving West and me alone on the couch.

Despite being together all day, we haven't spoken much. A tense awkwardness hangs between us—not only because we're not touching, but because we now have to figure out our sleeping arrangements. Sleeping in West's arms would be a dream come true, but I wish it was under different circumstances. I can tell by the expression on his face that he sees the way we both hurt Miles when he looks at me.

He doesn't speak, so I say, "If you want . . . maybe we can just sleep in separate rooms? Since Shawn is with Faye and Keely . . ."

West's pained eyes meet mine. He changed out of his funeral clothes into plaid pajama bottoms and a black shirt, while I'm in the volleyball sweats I packed. I never thought our first night together would be like this.

"Do you want that?" he asks, his voice gruff. I shake my head, and he looks away. "Neither do I."

We fall quiet, but I can't stop thinking about what Miles tried to tell me. Though I'm slowly putting the puzzle pieces together, I can't trust my own mind—but I do trust West.

"I need to tell you something," I say quietly. West's jaw tightens. "Miles was trying to tell me something the day of the barbeque, before you showed up, but I wouldn't listen to him. Then, before the crash, I accused him of being the guy outside Keely's window, and he tried to tell me something else."

"What was it?"

"That's the thing: I don't know, but it was about the guy outside Keely's house. I was so paranoid about him that I didn't even try to listen. But Miles knew something, West. One of the last things I heard him say was 'I know you guys lied.' And I remember Dean was really pissed off."

"But the van crashed before Miles could finish," West says, and I nod. "Dean could've crashed on purpose."

"Maybe."

"Jesus Christ . . . we need to tell the cops."

"The last time I accused someone of something, Miles—"

"Don't think about that. If it wasn't my brother outside Keely's house, it was someone else, which means people are still in danger. If Dean crashed on purpose just to shut Miles up, he must have something to hide."

"That's what I'm afraid of."

"Okay. There's nothing we can do tonight." West stands up. "So let's just get some sleep." He goes around to every window and door and double checks to make sure everything's locked. "Come on, let's go to bed."

West turns off the lights. With bated breath, I follow him to the same room I slept in the last time I was here. West closes the door, and the darkness engulfs us. I'm thankful the blinds are pulled shut, because I don't want to look into the forest and imagine myself running through those same trees.

Once West is under the covers, I crawl in after him. As soon as the heat of the blanket covers me, he pulls me to him, wrapping me in the warmth of his body. West buries his face in my hair and breathes in deep.

"Thank you for being with me today," he says.

"Of course . . . I love you, West."

"I love you too."

We're quiet after that, and it isn't long before West's breathing becomes slow and shallow, and his grip on me relaxes.

Once again, I can't sleep. Images of Miles pleading with me to listen to him haunt my mind. With everything going on, I haven't even used the bathroom in hours, so I slip out of bed.

"Where you going?" West asks groggily.

"Bathroom." I kiss his cheek. "Be right back."

West grumbles and curls under the blankets, instantly asleep again. My heart inflates, but I head into the empty living room, trying not to look at Brian's taxidermy. But as I'm making my way across the hardwood floor, something creaks behind me. I freeze.

Not this again.

Fear floods me, the crippling paranoia taking over, but I'm sick of being ruled by these emotions. West double checked that the doors and windows were locked—there's no way anyone could get in here. I run to the bathroom, and once I'm done, I go back out and hurry toward our room.

Something moves by Keely's door.

I stop in my tracks. The floorboard creaks again.

"Keely?" I whisper. "Is that you?"

Silence.

Clenching my eyes shut, I snap the elastic band against my wrist.

You're dreaming again. Wake up.

When I open my eyes, I find myself staring into the mirror above the fireplace. The cabin is inverted through it, and in the corner is a face.

I try to scream, but a hand covers my mouth and nose until I can't breathe. Kicking and flailing, I spot the man's obscured reflection in the mirror before my body weakens and I can't see anymore.

o o o

My vision fades in and out. The roof of a car, the soft fabric of a seat beneath me. The calm grumble of a vehicle moving. Then I'm surrounded by trees, and the night sky seeps through the leaves above my head. Someone carries me, but I can't see his face. I try to say *stop*, but the words don't come out. Everything is heavy.

He's taking me somewhere, but I'm too weak to fight him. I squirm in his arms, and he drops me to the ground. I feel nothing but the weight of gravity and the damp dirt on my hands, but through my disorientation, a memory leaks through the cracks.

That time Keely went missing in the forest, West caught her trail.

With weighted limbs, I roll the elastic off my wrist and drop it in the dirt, just as the person scoops me into his arms again.

I'm too powerless to do anything. I catch one last glimpse of the elastic, strewn among the leaves, before I slip into the black again.

27

I open my eyes to a sickly yellow light dangling above my head. A battery-powered lantern squeaks as it sways with the draft, and the smell of rotting wood permeates the air.

My hands are bound.

"Hey, you're awake. I was starting to think I'd have to do this while you were knocked out."

My vision adjusts to a man with his back facing me. His white shirt has stains on it—they could be dirt, sweat, or blood. My recollection returns in glimpses, and then all at once until my pulse explodes. When he glances over his shoulder, fear chills me to the bone.

"Dean," I breathe out.

"Hey," is all he says.

"What—what's going on? What are you doing? Where are we?"

"Take a look around."

Four walls made of logs encase us. It's a cabin rotting at the joints, and the roof looks like it could collapse at any second. Dean stands at some sort of workbench, but dark red stains the decaying wood. As my consciousness returns in full force, panic crashes into me. Metal tools hang on the walls and line the workbench. No, they aren't tools . . .

Knives. Some serrated, others long and sharp. A machete, a saw, and a long pair of scissors.

It's him. It's always been him.

"How?" I ask. "How did you get in the cabin?"

"Easy. I knew you were all going there, so I broke in before you even arrived. I waited in the closet."

"You were there the whole time."

"That's right. I heard everything." He scrapes metal against metal. "If it makes you feel any better, I didn't go there for you. I wanted Keely." He faces me with the knife in his hand, and I squirm against the chair he's strapped me to. There isn't a flicker of emotion in Dean's dull brown eyes—no anger, no hatred. Just nothingness. Blank, like he isn't alive at all. "But you were onto me, so now you have to go too."

"I don't understand," I choke out. "You went for Keely? Why?"

He takes a step closer to me, and I pinch my eyes shut. The floorboards creak beneath his boots. "Why do you think? She got way too involved with my cousin, and I really don't like the way he's changing because of her."

I think back to that time in Sea Breeze, when Keely told me that Shawn never dates.

No, Dean never *let him* date.

"Since I was dating Faye," Dean says, "I thought it'd be good for Shawn to have a girl around, but then he started acting differently. I tried to get rid of her before, but he panicked and said he'd break up with her as long as I didn't hurt her."

"You mean in the forest, when Keely went missing?"

"Yeah. Since you're going to die anyway, it doesn't matter if you know." He shrugs. "I'd planned on taking her here that night, but my cousin was so upset . . . I decided to stop for him."

He says it like it was a favor. I want to throw up, but I can barely even breathe.

"After that, Shawn promised me and him would be back to the way we always were, but he just couldn't stay away from Keely. So really, this is his fault."

"I don't understand," I whimper.

"I think you do."

This can't be happening. "What are you going to do, Dean?"

"First"—he sharpens his knife against a block—"I'm going to kill you. Then I'm going to kill Keely."

"No, please, you can't. Please let me go. Please." I'm already a cry-ing, sputtering mess. I wish I could wake up, or know this was one of my nightmares, but no matter how hard I bite on my lip or kick and tremble, I'm still trapped in this cabin with him.

"Hey, it's okay," Dean says. "No one's coming for you, so you should probably just make peace with yourself."

My body shakes against the restraints. I want to cry more, scream, beg for my life. But an awareness solidifies like a layer of ice around me: it won't change anything. Dean's knife glimmers in the swaying light.

"I think West should be the one to find you," he says. "I'd pay to see the look on his face, but no, I can't go down for this. I need to be careful. I think I'll dump you in the river, let you wash up somewhere far from here. They'll try to find you, but no one ever will. Then, someday, weeks from now, someone in another town will report a body, and it'll be ID'd as you. Honestly, I think I'll enjoy watching West suffer for it. He's such a control freak, but he couldn't even stop me from taking you. You know him pretty well, how do you think that'll make him feel?"

"Dean, please, you don't have to do this. Just let me go. I won't tell anyone. Please let me go."

"Answer the question! How will it make him feel?"

"Devastated."

Dean smirks. I hate that I've told him what he wants to hear. I hate that he's getting pleasure out of the idea of hurting me, hurting the people I love.

"Honestly, I always liked you, Olivia." He drags the knife along the arm of the chair. "You react to things. You're skittish, like a squirrel."

A pain like I've never experienced pierces my thigh. It consumes my whole body and lights my nerves on fire. I scream, and the knife makes a slicking sound as Dean pulls it from my thigh, covered in blood. My head becomes light as he holds it over his face and observes the blood dripping down the blade. Warm red leaks through my gray sweatpants, but the pain subsides enough for me to cry uncontrollably. If I focus on the tears, it's easier to push through the pain.

"Hey, it's all right," Dean says, and the feigned emotion in his voice makes me sick. I choke on my own cries. This can't be the last place I see, the last voice I hear. When Dean rounds the chair and brings his hot, sour breath to my ear, it isn't his voice—it's Miles's.

"*I tried to warn you, Liv.*"

Then Dean says, "Shh, it's okay. Miles is dead, too, at least you're not the only one. Does that make you feel better?"

"Why are you saying this? Please—just let me go. I won't tell anyone I saw you, I promise."

"You and I both know that's bullshit." The cold edge of a blade presses softly against my throat.

Stall him. Stall him. Stall him.

"Wait!"

The knife lifts.

"What about Miles, Dean? Was he really onto you? Is that why you crashed?"

He laughs once and lowers the knife. I watch it as he paces around. "Smart girl. Miles didn't know shit, really, but he'd figured out that Shawn had lied about where I was the night someone went to Keely's house, so he was suspicious. But the guy had something against me since I started dating his sister."

How could I ever think Miles didn't care about his sister being abused? I didn't know him at all. I never did.

"Anyway," Dean says, "that was me outside of Keely's that night, and it wasn't the first time I'd come around. I wanted to get rid of her, but I didn't want to get caught. Then Miles started running his mouth in the van. How pathetic is that? He cared so much about your opinion that he was going to try to sell me out right there, even though I was the one driving."

"He probably didn't think you would crash just to stop him."

"Clearly he was wrong."

"But do you feel anything at all? For killing him?"

"What do you want me to say? That I'm torn up with guilt? Hendricks had his perks. I wanted to shut him up, but I didn't want him dead. But I'm not sorry I killed him. Just sucks that Faye is so mad at me—I really do like her. Something tells me she'll get over it."

It's almost like he's gloating, like he's proud of what he's done. Every second I keep him talking is another second I have breathing. Another second someone has to find me.

"What about the animals?" I ask. "Did they annoy you like Keely did?"

"Right, you were pretty interested in who was doing it. It was hilarious watching you wonder. Honestly, I just did that to see people's reactions, but the thrill of it faded. This, on the other hand . . ." He runs the knife up my arm. "Are you scared?"

"Aren't you? Of going to jail?"

"Yeah, I do like being free. What does it feel like? To know you're about to die?"

Please, West, Mom, Dad, someone.

"I asked you a question," Dean says, and the knife is on my throat again.

"Don't," I beg. "Please—don't. This can't be happening. I—I recovered. I swam again. I was going to be okay. Please don't do this."

"That's it. Let it all out."

A phone vibrates on the desk, and the knife is off me again. Hope leaps inside me, because we're close enough to town to have a signal.

"Is that mine?" I ask.

"You really think I'd bring your phone? It has a GPS on it. Yeah, that's right. No one's coming for you, Olivia. Let that sink in."

It does sink in. The same way the blood from my thigh soaks into the wooden floor.

"Say a word and I'll kill you," Dean says to me before he answers the phone. "What, Shawn? I'm busy, why aren't you asleep?"

Shawn. If he's calling, maybe he woke up, and maybe the others did too. Maybe West noticed I never came back to bed, and now they're all looking for me. I tug and tug at my restraints until something cracks, and the pain shocks me.

"Man, I'm at home," Dean says. The way he's slipped back into his usual demeanor terrifies me. "How are you calling me? I thought you were at Hendricks's cabin. Why'd you go back to town?" Pause. "She's probably wandered off again into the woods and having one of her meltdowns. That chick is nuts."

The sudden hope that they're looking for me gives me strength, and I scream as loud as I can. "We're in the woods! A cabin!"

Dean hangs up immediately and storms toward me. "What the fuck!" His shout scrapes my ears, and he picks up the knife. A scream cuts my throat as I shove him into the wall with the chair. My hand breaks free from the zip tie, and I run. Tearing through the front door, into the dark woods, the throbbing pain from the stab wound in my thigh causes me to buckle, and the forest floor cuts into the bare soles of my feet. I land in the ground and dare to look back.

This is the same cabin we found in the woods the day Keely went missing.

Follow the river. The river leads to the ocean. The ocean leads to freedom.

He's going to kill me, so I bolt. I don't get far into the brush before Dean slams into me and hurls me to the ground. Another scream and fire-hot pain stabs my shoulder. Dean's knife. The pain is excruciating, like he's snapped the muscle in my shoulder right in half, but I kick him hard in the groin. He winces and drops the knife. Scrambling to my feet, I tear through the forest the same way I did the night of the crash.

This time, it is real.

"Get back here!" Dean yells, but I don't stop.

The overcast sky has veiled the moon, so the forest morphs into one black, menacing object. But that means Dean can't see either. Instead of going straight, I veer on a sharp angle and run until my foot catches a branch, and I fall.

Crumpling up against a tree, I ration what little breath I have left. Time ticks by slowly, and I can't hear Dean anymore. Both my thigh and my shoulder are bleeding, and the darkness around me becomes white. I'm losing too much blood. If Dean doesn't kill me, this will.

No, I can't give up. I have to live—for West, for my parents, for myself. I need to stop the bleeding, so I shred a piece of my shirt and tie it tightly around my thigh before pressing my hand over my shoulder wound. When I conjure the strength, I keep limping through the forest.

Something flashes through the woods. All my pain is defeated by the hope of being found. If I scream, Dean will hear me—but so will the police. I have to risk it.

"Help! Help me!"

My body slams into the ground, and my back cracks against a log. I whimper as Dean's hands wrap around my throat, eyes narrowed on mine like silver slits in the night.

"Stop," I say, weakly hitting his arm. "Please, stop."

He squeezes, and pressure builds inside my temples. The blackness of the forest fades to white.

"You're done. You hear me? You're *done*."

Maybe I am. I fought, I really did, but it hurts too much. *I'm sorry, Miles. I should have listened. I'll see you soon.*

The pressure lifts, but the light stays. Then my lungs fill with air, and my eyes adjust to cops surrounding me with flashlights, their guns pointed right at Dean, who stands with his hands up. They made it. I'm alive.

My head gets woozy and warm liquid leaks through my fingers, gripped to my shoulder. Someone scoops me into their arms.

"It's okay, Olivia. You're going to be okay."

Roger has saved me yet again.

○ ○ ○

Somewhere on the walk out of the forest, I passed out. When I come to, an ambulance and several cop cars wait for us on the road. Handcuffed, Dean is shoved into the back of a cruiser as a paramedic bandages my wounds.

"The good news is, it isn't bad," she tells me and smiles warmly. "You didn't lose that much blood—it was the shock that made you faint. You're a really tough girl, Olivia."

"Thank you," I say with a slight laugh, still in disbelief.

Roger places his hands on his hips. "Olivia, your parents are on their way. We'll need to get an official statement from you, but Keely and the others are over there waiting, if you want to see them."

Back in that cabin, I believed I'd never see anyone I love ever again. So when the paramedic is done patching up, I hurry around the side of the ambulance, where Keely, Faye, and West wait for me. Keely traps me in a hug even before West can, but as soon as we pull away, I'm in West's arms.

"I'm so sorry, Olive," he says, smoothing down my hair. "I wasn't there to protect you. I'm sorry."

I say nothing, just bury my face in his shirt and cry. Composing myself, I pull away and wipe my eyes.

"I'm really sorry, Liv," Faye says. "I knew Dean was screwed in the head, but I had no idea he was capable of this."

"It's not your fault . . . but I still don't understand how you all got to me so fast."

"Hey guys," someone cuts in. We all turn to Shawn, who has a cop with him. He averts his stare like a guilty dog.

"Stay away from me, Shawn," Keely spits.

He holds his hands up. "Keely, I'm sorry. Just let me explain my side to Olivia."

"You've got five minutes," the cop tells him. "Then you're coming to the station with us."

Shawn nods. He doesn't need to say it.

"You knew, didn't you?" I ask.

"Of course he knew," West says. "He's been covering Dean's ass this whole time."

"It's not like that," Shawn says. "Okay, it sort of is, but . . . I didn't know he'd go this far. Please, Olivia. Let me explain. I feel horrible."

I glance at the others before stepping away with Shawn.

"When West said you were missing from bed," Shawn says, "I had this sinking in my gut, and I just knew Dean was responsible. He'd been threatening toward Keely before, but . . . anyway, when I heard you scream in the background of the call about a cabin and the woods, I knew exactly where you were."

I never want to think about that horrible place again.

Shawn continues, "We found that place when we were kids. It started out as us playing a game—like, pretending to be real hunters. But then Dean started killing animals for real. It began with BB guns, but then he learned how to build traps, and he killed them by hand from there. It freaked me the hell out, so I told him he'd get in trouble if he kept doing it, and for years, I thought he'd stopped . . . but when the dead animals started showing up in town, I knew. I didn't have the balls to go back to that cabin, but I don't think he ever stopped killing there. It was where he wanted to bring Keely the night . . ."

"He told me," I say. "He'd planned on bringing her to the cabin the night she went missing."

Dean was the footprint, the unknown man in the woods. He was the one who'd spied on Keely's house that night—he really was there for her, not me. It was all part of his sick plot to kill her. Everything leads back to him.

"Yeah, but I was there too," Shawn says. "Dean said she was too drunk and that he was going to drive her home, so I insisted on coming with him. But then he told me he wanted to take her to the hunting cabin, and I totally freaked. I had to beg him to let Keely go. I promised I'd break up with her, but . . . somehow, Keely and I just kept talking."

"*Somehow*? You should have told the police, Shawn. What is wrong with you?"

"I'm a coward, okay? I was terrified. I had no idea what he was going to do. We're family, and he's always freaked me out, but I've never betrayed him. I thought if I did, he'd kill me first." Shivering, Shawn hugs himself. "Part of me knew what he was really capable of, but I just wanted to ignore it, you know?"

"You are a coward, Shawn." I pause. "But at least you eventually helped."

He nods, face pale, before the officer takes him away.

All of the blame isn't on Shawn.

Miles tried to warn me something was up with Dean, but I wouldn't listen. And maybe if I had just gone inside the cabin that day in the forest, they would have caught Dean sooner, and Miles wouldn't be dead.

But it doesn't matter what I could have, should have, or would have done. What matters is what I *did*, and what happened because of it, and how I'll move on from here.

Miles might be gone, but at least Dean Bowman won't be able to hurt anyone else.

28

It's hard not to itch underneath the bandages wrapped around my shoulder and thigh. It hurts less now that it's healing, but stab wounds are a lot more intense than scrapes.

My parents and West stand in a circle with Keely's parents in the carpool lot, and the wind blows sand all around us. The midday sun beats down on us. By nightfall, I'll be back in New York. For real this time.

"I'm really sorry," West says to my mom. "I promised you I'd keep Olivia safe, and I failed."

Mom touches West's arm with an empathetic smile. "West, no one could have anticipated that. We don't blame you."

Dad nods. "This is on no one but that Dean kid. You still helped get our daughter safe to us, and that's all we care about now."

West shakes Dad's hand and hugs Mom, thanking them.

"What you did was really brave, Olivia," Roger says. "Stalling him until we could get there was the right move."

Keely gives me a tight smile, though her skin is still sallow from yesterday's horror. I recognize the look in her eyes—the confusion, the terror. I see it in the mirror every day.

"I just can't believe he really wanted to kill *me*," Keely says. "I never did anything to him!"

"He said it was about Shawn, but I also think he just wanted to kill someone," I say. "I saw it in his eyes when he had me in the cabin— there was nothing there. Any emotion Dean ever showed us was fake."

"Still, I majorly have the creeps. I'm so sorry he took you instead, Liv."

"Don't. I got away from him, Keel. I'm glad it was me instead of you. I can take it."

"Yeah . . ." She nudges me teasingly. "You're way stronger than me. I doubt I would've made it out alive."

"Don't even joke about that, Keely," Sun says.

Roger puts his arm around Sun and says, "We do feel for Derek Bowman, Dean's dad. I really think he had no idea what his son was doing. He's a single guy, lost his wife a few years back. The good news is, Dean's being charged with premeditated, aggravated attempted murder, so he's facing hard time in prison. We're lucky the guy just turned eighteen. Your testimony will be crucial, Olivia."

The thought of returning and facing Dean sickens me, but I nod. Thankfully there's no courthouse in Caldwell Beach, so we'll be going to a different town when I need to testify against Dean.

My heart hurts. I step away from the circle, and West puts his hand on the small of my back. "You know, you're stronger than you give yourself credit for."

"Not really." I almost laugh. "Apparently I didn't lose as much blood as I thought, but I still fainted."

"Yeah, but it's got to hurt. I mean, I've never been *stabbed* before. You're badass as hell for surviving that."

"Olivia," Dad says, "come on, it's time to go."

I meet West's eyes, then lift up on the tips of my toes and kiss him on the cheek one last time. He inhales a sharp breath as I pull away. I'll miss his smell, how safe he makes me feel, how his arms are like an island while I'm lost at sea. But this was bound to happen. I have to keep swimming on my own, and I can't do that if West is always carrying me.

So, I let him go. "Goodbye, West."

His smile is broken. "Bye, Olive."

After I give Keely another hug, I thank Sun and Roger and get into the backseat of my parents' car. Everyone waves to us as we drive away, and I stare out the back window until I can't see them anymore.

Away from them, I feel hollow. My emotions are brittle. This summer has drowned me, but it still hurts to say goodbye to Caldwell Beach a second time.

I was born here. I almost died here. And in coming back, everything has changed. I don't know who I'll be from now on, how I'll sleep at night, if my dreams will swallow me whole. If I'll be sane or senseless or mad from my memories.

But I know I'll be back again, when I'm ready.

EPILOGUE

TEN MONTHS LATER

There's so much more pollen here than there is in New York. Without the buildings and skyscrapers, balls of spring fluff drift over my nose and make it itchy. The gravestone in front of me is an extravagant, blue-gray granite, and the afternoon sun brightens every grain of the rock like a million tiny lights. Engraved on it is *Miles Hendricks*, along with his birth year and the day he died. He was seventeen.

That's such a short life.

I'm so sorry, Miles.

Tears sting my eyes. Dr. Levy didn't want me coming back to Caldwell so soon, but ten months is a long time when you have unfinished business weighing on you as heavy as the ocean. My new medication is working, and as of last month, Dean Bowman was officially convicted. For kidnapping, premeditated attempted murder, aggravated assault, vandalism—the list goes on. He was given thirty years in prison and a restraining order against both myself and Keely—even if he ever managed to get out of jail, he could never come near us again.

The case against him was strong. As if to gloat more, he'd confessed to the animal killings, which added to the judge's decision to lock him up for a long time. Dean had attempted to kill me, and the entire jury agreed that he was a serial killer in the making. I'll never forget how scared I was taking the stand, having to face the man who almost took my life, but I did it. And now, I really am ready to move on.

"Olive?"

Wiping my cheeks, I turn around. West wears a black T-shirt and the blue swim trunks I asked him to bring. His dark hair has grown longer, falling in pieces over his forehead, and his eyes are tired, like he has smudges of motor oil beneath them.

The seasons have changed. We have too. My hair now reaches the middle of my back, and the stress of the past ten months has caused me to drop ten pounds. I lost my appetite for a while as I adjusted to my new meds, but I'm doing better now. Eating more. It's all progress. But I'm suddenly insecure about how skinny I am.

West scratches the nape of his neck. "How are you?"

"Okay." I look down at Miles's grave. "I know it's weird to meet in a cemetery, but I wanted to see him before I did anything else. I needed to."

"Yeah." West stands beside me. "I'm due too."

An oak tree canopies the grave and shields us with its shade. It's a pretty place for Miles to be buried—rolling hills, a fountain with a sculpture of an angel. Plenty of nature.

"My mom found these home movies she made when I was a kid," I say. "You know, before I left Caldwell the first time."

"Oh yeah?"

"Yeah. Miles is in most of them. He was a really sweet kid. He's always smiling and laughing in the videos, and he's always following me around."

"You're going to make me cry if you keep telling me that stuff."

"Sorry."

"It's okay."

When I left Caldwell ten months ago, West and I took a break from talking to each other. We waited a month before we started talking every day—through FaceTime, on the phone, even webcam. But this is my first time seeing him in person since then, and it's surreal. He wanted to visit me on Christmas but wasn't able to because of work. Plus, he now spends every weekend with Amelia, and it's important for him to be with her.

But I think the real reason neither of us has tried to see each other until now is because we weren't ready.

I reach into my purse and pull out a folded piece of paper. Smiling, I hand it to West, and he hesitates before he unfolds it.

"Holy shit," he says. "You got into the University of Maine."

"Yep." I rock on my heels. "Marine Sciences."

His smile stretches his face. "That's amazing, Olive. You're going to be a scientist."

"I guess so. I just really like fish and things."

He chuckles and hands back my acceptance letter. "I know you do. But this also means . . ."

"I'll be a *lot* closer than New York."

"We can finally be together for real."

"Finally," I say, but the smile melts off my face. I touch my wrist out of habit, although the elastic is gone. "West, if we're going to move forward, there are still things I need you to know about me. Before the crash, I freaked out—"

"I know. Faye told me."

"Why didn't you ever bring it up?" My voice breaks.

"Because it doesn't matter. What happened, happened. I don't even hate Dean for it anymore. I mean, he's in jail, so, no point."

"When I was driving into town with my parents, I felt like everyone was looking at me. Like everyone blames me for what happened to Miles."

"Trust me, that's not true. What happened last summer is a tragedy. That's all anyone says about it."

"There's something else I haven't told you."

He doesn't look surprised. "What is it?"

"My psychiatrist thinks that because Miles was with me the night I fell off the cliff, I began to subconsciously associate the event with him. The thing is, all last summer, I was having nightmares about Miles. Nightmares that he wanted to hurt me and drown me. Then, when I woke up after the crash and had another episode . . ."

West crosses his arms. "What'd you see?"

"It was more than seeing. I felt, heard, and saw Miles chasing me through the forest to your parents' cabin. Then he tried to drown me."

"Wow. That's . . . intense."

"Yeah. Dr. Levy said it was a dream, and I confused it with reality. But it haunts me every night. It messes me up that my last memory of Miles wasn't even real, that my mind could create something like that." When West doesn't reply, I ask, "Do you hate me?"

"What? No. Why would I hate you?"

"I don't know."

"You didn't ask for any of that, Olivia. No one would."

The leaves flutter above our heads. A chipmunk climbs the trunk of the tree, and West's arms wrap around me, encasing me in warmth. I breathe in the familiar smell of earth on his cologne. When we pull away, we're both crying.

"Damn it." West laughs and wipes his eyes. "I told myself I wasn't going to cry."

I can't help but smile. "Me too. Maybe we should get out of this graveyard. But there's one more thing I have to do first." I reach into my purse and pull out three stones. I open my palm, and West frowns.

"Are those—is that sea glass?"

"Yep. Miles gave them to me."

To my surprise, he smiles. "That little shit. I recognize their shape and color and everything. When did he give them to you?"

"Last summer."

"Why didn't you tell me?"

"I guess I didn't want to create more drama between you two."

"It doesn't matter now."

With a smile, I put one in West's hand. "There's one for you, one for me"—I set the third stone on Miles's grave—"and one for him. At least this way, a part of us will always be together."

He slips it into the pouch of his backpack. "Thanks, Olive."

"Come on, let's get out of here."

"Where to?"

"The cliffs east of the lighthouse."

As the sun drops to the horizon, the shadows from the trees stretch over the streets like arms. West and I hold hands and walk the sidewalk to the beach, by the fish 'n' chips shop shaped like a pirate ship, past Coffee Cabin and Caldwell Body Shop. When we reach the shore, a twinge of nervousness touches me at the red lighthouse perched atop the cliff. But that isn't where we're going.

I jump on West's back, and he gives me a piggyback ride as we head east. Grapefruit-colored streaks paint the sky. A content, peaceful happiness washes through me, so I take out my phone and start filming.

"Hey," West says, "get that thing out of my face."

"No." I laugh. "Maybe I want to remember this forever."

Mom's home movies inspired me. They make me feel immortal.

When I watch them and see Miles, West, and me as kids, I like to think somehow, somewhere, that part of us still exists. Even if we've aged—even if one of us died—nothing will change the fact that we were *there*.

Once we reach the cliffs, West sets me down. The grass is cool on my toes through my flip-flops. I drop my purse and take off my clothes until I'm only in my blue bathing suit.

"So now we're stripping?" West lifts an eyebrow.

"We're going swimming." Rolling my eyes, I nod at his shorts. "Why else would I ask you to wear those?"

He laughs and peels off his shirt. "Well, I figured, but are you sure?"

"I'm sure! I've been practicing. Turns out I actually love diving boards, and I'm a pretty good swimmer."

"Well then, after you."

The water stretches endlessly to the sun. With one last smile at West, I run toward the edge of the cliff and jump.

I land in a deep sea of cerulean. Safe, alive, and finally free.

THE END

ACKNOWLEDGMENTS

Sometime in 2018, I purchased a candle by the name of "Sea Glass"—something that would eventually inspire me to write a story with sea glass somewhere in it, a story I'm now proud to call my debut novel. Don't ask me how the simple name of a candle could inspire a psychological thriller about serial killers and mental health, but here we are. Thank you, candle!

To Meg, who has seen the best and absolute worst of my writing: thank you. You've done more for me than I can ever express. Just having someone as talented and intelligent as you believe in me all these years has kept me afloat, so really, I can't thank you enough.

To my parents and my sister, for helping me become who I am and giving me the space to learn and grow. I wouldn't be who I am today without you, even though I kept my writing a secret from you for so long. Thank you for supporting me and being there!

To Deanna, Monica, Leah, Taylor, Ashleigh, Jen, and everyone at Wattpad and Wattpad Books who took a chance on my story: this experience has been invaluable, and I hope we can continue to work together and accomplish great things. To Allen Lau and Ivan Yuen: thank you for creating such a fantastic app and providing so many opportunities for young writers.

To all the friends I've made on Wattpad over the years: Meg, Kell, Lynn, Stef, and Katelyn (West's biggest fangirl), and everyone else I've interacted with along the way: thank you all so much, you've all played a role in my writing, whether we just chatted for a while or exchanged reads. I'll always be grateful to you.

And lastly, to my Wattpad readers, to everyone who has supported me online and read my stories: you know who you are, and "thank you" doesn't express how grateful I am. I wouldn't be here without you.

I hope to see you next time.

ABOUT THE AUTHOR

Taylor Hale was born in southwestern Ontario and started writing on Wattpad in 2015. When she isn't writing, she can be found bartending at a live music venue, and thinking up her next idea. *The Summer I Drowned* is her first novel.

wattpad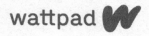

Where stories live.

Discover millions of stories created by diverse writers from around the globe.

Download the app or visit www.wattpad.com today.

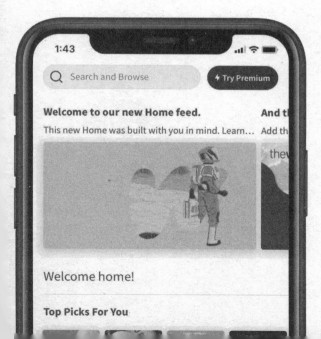

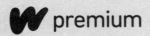

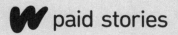

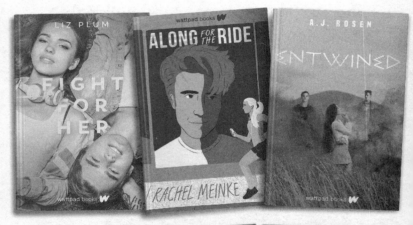